Jewels

By the same author

Bombs Have No Pity
(with Lieut. Col. George Styles, G.C.)

Robert Perrin

Jewels

Routledge & Kegan Paul
London and Henley

First published in 1977
by Routledge & Kegan Paul Ltd
39 Store Street,
London WC1E 7DD and
Broadway House,
Newtown Road,
Henley-on-Thames,
Oxon RG9 1EN
Set in 11 on 12pt Baskerville
by Kelly and Wright, Bradford-on-Avon, Wiltshire
and printed in Great Britain by
Lowe & Brydone Ltd

British Library Cataloguing in Publication Data
Perrin, Robert

Jewels.
I. Title
823'.9'1F PR6066.E7/

ISBN 0 7100 8700 4

To my wife Sonia and our children
Jeffrey, Lisa and Daniel

Contents

Illustrations

I

Conduct unbecoming

The time was half past seven on the evening of 23 January 1900, slightly more than three months after the mighty Empire of Queen Victoria began its war against the Calvinist farmers of the self-proclaimed Boer Republic in South Africa.

On this evening, beginning to chill after the heat of the day, seventeen hundred officers and men of Her Majesty's Imperial Army gathered on the reverse slope of Three Tree Hill, a small part of the Tabanyama range of mountains in northern Natal. For two weeks the British Army had been skirmishing with the Boers in the area, trying to break through to the beleaguered town of Ladysmith about a dozen miles away. These soldiers were ill-commanded by their generals, bravely led by their officers, and thoroughly disheartened after fighting four indecisive and somewhat disastrous battles against the Afrikaans farmers. The reverses at Belmont, the Modder River, Magersfontein and Colenso had shocked a British people who had believed its soldiers to be invincible and its generals to be all-wise, particularly in putting down revolts from ill-equipped natives who, apparently, failed to realise the self-evident blessings of belonging to the greatest empire the world had ever seen.

But on this night confidence was running high once again. The betting was two to one on that Ladysmith would be relieved within a week and the Boer finally given a firm beating. The waiting soldiers were drawn from the Lancashire Fusiliers, the Royal Lancaster Regiment, and from a cavalry unit, raised locally, called Thorneycroft's Mounted Horse. This was a unit of uitlanders, men who had come to South Africa for many reasons but who had all been denied equal rights in the Afrikaans state of Transvaal, a state grown rich after the discovery in 1886 of the vast gold fields at Witwatersrand. This was the state proclaimed a republic nation by its original settlers, the Boer farmers of Dutch and German descent, who had trekked across the arid wastes of the veldt to escape the influences of the British settlers in the more southern parts of South Africa.

Tonight the uitlanders were given the honour of leading the attack on a small mountain called Spion Kop, and Lieutenant Colonel A. W. Thorneycroft called his officers and men around him before the assault began on the mountain crest that rose 1,470 feet above the waters of the Tugela River, winding two miles below. If this crest could be captured and secured then the road to Ladysmith would be open, or so thought General Sir Redvers Buller, the commander of the British Army.

Colonel Thorneycroft, bald, moustached, and a bull of a man at twenty stone, was typically clipped and laconic in his briefing.

'We are about to attack Spion Kop. Make no noise. It's bayonet work only. No shots are to be fired. No smoking. No talking. Keep in close touch with one another.'

One of his lieutenants, Richard Howard Gorges, was particularly touched by the colonel's closing words. 'The honour of the regiment is in your hands. I can trust you all to do your duty.'

Honour and trust were words that hadn't been used to Lieut. Gorges ever since he'd been exiled from his home near Dublin by an outraged father, who had discovered him masturbating in a barn with one of the stable lads. That had been three years before, and since then Gorges, appearing older than his years with his height, trimmed moustache, and good looks, had learned many other vices as an enlisted man in the Cape Mounted Police. Now he listened with affection and pride to Col. Thorneycroft, a man he'd come to regard as his 'father' since his commission into his regiment at the outbreak of the war.

All Thorneycroft's men removed their cavalry spurs before they began marching in fours towards the lower slopes of Spion Kop. Soon a faint drizzle of rain faded. The night was dark with the stars shining only thinly. In the distance occasional rifle fire could be heard as British and Boer sentries exchanged desultory shots along the further slopes of the mountain range.

Suddenly, out of the darkness, a white English spaniel bounced up to the officers in the lead of the march. Gorges clicked his fingers and the dog came to his side. The lieutenant fondled him, scratching behind his long ears. The dog, wagging its feathery tail, didn't bark. A corporal was detailed in a whisper to lead it to the back of the column. He put a pull-through, used for cleaning rifles, round its neck, and the dog trotted off again into the darkness with its new handler.

Soon the soldiers' light brown uniforms were sodden from the long grass through which they were passing. The only sounds were the low swish, swish as hundreds of feet moved through the grass, the fluttering of the wings of small birds disturbed by the marchers, and the occasional screech of an owl. The grass gave way to rocks and the path began ascending steeply. The men rested frequently as scouts scrambled ahead to check that the Boers were still unaware of the impending attack. The top of Spion Kop was covered, as usual, in mist. The scouts returned. 'We can hear the Boers talking.' The whispered order went down the column, now moving over hard baked clay soil. 'Rise. Advance. Make no noise.'

Soon the crest was reached, and the line of men spread along its edge. Now, on hands and knees, far from their horses way below, the uitlanders of Thorneycroft's Mounted Horse crept towards the Boers. Eighty yards . . . seventy yards . . . and then a commotion, a crash, as an overloaded Royal Engineer towards the back of the advancing troops dropped some picks and shovels.

'Wie's daar?'

The challenge from the Boer sentry had been expected for minutes. The cavalrymen dropped flat on the hard soil as the Boers began firing. The bullets of their Mauser rifles cracked and whipped across the crest. Then the men with Thorneycroft heard the clicking of bolts. The Mauser magazines were empty. Thorneycroft was on his feet in an instant.

'Charge!'

His men, with the Lancashire Fusiliers on their right, sprang up and raced forward, bayonets out-thrust, yelling and screaming. Gorges felt no fear as he led his section towards the Boer sentries, now visible through the mist under a half moon. The Boers ran without attempting to reload. The garrison, about a hundred men from the Vryheid Commando, stumbled up from under their sleeping blankets, some in stockinged feet, and joined the fleeing sentries. Gorges saw one of them overtaken by a huge officer of the Lancashire Fusiliers. The Boer turned at the last moment and took the lieutenant's bayonet in his stomach. He bent as the steel punched into his body; his hands gripped the end of the bayonet and the muzzle of the Englishman's rifle as, screaming, he was lifted into the air and flung up and away like a ripe stook of corn.

In three minutes it was over. Spion Kop, so formidable from a distance, had been captured. Gorges clasped hands in delight with a fellow officer as they stood round the huge bulk of their colonel.

'Three cheers, gentlemen – and let them hear us down below.'

The cheering was heard and three star shells lit the sky in reply from an artillery battery on Three Tree Hill. The long climb and short fight – if it could be called a fight – had lasted a little over five hours, and the victorious British troops began digging in along the summit. But their trenching tools struck rock less than two feet below the surface. Gorges and his section took an hour to make a shallow trench but, in the flush of excitement, it seemed enough. They eased their back packs and rested, many falling asleep immediately with their soldiers' long training in taking cat–naps.

The wasted and lonely teenage years of Lieutenant Richard Howard Gorges seemed to have ended in this moment of British valour at arms.

It was shortly before two o'clock on the morning of 24 January 1900.

The mist swirled still around the crest as the men wakened from their fitful sleep. Then, suddenly, it cleared and the general feeling of elation and confidence vanished. In the dark and mist, the British force had mistaken the true crest of Spion Kop. This lay slightly lower, about 200 yards away to the left and about 50 yards to the right. The mist swirled back again to cover the mountain as sappers hurried forward to try to build new defensive positions. But here the rock was even closer to the surface, and only makeshift cover was possible with the inadequate trenching tools carried by the Royal Engineers.

To the observers below at headquarters the mountain was still covered in mist but, just before eight o'clock, it cleared suddenly on the crest. The sun had risen in a perfect blue sky on 1,700 men lying in an area 400 yards wide and 500 yards long.

The Mausers of the Boers began cracking again. The first casualty was a British officer sitting by a rock who slumped slowly onto his side, his hand still holding a half-eaten sandwich of Gentlemen's Relish.

The Boer riflemen were at nearly point blank range behind the rocks of a small rise called Aloe Knoll. Their artillery, Krupp howitzers and Vickers mortars, had an arc of fire of more than 120 degrees, and it was completely safe from the British artillery on the southern slopes of Spion Kop. For the men of the Boers' Carolina Commando on Aloe Knoll it was like shooting ducks in a barrel. But the most devastating enemies of the British were the whirling, red-hot pieces of shrapnel that continually swept their position. The shallow trenches gave little, if any, protection against the merciless, incessant barrage.

An hour after it began the Boers counter-attacked. Gorges saw them dodging from rock to rock, firing from the hip. The British fire was accurate in return but soon the Boers were over the crest, and the bearded farmers closed with the uniformed troops.

'Bayonet the bastards. Push 'em back.'

Boers fell, pierced in throat or chest or stomach, but their rifle fire was withering at close quarters. Soon it was hand-to-hand fighting. Gorges struggled with a Boer, his Mauser now slung across his shoulders, hunting knife gleaming in the fierce sun.

'Verdomme rooinek,' grunted the Boer. The two men swayed, locked in private battle amongst so many other life-or-death struggles swirling around them. Gorges and his assailant cannoned off other men, but still the young officer held the Boer's knife hand away from his body. Suddenly the Boer lurched against Gorges, a reddening hole in his striped shirt, shot by a British trooper at close range.

'God verdomme. God.' He fell away, and Gorges began firing at another target. Soon, though, it was clear that the Boers had overwhelmed the crest, and the British began moving back into the makeshift trenches they had dug during the night. Spion Kop became eleven hours of hell as shrapnel barrages swept the summit. They stopped only to be followed by further charges by the Boer riflemen. Water ran short and the screams of the wounded, the groans of the dying, were everywhere.

The scenes that day printed themselves on to the mind of Richard Howard Gorges. His friend, Needham, bleeding profusely from two chest wounds, propped against a boulder, still firing at the oncoming Boers. A cigarette hung loosely from his mouth. Then a third shot hit him, blowing the top of his head into a shower of pink and grey fragments, misting the air around him for a moment. Two officers, still in their teens, scarcely older than Gorges, firing until they fell dead across each other. . . . A messenger arriving from headquarters below the mountain with words of command for Col. Thorneycroft, and falling dead before uttering a word, hit in the mouth by a Boer sniper's bullet.

That unspoken command reached Thorneycroft later. He had been promoted to the rank of general and placed in full command of the carnage that was Spion Kop. The fighting went on through the morning and into the afternoon. A section of Lancashire Fusiliers, who'd taken the worst of the close range sniper fire, began waving white handkerchiefs. The Boers came out from behind their boulders to accept the surrender and lead the soldiers off the crest.

General Thorneycroft, hobbling now from an injured ankle, rose hugely from his trench.

'I'm in command here,' he shouted at the Boer leader, De Kock. 'Take your men back to hell, sir. I allow no surrender.'

But surrender of a kind there had to be. The British were exhausted by early evening, despite reinforcements. Hardly any were unscathed. Gorges himself had a bloody handkerchief round his temple, staunching the blood from a wound caused by a nearly spent fragment of shrapnel. As twilight fell the Boers' attacks slackened off. The soldiers began making jokes, but their laughter was wild and hysterical. The small headquarters unit on the crest of Spion Kop were unaware, through inadequate signalling arrangements, of plans to outflank the Boer. At main headquarters, beyond the Tugela River, there was confusion, and dissension.

General Thorneycroft looked at the bodies around him and heard the cries for water from the parched throats of the wounded.

'My poor boys . . . my poor boys.'

Shortly after nine o'clock in the evening, the decision was made to evacuate the mountain. As Winston Churchill, the war correspondent, scrambled up Spion Kop with a message for General Thorneycroft, he passed men stumbling down the mountain, some crawling, their hands bleeding from the hard rock. At the summit Churchill found Thorneycroft sitting in a trench, surrounded by his officers and the remnants of his regiment. Despite Churchill's assurances that reinforcements were on their way, Thorneycroft could not be persuaded to stay. His exhausted men started down from the blood-soaked clay and rock of Spion Kop. On the way down they met reinforcements, carrying a note from headquarters for the limping general.

'I can't read this,' muttered Thorneycroft. 'The writing is too small.'

Churchill took the note from his hands and read it.

'The note says you're to hang on until new trenches are dug. General, it says you're to hang on.'

'I've done all I can and I'm not going back.'

The young war correspondent helped the exhausted general as they continued downwards. Spion Kop was over. Lieut. Gorges's – and Britain's – day of glory had ended in a nightmare.

The next morning the Boers carried their sixty or so dead from the mountain, wrapping their bodies in blankets. Some cried openly, tears streaking the dust on their faces; as they watched the British stretcher parties searching for any living among the dead who, at times, were piled three high upon each other in the trenches, or what passed for them. The 243 British who had died in the battle were buried where they lay. But most of those who spent the night on the mountain without water or medical aid were to die later.

The wounded from Spion Kop received a rapturous welcome when they returned to Cape Town. Crowds pressed round the hospital train, flowers were thrust through the open windows, and the walking wounded, like Richard Gorges, had to endure the smacking kisses of the elderly, straw-hatted matrons on the station platform. They had to be rescued by nurses who helped them to carriages for the drive back to the military lines at Cape Town Castle. Here, a month later, Gorges heard the news of the Relief of Ladysmith.

Spion Kop hadn't really been necessary at all. Another way round the Boer positions had been found. The news added to this bitterness for those he liked to call 'the remote fools who never hear a shot fired except through their telescopes'. This saying was to be quoted again and again round the Castle, the establishment of the British Army in South Africa. It was a fair reflection of the feelings of many young officers.

Within weeks, though, the Boer War, as a war of set battles, was over. By early summer, Johannesburg and Pretoria had fallen. For the next twenty months the Boers were forced to use hit-and-run guerrilla tactics against British troops spread in blockhouses and small forts across the Transvaal, Orange Free State, Northern Natal, Basutoland, and the Northern Cape Colony. The natural bitterness of a guerrilla war was exacerbated when concentration camps were set up for the wives and families of the Afrikaans fighters. Disease swept these camps and thousands died, both the guarded and their guards.

But life for Richard Gorges, now based at Cape Town, except for occasional forays up country, was more pleasant. As a survivor of Spion Kop he was a figure to be admired by officers newly arrived from England. Even his heavy drinking, acquired with the Cape Mounted Police, was admired. He never made a fool of himself at the interminable and incessant parties in the clubs and hotels patronised by the military officers along and near Adderley Street in Cape Town. By general opinion,

Richard Gorges, now promoted a captain of cavalry, was a 'man's man'.

But Gorges had other reasons for enjoying his life in Cape Town. He lived in officers' quarters at the Castle, looked after by a teenage Malay boy called Peter, who came from the city's Woodstock district. Slim, coffee-coloured, always smiling, Peter cleaned up the captain's quarters, prepared his baths, cleaned and pressed his uniforms, and acted generally as any Army batman would do for the more senior officers on the general staff. His English was adequate, learned from the seamen who frequented the Woodstock district. And early on in working for Richard Gorges, he had perfected other ways to please his British captain. These, too, he had been taught by the seamen who went to Woodstock in search of the shanty area's nefarious delights. It had begun one morning when he'd entered Gorges's bedroom with his usual pot of tea and glass of brandy.

The room was half in darkness with the sun beginning to find its way through the window blinds. Gorges, still half asleep, lay on his side, naked. The light caught the lower half of his strong, lean body. The Malay boy watched him gently playing with his hardening manhood. The Malay, without a word, placed the tray on the bedside table, straightened up and began unbuttoning his shirt. Then he opened his belt and let his grey trousers slip to the floor. Like most young men from the Woodstock he wore no underclothes. Still without a word, he knelt by the bed and gently began stroking 'his captain'. As he felt the other's hands, Richard Gorges opened his eyes and smiled. The young Malay smiled back. Gorges shifted across the bed and the Malay boy stood up, showing his slim, lithe body. He knelt on the bed and slowly lowered himself so that he lay, curled slightly, facing Gorges. The filtering sun contrasted the hues of the two men's skins as they embraced, hands around each other's buttocks as they pulled themselves close. Gorges bent his head down and kissed the smooth skin of the Malay boy's cheek. Then they fell apart, lying on their backs, hands reaching across their bodies. Slowly, at first, then faster, they caressed each other. When it was over Peter reached over the side of the bed, picked up his shirt, and gently wiped first Gorges and then himself.

'Captain happy?'

Richard Gorges didn't reply. He reached across the bed and clasped Peter round the waist. He squeezed slightly, affectionately, and nodded. So it began. In the weeks that followed Gorges came to learn all of the Malay boy's body. In his locked bedroom in Cape Town there was little fear of that experience, years back, occurring again; little fear of the door bursting open and his irate father staring down at him, first surprise, then shock, and then anger registering across his face. There was only the lapping warmth of Peter's body and the demanding thrusts of his firm buttocks as they pressed invitingly against Gorges.

Outside that bedroom the relationship remained one of master and servant. But, once inside, it was of equals searching for new sensual delights. But after some weeks the nagging fear of discovery began to reassert itself.

'Is there anywhere else we can meet?' Gorges asked the Malay boy one morning as they lay together.

'My home, Captain. There's only my sister. No mother. No father. My sister don't mind. She got sailors.'

The next evening Gorges followed his Malay boy through the crowded alleys of Woodstock, past the wooden, open-fronted shops, through the cries of Cape Town's multi-racial bazaar, to Peter's home. This was above a shop selling spices, and was reached by a flight of steps alongside the building. Inside there were two rooms. The first contained a couch, two chairs and a table, and in the corner, curtained off, was the cooking area with a small stove. Gorges noted idly that two of the pots hanging on the wall were undoubtedly War Office property. So his young friend, thought Gorges, had been pilfering. Well, he reasoned, so did every civilian who worked with the growing British garrison. But it was the second room, the bedroom, that delighted Gorges. A scent of incense, mingled with the smell of spices from the shop below, hung in the air. There was a dressing table with a small stool, but dominating the room was a large wooden bed with a fringed canopy. At its side was a small table with an ornamental oil lamp.

'My mother bring from home,' explained Peter, pointing at the bed. 'We come here then she die from tummy sickness.' He spread his hands expressively.

'Dysentery, I suppose,' Gorges murmured to himself as he stood just inside the bedroom. He turned as he heard a small sound behind him. Standing by the table, one hand resting on it, was a girl about the same height and age as Peter. Her gleaming black hair hung over her shoulders, tumbling down the front of a dark-green cheongsam.

'This my sister,' said Peter, moving towards her. 'She called Ann-Su.'

Richard Gorges was struck by the smoothness of her skin, so like her brother's. He noted that brother and sister both had almond-coloured eyes.

'Hello, Ann-Su,' he said, taking her tiny hand. There were moments of silence, broken by Peter.

'This my Captain, Ann-Su. He come here sometime.'

'But what about her, Peter? Where will she go?'

'No worry, Captain. When we here, she sleep couch', explained the Malay boy. 'I sleep couch when she got sailor.'

Ann-Su lowered her eyes and smiled up at Gorges from under her long eye lashes.

'Not necessary if Captain like,' she said quietly, almost in a whisper.

Gorges looked at her and then at her brother. He felt excitement growing in him. He looked again at Peter with a question in his eyes.

'Okay with me, Captain. Together nice, eh?'

That night Gorges experienced the depths of depravity and the heights of pleasure. The three bodies, two slim and smooth, the other hard and angular, twined together. At times Gorges wasn't sure in which body he was buried. Tongues licked, teeth nipped, hands caressed. Gorges reflected later, as he returned to the Castle with Peter following him, that quite obviously the young Malay brother and sister had been practised in their bedroom arts for quite some time. But it was a night, he was certain, that would have to be repeated as soon as possible. And so it was.

In January 1901, the SS *German* arrived in Cape Town, after her three weeks' voyage from Southampton, and disembarked more British reinforcements at the South Arm jetty; amongst them were men of the 3rd Battalion of the Royal Irish Fusiliers. For a month they were billeted under canvas just outside Cape Town, and it was during this time that Richard Gorges met a new friend who was to dominate his later life.

As was his usual custom, Gorges called at the officers' club just off Adderley Street for a drink and a chat after a tiring, sweaty day drilling troops and inspecting stores. This evening a group of the newly-arrived officers from the Royal Irish Fusiliers, wearing mess uniforms, were lining the brown mahogany bar swapping their first impressions of South Africa.

'What gets me down is the heat during the day,' said one officer in a soft southern Irish brogue.

'But what you have to remember, old boy,' said Gorges, joining the group, brandy and soda in his hand, 'what you have to remember is that it can get damn chilly at night out in the veldt.'

'By the way,' he continued, 'I hope you don't mind me butting in. The name's Richard Gorges. I'm with Thorneycroft's Horse.'

The magic name of Thorneycroft of Spion Kop guaranteed, once again, admiring glances and a steady flow of questions and glasses of brandy.

'I say, Gorges, this damned language these Boers use. For instance, does veldt mean the desert?'

'Well, it can do. But really the veldt is everything between here and there. It's the country outside the towns. It can be desert; it can be farmland; or it can mean fairly hilly country. Out here you've got to remember everything's distance. It's a big place. So really everywhere that's not a town is the veldt.'

Gorges went on, jabbing his cheroot to emphasise the point: 'But I tell you this, those Boers live, sleep, and eat on the veldt. They can see you coming for miles and yet you can't see them until you're right on top of them. It's devilish difficult out there. Believe me, I've had some.'

His stories of the veldt and of Spion Kop dominated the conversation, and the Fusiliers' officers invited Gorges to join them for dinner. As he sat down he turned to his companion on the left, a lieutenant in his early twenties.

'I'm sorry, old boy. I didn't quite catch your name in the introductions.'

'It's Shackleton. Frank Shackleton.'

They shook hands, half-rising from their straight-backed chairs. Gorges was a head taller than the clean-shaven, even-featured lieutenant.

'Shackleton, eh. No relation by any chance to that chappie Shackleton who's off to the South Pole with Captain Scott?'

'He's my elder brother, actually.'

'Well, bless me, my dear chap,' said Gorges expansively. 'That certainly calls for some wine. Brother of that Shackleton, eh? We'll have to drink a toast to Scott's success. Though, if you don't mind me saying, give me the heat and the flies here rather than all that ice and those penguin birds!'

The two men laughed and from that moment were friends. Shackleton envied Gorges's experience and reputation; Gorges envied his companion's obviously high connections in society. During dinner they compared their backgrounds. Shackleton explained how his father, a doctor, had moved from County Kildare to Dulwich, near London, where he now had a flourishing practice. Gorges, for obvious reasons, was more reticent about his family background, merely saying he'd followed his father, once a lieutenant-colonel in the Indian Army, in the family tradition of soldiering in the colonies. Why he'd followed that family tradition in such haste was something not to be mentioned. The conversation between the two men went on over brandy and cigars, served as they sat in the well-upholstered chairs of the club's lounge. By now, despite their differences in rank, they'd slipped easily onto Christian-name terms.

'What were you doing, Frank, before you volunteered?'

'Well, it wasn't much of a job really. I was an assistant to an assistant at Dublin Castle.'

'Oh – in the civil service?'

'Not really. I was working in the office of the Ulster King of Arms. You know, looking up old family trees and mottoes and all that sort of thing.'

'Pretty boring, eh?'

'No. Not at all, actually. I've always been interested in genealogy, and it's a pretty responsible department, you know, Richard. We've got to arrange all the ceremonies for the Viceroy, look after the Crown Jewels, all that sort of thing.'

'Crown Jewels, old boy? I thought they were in the Tower of London.'

'No – I mean the Irish Crown Jewels. Well, that's what they're called although, to be absolutely precise, they're the ceremonial jewels belonging to the Order of St Patrick.'

'Well, I don't know, Frank. It sounds a pretty fine position to me.'

'Yes, I suppose it is. When this lot's over I'll probably go back to it.'

The evening ended with Gorges and Shackleton making arrangements to meet the next day for a lunchtime drink at Cape Town Castle. Gorges was delighted with his new friend, well-connected socially and first-class company. Good-looking too, he mused to himself, as he strolled back to his quarters, and a nightcap of his favourite Van Houten's cocoa laced, as usual, with brandy by Peter, who always waited up for his captain's return.

It was Frank Shackleton who raised the subject first as he and Richard Gorges dined together during the second week of their friendship. He was very blunt about it.

'Richard, what do we do about women and that sort of thing in this place?'

'Well, that's one of the problems, old boy. It might seem like the Wild West out here, even compared to Dublin, but, frankly, those sort of things just don't happen here. I suppose it's all to do with all that Boerish puritanism?'

'Boerish? Or boorish?'

The men laughed. 'That's not bad, Frank. Boerish or boorish! But, sadly, that is the situation.'

Shackleton looked dismayed. But Gorges continued quickly. 'As I said that, sadly, is the situation unless. . . .'

'Unless what?'

'Well, unless you happen to have a friend who knows a friend who can arrange these things.'

'Do you know such a friend, Richard?'

'It could be arranged, old boy. I take it you don't object to coloured people?'

'Coloured? Not the natives, surely?'

'Oh, certainly not, Frank. I mean . . . well, they're kaffirs. Not done. Not done at all.'

'What then?'

'Well, my friend has some friends among the Malays. I wouldn't exactly call them natives, would you?'

'I don't know,' said Shackleton hesitantly.

'I tell you what, old boy,' replied Gorges quickly, 'I'll get my friend to arrange something, arrange for you to meet somebody and, I mean, if you don't like her . . . well you don't have to do anything, do you?'

'All right then, Richard,' said Shackleton, throwing down his napkin and beginning to rise from the table. 'Arrange something and we'll see.'

Two nights later, Gorges and Shackleton went to the Woodstock district. They threaded through the narrow alleys until they came to the spice shop.

'This is the address, Frank. Now you just go up those stairs at the side and go in that door.'

Shackleton looked worried and embarrassed. 'I'm told her name is Ann-Su,' said Gorges. 'She might be exactly what you're looking for.'

'I don't know, Richard. I don't know,' said Shackleton looking nervously around. 'I mean – what if anyone from the regiment saw me.'

'They don't come down here, old boy. They stick to the club or the mess. Don't worry.'

'Are you sure?'

'I'm sure. Just go on up there and enjoy yourself.'

Frank Shackleton walked up the stairs, turned to look down at Gorges as if for reassurance, and then continued upwards. He knocked at the door and, after a moment, it opened. From the street, Gorges couldn't see who was behind the door but he knew it would be Ann-Su. Anyway, that's how he'd planned it with her brother. Another few seconds and Shackleton went through the door and it closed.

'All okay, Captain?' Peter had been watching from an alleyway across the narrow street and approached Gorges.

'Fine, Peter. Just fine. Let's give them ten minutes and then we'll go in.'

To pass the time Gorges haggled desultorily with some of the street tradesmen, amused at the way they liked the bargaining more than they did the actual selling. Then, with Peter, he returned to the spice shop and quietly began climbing the wooden stairs. Peter opened the door and, motioning Gorges to be silent, led him into his home.

The outer room was in darkness but a sliver of light shone from under the bedroom door. Gorges tip-toed to the door and listened for a moment, ear pressed against the wood. He turned back to Peter and nodded. The two men began undressing. Peter was naked in a moment. Gorges took longer, struggling with the buttons of his waistcoat. When they were both naked, they embraced for a moment, both obviously excited at the feel of their skins against each other, and at the prospect of what lay before. Peter slid to his knees, kissing Gorges's body, before fastening his mouth on him. Gorges almost succumbed, throwing his head back in pleasure. But then he put his hands on either side of Peter's head and pulled him gently from his body. Peter looked up, lips wet, and saw Gorges nod towards the bedroom door. The Malay boy got up and moved to the door. He grasped the handle and turned it gently. He'd oiled the hinges and lock especially that very day, so there was no noise as it swung open. Gorges stood by him, hand on his waist, as they looked in.

Ann-Su's jet-black hair was spread across the pillow, gleaming in the subdued light of the oil lamp. Her head tossed from side to side, small mewing sounds coming from deep in her throat. Her hands were clasped tightly round Shackleton's neck and her calves and ankles gripped just above his pumping buttocks. Her eyes opened and she saw her brother and 'his Captain' at the door.

'Me kant, tuan,' she breathed into Shackleton's ear.

'Kant?'

'Me turn, tuan,' translated the girl, easing herself from under Shackleton and turning him onto his back. Then she straddled him, keeping her head close to his, her hair hiding his face, just as she'd been instructed by her brother.

Gorges and Peter slipped into the room and stood either side of the bed. Then Ann-Su raised her face from Shackleton's and leaned back, supporting herself on her knees and her hands on either side of his body, as it moved in rhythm with hers. It was then that Shackleton, beginning to moan with delight, saw first Gorges and then Peter. His eyes, glazed with pleasure, widened. His mouth opened to say something but Ann-Su covered it with hers as she leant forward again, her small breasts with erect nipples crushing against the hairs on Shackleton's chest.

Gorges and Peter knelt on either side of the bed and began caressing the heaving bodies and each other. Soon the four bodies were joined together, and Frank Shackleton learned of sensations he'd never imagined could exist. He learned that male and female bodies could be interchangeable, each capable of giving pleasure.

Next morning, the two British officers walked back through the Cape Town dawn. They hardly exchanged a word and Gorges was determined it was not he who would break the silence. Suddenly Shackleton stopped and turned to his taller companion.

'Richard, I want to say I was shocked and ashamed when I first saw you and that boy there, but now I'm not. That was the most incredible experience of my life.' Gorges smiled.

'That's all right, old boy. We'll have to do it again sometime.'

The two officers laughed into each other's faces, clapped each other on the back, and continued on their way.

Twice more Shackleton and Gorges went back to Woodstock and the bedroom above the spice shop. Each time their bodies demanded more delights. Once they stood, caressing each other, and watched the Malay brother and sister bring themselves to their climaxes with just tongue and hand. Once Peter and Ann-Su lay together watching the two Englishmen making love, Shackleton now uninhibited in either heterosexual or homosexual embraces. But soon orders came for the Royal Irish Fusiliers to move up country.

'We're going to a place called Brandfort, Richard. We're to man the blockhouses around the railhead.'

'Don't worry, old boy. It'll be a bit boring but I doubt if the Boers will trouble you there. You'll be back in Cape Town in a month or two. I'll still be here, I bet.'

The two men got gloriously drunk at the farewell party held in the Fusiliers' mess. Even Gorges, for once, was overcome with the amount of liquor he consumed. But he managed to nurse his hangover down to the railway station to shake Shackleton's hand before the battalion boarded their armoured train.

In Cape Town, Gorges continued his life of pleasure, punctuated by occasional bursts of intensive activity, as new recruits came in for training and new supplies arrived. News from up country took a few days to filter back – usually news of ambushes on the veldt, skirmishes around blockhouses, or reprisal raids on the farms of uitlanders. Once, Gorges heard of a skirmish near Brandfort, but he thought nothing more of it until he received a message from the Army hospital at Wynberg.

'Lieut. F. H. Shackleton, Royal Irish Fusiliers, has been seriously wounded and asks if you can visit him.'

Gorges requested and received immediate permission to travel to see his friend. He found Shackleton, head and arm bandaged, in a long, airy ward at the hospital in the small South African township.

'How are you, old chap?'

'Not too much, Richard, as you can see. Blasted Boer sniper got me. Didn't even see him. Blast it.'

'Don't worry. You'll be up and about soon.'

'That's the rub. One caught me just above the elbow and the doctors think it's smashed up the muscles a bit much. They're going to send me home when I leave here.'

Gorges' dismay showed in his face. 'Not back to England, you mean?'

''Fraid so. They say I'll be travelling next week in the *Umbria*.'

'Oh, bad luck, old boy. Just here a few months, getting to know the place, and off you go again. We'll miss you.'

The two officers chatted for more than an hour, neither mentioning their nights above the spice shop, before a nurse told Gorges he'd have to leave and allow Shackleton to rest.

'I'll come to see you off in the ship before you go, Frank,' promised Gorges as he walked down the long ward away from his friend.

After Shackleton had left in the *Umbria*, along with hundreds of other wounded officers and men, Gorges continued his rather lonely life of work, drinking, and the pleasures of his companions in Woodstock. By now, no longer one of the few veterans in Cape Town who could tell of meeting the Boer at bayonet's length, his stories of Spion Kop and the Cape Mounted Police were beginning to lose their thrall amongst those who once hung on his every word. His drinking increased along with his visits to the bedroom above the spice shop. Within a few months, rumours began to circulate amongst the troops about a cavalry officer who 'kept' a Malay brother and sister in Woodstock. The later private Army inquiry never established where these rumours started, but Gorges always believed they began with an indiscreet word from Ann-Su while she was entertaining another member of the British forces. As the rumours began to circulate upwards into the officers' messes, Gorges was amongst the least of the suspected. Certainly, he was becoming a bit of a hard-drinking bore but he was a 'man's man' with seven clasps already to his South African campaign medal. But one morning, in May 1902, the world of Richard Howard Gorges crumbled again.

The previous night he'd dined and drunk particularly well and decided not to let Peter return to Woodstock. Instead, they stayed in the officers' quarters at the Castle. Before they retired to bed, Gorges plied the Malay boy with brandy, with the result that neither of them awoke when a fellow officer called at Gorges's quarters to inquire why he'd not appeared for breakfast in the mess. The bedroom door, through drunken forgetfulness, was ajar, and through it the officer saw Gorges and Peter lying naked on top of the bed. He reported immediately to the adjutant of the regiment, and Gorges was placed under arrest in his quarters. The still-befuddled Peter was tossed unceremoniously out of the Castle.

'Shall we court-martial Captain Gorges?' asked the adjutant.

'Court-martial him. Court-martial him,' boomed the redoubtable General Thorneycroft when he was told of the affair. 'I'd shoot the brute. I wouldn't try him.'

'But we can't shoot him, sir, without a trial?'

'Then kick him out of the regiment. At once, do you hear, at once.'

Thus sentence was pronounced on Richard Howard Gorges by the man he'd come to regard as his 'second father'. It was his second sentence of exile in less than ten years. He was ordered to report to the officers' mess at noon the next day, bringing with him his resignation in writing, relinquishing his commission in Thorneycroft's Mounted Horse.

'No explanation is to be given in your letter for your resignation. Nor will one ever be written down in the regiment's record,' said the officer who brought the news to the hapless Gorges. 'Just bring your resignation to the mess at noon. And get packed ready to leave the Castle immediately afterwards.'

As Richard Gorges, wearing civilian clothes, approached the mess at noon, he sensed a quietness about the area outside. Usually at this time, with the sun at its zenith, there would be small throngs of officers gathered under the shade of the balcony, drinks in hand. This day, there was only one officer standing there. As Gorges approached the double doors of the mess, the officer moved aside and opened them. Gorges stood at the threshold for a moment, eyes accustoming themselves to the cooler light inside. Twenty yards directly ahead of him, standing by the mantelpiece and under a large portrait glorifying the regiment's action at Spion Kop, stood General Thorneycroft. Drawn up in two lines, between Gorges and the General, were the sixteen officers of the regiment.

Gorges sensed what was to come but he had to go forward, his legs moving almost of their own volition. He marched through the ranks of fellow officers and held out his letter of resignation. The General took it without glancing downwards at it. His eyes pierced into Gorges's brain. He spat out one word very quietly.

'Swine.'

Then General Thorneycroft spun on his heel, turned his back on Gorges, hand clasping the letter behind his back, and looked up at the large painting.

The tall figure of Richard Gorges waited a moment and then turned. Before him was the open door. He began marching towards it, the second pace hardly taken when the first heavy cavalry boot crashed into his buttocks. He half staggered but continued at a measured pace as each officer kicked him in turn. At the door he paused, waiting for the last kick which pushed him, off balance, on to the steps of the balcony. The door behind him slammed shut. As he walked out into the fierce sunshine tears of humiliation began trickling down his face.

On 23 May 1902 the life of Richard Howard Gorges in South Africa had ended.

2

Just a jape

Thirty minutes after midnight on 18 March 1906, there was little doubt that the newly-knighted Sir Arthur Vicars, Ulster King of Arms, Registrar of, and Knight Attendant on, the Order of St Patrick, was becoming very tipsy indeed. He swayed slightly as he stood before the glowing coals in the fireplace of his gaslit office on the first floor of the Bedford Tower in Dublin Castle. Around him were his staff and some of their friends, invited by Sir Arthur to celebrate the successful end to the social season in Ireland. In the yard below horses' hooves clattered on the cobbles pulling the carriages of the social élite away from the final ball of the season, in St Patrick's Hall at the Castle. The season always placed an extra burden on Sir Arthur and his staff, with all the worries about which lord took precedent over which knight in seating arrangements at dinners, or positions in processions with the Viceroy of Ireland, Lord Aberdeen, or even the annual headache about the order in which debutantes should be presented to the Viceroy. The season gave Sir Arthur, working closely with the vice-regal staff, little chance of studying the complicated genealogy of the Irish aristocracy. But he did enjoy the pageantry of the season, and this season, which had begun the previous Christmas, had gone without a hitch.

'Gentlemen,' he slurred slightly, 'Gentlemen, I want you to raise your glasses and drink a toast to the present company. I think we deserve it.'

The nine men with him raised their glasses of champagne and drank the toast.

'Present company.'

Sir Arthur stumbled slightly on the edge of the carpet by the fire. 'Horlock, I think we need some more wine.'

Charles Horlock, his personal secretary, nodded benignly and left the room to go to the office next door, where half a dozen bottles of champagne had been placed in ice buckets.

'I say, the Viceroy was in good form tonight, wasn't he, sir?'

Sir Arthur looked blearily at his nephew, Peirce Gun Mahony, who was Cork Herald on his staff.

'Eh, what, Peirce?'

'I said the Viceroy seemed to have a splendid time. Hardly off the floor during the quadrilles.'

'Yes . . . yes . . . quite a success.'

Horlock returned to the room, dominated by a large leather-topped desk which had been lifted into a corner to provide more space. The champagne corks popped and glasses were refilled.

'No more for me, thanks,' said Frank Bennett-Goldney, a thickly-set man who was due to become Athlone Pursuivant. 'I've got to return to the Shelbourne and get changed. I'm catching the mail boat back to England.'

Bennett-Goldney exchanged good-byes and left. Apart from his expected sinecure in Dublin he was also Mayor of Canterbury, and nursed ambitions to become Member of Parliament for that constituency in Kent.

'Dammit,' said Arthur Burtchaell. 'When he becomes Athlone he'll have to spend more time here than he does now.'

'Now, now, Arthur,' Ulster King of Arms gently chided his chief secretary. 'You know he's a very busy man, and anyway he doesn't like being away from his mother for too long. Don't be an old grouch, Arthur. Enjoy yourself and get me another glass of wine, will you?'

'Do you really think that's wise, sir? Your head you know.'

'Yes, I do know, Arthur. But tonight is special, what?'

Sir Arthur swayed as he held out his glass. He surveyed the rest of the company through eyes which were rapidly finding considerable difficulty in focusing. Peirce Mahony was discussing the new play at the Abbey Theatre with Esme Percy and Peter McEnnery. Percy, with his perfect actor's profile, held himself in conversation as if he was constantly on stage, continually being watched through opera glasses. In contrast,

McEnnery, whose father's estate spanned prime hunting country outside Dublin, looked a red-faced farmer, almost bursting out of his evening dress.

But Sir Arthur enjoyed the contrast in the group. Percy, so witty and sharp; McEnnery, generous and down-to-earth; Mahony, conscientious and loyal. Good friends all, he thought.

A shout of laughter from another part of the room, over by the large windows now curtained in a deep red velvet, made Sir Arthur turn. He swayed more noticeably as Burtchaell handed him his refilled glass. He walked unsteadily, weaving slightly, towards this group.

'What's the joke then, Frank?' he asked his Dublin Herald, Frank Shackleton.

'Well, sir, Richard here was telling the latest tale about Daisy Warwick.'

'You mean Lady Warwick, don't you?' It was a gentle reproof. Sir Arthur Vicars didn't like too much familiarity with the socially famous. Especially one who was the mistress of King Edward VII.

'Yes, sir. Lady Warwick.'

'Well, then, what is this latest tale?' He turned to the man on his right, the only one in the company wearing military uniform. 'Come along, Captain Gorges, tell us.'

Richard Gorges took the cheroot out of his mouth and smiled. 'Again, Sir Arthur?'

'Go on, Richard, it's so ripping,' urged the other two in the group, Peter Simpson-Jones and John Hillman, both newly arrived from university to work in the vice-regal office before joining the Foreign Office. 'Let's hear it again.'

'Well, I'm told that Lord Charles Beresford has been taking advantage of His Majesty's absence on the Riviera. He was invited to the Warwicks' for the weekend and thought he should try to re-establish his reputation with Lady Warwick, if I can put it that way.'

The group guffawed with the exception of Sir Arthur Vicars, who merely smiled weakly.

'Beresford', resumed Gorges, 'went a-calling after the house had retired. He got to the room where Daisy Warwick usually sleeps, opened the door, rushed in wearing his nightgown, and jumped on the bed shouting "Cock-a-doodle-do".'

'What?' muttered Sir Arthur, as the others, who'd already heard the story, collapsed into laughter again.

'Cock-a-doodle-do, that's what Beresford said.'

'What's so funny about that, Gorges?'

'The joke is Lord Beresford had picked the wrong room, you see. He'd jumped into bed with the Bishop of Chester and his wife!'

Simpson-Jones and Hillman were gasping with delighted laughter. Sir Arthur Vicars seemed stunned at the enormity of the scandal he'd just heard. Richard Howard Gorges looked across at Frank Shackleton and winked.

Four years earlier, within days of his disgrace in South Africa, Richard Gorges had left the colony and returned to England. He had little money left and soon applied for a commission in the Royal Irish Regiment. His obvious experience, his South African campaign medals and clasps, and a letter of recommendation from Frank Shackleton, had ensured his success. No word of the circumstances of his resignation from Thorneycroft's Mounted Horse had reached his new regiment, and Gorges had explained it by saying he had had to return from the colony for family reasons. Indeed, his father had died in the previous month.

'And anyway, sir,' he told the adjutant of the Royal Irish Regiment, 'I think you'll agree I've done my share of fighting, what? Spion Kop and all that. Actually, the war's as good as over.'

He was commissioned as a captain and made an instructor of musketry. His first posting with the regiment was to Portsmouth. Gorges enjoyed his life at the great naval port on the south coast, and his round of duties with musketry work at Hilsea Lines, the big ceremonial parades on Southsea Common, or the smaller church parades at the Garrison Church, in the shadow of Portsmouth Cathedral and Southsea Castle. It was an agreeable time. The slight scar on his forehead, from the Boer shrapnel, set him apart from the officers of his own age, and guaranteed him the attention in the mess that had begun to wane in Cape Town.

His other appetites were satisfied by fumbled assignations with young sailors in grubby rooms along Queen Street, leading from Portsmouth Dockyard, or in the more comfortable and relaxed surroundings of a set of rooms he'd rented in Alhambra Road, just off the promenade at Southsea, the holiday part of the naval city. The train services to London were frequent, and he travelled to the capital at least once a month to meet Frank Shackleton.

Early in 1903, Shackleton had left the Army with a disability pension and begun working with a firm of brokers in the City, the financial heart of the great Edwardian Empire. Shackleton had kept in touch with Dublin, and was appointed Gold Staff Officer to Ulster King of Arms for King Edward's visit to Ireland in 1903. But, apart from these less than onerous duties, Shackleton was intent on making his fortune. His brother, Ernest, had returned, a figure of note, from Captain Scott's unsuccessful Polar expedition in 1901, and was beginning to talk of forming his own expedition to make the dash to the South Pole. To raise money, Ernest looked at schemes for mining in Bulgaria, for running a fleet of taxi-cabs, for setting up a whaling factory. The brothers Shackleton, Ernest and Frank, had the same driving charm, the same good looks, the same determination to make a fortune and live as one of the landed gentry. The differences were in their sexual tastes and in their methods of acquiring their fortunes. Ernest had received a head start with his marriage to the daughter of an extremely wealthy lawyer. Frank had to rely more on his wits. There was brotherly regard between them, but also an innate rivalry.

'I think I'm on to something big this time,' confided Frank Shackleton to his friend, Richard Gorges, one day in the summer of 1904. They lay sprawled across a couch at Shackleton's flat at 44, Park Lane, the smartest part of London's Mayfair. 'This time it really looks good.'

'What is it?' queried Gorges, leaning across to refill his glass with hock.

'I've been let in on the ground floor of a scheme to buy a forest – a whole forest, mark you – in Mexico. This company has got the option on it and they've invited me to help promote the scheme. We're calling it the North Mexico Land and Timber Company. Once we've raised the capital we should make a real killing.'

'Are you that certain?'

'Richard, my dear friend, I'm so confident about this that I'll even let you buy into it.'

'Not much chance there, old boy. You know I'm fairly short of the ready. Always looting my friends.'

'Don't worry. There's plenty of time.'

'That's just not what there is,' said Gorges, putting down his glass and turning towards Shackleton. 'I've got to catch a train back to Portsmouth in a couple of hours. There's not much time today.'

Shackleton smiled at the neat way his friend had steered the direction of the conversation. Gorges stood up and began unbuttoning his waistcoat. . . . Later, as Gorges puffed a cheroot and sipped some wine from the bottle in an ice bucket at the bedside, he had some news for his friend.

'It's on the cards, Frank, that the regiment will be moving back to Ireland next year. The talk in the mess is that we'll be based at the Curragh for three or four years.'

'Well, well, Richard. With my connections at Dublin Castle we should have a marvellous time.'

In fact, it was Shackleton who moved first to Dublin on a more permanent basis. Delighted with his earlier work, Arthur Vicars appointed him Dublin Herald on his staff.

'I won't be able to spend all my time in Ireland,' said Shackleton as he was offered the post. 'I've got a lot of business in London, as you know.'

'Don't worry, Frank. I realise you're a coming man in business, but really your duties here will be more ceremonial than anything else. There'll be busy periods when I'll need your help but I'm sure we can fit these in with your plans.'

Shackleton was delighted with his social elevation. But there was the problem of where to stay in Dublin.

'I doubt, sir,' he said, 'If my funds would stretch to a suitable hotel like the Shelbourne or the Gresham, or Buswell's when I am in Dublin.'

Vicars thought for a moment, hands straightening some papers on the desk in front of him.

'I tell you what, Frank. I'm thinking of moving from my present rooms in Wellington Road. They're much too small now the office is getting bigger and there's more entertaining to do. Why don't we rent a place together?'

The arrangement seemed ideal. Vicars and Shackleton moved to a semi-detached Victorian villa at No. 7, St James's Terrace, Clonskeagh, in Dublin, agreeing to share all the household expenses. They engaged a cook, Elizabeth Darcy, a manservant, Frederick Pitt, and a coachman, Arthur Phillips, to run their new establishment.

Three months later, Captain Richard Gorges arrived at the Curragh, the huge military camp thirty miles outside Dublin, to continue his duties as musketry instructor with the Royal Irish Regiment. But in those few months the relationship had changed somewhat between Ulster King of Arms and his Dublin Herald, for – although luxurious by the standards of the appalling Dublin slum tenements – the villa in St James's Terrace could be cramped at times. The closer relationship, or perhaps understanding, between the two bachelors began, quite naturally, around the bathroom. One morning, Vicars, ever mindful of how Lord Fingall had once defined a gentleman to him as 'one who tells the truth and takes a bath every day', opened the bathroom door without knocking, and saw Shackleton lying in the bath, gently soaping himself. The sight of the young, battle-scarred body before him shocked Vicars. He left the bathroom immediately, apologising for his intrusion. But as he lay in the same bath later the memory of Shackleton's body returned to excite him. He hadn't thought of men in that way before, but he'd wondered often why other men's talk about the beauties of such and such a woman had failed to arouse much response in himself.

At breakfast, just after nine o'clock, he helped himself to some fried whiting from the warming plates on the sideboard, and apologised yet again to Shackleton for interrupting his bath.

'Should have knocked, Frank. Sorry. Quite inexcusable.'

'Don't be so silly, sir. In the Army you get quite used to that sort of thing. I mean, after all, we're both men. Put it from your mind, please.'

But, that evening, Vicars returned to the subject. While Shackleton nursed a large brandy in their drawing room, he sipped his second glass of port. He had no head for drink and even one glass served to loosen his inhibitions.

'Frank, this morning . . . well, I mean . . . it was the first time I've seen a man's body like that and . . . well, it did shock me a bit.'

Vicars went on hurriedly, 'I mean, Frank, not your wounds, but, well, just a naked man. I can tell you I've been disturbed about it all day.'

Shackleton smiled at the man sitting opposite him, relaxed in the armchair covered in dark printed chintz.

'As I said this morning, put it from your mind. It's not the "poses plastiques" after all.' He laughed at his companion's puzzled expression. 'You mean you haven't heard of "poses plastiques?"'

'You mean. . . .'

'Yes. Young boys standing up before men without any clothes on.'

'Good lord, no. I wouldn't like that.'

'Some people do, sir, as you well know. Some very highly placed people at that.'

'Of course, I've heard some rumours, but surely it's all very wrong and unnatural? I mean, well, it's abominable.'

'Judge not, sir, judge not.' Shackleton wagged his finger, almost in reproof. 'Love between men has been happening long before the coming of Christ. You just have to read the Greek classics.'

'I know, Frank, but nowadays?'

'Nowadays the abominable thing is to be found out. Our gracious majesty can have an affair with any common actress, as you well know, and everyone thinks that's jolly normal and something to be applauded. Any other vice is therefore abominable, to use your word. But it still goes on.'

Vicars was taken aback by Shackleton's liberal attitude but, even after two glasses of port, he couldn't bring himself to put the question to Frank Shackleton, Dublin Herald, that was now firmly in his mind. However, the arrival of Captain Gorges in Ireland three weeks later meant he never had to put that unspoken question. It soon became apparent even to the unworldly gentleman, now just turned 40 years of age and soon to be knighted, that there was a lot more than common friendship between Shackleton and Gorges. The two men, outwardly like any other young eligible bachelors, took strolls together through Phoenix Park on Sunday morning, or went out to the Strawberry Beds, on the north bank of the River Liffey, that other favourite place of relaxation for Dubliners on a sunny weekend. Gorges cut a dashing figure at the ceremonial parades at the Curragh or in Phoenix Park, and he and Shackleton were in constant demand at weekend hunting parties, at the great houses that abounded within twenty miles of the Irish capital. Life in Dublin, at that time, had an infectious gaiety to be found in few European capitals, and the Fenian troubles before the turn of the century seemed to have been forgotten. Terrible poverty still afflicted the west of Ireland but in Dublin, in the summer of 1905, Frank Shackleton and Richard Gorges led a sweet life.

But Vicars's suspicions about Shackleton hardened from doubt to firm conviction one Monday morning in early October, when he returned earlier than usual from a weekend with the Earl and Countess of Fingall. He let himself quietly into the villa in St James's Terrace and went upstairs, to change from his weekend tweeds into his everyday working clothes of frock coat and light grey striped trousers. From Shackleton's room, next door to his, he heard laughter and two voices. Vicars, without really thinking, went across the landing, knocked on the door, and, without waiting for a reply, entered. Shackleton looked round, surprised. He was dressed only in a towel, obviously fresh from a bath. Lying in bed, the sheets half covering his naked chest, was Richard Gorges.

'Good morning, sir,' said Shackleton, quickly regaining his composure and smiling slightly. 'Back a little early from the Fingalls', aren't you?'

'Yes, Frank, yes,' muttered Vicars, his eyes fixed firmly on Gorges. 'I didn't realise you had invited a guest for the weekend.' He turned hurriedly. 'I'll see you at breakfast.'

The meal was eaten in a strained silence, although Shackleton and Gorges made occasional attempts to draw Vicars into a conversation about his weekend with the Fingalls. Later, at Dublin Castle, Vicars called Shackleton into his office.

'Frank, I think you should have told me that you'd invited Captain Gorges to stay while I was away.'

'Why, sir?' Shackleton realised this was to be something of a formal interview.

'Well, you know. . . .'

'Know what, sir?'

Vicars became exasperated. 'Let me be perfectly plain, Dublin. What is this friendship you have with Captain Gorges, because to me it seems to go a long way beyond what might be considered a normal friendship?'

'Sir, we served together in South Africa. We are very close friends.'

'That's not what I mean, Dublin. Are you and he . . . well, I mean, do you and he . . . dammit, sir, you know what I mean.'

Frank Shackleton looked calmly down at Ulster King of Arms seated behind his desk. 'You want the truth, sir, and the truth is that Richard Gorges and I are very special and close friends. We share a common interest.'

'You mean?'

'Yes.'

Vicars buried his head in his hands. 'Good lord, Frank, I never thought. The scandal. The scandal.'

'What scandal?'

'The scandal.'

'There'll be no scandal, sir. After all, you and I share the same house all the time when I'm in Dublin, and nobody turns a whisker at that.'

'I shouldn't think so.' Vicars looked up angrily. 'The very idea.'

'Well, then, where's the scandal between Richard and myself? Only you know he's a special friend, so I cannot see the harm or the scandal. We are naturally very discreet in our behaviour.'

'I should hope so, Frank. I should hope so. But I'll have to consider the position very carefully. I'll talk to you later at dinner.'

Vicars thought long and hard during the day in his office and during the early evening at his club in Kildare Street. And the more he thought the more he realised he was compromised and that there was little he could do.

At dinner at St James's Terrace, the two men ate their galantine of chicken in silence. Shackleton knew Vicars had to speak first. The older man put down his knife and fork abruptly.

'Frank, it's quite clear that you cannot have Captain Gorges to stay here again. You can, of course, bring your friends, including him, here for dinner or a drink, but you must not have them stay the night. Do you understand?'

'Certainly. We share this house and I wouldn't do anything to upset you, sir.'

'Obviously, the fact that you and Captain Gorges are, what you call, special friends has come as a great shock to me. But, as you yourself said, judge not. I think you're right. I shall not judge.'

His eyes pleaded across the dining table. 'But, Frank, for heaven's sake, be discreet. The scandal could bring down Dublin Castle itself.'

'You have my word, sir. There'll be no scandal.'

Over the next months Shackleton invited Gorges often to St James's Terrace, but only for dinner. Gradually, Vicars became used to their friendship, and even began to warm to the other friends the two men introduced into the circle. To his surprise, his nephew, Peirce Gun Mahony, was invited often and seemed to revel in the company with its heavy drinking, its slightly risqué jokes, and its long discussions about the theatre, fashion, and the arts.

But Vicars's notoriously slight head for alcohol meant he usually retired to bed before the evening's parties were over. His departure was the signal for Shackleton or Gorges to lock the doors, dim the lamps on the gaselier, and allow its soft light to reflect off the rose-coloured silk of the fringed shade, and onto the more intimate activities of their circle of friends. Clothes were flung carelessly into corners as couples paired off in passioned embraces. It was strange, thought Shackleton more than once, how married men even, once they'd shed their inhibitions along with their clothes, began to delight in the other face of love. And so it continued through the social season of 1905–6, ending with the celebratory party in the office of Ulster King of Arms, above the Upper Yard of Dublin Castle.

By two o'clock in the morning of 18 March 1906, Sir Arthur Vicars lay, or rather sprawled, on a comfortable, leather-covered settee pushed to one wall of his office. The stud of his stiff white wing collar was undone, and his white bow tie hung over the silk lapels of his tail-coat. His curly brown hair, with its middle parting and greying sideburns, fell dishevelled over his high forehead. His trim moustache, streaked a little with grey, quivered slightly as he snored quietly in a drunken sleep.

Around him his celebratory party continued, though the company had been reduced. Arthur Burtchaell and Charles Horlock had left, knowing that with Ulster King of Arms in the condition he was, they would be carrying the burden of the office's work later in the day. Peter McEnnery had left as well, having a hunt to lead that day in Co. Meath. The six who remained, drinking the last bottles of champagne, were Frank Shackleton, Richard Gorges, Peirce Gun Mahony, Esme Percy, Peter Simpson-Jones, and John Hillman. It was Percy who suggested the idea first.

'Don't you keep the Crown Jewels in this building?' he asked Shackleton.

'Certainly, my dear old acting friend. They're in a safe in the library downstairs.'

'Couldn't we have a peek at them? I've always wanted to see them.'

'Not possible, old boy,' said Shackleton, draining his glass and reaching for the bottle again. 'I haven't got the key to the safe. Only dear old Sir Arthur over there carries that.' He gestured towards Ulster King of Arms sound asleep on the sofa.

'But he wouldn't know if we just borrowed the key and had a look, would he?' chimed in Simpson-Jones. 'I think it's a marvellous idea.'

Shackleton shrugged. 'Well, I don't see why not. Can't be any harm in it while I'm here. After all, I am Dublin Herald.'

'Where does he keep the key?' asked Percy.

'On his key ring, I believe.'

The group looked across at Sir Arthur. The chain of his key ring hung across the front of his trousers.

'I'll get them,' said Peirce Gun Mahony, suddenly feeling protective towards his recumbent uncle. He crossed the room, gently detached the chain from its trouser fastening and, pulling slowly, drew a set of keys from the right pocket. He handed the keys to Shackleton. Sir Arthur shifted uneasily on the sofa, but continued snoring.

'Right, gentlemen, follow me,' said Shackleton, leading the group from the room, along a corridor and towards a circular staircase. This wound down into the hallway off the portico of the building. Shackleton led them directly across the hall, through a small archway and a set of doors, into the library of Bedford Tower. Twenty feet away, against the further wall, was the safe containing the Irish Crown Jewels.

Peirce Gun Mahony turned up the gas lights, and the six men approached the safe. Shackleton held Sir Arthur's key ring to the light and selected what he knew to be the key to the Radcliff and Horner safe. He slipped the key into the upper lock and turned it without a sound. Then he grasped the central handle on the door of the safe. This, too, moved without a sound and the safe swung open. Inside were a number of documents and half a dozen boxes.

'Which one is the jewels?' he asked Mahony.

'They're in the biggest box, Frank. The red morocco one. The other boxes hold the gold collars of St Patrick and some family jewels of mine.'

Shackleton crouched down and lifted out the large red morocco case, placing it on top of the safe. The others crowded around him as he opened it. Inside, wrapped in tissue paper, were two large pieces of jewellery. Shackleton carefully unwrapped the paper round them, and their brilliance flashed even in the half light of the library.

'These, gentlemen,' said Shackleton, 'are the Irish Crown Jewels, the jewels of the Order of St Patrick.'

'Aren't they incredible?' exclaimed Gorges, almost in a whisper. 'Aren't they just incredible?'

'Let me explain,' said Shackleton, holding up the larger of the pieces. 'This is the Star and its eight points are made from Brazilian diamonds. The shamrock in the middle is made of emeralds, and it's laid on a ruby cross. Now, look round the cross, that's the motto of the order 'Quis Separabit?' and the date of the founding of the order MDCCLXXXIII, or 1783 in other words, all picked out in rose diamonds. Magnificent, isn't it?'

The group of men were silent in their awed admiration. Shackleton picked up the second piece.

'Now this is the Badge. As you see, its inner trefoil of emeralds is laid on a ruby cross, and surrounded by this blue enamel band, with the motto and the date again picked out in rose diamonds. This outer circle is made out of the largest Brazilian diamonds, and the Irish harp and the loop on the top are also made out of diamonds.'

As he turned them in the half light, the diamonds flashed and sparkled, reflecting in the eyes of the men staring at them, transfixed by their beauty.

'How much are they worth?' asked Simpson-Jones.

'I should think they're without price as they are,' replied Shackleton. 'But if you broke them up, well, who knows? There must be hundreds of diamonds in them. Must be worth a fortune, eh? Must be.'

'I think they're insured for £20,000,' Mahony broke in. 'I recall Sir Arthur telling me that.'

'A fortune, indeed,' muttered Gorges. 'That's more than five hundred times what an ordinary working chap would earn in a year.'

'Yes, they're quite priceless,' said Shackleton, beginning to wrap the jewellery in tissue paper again.

'I say, you chaps,' said Simpson-Jones, somewhat hesitantly, 'Wouldn't it be a jape if we pinched them?' He giggled.

'Don't be silly,' said Shackleton, looking at him severely.

'No, I don't mean really pinch them, Frank. Just purloin them for the rest of the night and send them back to Sir Arthur in the morning. Give him quite a shock, eh?'

'It would be a ripping jape,' laughed Hillman. 'It would certainly teach Ulster not to drink too much champagne anyway.'

Mahony was against the idea. 'If the Viceroy found out there'd be the devil to pay.'

'Oh, I don't know, Peirce,' said Shackleton, warming to the idea. 'If Simpson-Jones and Hillman locked them in the vice-regal office the jewels couldn't come to any harm. I think it's a good jape.'

'Think it could be fun,' said Gorges rather vaguely. His mind was still filled with the beauty of the jewels and their value.

'Seems you're outvoted, I'm afraid, Peirce,' said Shackleton.

He put the jewels back in their case and handed it to Simpson-Jones. Then he locked the safe.

'Peirce, you go and put these keys back in Sir Arthur's pocket and I'll go and make sure the jewels are locked safely in the vice-regal office.'

Mahony took the keys upstairs while Shackleton and the rest crossed the portico of the building and opened the front door. The patrolling soldiers took little notice of the group as it crossed into the vice-regal office. Security was always tight at Dublin Castle, the headquarters of the British administration in Ireland, but the guards had been warned by the officer of the watch that there was likely to be a late party in Bedford Tower. Anyway, the sight of Captain Gorges in his uniform, accompanying Dublin Herald, was enough to allay any doubts they might have had. After Shackleton had satisfied himself about the strength of the lock in the drawer of Simpson-Jones's desk, the party returned across the courtyard to the Bedford Tower.

'Call up Sir Arthur Vicars's carriage, soldier,' ordered Gorges.

'Straight away, suh!'

When the group returned to his office, Sir Arthur sat slumped on the settee. His nephew had woken him after fixing the key ring to his trousers and replacing the keys in his pocket.

'Dear me. Oh, dear me,' slurred Ulster King of Arms. 'Seems I've had a little too much wine.' He tried to stand but fell back into the depths of the settee.

'Don't worry, sir,' said Mahony. 'Give us your arm and we'll see you to your carriage.'

With his nephew on one side and Shackleton on the other, Sir Arthur was helped downstairs and into his carriage, driven by Phillips, his coachman. Shackleton returned with him to St James's Terrace and, with the help of Pitt the footman, put him safely to bed. The rest of the group used carriages waiting outside Dublin Castle to reach their homes, while Captain Gorges begged a bed from the officer of the watch.

Shackleton managed four hours' sleep and breakfasted alone at St James's Terrace, forcing down one of Mrs Darcy's chicken omelettes after refusing, with an inward shudder, her offer of wholemeal porridge and kippers. He left for his office in Dublin Castle as Sir Arthur struggled awake, dry-mouthed and with a fearsome headache.

'I'll send Phillips back for Sir Arthur,' he told Pitt as he hurried down the steps of the villa. The problem that excited him now was how to return the Crown Jewels. In fact, he'd been in his office for scarcely five minutes when Simpson-Jones was on the telephone to him from his office across the Upper Yard. The same problem was exercising his mind.

'What shall we do, Frank? I don't want to hang onto the jewels longer than possible. I can't really hand them over to Sir Arthur myself because he might report me to the Viceroy and that'll mean the end of me for the Foreign Office. And I don't think we should entrust them to the messengers.'

'You're right, old boy. I'm afraid your jape has become a bit of a devil.'

'My jape? We were all in it together,' said an indignant and rather frightened Simpson-Jones.

'Well, you suggested it in the first place, didn't you, old boy?'

'But . . . but we all agreed. Don't put it all on me.'

'Oh, let's stop this squabbling and think how we can return them.'

'Is Sir Arthur in his office yet, Frank?'

'No. And I doubt with his hangover if we'll see him much before lunch. I've just sent his carriage back for him.'

'Well, what about if I simply popped the jewels over to you and you put them on his desk. Isn't that the safest way?'

'It'll be a bit of a shock for him in his state.'

'But, Frank, wasn't that the whole point of the jape?'

'Uhmm . . . you could be right.' Shackleton thought for a moment. 'All right then, let's do that.'

'I'll be over straight away.'

A few minutes after mid-day, Ulster King of Arms arrived at his office, immaculately shaved and dressed but feeling more than a little worse for wear. He saw his tray filled with letters; he noticed that all traces of the night's celebrations had been cleared away by Mrs Farrell, the cleaning woman, and her son, Seamus; and then, almost with disbelief, he saw the red morocco case planted squarely in the middle of his large blotting pad. Surely it couldn't be? he thought. Surely not? With unsteady hands, he opened the case and saw the Star and the Badge wrapped as usual in tissue paper. But how? And why?

Sir Arthur hurried into the next office, clutching the morocco case. 'Frank, what's this doing out of the safe? What are the jewels doing on my desk?' Shackleton heaved a sigh, got up from behind his desk, and walked up to Sir Arthur.

'Now, don't worry, sir. They've not been in any danger. It was all a jape.'

'A jape? A jape? What on earth has been going on? You must tell me, Frank.'

So, rather shamefacedly, Shackleton explained the night's events. Sir Arthur's face reddened, first with embarrassment and then with anger.

'I'll take this to the Viceroy, Dublin. He shall hear of this. It's monstrous.'

'But, sir, no harm's been done. And,' he added gently, 'none of this would have happened if you hadn't fallen asleep. Believe me, sir, it was simply a harmless jape.'

Sir Arthur's mind whirled with fatigue, pain, and now bewilderment. But even in this sorry state of mind he could comprehend that, for the second time in a year, he'd been compromised. And that, for the second time, his Dublin Herald, Frank Shackleton, had been involved.

'What part did Captain Gorges play in all this, Dublin?' he asked sharply.

'No more than anyone else, Sir Arthur. It was just a silly jape. Like you, we'd had too much champagne.'

'I am not satisfied, Dublin. I think you are too much influenced by others, particularly by Captain Gorges. I must warn you against him.'

Then Sir Arthur shrugged his shoulders in resignation. 'I suppose you're right, Frank. I'll have to regard it as a jape caused by too much wine. The main thing is the safety of the Crown Jewels. I'll put them back in the safe.'

He began to leave the room, holding the red morocco case close to his chest. Suddenly he stopped and turned.

'Obviously, Frank, I'm going to have to think more closely about security here. I shall have to take more care of the keys. Quite clearly.' He shook his head sadly as he left the room, shoulders drooping, a picture of dejection. In contrast, some miles away, approaching the Curragh military camp, Captain

Richard Howard Gorges was in an excited and very thoughtful frame of mind.

On that chilly March day in 1906, it had just occurred to him that if the Irish Crown Jewels could be 'stolen' once, then they could be stolen again.

3

Daisy Newman's 'entertainments'

In all their 690 years the dank corridors of Dublin Castle hadn't heard so much laughter as news of the jape spread through the overcrowded offices of the British bureaucracy in Ireland. The walls that wept usually with damp from the River Poddle, running beneath the Castle, cried now with laughter. When civil servants met Sir Arthur Vicars, scurrying back and forth with genealogical reference books, officious and meticulous, they could barely restrain themselves from laughing openly to his face. The laughter wafted along the quays of the River Liffey and into Phoenix Park. The Viceroy, Lord Aberdeen, heard the story from his son, Lord Haddo, permitted himself a mild guffaw and summoned Sir Arthur to see him.

The carriage of Ulster King of Arms was being re-upholstered that day early in April 1906, so Sir Arthur decided to walk to the Vice-Regal Lodge in Phoenix Park. As he hurried across King's Bridge, passing above the Guinness barges moored along the Liffey, and approached Park Gate, his mind reviewed all the security arrangements for his office. He knew instinctively that this was the reason for his summons. It took only twenty minutes before he glimpsed the white Ionic columns of the Lodge through the trees, just breaking into full leaf along the carriageway.

Sir Arthur waited in an anteroom for a few minutes before he was ushered by a footman into the Viceroy's office. This overlooked the sweeping lawns of the official residence and Lord Aberdeen, his full beard neatly trimmed, rose to greet his visitor from behind a desk set at an angle in a corner of the large room.

'Well, Ulster, I presume you know what this is about?'

'I would think it's about the safety of the Crown Jewels, my lord.'

'Precisely. Precisely. The safety of the jewels!'

Lord Aberdeen turned away and stood looking out of the window at the lawn, hands clasped behind his back.

'I, of course, Ulster, have heard about the recent incident concerning the jewels. I must confess it worries me greatly.'

'But, my lord, it was a harmless jape. It was wrong, of course, very wrong, but a mere piece of foolishness caused by too much wine.'

'I shall accept your judgment of that, naturally – and personally, I think you're correct – but this harmless jape, as you choose to call it, does prove that the jewels are vulnerable.'

He moved away from the window, walked over to Sir Arthur, and clasped his forearm tightly.

'What you have to remember, Ulster, is that we're living in dangerous times. There are anarchists everywhere who would dearly love to steal the jewels to embarrass His Majesty as well as using them to buy guns and all their infernal equipment. And I don't mean just the Fenians. At present they seem satisfied with the hullaballoos they're causing in the House of Commons. I'm told there are even Russians touring Europe trying to raise funds for some sort of revolution against the Tsar.'

Lord Aberdeen walked to his desk and picked up a sheaf of papers. 'There's even a report here from the Royal Irish Constabulary that says one of them, a fellow called – how do you pronounce it? – Maxim Litvinoff, has been in Dublin contacting our own little band of anarchists. These are very difficult times, Ulster. We have to be on our guard.'

'But, my lord,' Sir Arthur broke in, 'what more can I do? You know for years I've been worried about the jewels. I told your predecessor, Lord Cadogan, about it. I wanted a flat built for myself in the Bedford Tower and the jewels could have been placed there in complete safety.'

Sir Arthur spread his hands hopelessly. 'Then he was replaced by Lord Dudley and the whole idea fell through. Next the Board of Works built a strongroom in the Bedford Tower for all the books and manuscripts that are my responsibility, and they made the entrance too small for the safe containing the jewels to go into the strongroom.

'I mean, my lord,' Sir Arthur continued, shrugging his shoulders, 'what more can I do?'

'What about the keys to the safe, Ulster?'

'I've got the only two keys. One I've secreted at my residence. The other I always carry with me. I even sleep with it under my pillow. It's always with me.'

'On your key ring, I heard,' the Viceroy interrupted, a note of sarcasm creeping into his tone.

'But, where else, my lord? Where else?' Tiny beads of perspiration began to form on Sir Arthur Vicar's brow. 'After this latest episode I even asked West's the jewellers to make me a chain so that I could carry the second key around my neck. But they pointed out that that would mean I would have to virtually undress every time I wished to open the safe!'

'I see your point, Ulster. It is devilishly difficult.'

Sir Arthur, sensing sympathy in the Viceroy's attitude, hurried on. 'I mean, my lord, could the jewels be in any safer place? There's not a way an outsider can get to them. The Castle, after all, is patrolled by the constabulary and the military. Indeed, as you know, my lord, the military even use the basement of the Bedford Tower.'

'Yes, I suppose you're right, Ulster. The only danger lies within, as we've seen.'

'But, my lord. . . .'

'Can you vouch for all your staff?'

'Of course, my lord. Absolutely.'

'Of course, Ulster.' The Viceroy smiled amiably. 'And I don't think we have to worry about you running off with the jewels, do we?'

Lord Aberdeen laughed and the atmosphere in his office relaxed.

'Come along now, Ulster, don't look so solemn. Have a glass of sherry.'

'Thank you, my lord, but you know . . . my head.'

'Come along now, Ulster. One glass won't hurt, and I want to hear how the plans are progressing for the Exhibition next year, as well as His Majesty's visit. You're going to have a busy time.'

The two men sat in silk-covered armchairs as they discussed the plans for what were to be the momentous events in Ireland in 1907. Or so they appeared to be at the time.

That summer in 1906, a particularly fine one by any standards, Frank Shackleton continued with his plans to make a fortune in Mexico, and Captain Richard Gorges pursued the delights of an officer in an easy-going peacetime Army. Shackleton spent more and more time in London, chasing the crock of gold at the end of his Mexican rainbow. He had formed the Celtic Investment Trust to raise the £1,000,000 needed to finance the company that had obtained the vast land option in Mexico. His brother Ernest, too, was trying to raise money for his expedition to the South Pole and, in fact, was meeting more success than Frank.

'I've got this stockbroker, Frank Alden, interested in the scheme,' Frank Shackleton told Gorges one day in August, as they relaxed after a strenuous game of tennis at the Spa Hotel at Lurcan, just outside Dublin. 'Alden says he wants an independent team of forestry experts to go to Mexico to look at the land, and if their report is favourable then he says he'd be willing to underwrite a shares issue to the public.'

'That sounds marvellous,' said Gorges, sipping a lime juice liberally strengthened with London Gin.

'Well it is and it isn't, Richard. It's going to cost an awful lot of money to send them there, and my overdraft is getting pretty high even with the goodwill at Cox's Bank and all that. But if we can get that survey – and I'm sure it'll be a first class report – then the backing of Alden of Throgmorton Street will guarantee the success of the shares issue. And when that happens we're home, dry, and set for life.'

'How much do you need?' asked Gorges, adding hastily, 'Not that I've any to spare.'

'Well, I should think £10,000 in the next year would see me through. Once that report confirms the value of the forest then Cox's will be good for the rest.'

'That's a lot of money. An awful lot. Haven't you got any shares? I remember you saying. . . .'

'Oh, you mean those things I bought in the Montevideo

Public Works Corporation. They're already placed as security on my overdraft. Not that they're worth much.'

The rattle and hiss of the steam tram from Dublin, passing the hotel's entrance, brought the two friends back to reality.

'I think we'd better go and change, Frank. Don't want to catch cold, you know.'

They smiled at each other. Since the incident at St James's Terrace with Sir Arthur, they'd found this hotel an ideal meeting place. Gorges booked a room for the night, which gave them the chance of a game of tennis and, more importantly, the certainty of a few hours' undisturbed company.

'You take the bath first, Frank,' said Gorges as they entered the spacious hotel room, the shades pulled down to keep it cool from the heat of afternoon sun.

'No – all I want is a rub down with a wet flannel and a dry towel,' Shackleton smiled at Gorges. This was his invariable answer, almost a code phrase between them.

'Let me do it,' said Gorges, going into the adjoining bathroom and re-appearing with three large fluffy towels, which he spread carefully over the coverlet of the double bed. 'I'll get the flannel and soap.'

When he returned to the bedroom he'd shed his white shirt and white flannel trousers. Shackleton lay naked, face down on the towels. Gorges began rubbing the flannel over his friend's back, gradually working down to his tight buttocks, drying the skin with a small hand towel.

'Turn over, Frank.'

Gorges avoided deliberately the obvious sign of his friend's excitement and began washing his shoulders and chest. He moved down, still washing and drying gently, towel occasionally flicking against Shackleton's quivering body.

Then Gorges bent over Shackleton and kissed his chest, moving his hands and mouth downwards, first to caress and then hold his friend's maleness. Later, they reversed roles and it was Gorges's turn to moan and twist with delight. The bond between the two men was so complete that total intimacy of action or thought was now commonplace.

'Frank,' said Gorges, as they rested side by side, 'there is a way out of both of our money problems. I've been thinking about it a deal recently.'

Shackleton raised himself on one elbow and looked down into Gorges's face. 'I wish there was, dear Richard. If only there was.'

'Well, to be truthful, it's an idea that came to me after that jape last March. I thought to myself – if they can be pinched once, as it were, then they can be pinched again.'

'You mean, we steal the Crown Jewels?' said Shackleton, an incredulous note in his voice.

'Why not?'

'It's unthinkable.'

'Why? They're only a load of old diamonds, kept in a safe and rarely worn by anyone. Let's face it, they're pretty useless.'

'But they're the Crown Jewels!'

'I remember you telling me that they're really the jewels of the Order of St Patrick.'

'Same thing, Richard. Same thing.'

'Well, they aren't like the real Crown Jewels in the Tower of London, are they? In reality, they're simply the baubles of a club for doddering old Irish aristocrats. Anyone would think the Empire would fall if they vanished. The amount they're seen in public, they might just as well have vanished already, come to think of it.'

'You are serious about this, Richard, aren't you?' said Shackleton, surprise in his voice.

'Of course I am, old boy. Between us we could pinch them and live happily ever after. What about that hacienda on your timber plantation in Mexico? Just think of that.'

'That's what I am thinking about, Richard.' Shackleton lay back, rubbing his chin reflectively. 'You know, it's not such a silly idea after all. It would solve our problems . . . but, no, we'd never get away with it. No, it's impossible.'

'It's not impossible. At least let's talk about it. We've got the rest of the day.'

'All right then, but I don't think it's at all feasible.'

The two men dressed, ate a light tea of cucumber sandwiches and sesame cake in the hotel's spacious lounge, and strolled through the grounds, straw boater hats at a jaunty angle, discussing the idea that was shockingly new to Shackleton, but which had become something of an obsession to Gorges. For Gorges, whether he knew it consciously or not, his idea had become something more than a plan to obtain badly-needed money. Twice cast out and humiliated by people he'd regarded with total affection and loyalty, this scheme, nursed over many months, was to be his revenge, his way of striking back at those figures who had so wounded him.

'You see, Frank,' explained Gorges, as the two men stopped to sit on a secluded bench in the hotel's garden, 'it would be easy to engineer another kind of occasion when Sir Arthur would be incapable. This time, though, we wouldn't take his keys, we'd make wax impressions of them and have our own keys cut.'

'But wouldn't that be dangerous? In the hue and cry surely all the locksmiths in England, let alone Ireland, would be questioned by the police, and one of them would identify us? Then there's the whole problem of disposing of the jewels. We'd be identified again, surely? And that's even if we could find someone willing to buy them and then dispose of them. Remember there'll be an absolutely tremendous hue and cry.'

'Yes, of course. I've thought of all those things. Quite obviously we need someone who knows the criminal fraternity to help us, someone totally unconnected with us or the Castle.'

'But where . . .?' Shackleton interrupted.

Gorges held up a hand for silence and continued, 'I think I've got just the person. A woman called Daisy Newman.'

'Newman?'

'Yes, Miss Daisy Newman. Actually, she runs a very discreet business catering to the needs of people like you and me.'

'The needs?'

'You know . . . remember Peter and Ann-Su back in Cape Town?'

'Oh, I see. Where?'

'Right here in Dublin. An establishment in Ballsbridge.'

'But, Richard, how do you know she'd help?'

'Well, I've visited her when you've been away in London, and my impression is that she's pretty thick with the criminal fraternity, or knows people who are.'

'Wouldn't it be a risk bringing her into such a notorious robbery?'

'I think not if we pay her enough. She's already told me she's looking for money to open a similar establishment in London.

She thinks she's getting too well known in Dublin.'

Shackleton remained unconvinced. 'Who'd do the actual robbery, Richard?'

'I would. There are so many Army officers milling around the Castle all the time that I'd be inconspicuous.'

'But the sentries outside the Bedford Tower would recognise you.'

'Surely. But then I wouldn't go in the front entrance. I'd use the basement where military stores are kept. I'd go in through the basement and up into the library where the safe is. It would be quite easy for me to borrow the keys to the basement and have copies made. I've been to the basement stores a few times already on proper military business. I know the layout. All I'd need would be the key that opens the door to the library from the basement. And that's easy enough to get.'

'It's all pie in the sky, Richard, old friend,' said Shackleton.

He went on firmly, 'We'd never get away with it. The Dublin detectives aren't all that clever, but even they would realise the robbery would have been done by someone who works inside the Office of Arms.'

'Of course, they would, old boy. But what if you were in England throughout the whole period of the robbery? You'd have a perfect alibi.'

'But if I was away how would you get invited to Sir Arthur's to get the impression of the keys?'

'Don't you see it, Frank? We'd use Peirce Gun Mahony.'

'That's ridiculous. Peirce wouldn't help rob his uncle.'

'He wouldn't know he was doing it, Frank. He might realise afterwards what had happened – in fact, he probably would – but he wouldn't dare speak out. If it came out that he had tastes like we do then, as a supposedly happily married man, he'd be totally disgraced. I'd stake my life on his silence.'

'It's all a bit far-fetched for me, Richard, I must say.'

'No it's not,' insisted Gorges. 'Let's go and have a bite of dinner and a bottle of wine and you think some more about it.'

Richard Gorges was convinced he could persuade Shackleton to take part in the robbery, but he realised his best approach was to allow his friend to brood over the tentative plans. Indeed, Shackleton did remain fairly silent over dinner in the hotel dining room as he mulled over what Gorges had outlined. But as the two men ordered brandies, he began discussing the idea again. He had half made up his mind.

'What you've worked out does make sense, I see that. And I agree with what you say about Peirce. But there are two things worrying me at this stage. One is this woman of yours, Daisy Newman, and the other is the effect the robbery would have on Sir Arthur.'

'Let me take those in reverse order,' replied Gorges, drawing heavily on his cheroot. 'First, Sir Arthur. Well, I don't think the police will suspect him. They're not that cretinous. I think he'll have some explaining to do about the security of the jewels, but that's all. For a time, things will obviously be hot for him, but then it'll all simmer down.'

Gorges spoke with conviction because he knew Shackleton was fond of the Ulster King of Arms. He nursed different feelings himself, having heard that Sir Arthur had warned Shackleton about him. As far as Gorges was concerned, Ulster King of Arms could go to the devil – and in full regalia as well. But he hid his true feelings and continued.

'Now this woman, Daisy Newman. Well, the only way you're going to be convinced about her is by meeting her. I'll arrange something, say, tomorrow night.'

'The night after would suit better, Richard, if that's possible. The Viceroy is holding a levée tomorrow which I've got to attend in full dress. Let's make it the night after.'

'I will, Frank, I will,' said Gorges, sensing victory. 'And be prepared for some surprises. Miss Newman runs quite an interesting establishment.'

The house, tall and early Victorian, stood in its own grounds in a leafy avenue not far from the main road leading from Ballsbridge to Dublin. In the gathering dusk of a warm autumn evening, Shackleton and Gorges walked up the driveway towards the front door. Gorges banged the ornate knocker and, almost immediately, the door was opened by a boy in his middle teens, dressed in a green footman's uniform.

'Good evening,' said Gorges. 'We are expected by Miss Newman.'

'Yes, sir. May I take your coats and sticks?'

The boy ushered them into a drawing room off the hallway, comfortably furnished with two long chintz-covered sofas, a glass-fronted sideboard containing sparkling cut-glass crystal ornaments and, to Shackleton's surprise, mirrors that covered two walls from ceiling to floor.

They waited only a few minutes before the door opened and a woman in her early thirties, dressed in a green silk evening gown, entered the room.

'Good evening, Captain.'

'Hello, Daisy,' said Gorges, rising from the sofa.

She turned towards Shackleton. 'You must be the friend the Captain mentioned to me. Welcome to my house,' she said in a soft Dublin brogue.

The woman held out her hand formally and Shackleton took it without speaking. He was still bemused by his surroundings and the appearance of Miss Newman. He'd been expecting something sordid and vulgar, but this was like calling at any respectable house for, perhaps, an evening of bridge. Miss Newman, auburn hair hanging over her shoulders, was slim and elegant, sharp-featured yet attractive, not at all the blowsy female Shackleton had been expecting to meet. Gorges broke into his thoughts.

'I told you, Frank, you were in for a surprise.'

'Would you care for a glass of wine here or shall I have it served in your room, Captain?'

'In the room, please, Daisy.'

'Shall we discuss your business now – you did say you wanted to talk about business, didn't you? – or shall we have the entertainment first?'

'I think the entertainment first, Daisy. Don't you, Frank?'

Shackleton, startled out of his reverie by the question, merely nodded.

'Your friend doesn't say much, Captain. I have a feeling he expected something different.'

She moved to a velvet cord and pulled it once. The footman entered the room.

'John, show these gentlemen to the usual room.'

Gorges followed the footman up the thickly carpeted staircase with Shackleton trailing behind, still trying to gather his thoughts.

'Your room, gentlemen. I think everything has been made ready.'

The young footman opened a door leading off the first landing and stood to the side as Shackleton and Gorges went in. It was a large high-ceilinged room furnished with three armchairs, a sofa, and a nest of wooden tables. The footman re-entered the room and placed an ice bucket containing a bottle of champagne by the sofa. Shackleton looked round in bewilderment. There was no bed.

Gorges laughed. 'I know what you're thinking, Frank. It was exactly my reaction the first time I was brought here. But look at this.' He moved to a wall that was covered by a tapestry and pulled a cord at its side. The tapestry slid across revealing yet another large mirror. Shackleton gasped.

'Good lord! I can see into the next room.'

'Precisely, old boy. Let's have some wine and you just wait a moment.'

Shackleton sat in one of the armchairs, sipping his champagne and looking at the bedroom next door through the mirror. Suddenly, he saw Daisy Newman enter it, still dressed in her evening gown, followed by a younger woman, blonde and more buxom, wearing a maid's uniform. Neither of the women gave any indication that they knew they were being watched.

Daisy Newman sat at a dressing table and the maid began brushing her hair. After a few minutes she stood up, facing the mirror and the two men watched as the maid began unbuttoning her silk gown. It fell round her feet and she stepped out of it, wearing now a chemise and a white petticoat over dark stockings. These, too, were removed gently by the maid, and soon Daisy Newman stood naked. The maid, still standing behind her, began caressing her small pointed breasts, and the two men in the next room, now leaning forward in their armchairs, champagne forgotten, watched her nipples harden and rise. Then Daisy turned and embraced the maid, kissing her deeply on the mouth.

'Good lord, Richard,' Shackleton murmured, as the maid's clothes quickly joined Daisy Newman's on the carpeted floor.

'A bit different, what?' said Gorges in a rather strained voice. 'A bit different.'

The older woman now lay on the bed, her legs outstretched towards the mirror, as her maid sank to her knees and buried her head into Daisy Newman's trimmed pubic hair, licking and sucking. The two men, visibly excited by the display before them, saw Daisy fumble for a cord by the side of the bed. A bell tinkled on the wall beside Gorges.

'That's the signal, old boy. As they say, let's go and join the ladies. . . .'

Two hours later, thoroughly satiated and somewhat exhausted, Shackleton and Gorges, freshly bathed, returned to the drawing room to find their hostess ready with a decanter of brandy. She was dressed again in her silk evening gown, and acted as if nothing untoward had happened, unrecognisable now as the wild-haired, voracious woman of not so many minutes before, who'd lain sobbing and moaning, sandwiched between the thrusting bodies of her two guests.

'A drink, gentlemen.'

'Of course. Thank you.'

'Now this business you wanted to discuss, Captain.'

'Well, Daisy, it's quite possible that in the near future Frank and myself might be acquiring some jewellery in rather unusual circumstances. We wondered – or rather I wondered – if you might know of anyone who could help us dispose of the jewellery without it coming to the notice of the authorities.'

'I can presume, gentlemen, this jewellery might be considered by the authorities as being stolen at the time you acquire it.'

'You can so presume, Daisy.'

The woman smiled engagingly. 'Well . . . who would have thought?'

Shackleton looked at Gorges in alarm. Had his friend misjudged the woman's character?

'No – don't worry yourselves. I could help you . . . perhaps. But it would depend on the terms.'

'Oh, don't concern yourself on that score. We would be willing to pay handsomely for your help,' said Gorges.

'How much?' came the blunt question from Daisy Newman, her sharp features hardening.

'I should think about two thousand pounds,' said Gorges, flatly.

The woman's eyes widened a fraction.

'For that money I could indeed help you. Or, at least, I could introduce you to people who could help you. What do you need?'

'First,' said Gorges, 'we shall need a locksmith in Dublin who can cut some keys quickly, and well, and then keep very silent about it.'

'That's easy,' interrupted Daisy Newman. 'There's a man I know just off Sackville Street who can be trusted.'

'Good. That's splendid. Then we shall need someone to buy the jewels from us and dispose of them in a different form.'

'You mean, break them up?'

'Precisely.'

'Captain, will there be much hue and cry over these jewels?'

'Considerable, I fear,' said Shackleton, gloomily, 'very considerable.'

'Then it would be better if the jewels were taken from Dublin and disposed of in London. I have a cousin there who will undoubtedly know of a man willing to undertake the work. I shall write to her at once.'

'Capital, Daisy. Absolutely capital,' said Gorges slapping his knee in delight. 'I knew all along you were the woman we needed. Send me a message at the Curragh when you have heard from your cousin in London, and we shall meet again.'

'I'm always pleased to be of service to you, Captain Gorges. You know that.'

'Thank you, Daisy, for your help and, of course, for your hospitality.'

'It was indeed a pleasure.'

The two men left the drawing room to be met in the hallway by John, the footman, holding their coats and sticks. He handed Gorges an envelope.

'Your account, Captain.'

'Thank you, John. Goodnight.'

As they walked down the driveway, Shackleton was still remembering the scenes in the bedroom with the see-through mirror.

'Amazing woman that, Richard.'

'Indeed.'

'And that maid girl, Millicent. Amazing too.'

'So she should be, old boy. That was Daisy's sister.'

'Good lord . . . and John?'

'The footman? He's their brother, of course. I told you it was a surprising house, didn't I?'

A fortnight passed before a message arrived for Gorges at the Curragh asking him to contact Daisy Newman. The next evening he went to her house in Ballsbridge.

'We cannot be too long,' she said, when Gorges had been shown into the drawing room. 'I have some other gentlemen arriving for an entertainment.'

Gorges was disappointed. He'd hoped to make full use of all the services offered by Daisy Newman, as well as conducting their other business.

The woman sensed his feelings. 'There'll be other times I'm sure, Captain, when your stay can be longer. But tonight it must be brief.'

She handed him a folded piece of paper. 'Here is the address of a man in London who might help you in your enterprise. He has been warned by my cousin to expect a visit from a gentleman in Dublin. As a way of identifying yourself you can mention my name.'

'And the locksmith?'

'I think it would be better since he is in Dublin if I were to contact him when the occasion arises. How can I put it . . .? Well, shall we say we have more than a nodding acquaintanceship.'

Daisy Newman rose from her chair and pulled the bell cord.

'I apologise for the rush but I do believe it's best if my gentlemen callers do not meet each other. It could give rise to embarrassment.'

'Certainly, m'dear,' muttered Gorges. 'I shall be in contact with you very shortly.'

As he walked away from the house he looked at the name on the piece of paper he'd just been given: Mr Rufus Levinson at No. 17c, Club Row.

It proved impossible for Gorges to obtain leave from his regiment immediately, so it was Shackleton who found himself pushing his way through the crowded, narrow streets of the

East End of London the following week. Shackleton wondered still at times about whether the robbery should go ahead. But, under Gorges's continual pressure, he saw little harm in contacting what he presumed would be a diamond merchant.

Rufus Levinson's office – if it could be called that – was a small room on the fourth floor of a scruffy building within hailing, and hearing, distance of the noise and bustle of the open market below in Club Row. Shackleton knocked and was admitted by a short middle-aged man, a full beard hardly masking the Jewishness of his features.

'Yes. You want something?' he asked suspiciously, eyeing the well-dressed stranger standing before him.

'Mr Rufus Levinson?'

'Who wants him?'

'I've come from Dublin,' said Shackleton, brushing the lapel of his frock coat as if the dust of the grubby room had already dirtied him. 'Miss Newman gave me this address.'

'Ah, yes. A man from Dublin. I was told to expect one. I am Rufus Levinson.'

'Yes. I thought so.'

'You can't be too careful, you know,' said Levinson, explaining his early evasiveness in an apologetic tone. 'Take a seat, please.'

He moved crab-like to one side of a stained wooden table, and Shackleton lowered himself carefully on to a wicker-backed chair.

'You have something for me to see?' asked Levinson.

'No, no. Not yet. I'm merely trying to ascertain if you would be interested in disposing of some gems that might come into my possession.'

Shackleton took out a sketch of the Crown Jewels he'd made from memory and tossed it in front of Levinson.

'You'll see I've marked which stones are rubies or emeralds and which are white and rose diamonds.'

Levinson studied the sketch and then looked sharply up at his visitor.

'You're going to steal these?'

'We might acquire them,' replied Shackleton, with a careless shrug.

'I know about these jewels,' said Levinson. 'Who in the diamond business doesn't?'

'Are you interested, Mr Levinson?'

'Interested? Interested? Of course I'm interested, but I tell you this, my friend, these jewels would have to go abroad to be worked on. If these are stolen the market round here will be swarming with constables searching for them. No one would be safe.'

Shackleton explained that there might be a few days' grace before the robbery was discovered.

'That would be a blessing. If they could reach Paris before the hue and cry started then there would be no trouble.'

'How much will you pay for them, Mr Levinson?' Shackleton asked sharply.

'That's very difficult to say, Mr . . . er . . . Mr?'

'It would be better if you called me Mr Newman,' said Shackleton.

'Well, Mr Newman, then, as I said it's very difficult to place a value on these jewels.'

'They're insured for more than £30,000,' lied Shackleton, sensing what was to come.

'Oh, yes, they would be,' said Rufus Levinson, nodding in agreement. 'But they're insured for their present state, as they are. When they're broken down just into gems . . . well, who knows?'

The diamond merchant thought for a moment. 'And, of course, there's the danger of handling them even.'

'How much, Mr Levinson?' persisted Shackleton.

'These are the only jewels you'll be acquiring, Mr Newman?'

Shackleton was silent for a moment, thinking of the other cases of jewels in the safe – the Mahony family jewels and the gold collars of the Knights of St Patrick. Why not, he thought to himself.

'There could be some others – some gold, jewels, and what I presume to be some smaller diamonds.'

'Right,' said Levinson, as if coming to an instant decision. 'Sight unseen, I'll give you £10,000 for the lot.'

'Not enough,' replied Shackleton abruptly.

'But the danger, Mr Newman . . . you must realise these are famous pieces.'

'It's not enough.'

The haggling went on for more than fifteen minutes, each man realising that a deal would be struck eventually.

'My final offer, Mr Newman – £14,000.'

Shackleton did some mental arithmetic working out his share after Gorges and Daisy Newman had been paid. His share wouldn't be the £10,000 he'd hoped for – in fact, not much more than half that figure – but it could help him through.

'Make that 14,000 guineas and we have a deal.'

Levinson reacted with mock horror. 'Guineas, yet!' He paused. 'All right then, Mr Newman, 14,000 guineas it will be.' He'd been prepared to offer another £1,000 as his limit, so an extra £700 wasn't that bad.

The two men shook hands. 'When can I expect the merchandise, Mr Newman? I shall have to have time to contact my friends on the Continent.'

'To be frank, I don't know, Mr Levinson. But we shall give you sufficient warning.'

Shackleton was glad to get away from the grimy office, with its incessant noise of people in the market nearby clamouring to buy and sell. He hailed a horse carriage and retired, with a large brandy and soda, into the quiet confines of the Junior Army and Navy Club in St James's Street, to consider his position. His fellow club members saw he was deep in thought, slumped in a high-backed upholstered chair by the window, so they didn't approach him.

What to do? He realised he was nearly at the point of no return. His bank was pressing him to reduce his overdraft and Wilton's the moneylenders were becoming urgent in their inquiries about two amounts, totalling £1,300, he had borrowed, although he had wheedled Sir Arthur Vicars into guaranteeing the bills. There was no help likely from his father, since the family savings had been sunk into his brother Ernest's Antarctic expedition. He felt his dream of fortune in the lush forests of Mexico beginning to fade. And then there were the jewels. . . . Could he be certain of Gorges's tentative plan? In essence, once the keys had been obtained, the plan could hardly fail. And if he established a strong enough alibi there could be little danger to himself. It was the only way.

Shackleton put down his glass and signalled a waiter.

'Yes, Mr Shackleton?'

'Parkes, get a telegraph form for me, please.'

The telegraph to Captain R. H. Gorges, c/o Officers' Mess, Royal Irish Regiment, The Curragh, Ireland, was brief and to the point.

'Agreement reached in London on monies. Will return Dublin next week to finalise details of movement. Regards FRS.'

It was date-stamped 15 September 1906, at South Audley Street Post Office, not far from Shackleton's club.

The robbery of the Irish Crown Jewels was now inevitable.

4

Key to a fortune

On 12 February 1907 Ernest Shackleton called a news conference in the mahogany splendour of the Royal Geographical Society in London, to announce that he had now obtained enough financial backing to mount an expedition which would attempt to reach the South Pole for the first time during the following two years.

'Gentlemen, this is not to say I have fully drawn up my plans for this great expedition,' he told the reporters scribbling down his every word. 'But it does mean that the expedition will definitely take place.'

His announcement received wide coverage in the newspapers, and Frank Shackleton read a full account in *The Times* as he sat at breakfast in Dublin. He felt a slight twinge of envy at the fame his elder brother was enjoying, but this was softened with natural family pride. He smiled to himself as he read of his brother's plans 'not being fully drawn up'. His own plans, he thought to himself, were much more advanced. In fact, since his firm commitment to Richard Gorges the previous September, their plans to steal the Irish Crown Jewels were almost complete. 'I'll reach my goal before you this time, Ernest,' he muttered, half to himself, as he pushed the remains of a plate of Mrs Darcy's excellent kippers away from him.

'Eh? What was that, Frank?' asked Sir Arthur Vicars, looking round the corner of his outspread copy of *The Times*. 'Something about your brother, eh? First class chap . . . it'll mean a knighthood at least if he makes the Pole this time. Might even mean you'll have to draw up his coat of arms, eh!' Sir Arthur was in ebullient form that morning. His star as

Ulster King of Arms was near its zenith. Within six months he would proclaim open the Irish International Exhibition in Dublin, and then welcome the Royal Family to the island. His plans, too, were going ahead steadily, though, as usual, fussily. He was totally unaware – and, in fact, wouldn't have believed even if told – that the man sitting opposite him at the breakfast table had already sown the seeds not only of his own destruction but that of many others.

Since Frank Shackleton's agreement to the robbery, Richard Gorges had concentrated on becoming a familiar figure with the officers and men garrisoned at Dublin Castle. He took every opportunity to drink and dine in the various messes and soon was an accepted figure, a figure to be seen, but a figure so familiar that he wasn't noticed. In early November he'd arranged another meeting with Daisy Newman at her house. As previously, the entertainment came before the business, but this time, as a variation on the familiar theme, Gorges enjoyed himself with Millicent, Miss Newman's sister, and then later with her brother, John.

'Daisy,' said Gorges as they drank champagne together afterwards, 'this establishment of yours is quite, quite remarkable. You can cater for any whim at all. How did you do it?'

'It was really a matter of financial necessity, dear Captain. Our parents died when I was only fourteen years of age, and the only way I could get out of the tenements was in this way. I raised Millicent and John on the money I earned working at night along Sackville Street, and somehow – I don't think there was a conscious decision – they joined me when they were old enough.'

'What are you planning to do with the money you'll get from our business arrangement?'

'Well, I shall certainly leave Dublin. My cousin in London tells me that a similar establishment to this would be a success in, perhaps, a suburb like Ealing.'

'Perhaps so, Daisy. Perhaps so. But we're still some way from realising our plans. Next Tuesday I shall be obtaining a key which must be copied and returned within an hour at the most. Will your locksmith be capable of obliging?'

'Captain, he is one of the best in Dublin, as I've already told you.'

'Thing is, Daisy, I think it better if I don't meet him. Possible identification and all that. . . .'

'Certainly. I understand. I'll take the key to him and return it to you.'

'Splendid. Well, I suggest we meet outside Buswell's Hotel at one o'clock on Tuesday. I shall lunch there, and you can leave the original key and the duplicate key for me in an envelope at the porter's desk while I'm finishing my meal.'

Gorges had deliberately chosen the lunch period at Dublin Castle as the time of the first part of the operation. It was when there was the most activity in the yards of the gloomy castle, with soldiers going to their barracks for lunch, officers heading for drinks in the mess, and carriages clattering back and forth with the civil servants leaving for their luncheon appointments. A perfect time not to be noticed, thought Gorges, as he marched into the basement store under the Bedford Tower. It was manned, during this lunch period, by a young corporal standing in for the quartermaster sergeant-major. The corporal stiffened to attention as Gorges entered the store and handed him a requisition form for some specialised small-bore rifle targets, which he used sometimes during musketry practice at the Curragh.

'There's none to be found down at the Curragh, I'm afraid, corporal,' he said. 'I'm sure you must have some here.'

'I don't know, sir. I don't think so.'

'Don't think, corporal,' snapped Gorges. 'Just don't think. Go and look.'

The corporal reddened at the rebuke. 'Suh!' He walked, back stiff with resentment, through the shelves of equipment, checking each item. As soon as he was out of sight, behind the shelves, Gorges slipped round the counter and lifted the set of keys off a hook set on a board on the wall. The corporal returned from the dark recesses of the basement.

'I can't find any of these sort of targets, sir. Really I couldn't.'

Gorges pretended annoyance as he picked his requisition form off the counter. 'Corporal, you didn't look properly. I shall return when the QSM is here. Perhaps he can jog your memory.'

'Suh!'

Gorges strolled out of Dublin Castle, acknowledging the salutes of the sentries, and then hurried along the streets, trying to avoid the muddy cobblestones, to Buswell's Hotel. Daisy Newman, who'd been pretending to window-shop, watched his approach and, as he neared the hotel entrance, moved towards him. To anyone watching it would have seemed as if the army officer and the smartly-dressed lady collided purely by accident, neither looking where the other was going. Gorges spun round.

'My dear lady, I do apologise. Most frightfully sorry. Are you at all hurt?'

'Not at all, Captain. Think no more of it,' said Daisy, quite loudly, as she placed the keys, handed over by Gorges in the collision, in her large purse.

Daisy Newman walked off towards Sackville Street as Gorges saluted and went on into the hotel. The locksmith's shop was in a side street just before the Gresham Hotel. The sign above it was simple – 'Locks Fitted – Keys Cut'. A bell tinkled at the back of the shop as Daisy opened its door and entered. The curtains behind the small counter, displaying various kinds of locks and keys, parted and a tall grey-haired man, wearing a leather apron, came into the shop. His face lit up when he saw his visitor.

'My dear Daisy, how are you?' He hurried round the counter to clasp both her hands in his.

'I'm very well indeed, Frank Robinson, and how are you?'

'Busy – but never too busy for you, Daisy.'

The locksmith, a widower in his mid-fifties, had been one of Daisy's earliest customers when she'd first walked the streets in Dublin, but their sexual relationship had deepened over the years into a genuine fondness. Robinson couldn't afford – nor wanted – to visit her house in Ballsbridge but for the last two years they'd holidayed together, as man and wife, at a small hotel in Kingstown. The truth was that Frank Robinson was deeply in love with her. Often he had proposed marriage, but Daisy had always refused. 'You don't want to marry a woman who lives like I do, Frank,' she used to reply. 'Find a respectable girl who can help you in your shop.'

This day, though, there could be little time for pleasantries.

'Frank, I want some keys cut quickly. You remember a few weeks ago I said I would be calling.'

'Yes, of course, Daisy. How long can you wait for the keys?'

'Less than an hour.'

'Right. Give me the keys here.' Daisy handed him the ring taken from the basement stores, with the three keys hanging from it.

Robinson looked at them. 'These are simple enough. Now you go shopping or whatever and return within the hour. Off you go now, Daisy, I've work to do.'

So it was, just over an hour later, that Gorges, having sampled an excellent cold buffet washed down with a bottle of hock, stopped at the porter's desk in the crowded lobby at Buswell's, and asked if a package had been left for him. The porter handed him a bulky envelope, and Gorges flicked him a penny for his trouble. He walked to the gentlemen's lavatory and, in the privacy of a cubicle, took out the two sets of keys. The newly-cut set gleamed in contrast with the dullness of the original keys he now had to return. He hurried back to Dublin Castle, getting splashed by mud from a passing horse carriage on the way and went directly to the storeroom beneath the Bedford Tower. A sergeant-major, a bewhiskered veteran quartermaster of many colonial campaigns, was now behind the counter.

'Good afternoon, Q.'

'Hello, sir. Captain Gorges, isn't it?'

'That's right. Q, I need your help.'

'Yes, sir. Corporal Johnson said you'd called while I was out at lunch. Said you wanted some of those new small bore targets. Well, I'm afraid we're not holding them here. Perhaps you could try Royal Barracks over the river, sir.'

'Small bore targets, Q? I didn't want those. I'm afraid your young corporal must have mixed me up with someone else. All I wanted were a few dozen pistol targets. I've got an officers' shoot at the weekend and my armourer has run a little short.'

'Corporals!', the QSM snorted in disgust. 'They're worse than ruddy privates, if you'll pardon the language, sir. I'll get the targets for you.'

The sergeant-major turned and went to the back of the storeroom, where Gorges already knew the targets were kept.

Swiftly, he slipped behind the counter and placed the key ring back onto its hook.

'Here you are, sir,' said the sergeant-major, returning to the counter. 'I can manage to let you have four dozen targets – if that's all right.'

'Very good, Q. First class.'

'Just sign here, will you, sir?'

Gorges signed the requisition form and strolled out of the store, targets under his arm, and a set of keys jingling in his pocket. The first part of the plan had worked to perfection. Indeed, it gave Shackleton and Gorges an added and unexpected bonus. When Gorges showed his friend the newly-cut keys, Shackleton asked which one opened the door to the basement store.

'Don't know, old boy,' replied Gorges. 'But be certain one of them will.'

'But then what are the other keys for?'

'Haven't an earthly, Frank. Probably for some of the store cupboards.'

Then the same idea that had been forming in Shackleton's mind struck Gorges.

'I wonder . . . one of them couldn't be the key for the door from the basement to the library hallway?'

'I'm wondering that too, Richard.'

Shackleton paused, then added, 'Give me the keys and I'll check. Leave it to me.'

The next day, Shackleton went into the Office of Arms in Bedford Tower. He walked through the empty hallway and into the library. To his left was the room used by the office messenger, William Stivey, a naval pensioner, who had a desk set just outside the strongroom, built by the Board of Works at Sir Arthur Vicars's request; the strongroom with an entrance too small for the safe standing on the opposite side of the library.

Shackleton wandered casually into the messenger's room.

'Morning, Stivey.'

'Good morning, sir,' replied the ruddy-faced old sailor, fingering his stiffly waxed white moustache, yellowing at the edges from the strong tobacco he used.

'Everything all right? Not working you too hard, I hope?' asked Shackleton.

'No, sir. No complaints,' smiled Stivey.

'Right-ho then, carry on.' And Shackleton, now satisfied of Stivey's location, returned to the hallway. There, in a corner just under the spiral staircase, was the door to the basement. Looking about him to make sure he was unobserved, Shackleton went to the door, pulling the three newly-cut keys from the pocket of his frock coat. The first one didn't even go into the lock; the second one did, but wouldn't turn; the third one slipped in and, even before it clicked the lock open, Shackleton sensed that this was the right key. He locked the door again, pocketed the keys, checked again he'd been unobserved, and then, whistling under his breath, began mounting the staircase towards his office.

'That's simply tremendous,' was Gorges's response when he heard the news. 'Two keys at one go. Capital. Now we've no problem of how to get into the Tower. All we've to do is worry about getting the key to the safe.'

'Yes – and that's going to be a problem,' said Shackleton, shaking his head. 'Ever since that jape last March Sir Arthur has watched his keys like a hen looking after her chicks.'

'Don't worry, old boy. We'll work out a plan.'

As the Dublin Season swirled its petticoats into 1907, Shackleton and Gorges went the rounds of balls, dinner parties and weekends in the country, making visits about once a fortnight to Daisy Newman's residence, continually trying to finalise their plans. The discreet parties that ended in total indiscretion still continued at No. 7, St James's Terrace, and Shackleton had taken to bringing friends over from London to join them.

'Is it wise?' asked Gorges one evening as the two men dined at the Spa Hotel. 'Aren't you bringing too many people into the circle?'

'No – don't you see, Richard? The more people involved, the less the spotlight will fall on us. And anyway things are so dashed hot in London at present for people like us, that parties like ours in Dublin are the only chance some of our friends have to really let go and enjoy themselves.'

'Why are things so hot in town?'

'I'm not sure. But some of my friends there have heard that Scotland Yard are even compiling a special dossier on anyone with interests remotely like ours.'

'It sounds pretty damnable to me!'

'It is – and that's why I think it's only fair to occasionally invite people over to Dublin.'

'I can't say I like it too much, Frank, but I don't suppose it can do any harm once in a while.'

'Forget it,' said Shackleton, looking round to check no one was within earshot. 'Let's consider more important things. For instance, when does the operation go ahead?'

'The best time in military terms, old boy, would be the time of maximum confusion, what? When could that be?'

'I should have thought sometime between the opening of the International Exhibition and the Royal Visit – between the middle of May and the beginning of July. That's when the Office of Arms is going to be overwhelmed with work. There'll be so much toing and froing that a whole battalion of fusiliers could march through the place without being noticed.'

'Excellent, Frank, but what about your movements? We don't want you in Ireland when I go into action. People inside the office will be the prime suspects.'

'Naturally . . . well, I shall have to be here for the Exhibition and its first couple of weeks. There are one or two ambassadors and commercial attachés coming over from London and I shall want to meet them, mainly, I must admit, for reasons of personal business.'

'Then what?'

'Well, I shall have to be in Dublin for the Royal Visit, of course, but I was planning to stay in London for a couple of weeks before that. There are so many loose ends to tie up trying to finance this Mexican venture.'

Gorges pulled out a small leather pocket diary and began looking at the dates.

'When will you have to return to Ireland for the royal shenanigans?'

'Let's see . . . they're arriving on 10 July. . . .'

'That's a Wednesday. . . .'

'I'd have to be here by the Monday.'

'That's 8 July.'

'Right.'

Shackleton reached for his own diary. 'Now let's see . . . in fact, that weekend I'm due at Penhurst staying with Lord Ronald Gower. I think I've got the old bohemian interested in my Celtic Investment Trust.'

He flicked the thin pages, edged with gold foil. 'On the 4th I'm dining at the Ormondes . . . yes, those are the only two firm dates I've got. I suppose I'll be dropping in to see Ernest to discover how he's getting on – by the way, he's set up an office in Regent Street for the expedition – but otherwise I'll be pretty footloose.'

'I think then that's the week we do it, Frank, when you can establish a firm alibi over the water. The first week in July.'

'That's agreed. But remember, Richard, we still haven't solved the problem of getting the impression of the safe keys.'

'Hang on, let's get some more brandy,' interrupted Gorges. 'Give us time to think.' He beckoned a waiter and gave the order, adding, 'Better bring the bottle and some more coffee as well.'

When the brandy and coffee were on the table and the waiter had retired, Shackleton, who had been idly flicking the pages of his diary, leaned over the table towards Gorges, holding the diary open at one entry.

'That's it, Richard. That's when you get the impression,' he said excitedly.

Gorges took the diary and looked at the entry. For 30 June, in Shackleton's distinctive, flowing hand, was written – 'Birthday. P.McE.'

'Peter McEnnery's birthday?'

'That's right, Richard. Now I'll be away but I bet I can persuade Sir Arthur to put on a dinner party at St James's Terrace for him. The old boy's pretty fond of Peter, you know.'

'Yes', said Gorges drily. 'And so are quite a few others.'

Shackleton laughed and then continued, 'But don't you see? I'll arrange for you to be invited – Sir Arthur won't refuse – along with Esme Percy, Peirce Mahony and the others. It'll be the perfect opportunity to get Sir Arthur tiddly. I'm sure he'll stumble off to bed early, as usual, and that's your chance.'

'How?' said Gorges, slightly puzzled. 'This time I can't be seen with the keys.'

'Well, after Sir Arthur has gone to bed, you can get the others to cut loose, can't you? Then they won't notice when you sneak upstairs to Sir Arthur's room. Knowing him at the moment, the keys will be under his pillow – and there you are.'

'Under the pillow! But I'll disturb him.'

'Not when he's tiddled, dear friend. The eruption at Vesuvius wouldn't wake him up.'

Shackleton went on, firmly convinced of the plan, 'I think it's your only chance. He really is funny about those keys nowadays.'

'If you say so, Frank. That means I get the keys copied on the Sunday, that would be the 30th, and go into the Tower during the week.'

'Yes. But I wouldn't arrange anything with Daisy Newman's locksmith yet. Let's leave that until well after the Exhibition.'

The sun glittered off the swords, scabbards and polished harnesswork of the 5th Hussars as they clattered and clinked their way out of Dublin Castle on the morning of 4 May 1907. They rode in escort to the open carriage taking Lord and Lady Aberdeen to the official opening of the Irish International Exhibition, a display window for Irish industry and culture.

Crowds lined the road to Ballsbridge as the carriage and its escort made its impressive way through the stately squares and avenues of the Dublin suburbs, an elegant façade to some of the worst poverty in Europe. The poor, men in caps and mufflers, women in shawls holding children without shoes on their feet, mingled and jostled on the pavements with the better-dressed and better-fed middle-class families, their children in bonnets and sailor hats, waving small Union Jacks, all trying to get the best view of the Viceroy's stately progress.

Everything was ready at the International Exhibition grounds, though teams of gardeners were feverishly renewing multi-coloured bedding plants, ruined in a late April storm. The huge glass dome of the great central hall shone out as lines of soldiers in red tunics, black trousers, and polished helmets, held back the crowds pressing round the entrance. Inside, by eleven o'clock, the élite of Ireland had taken their seats in the Concert Hall, nodding recognition to each other, shuffling in their chairs, and gently fanning themselves with programmes of that morning's event. The ladies constantly readjusted their dresses, trimmed and draped with Irish lace. The men, great landowners grown rich on centuries of land enclosures, fingered the pearl or diamond pins on their stocks, catching each other's eyes occasionally, and smiling conspiratorially, as the social élite do, ever relishing their membership of a charmed circle. A massed choir of more than three hundred, at the far end of the hall, covered the noise of the murmured gossip, and the steps of the ushers, as they showed in late arrivals and people shuffled back their seats to let them through the rows.

Just before noon, sounds of cheering outside filtered into the hall as Lord Aberdeen's procession entered the Exhibition's grounds. A wait of a few minutes, and then the orchestra struck up with a stirring selection from Wagner's *Tannhauser* as the official procession entered the hall. First came the builders and architects, then the members of the Exhibition's executive council, followed by the mayors of Irish cities, representatives of foreign governments and the armed services, and finally the Viceroy's immediate procession.

Frank Shackleton, Dublin Herald, felt uncomfortably warm in his glittering yellow and silver tabard as he walked behind the Knights of the Order of St Patrick. Behind came the senior members of the Viceroy's staff and then, alone, Ulster King of Arms, white ruffle round his neck, gold-tipped stick of office in his right hand, the sun's rays through the glass roof reflecting off the embroidered heraldic lions and harps on his tabard, and the gilt crown on his head. A few steps behind walked Lord and Lady Aberdeen. The heralds of the Office of Arms gathered around the two throne-like chairs set upon a dais. There were speeches of self-congratulation, normal, indeed obligatory, on such occasions, and the presentation of a gold key to the Viceroy.

Yet another key, thought Dublin Herald, his mind far away from the ceremony going on around him. His thoughts fixed also on the insignia jewels of the Order of St Patrick, glittering on the breast of the Viceroy's uniform. Keys and jewels . . . keys . . . jewels . . . keys . . . jewels.

The Viceroy signalled to Ulster King of Arms, and Sir Arthur Vicars, a resplendent figure, stepped forward slightly, and in his most official voice announced: 'By command of His Excellency, I proclaim the Exhibition open.'

Trumpets drowned the echoes of the last public pronouncement ever to be made by Sir Arthur as Ulster King of Arms.

'Daisy, m'dear', said Gorges, 'We must discuss business now.'

The woman, lying on her bed, reached up and tweaked his moustache.

'Now, my lovely Captain? You know I never discuss business like this. Take a bath and we'll talk downstairs.'

'No, I especially asked to come here when your sister and brother were out because there must be no chance of them overhearing. If we go downstairs they might return and learn something. It's better here,' insisted Gorges. 'And anyway it's more friendly,' he added, bending down and softly kissing her between the two dimples above the curve of her slim buttocks.

'All right then, but no more of that, ' said Daisy, rolling over onto her side. 'I'm quite sore enough as it is.'

Gorges laughed. 'With you, Daisy, I could give up my other pleasures altogether. Sir Lawrence Jones recently told Frank that a doctor asked the undergraduates at Oxford about sex. The general opinion was that nine out of ten women are indifferent to or actively dislike it. The tenth, said these youngsters, who would enjoy it, would always be a harlot. You are the tenth woman and yet I would never call you a harlot.'

'The business, Captain, the business,' insisted Daisy Newman, smiling indulgently at the compliment.

'Right, m'dear. Today is the 21st of May. Our operation will take place within the next six weeks. There are two things I want from you – first, instructions from your locksmith about taking wax impressions of keys, and second, I shall want you to take a trip to London during the first week of July.'

Daisy Newman sat up on her knees, legs pressed close together, looking down at Gorges, a serious expression on her face. 'The first is easy enough – my locksmith will do anything for me – but the second . . . well, it's the first time you've mentioned it.'

'I know, Daisy, but Frank and I have decided that you're the person who'll have to take the jewels to London. He'll be there already during the robbery and I can't suddenly skip from the regiment like that. It would cook my goose.'

'But, after the robbery, surely there'll be searches everywhere. I might be caught with the gems, and then what?'

'Don't worry, m'dear. The way it's planned you'll be on your way back to Dublin before any hue and cry is raised.'

Gorges added quickly, sensing her indecision, 'That's the truth, Daisy, and, of course, we'd give you, say, another £200 for making the trip.'

'Well . . . if what you say is true, I don't suppose there's any harm. All right, I'll do it.'

Daisy got off the bed and walked to a chair to pick up a silk dressing gown. Gorges watched her lithe body move, the deep furrow of perfect skin of her back meeting the twin rises of her apple-shaped buttocks, and felt a quiver of excitement. She turned, tying the sash of her gown, and noticed his growing excitement.

'Now, no more of that. I say never mix business with pleasure, not that it's never but a pleasure doing business with you. But this business about the jewels is serious.'

Gorges sighed, as if with mock disappointment. Only he knew how real his actual disappointment was. With Daisy Newman he could act out every fantasy in his fertile mind.

'About these wax impressions, dear Captain Gorges,' said Daisy, as she sat at her dressing table and began brushing her hair. 'I'm sure my locksmith will want to know what sort of keys you're dealing with. I've always understood from him that taking impressions is an expert business.'

'They'll be the impressions of a number of keys, ordinary keys, but the one I'll be really interested in will be of a key to a safe.'

'He'll want to know what sort of safe.'

'It's a Radcliff and Horner safe, fairly old.'

'Wait – I'll write that down,' said Daisy, fumbling in a drawer for pencil and paper.'

'A Radcliff and Horner?'

'That's right.'

'Well, I'll tell my locksmith all this and then let you know. Can you drop by in three days' time?'

'A pleasure, m'dear,' said Gorges, now standing behind her. slipping his hands down the front of her dressing gown. Daisy felt his excitement pressing into her and turned her head to protest. Gorges covered her offered mouth with his, his hands now untying the sash of her dressing gown. For Gorges, business and pleasure could always mix. And, if the truth were known, the same applied to Daisy Newman, particularly where this young and handsome Army officer was concerned. But three days later she had anything but good news for Captain Richard Howard Gorges of the Royal Irish Regiment.

'My locksmith says it's easy to get wax impressions of ordinary keys. Basically you just press them firmly into the wax. But he couldn't guarantee that such an impression would work on the key to a safe.'

'For heaven's sake, why not?' asked Gorges, now becoming somewhat alarmed.

'Because he says it wouldn't be accurate enough. Apparently the key to a Radcliff and Horner – that was the name wasn't it? – has to press seven levers before opening the safe lock. Anyway it's something like that, and he says a wax impression probably wouldn't give him a good enough basis to work on.'

'Well, what does he suggest then?' said Gorges, a note of desperation in his voice as he began to see his whole plan crumbling before him.

'The locksmith says the only certain way of getting an impression from which to cut an accurate key is by using plaster of Paris.'

'Plaster of Paris . . . good lord.'

'Yes, you press the key between two bits of plaster, let the plaster harden, and then you have a perfect impression.'

'That's not too bad,' sighed Gorges with some relief. 'And from that plaster impression your man can cut a duplicate quickly?'

Daisy lowered her eyes beneath their full lashes, keeping the bad news to the last. 'No, he can't. He says to get a perfect fit, a duplicate guaranteed to open the safe, he'll need at least a day's work.'

'Oh, no,' groaned Gorges. 'It won't work then. The original key has to be returned within minutes or the whole scheme is so much dung from a Donegal cocksparrow – if you'll pardon the expression, m'dear.'

He went on despondently: 'Plaster of Paris impressions by an expert, a day's work cutting the key . . . no, it's just too much.'

The woman tried to cheer him up. 'The impressions don't take long to make when you know what you're doing. Five minutes at the most, I'm told.'

'But don't you see, Daisy?' said Gorges wearily. 'I won't have the time to get the keys to your locksmith. There's no time.'

'Well, then the locksmith must come to you,' replied Daisy brightly.

'What?' muttered Gorges.

'I said, dear Captain, the locksmith must come to you. If he's waiting outside the place from where you are going to purloin the keys, then he can make the impression himself and hand the keys back to you. After that he can go away and do his work with no fuss or hurry.'

'That's marvellous,' said Gorges delightedly, his depression lifting. With a smile, he began to hum and then sing softly,

'She never once has blundered
And at touching for a hundred
What an artist! She's the smartest, the smartest girl in town.'

'Am I really, dear Captain?' said Daisy, recognising Marie Lloyd's latest song. 'Am I really the smartest girl?'

'You certainly are, Daisy. You certainly are. I could hug you.'

'Well, why don't you? You've still got plenty of credit on your account here. . . .'

After Gorges had explained the new idea to Shackleton, the two friends agreed the scheme was nearly perfect. They went through it in fine detail for hours on end.

'It's just as well we didn't have to rely on Peirce Gun Mahony to get you into Sir Arthur's home,' said Shackleton after they'd finished their discussion.

'Yes,' agreed Gorges, 'I heard he'd been taken ill.'

'He's gone down to the country to rest and then he thinks he'll finish his convalescence in London. He wants to make sure he's fit for the Royal Visit.'

'After the jewels are gone, I doubt if anyone will be fit for the visit,' laughed Gorges.

Shackleton nodded. 'Yes, it's going to be a terrible shock for them all. But it has to be, I'm afraid.'

'Don't fret,' said 'Gorges. You just get over to London and start establishing your alibi. I'm quite happy about the plan. Bit of damned excitement at least. Night manoeuvres and all that, what?'

Frank Shackleton left for England on 10 June, the same day that Sir Arthur Vicars entertained his friend, William Chamney, and John Hodgson, a noted expert in antiques, who was librarian to the Duke of Northumberland, caring for his fine collection of rare volumes at Alnwick Castle. The company at dinner was so delightful to Ulster King of Arms, the conversation about his beloved antiques so stimulating, that he invited Mr Hodgson to visit him the next day at the Bedford Tower. The antiquarian was delighted with the thousand and more rare and richly-bound volumes on genealogy that were in the library, many placed there at Sir Arthur's own expense.

'Now look in here, Mr Hodgson,' said Sir Arthur, leading him into the strongroom. 'Just look at these.'

There, in a glass case secured by four locks, were two silver maces, a jewelled sceptre, the Irish Sword of State, and other smaller pieces of regalia belonging to the Knights of St Patrick.

'Magnificent. Absolutely magnificent,' breathed Mr Hodgson. 'Can I examine them?'

'Of course,' said Sir Arthur. 'But I insist on showing you something else first.'

The antiquarian was loath to leave the strongroom but Sir Arthur, grasping him firmly by the arm, led him across to the safe standing forlornly alone in the library. He opened it with the key ring he took from his pocket and removed the prized red morocco case.

'These are the Irish Crown Jewels, Mr Hodgson,' he explained, unwrapping the tissue paper around them.

Mr Hodgson, to be frank, was more interested in the contents of the glass case in the strongroom, much older and more interesting to him, but he had to agree the jewels were fine pieces.

'Yes, they are, aren't they, Mr Hodgson?' said Sir Arthur, proudly holding the Star and Badge to the light to let their diamonds sparkle and gleam. 'They really are my pride and joy. No doubt, His Majesty himself is looking forward to seeing them when he visits us next month.'

Sir Arthur carefully wrapped up the jewels again, placed them carefully back in their case, and locked it in the safe. It was the last time he was ever to see them.

5

Captain Gorges raids the Castle

Mrs Darcy, worthy and simple cook that she was, had excelled herself in preparing the birthday dinner for Peter McEnnery, at No. 7, St James's Terrace on 30 June 1907. Pitt the footman had laboriously copied her menu on to the parchment sail of a small model silver galleon that sat in the centre of the glittering table, covered with stiff, shiny Irish linen, and glinting antique cutlery collected over the years by Sir Arthur Vicars. First there was a cold consommé of beef, followed by cutlets and fresh asparagus, and then an entire 12 lb Irish salmon. These were washed down with claret and then hock and, to cleanse the palates of the six men around the table, some champagne accompanying the sorbet ices. Finally Pitt brought in coffee, decanters of port and brandy, and a box of Havana cigars. Sir Arthur, flushed with food and wine, rose to propose the toast.

'Gentlemen – to our friend Peter on his birthday. God bless him.'

The others rose to drink the toast, turning towards McEnnery seated at the top of the table. He coloured slightly with embarrassment, and rose himself after the others had sat down.

'My toast is simple, gentlemen. To my friends.' He tossed the port down his throat and sat down. The other diners cheered him and filled his glass again.

Richard Gorges, who had tried to keep his consumption of wine to the minimum, noted with satisfaction that, of the entire company, Sir Arthur was already the worst for drink. McEnnery was well on the way, he reckoned, and the other three, Esme Percy, with his two friends, Derrick Moore and Patrick

Walker, were passing the decanters fast enough to suggest that quite an evening was ahead. He lit one of his own cheroots, permitted himself a generous draught of brandy, and waited for events to take their course.

By midnight, Pitt was summoned to the room again to help Sir Arthur to his bed. Ulster King of Arms had tried manfully to keep control of his whirling senses and, to Gorges's concern, was seeming to succeed. Then, suddenly, as is often the case with weak-headed drinkers, he slumped back in his chair and began snoring. The company, like Gorges, had been expecting this to happen for some time and clapped somewhat ungraciously when Pitt, a sturdy arm under Sir Arthur's left shoulder, led their host unsteadily out of the room.

'G'night, my friends,' muttered Sir Arthur. 'It's been a wonderful party. G'night.'

Pitt returned to the room after some minutes, and since McEnnery had been invited to stay the night, asked him if anything more was needed.

'Just some more port and brandy, Pitt, then you cut along off to bed,' drawled McEnnery, his face ruddier than ever. 'And thank Mrs Darcy for a first class dinner, will you? Absolutely first class.'

When more drink had been brought and the footman had gone, McEnnery looked across at Gorges, raising his eyebrows and inclining his head quizzically. Gorges nodded and went to the door and locked it. Then he turned down the gaselier until the room was bathed in a dim, pink light.

'Gentlemen,' said Gorges, surveying the expectant faces watching him, 'let the real birthday party begin.' To encourage the others, he swiftly drew off his tail coat, pulled off his white bow tie, and slipped out of his stiff-fronted evening shirt. Soon the others had joined him in varying states of undress, lying on the carpet or sprawled across the purple-covered sofa. Gorges moved from partner to partner until, disengaging himself from the embrace of Derrick Moore, he muttered, 'Scuse me, dear chap. Must find the gentleman's.' He pulled on his trousers, socks, and evening pumps, and went to open the door. As he unlocked it, removing the key, he looked back and knew, by seeing the interlocked bodies in the room, that his absence wasn't going to be noticed for some time. Nevertheless, he took the precaution of locking the door from the outside before starting to make his way upstairs. He knew that Pitt slept in an attic room, but still he moved on tip-toe. Outside Sir Arthur's room, off the landing on the first floor, he paused and listened. All he could hear were gentle snores from inside. The moment of truth, he thought to himself, as he half opened the door and looked in.

Sir Arthur lay under the covers of his bed, head turned sideways on the pillow away from the soft light of an oil lamp Pitt had left burning, at quarter wick, on the chest of drawers. The footman had managed only to half undress his master, and Sir Arthur still wore his evening shirt. His trousers and tail coat were draped over a dumb valet in the corner of the room. Gorges entered the room further and closed the door behind him. Slowly, half crouching, ready to drop for cover, he approached the bed. Sir Arthur snored gently on in a dreamless sleep. Gorges inched his hand under the white pillows trying to touch the key ring he hoped and prayed would be there. Soon, he could feel the pressure of Sir Arthur's head on his hand, but as yet no feel of any key ring. He lifted the pillows slightly, watching Sir Arthur's face intently for any sign of awakening, and moved his hand further. Suddenly, he felt the touch of metal. With first and second fingers he grasped the metal and pulled slowly. A key emerged first from under the pillows followed by the metal ring holding five others. Gorges picked them up one by one, so that they wouldn't clink together, and began his retreat from the bedroom, moving backwards, but always facing Sir Arthur to note any sign of disturbance. When he felt the knob of the door press into him, he turned and gently opened it an inch or so. He looked through the gap onto the landing, half-lit by the gas lamps in the hallway below, and saw and heard that all was still quiet. He took the stairs one at a time, occasionally pausing to listen again, until he reached the hallway. He listened at the door of the dining room and the silence within, punctuated by low moans, satisfied him that he hadn't been missed yet. Gorges moved to the hall stand, slipped his cloak around his bare shoulders, and went to open the front door. He didn't bother to slip back the catch since he was carrying one of Frank Shackleton's front door keys. Outside on the wide step, he looked up and down St James's Terrace. Nothing and no one were in sight except a hansom cab parked twenty yards down the terrace, the horse tethered to a gas lamp. He walked quickly to it and knocked on the door.

'Daisy?' he said quietly.

The blind rolled up and the window was pulled down.

'My dear Captain,' said Daisy Newman, looking through the window, a shawl over her head. 'Fancy meeting you at this time of night.'

Gorges kept his head turned as he knew Daisy's locksmith was also in the carriage. The less they saw of each other the better.

'Where's the driver?'

'We told him to return in an hour or so. He's discreet and thinks we're lovers.'

'Good. Here are the keys.' He passed them through the window. 'I'll be back in five minutes.'

'That'll be enough time,' replied Daisy as Gorges began walking back to Sir Arthur's house. He opened the front door quietly with Shackleton's key and went to the door of the dining room to listen again. Although it had seemed longer, an eternity almost, the whole operation until then had taken less than ten minutes.

Outside, in the carriage, Frank Robinson rubbed each key with an oiled cloth before putting them between small blocks of plaster of Paris, which he'd moistened from a bottle of water. He worked swiftly and expertly, pressing each block together. He waited a few minutes until he felt that the blocks were dry. He took a small chisel and a light hammer and, with a couple of taps, knocked the blocks apart again. The lightly oiled keys fell into his hands as he upturned the blocks. By the light of a small oil lamp, held by Daisy Newman, he could see that perfect impressions of the keys had been made. He had hardly finished threading the keys back on the ring when Gorges knocked on the carriage door. Daisy handed the key ring back through the window.

'All done, Daisy?'

'Every single one.'

'Right. I'll be in contact with you later.'

'Take care!'

'Be sure I will.'

Gorges re-entered No. 7, St James's Terrace, again using Shackleton's spare key, took off his cloak, and began climbing the stairs. He paused outside Sir Arthur's bedroom, listened carefully, but could hear only gentle snoring. He eased the door open and put his head round.

Ulster King of Arms lay in the same position as before, sound asleep, his head still turned away from the glow of the oil lamp. Gorges approached the bed on tip-toe, again watching for any movement, and gently slid the keys back under the pillow. He didn't bother to push them right under Sir Arthur's head, as he thought this would be an unnecessary risk. Then he retreated from the bedroom as before.

As he shut the door quietly behind him a sense of exultation gripped him. He could have shouted with delight. He stood on the landing for a few moments to allow his nerves to settle. He realised that he'd been holding his breath for almost all the time in the bedroom, so he took some deep gulps of air before going down the stairs. He unlocked the dining room door and went inside.

Derrick Moore, lying on the floor and enjoying, quite obviously, the skilled caresses of McEnnery, looked up and saw him.

'What took you so long, Richard?'

'Must have been the asparagus, old boy,' smiled Gorges as he undid his trousers and joined the others on the floor. He reckoned he couldn't have been away for much more than twenty minutes. The night was still young.

Later that day, 1 July, Frank Robinson began working on the keys in the workroom behind his shop. Five of the keys of which he had made impressions were simple to copy. It was the sixth key that needed care, the key to the safe. First, using small calipers, he measured every aspect of the impression in the plaster. These measurements he noted down. Then he melted some phosphor bronze in a small ladle held by tongs over a gas burner. When the metal was molten, he poured it into the block of plaster, both sides held together firmly with wire, through a small hole he'd drilled in the side. Robinson left this for four hours before cutting the wire and gently tapping apart the two pieces of plaster. Inside was a solid metal key, perfectly cast in its plaster mould. Robinson removed it with a pair of tweezers and laid it on his work bench. Then he measured it with calipers, comparing each measurement with the one he'd taken before. He smiled to himself with pride. Only two small adjustments needed to be made and then the key would be a perfect copy. He left it to cool and harden for another two hours before beginning to work on it with a small Ward file. He needed to make two nicks of 1/32nd of an inch each in the key's edge. When these were done, the key, just over 4½ inches in length, was complete. He rubbed the edges with fine emery paper to round them a little and then spent another ten minutes rubbing the key with an oiled cloth. Finally, he was satisfied. The key was as near perfect a copy as he could make. Without testing it, he couldn't guarantee it might not scratch the levers in the safe as it pushed them back, but he didn't think it would. Robinson wanted it to be perfect for Daisy. He guessed the key was to be used in some kind of criminal activity, because of the circumstances in which the impressions had been made, but he hadn't asked Daisy about the key's eventual use. He trusted her enough to know that he wouldn't be implicated in anything that might happen. He didn't want payment either, just her gratitude. The bell tinkling in his workroom broke into his thoughts. He glanced up at the clock on the wall. It was five o'clock, the time he'd told Daisy to call. He wrapped all the copied keys in oiled cloth, and put them in a large envelope before going out into the shop. It was Daisy.

'Here they are, love, just as I said they would be,' he said, handing her the envelope.

'Was it difficult, Frank?'

'Not half as difficult as getting you to marry me!'

'Oh, don't start that again, silly. I'm good enough for you to take on holiday, but that's all.'

She raised herself on her toes and kissed him lightly on the cheek.

'Thank you, dearest Frank.'

'I don't want your thanks, Daisy. Just be sure and call here again soon.'

'I will, dear. That's a promise.'

Two hours later, Richard Gorges flicked his cane against the peak of his uniform cap, acknowledging the salute of the doorman, and entered the Gresham Hotel in Sackville Street. He walked across to the porter's desk and asked if a package had been left for him. He was handed the envelope left earlier by Daisy Newman and, after tipping the porter a penny, left the hotel. Outside, in the middle of the wide street, was a rank of taxi carriages. He hailed one and gave the cabbie instructions to take him to the Spa Hotel. There, in his room, on the first floor, he examined Robinson's handiwork, particularly the largest key, which he knew was the one to the safe. To his eye it seemed a perfect piece of engineering.

Gorges ate alone in the hotel restaurant that Monday evening and, fortified by four large brandies, retired early to bed. He wanted to be fresh for the next day, the day he'd revenge himself against the Establishment that had twice tried to crush him; the day when he'd steal the Crown Jewels.

Gorges reviewed his plans in his mind as he breakfasted in the hotel dining room just before ten o'clock. He took a substantial meal of poached eggs on toast, grilled kidneys, strawberries, scones, and two pots of tea, because he didn't plan to eat again until after the robbery. After breakfast, he took the steam tram back into Dublin. He was due to meet Daisy Newman outside Alex Findlater and Company's store just before noon.

As usual, she was waiting, and the two of them began strolling along Sackville Street looking in the windows of the fine stores. In the bustle of lunchtime Dublin – horse trams clattering, children begging, shop girls pressing by during their short break, it was a very usual sight to see an Army officer escorting his lady, indeed his very attractive lady, dressed in a white blouse, pink flounced skirt, and a small boater pinned elegantly on her auburn hair. They could talk without fear of being overheard in the general hubbub around them.

'The keys look marvellous, Daisy.'

'Yes, my locksmith says they're near as perfect as he can make them. When are you going to use them?'

'Tonight, Daisy, tonight. And that means you'll be away to London on tomorrow's mail boat.'

'But there's no warning.'

'That's part of the plan.'

'But . . . but . . . my appointments? And what do I tell Millicent and John?'

'Just tell them you've been called away because your cousin in London is dangerously ill. Don't worry about it. Knowing those two, they can look after the business perfectly adequately. And, after all, you won't be away that long. You'll be back on Thursday evening at the latest.'

'But where will I have to go in London?' asked Daisy, as they threaded their way through the throng on the pavement.

'I'll tell you when I see you later tonight.'

'How late? I have an entertainment tonight.'

'I shall be at Ballsbridge by midnight, or just before, if all goes well.'

'They'll have left by then.'

'Right – and make sure your brother and sister are in bed by then. The less people who know the better.'

'Of course.'

By now, the couple had reached the main Post Office.

'Daisy, I shall leave you here because I must send a telegraph,' said Gorges, formally saluting her and turning to walk into the Post Office, between the massive pillars of its main entrance.

He filled in a telegraph form addressed to F. R. Shackleton at 44, Park Lane, London, W. It said simply, 'Expect Newman tomorrow with goods. Regards RHG.' The clerk behind the counter accepted it, hardly glancing at Gorges. Now his one problem was how to occupy the next hours before his plans began in earnest. For an hour he strolled along the quays by the River Liffey, once stopping to watch, along with other passers-by, a fight between two drunken women outside Jackson's Bar. It was just as well they were so drunk on Cork gin, he thought, or they might have killed themselves with the ferociously long hat pins they wielded as they swayed around each other. The brawl ended with a burly potman coming out of the bar and emptying a bucket of porter slops over them. The women ended lying bedraggled in the gutter, their mutual resentment now turned to maudlin rage against the potman.

Then Gorges decided to wander along the carriageway in Phoenix Park. That summer afternoon there was a polo match in progress between two teams from the Hussars. Gorges recognised some of the players from his evenings as a guest in their mess, and sat in a deck chair to watch the last hour of the match, later joining them in the pavilion for a few glasses of a refreshing fruit cup.

'Hello, Gorges,' said one of the players. 'What's the infantry doing here? Trying to pick up a few tips from the cavalry? Maybe you want to join us, eh?'

'Not at all, old boy. Used to be in a cavalry unit myself. Had enough of horses. Give me the infantry now.'

'You in the cavalry! Never. You haven't the seat for it.'

'Well, Thorneycroft's Mounted Horse of Spion Kop weren't exactly infantrymen.'

Gorges could have bitten his tongue as he said it. Ever since returning to Ireland he'd kept silent about his unit during the Boer War. He reasoned that the story of his disgrace – or the disgrace of an unnamed officer, at the very least – must have spread through the officer corps in the past few years.

'Thorneycroft's, eh,' said the Hussar officer. 'You were in Thorneycroft's? Damned fine regiment from what I heard.'

Another officer, who'd joined the group, interrupted: 'Wasn't that the regiment where one of the officers got booted out for falling in love with some coloured boy?'

'Not in my time,' lied Gorges angrily. 'You must be mixing it up with something else. And anyway, the Hussars can talk about disgrace, can't they? It wasn't so long ago the colonel of your 10th got cashiered for attacking some girl on a train.'

'Oh, come along, Gorges. Don't bring up that Colonel Baker affair again. Not fair, old boy. Not at all cricket.'

'Well, you started it.'

'Look, old boy, I was probably mistaken. I heard this tale at Aldershot last year from some johnny who'd been in Cape Town. He said Thorneycroft's, but he must have been mistaken. I'll contact him and find out the details and let you know when I next see you in the mess.'

'Do that,' said Gorges, putting down his fruit cup and preparing to leave.

'Hope you weren't offended,' said the Hussar officer, now apologetic.

'No – and anyway thanks for the drink. Most refreshing.'

As Gorges left the pavilion he heard the Hussar saying, 'Could have sworn it was Thorneycroft's. Oh well, it doesn't matter.'

Gorges cursed himself for his indiscretion. This would be the worst possible time for his past to catch up with him. He hailed a cab, passing along the carriageway, and directed it to the Spa Hotel. On the way, memories of his humiliation in South Africa came vividly back to him. Tonight, he thought, that score would be evened.

At the hotel, he took tea and then went to his room for a bath and to change into his mess uniform, short jacket, waistcoat, and trousers with wide red stripes down the legs. He also took his cloak with him as he left the hotel, although the evening was warm.

By half past six he was walking through the ornate archway of Dublin Castle, past the usual number of sentries and policemen. The Castle was comparatively quiet at this hour with the civil servants long gone to their clubs or their homes. To the sentries who recognised him, it appeared that Captain Gorges had been invited for dinner in the garrison mess. A totally usual event. Nothing out of the ordinary at all.

Gorges walked into Upper Castle Yard, saw the two sentries outside the front entrance to the Bedford Tower, and acknowledged their salutes, palms slapping their rifle butts, as he passed them and turned the corner of the building. He walked more slowly now, constantly watching for anyone, as he approached the entrance to the basement store. The area on this side of the Tower was deserted, as he knew it usually was. He stopped at the top of the steps leading to the store and took a last look round. No one was in sight. He turned quickly and hurried down the steps.

Gorges took out the set of three keys and unlocked the basement door. At a quarter to seven he was inside, the door locked behind him. He went to the back of the basement and tried to unlock one of the big cupboards where rifles were kept. The second key on the ring worked, and the cupboard swung open. Gorges saw it would be a tight fit, but he moved some of the Lee-Enfield rifles to the side, and made a space just large enough for himself to squeeze into. He pulled the doors closed and locked them. He knew he would have to wait in the cupboard for at least an hour. That was the time Frank Shackleton told him that one of the Dublin detectives, Detective Owen Kerr, usually took to make his thorough check of the Bedford Tower after the staff had gone home. Sometimes, according to Shackleton, the detective checked the basement, and sometimes not, merely testing the door in the hallway above that led to the basement. But this night, Detective Kerr was particularly meticulous in his search. About thirty minutes had passed, Gorges estimated, before he heard footsteps on the concrete floor of the basement. He didn't hear them approaching. Suddenly, they were just there, outside the store cupboard.

Gorges sucked in his breath and shrunk back into the darkness of his hiding place, pulling his cloak tightly around him. The steps stopped. Gorges began to relax again. Then he froze with terror as the door of the cupboard was rattled. Twice more the detective outside tried the lock. Then Gorges heard his footsteps again for a few moments. He didn't dare move inside the cupboard for fear of knocking over one of the rifles, so he had to let the sweat that had formed on his temples, under his uniform cap, drip into his eyes and run down either side of his nose. He held himself rigid, hardly daring to breathe, for at least another five minutes. Then he began to relax. The detective, he thought, must have completed his checks in the basement. But Gorges waited, counting silently to a thousand, before he decided it was safe to make his next move.

He slid the key into the lock of the store cupboard and turned it as silently as possible. The door swung open a little as the lock clicked, and Gorges listened, ears straining, for any sound. There was none. He pushed the door open, eased himself forward, realising for the first time the cramped position he'd been in, and stepped into the basement store. His eyes took a few moments to accustom themselves from the blackness of the cupboard to the half-light of the basement. He locked the store cupboard and moved towards the narrow staircase at the back of the basement. Gingerly, he began climbing its stone steps until he stood by the brown wooden door at the top.

Gorges pressed his ear against the cold wood and listened for some minutes. He could hear nothing and guessed that by now Detective Kerr must have completed his inspection and left the Tower by its front door. The key, tested by Shackleton turned the lock without a sound and Gorges stepped into the empty hallway. He shut the door behind him and pressed himself against the stone of the hallway, hidden from above and the side by the winding staircase. Again he listened and could hear nothing. By any reckoning, Gorges thought, the coast must be clear. He walked on the balls of his feet across the hallway, opened the unlocked door to the library, and went in.

The light by eight o'clock on this fine summer night was still bright enough to filter into the library through the sash windows at the front of the building. Gorges crouched low as he crossed the carpeted floor to kneel by the side of the safe, its size shielding him from any over-zealous sentry who might peep through the windows. Gorges thought this to be very unlikely as the soldiers on sentry duty outside the Bedford Tower usually kept their eyes firmly open for any officer or senior NCO who might be checking they were still alert, and not having a quick puff on a cigarette in the shadow of the columns at the entrance to the building. He took the duplicate safe key from his pocket and slipped it into the upper lock. There was no resistance as it went in and only a low click as it turned.

Inwardly, Gorges blessed the craftsmanship of Daisy Newman's locksmith. The key slid into the lower lock just as easily and turned with hardly any pressure. Gorges grasped the central lever, turning and pulling it, and the safe door, with the manufacturer's name crested in the middle, swung open silently.

The red morocco case was on the top shelf with other wooden boxes. Gorges opened it, unwrapped the tissue paper around the Star and the Badge and held them for a moment, marvelling, yet again, at their beauty. He took a large chamois leather bag out of the pocket in the lining of his cloak, and carefully placed the Star inside. The Badge was laid aside for a moment. Then he opened the six other wooden boxes. In five of them, again wrapped in tissue paper, were the gold collars worn by the Knights of the Order of St Patrick; in the sixth, the jewels belonging to the Mahony family, pearl necklaces, diamond and emerald brooches, and a fine diamond tiara. All these disappeared into the chamois bag.

Gorges refolded the tissue paper carefully and placed it back in each box. This was just one of the ideas Shackleton and he had worked out to confuse the inevitable police investigation. No ordinary burglar would be so neat, Shackleton had reasoned. Now Gorges began the second diversionary ploy as he crouched in the angle between the safe and the glass doors of the library shelves.

From the inside pocket of his mess jacket he took a small and very fine screwdriver. He picked up the Badge. A piece of blue ribbon was attached to it by a clasp fastened with two small screws. Gorges had to strain his eyes in the gathering gloom to see the screw threads, but Shackleton's estimate had been right, and the small screwdriver did fit them. It was delicate work, not helped by the nervous sweat on Gorges's palms, but after five minutes he had undone the screws. He put them, the clasp, and the Badge into the bag lying on his folded cloak, then neatly wrapped tissue paper round the piece of blue ribbon and replaced it in the red morocco case. Another little puzzle for the police, Gorges thought to himself. Then he stacked all the cases back on the top shelf of the safe and swung the door shut again. He pulled the central lever back into position but deliberately left the safe unlocked. Shackleton and himself wanted the robbery discovered as soon as possible, so that the former's alibi would stand investigation. Gorges placed the chamois bag carefully in the deep pocket of his cloak and then swung the garment around his shoulders.

Still crouching, he moved across the library and into the hallway. There was one more diversion to set up before he could leave. He went to the front door and quietly turned the Chubb lock and pushed up the catch to hold it open. Another lock on the outside of the front door which Shackleton said was never secured, would hold the door shut. Now, thought Gorges, the police will think the thief must have slipped past the sentries and gained entry through the front door. The neatly-folded tissue paper, the blue ribbon, and the front door – three things to occupy busy little police minds, thought Gorges, as he moved across the hallway and through the door to the basement. Three things, he thought with grim satisfaction, that would need a lot of explanation from Ulster King of Arms. He locked the door from the hallway to the basement behind him and, after waiting a few seconds to get his eyes used to the deeper gloom of the basement, moved down the stairs, past the shelves of equipment, and to the door leading out into the Yard.

Gorges opened this and locked it behind him. He stood at the foot of the steps for a moment listening for any footsteps on the cobbles, and hearing none, quickly ran up them and into the open. There was no one in sight as he began strolling round the Bedford Tower with its high, six-sided bell tower.

As he approached the sentries at the front of the building he began weaving slightly and returned their salutes with a perfunctory wave. As he'd hoped, the sentries assumed he had had one drink too many in some officer's room or other, and took little notice of him. Shortly before nine o'clock Gorges weaved his way, though with not too much exaggeration, back under the archway of Dublin Castle and past the salutes of more sentries and uniformed policemen. In his cloak lining he could feel the comfortable weight of the jewels that had taken him less than three hours to steal.

Still pretending to be a little unsteady, he hailed a cab from the long line of them waiting, as always, outside the Castle. This dropped him outside the Shelbourne Hotel, and Gorges entered the gates of St Stephen's Green opposite the hotel. Couples were still strolling through this favourite courting spot in the centre of Dublin, and Gorges sat on a bench and watched the world and its women go by. Strangely, he felt no emotion, rather an emptiness as if the tensions of the evening had drained him. He felt very tired suddenly, and had to force himself off the bench and towards the line of cabs outside the hotel.

This cab he instructed to go to Ballsbridge. It had been part of the plan deliberately to break his journey to Daisy Newman's, in case the police questioned the cab drivers outside the Castle about their most recent fares when the hue and cry was raised. Gorges himself, at that time on the evening of Tuesday 2 July, was fairly confident the robbery would be discovered the next day. Surely, he reasoned, a thorough check would be made when the front door of the Bedford Tower was found to be unlocked. He'd given a different impression to Daisy Newman, of course, but that was simply to make her less nervous about carrying the jewels to London.

Gorges's cab arrived at the end of the avenue leading to her house just after eleven o'clock. He paid off the cabbie under the gas lamp on the corner, and walked the remaining two hundred yards. The house was in darkness so Gorges assumed it was safe to approach. He stood outside the front door for a few moments, listening for voices, but heard none. Obviously Daisy Newman had been waiting up for him, because she opened the front door as soon as the first echoes of the knocker had died away. She was holding an oil lamp, wearing her silk dressing gown, and motioned Gorges to be silent as he entered the hall. He followed her into the drawing room, and waited while she pulled down the chain on the gaselier to get the by-pass, a small pilot flame, to light the lamp. When the room was lit she went to the drawing room door, opened it and listened for a few seconds. Then, satisfied that all was quiet in the house, she locked the door and turned to Gorges.

'You did it then, dear Captain?' she inquired eagerly.

'Did it? Did it, Daisy? Of course, I ruddy well did it,' said Gorges, a sense of exultation filling him for the first time. 'Yes, I did it.'

He hugged her tight, feeling her nakedness under the dressing gown. 'Oh, Daisy, I did it. It went exactly to plan!'

He fell back on the sofa, legs outstretched, cloak still wrapped round him tightly.

'Give me a drink, m'dear. A very large brandy. I need one.'

Daisy hurried to the sideboard and filled a crystal balloon glass almost to the brim. Gorges took a healthy gulp and felt the brandy warm his throat and empty stomach.

'Come here, Daisy,' he said, pulling her down onto the sofa beside him. The front of her dressing gown fell open slightly and Gorges saw the smooth curve of her breasts. A tremendous surge of excitement went through him and he pulled the woman to him and kissed her deeply, forcing her teeth apart with his tongue. Daisy struggled away from him.

'Where are they then? The jewels? Let me look.'

Gorges felt inside his cloak, pulled out the large chamois bag, untied the leather around its neck, and spilled the jewellery on to the carpet in front of the sofa.

'Holy Mother of God,' exclaimed Daisy, in a whisper, as she saw the tumbling diamond pieces, the rubies, the emeralds, the gold collars, the pearl necklaces. They lay in a pile, glittering and shimmering under the gas light.

'There they are, Daisy. There they are, on your own carpet. The Irish Crown Jewels and I stole them.'

'They're incredible. I didn't realise . . . the Crown Jewels . . . God, they're beautiful.'

Daisy slipped from the sofa on to her knees and, bending over, began running her hands over the gems, her auburn hair brushing the carpet.

'They're just beautiful, beautiful,' she whispered. Gorges looked down at her, noting the curve of her buttocks beneath the thin dressing gown. His excitement was uncontrollable. Daisy was oblivious to everything but the shimmering jewels and scarcely felt the hem of her dressing gown being lifted. She gasped with shock and pleasure as she felt Gorges enter her from behind. She, too, felt uncontrollable excitement as he thrust into her, pushing her face into the carpet, her eyes inches from the glittering white and rose diamonds.

'Oh, God . . . incredible, darling . . . it's incredible,' she moaned as she felt Gorges shudder inside her. They remained, panting, locked together, and then Gorges pulled away and stood up. He pulled Daisy up, her dressing gown now open, and hugged her to him. They stood silently together, holding each other tight, both still trembling with excitement.

'That was the best time ever with anyone,' said Daisy, her head buried in Gorges's shoulder.

'Must be the power of the jewels, m'dear,' laughed Gorges, pushing her away slightly, and looking down into her shining face. 'They're going to alter an awful lot of lives. You mark my words.'

The couple, all emotions spent, began picking up the jewels and putting them back in the bag, occasionally holding up a piece and watching it flash and gleam under the light.

Gorges sat back on the sofa and picked up his unfinished glass of brandy from the floor. Daisy, holding the chamois bag to her, sat down beside him.

'It's up to you now, Daisy. Have you made arrangements for the boat?'

'Yes, but I'm afraid. Suddenly, I'm afraid. It seemed quite a lark before but now it's awfully serious.' She looked down at the bag. 'The Crown Jewels. I never realised. I thought you were going to steal some ordinary gems.'

'Can't put 'em back now,' said Gorges. 'We've got to go ahead and get them to London. You must do it, Daisy. Don't you see?'

'I suppose so . . . yes . . . of course. What do I do?'

'All you've got to do is take them to this address and hand them to Frank. That's all . . . then you come back to Dublin.' Gorges felt in his mess jacket, pulled out an envelope, and handed it to the woman. 'All the instructions about getting to Frank are written here. It won't take you long.'

'All right then. I've arranged for a cab to collect me here at six o'clock to take me to the station for the train to Kingstown.'

'Fine. That means you'll be in London late tonight. Go straight to Frank's and he'll give you a bed for the night. Then come back on Thursday.'

'What are you going to do now?'

Gorges looked at the clock on the mantelpiece, and saw it was shortly before one o'clock.

'Can't go far at this time, Daisy. I suppose it's the sofa for me or. . . .'

'Or? Don't be silly, Captain dear. There's time yet and Millicent can give you breakfast after I've left. You can get a cab later.'

'Capital, Daisy,' exclaimed Gorges, putting his arm around her shoulders and giving a gentle hug. 'You've got the lamp. You lead the way, what!'

Just before ten o'clock that Wednesday morning, 3 July 1907, Daisy Newman boarded the boat at Kingstown. In a small carpet bag she carried her nightgown, wrapped round the chamois leather bag. As the boat pulled away from the quay, the Irish Crown Jewels given to that country's nobility seventy-seven years before by King William IV left Ireland for ever.

6

'*My God . . . the jewels are gone!*'

The Irish Crown Jewels were already an hour out to sea, on their way to London, Paris, and anonymity, when Sir Arthur Vicars began crossing the Upper Yard of Dublin Castle. He was late for work this morning of 3 July 1907, and was perturbed and still somewhat angry. The previous afternoon all his plans for the visit of King Edward VII, Queen Alexandra and Princess Victoria, so carefully fixed, had been dismantled by Lord Aberdeen. He had called Sir Arthur over to his office in the Castle, and broken the news that the Royal Family were not to stay in their apartments in Dublin but would sleep aboard the Royal Yacht at Kingstown during their visit, now just a week away.

'But why, my lord?' Sir Arthur had protested.

'Anarchists,' replied the Viceroy, darkly.

Ulster King of Arms groaned to himself. Not that again, he thought.

'Anarchists,' repeated Lord Aberdeen. 'If Their Majesties stay here at the Castle, then they could be in danger. As I've told you before, Ulster, these fanatics are everywhere.'

'But, my lord,' said Sir Arthur. 'All my plans have been drawn up on the basis that they'll be staying here.'

'Then you'll just have to change them, Ulster. I've already received confirmation that my suggestion has been accepted by His Majesty's advisers. They will carry out their full programme of visits but they will return each night to the *Victoria and Albert* at Kingstown.'

Lord Aberdeen didn't tell Sir Arthur that his suggestion had been received with some annoyance by King Edward. His

Majesty was well used to possible threats to his life and, after so many years travelling the world, took scant notice of them. But it was hard for him to ignore totally the advice of his representative in Ireland. Thus, the compromise plan was accepted at the last moment.

Sir Arthur, top hat set firmly and squarely on his head hurried to work the next morning having spent a near sleepless night revising the plans for the Royal Visit. To him, all the last-minute confusion was unnecessary and very unfair. But a change in plans there had to be, so the next few days were going to be extremely busy ones for the staff at the Office of Arms. Scarcely had he mounted the spiral staircase in the Bedford Tower and sat down behind his desk when the first distraction occurred. After knocking, William Stivey, the messenger, came in.

'Yes?' said Sir Arthur, rather testily.

'Sir, I've some worrying news.'

Sir Arthur threw down his pen in disgust. 'We've got enough worries as it is, Stivey. What's the matter now?'

'Well, sir, when I arrived for work this morning at ten o'clock I found Mrs Farrell waiting for me.'

'What on earth for, Stivey? She should have finished her cleaning well before then.'

'But, sir,' persevered Stivey, 'She said that when she arrived for work just after eight o'clock, she found the front door unlocked. The catch was up.'

'Is that so?' said Sir Arthur, sarcasm heavy in his voice. 'Is that so, Stivey?'

'Yes, sir.'

'Well, thank you for telling me.'

Stivey waited for a few moments, hoping for some instructions about what to do. But Sir Arthur was already busy with his papers again, and the messenger withdrew, feeling rather awkward. He'd thought it very important that the front door had been found unlocked, but obviously his superior didn't agree.

Sir Arthur, indeed, gave little thought to the news. Hadn't he lost his own front door key only a week before, and had to ask Detective Owen Kerr to let him into the building? He put his hand in his pocket and felt the reassuring weight of his key chain carrying the key to the safe. He dismissed the matter of the unlocked front door from his mind. Anyone could have left the latch up by mistake, he thought, and anyway he had more important things to worry about.

Daisy Newman reached Euston Station in London just before midnight that day, hailed a cab, and went directly to Frank Shackleton's rooms at No. 44, Park Lane. Shackleton had waited up for her, having received the telegraph from Richard Gorges, and had prepared a supper of cold cuts and a bottle of champagne.

'How was the journey, Daisy?' he asked as she entered his rooms.

'Smooth enough, Frank, but I must say I travelled expecting a hue and cry at any minute. I'll be glad when I get rid of these.' She put her carpet bag on a chair, opened it, unwrapped the chamois bag from her night attire, and handed it to him.

'There you are. They're yours now. I've done my part.'

Shackleton opened the bag and spilled the jewels on to a table, covered with a fringed and richly patterned cloth. He picked up the Badge of the Order of St Patrick and noted that Gorges had followed their plan by removing the piece of blue ribbon. A brilliant stroke that, he thought.

'Well done, Daisy. Well done, indeed. But you shouldn't have worried about any hue and cry. There's no mention of any robbery yet in tonight's evening papers. Probably the people at the Castle haven't let out the news.'

He realised that Daisy was still standing. 'Come and sit down, dear Daisy. I'm a dreadful host, I must say. Have some wine.'

'A glass would do well, Frank.'

After he handed her the glass of champagne, Shackleton was eager to hear every detail of what had happened in Dublin. Daisy first removed the wide-brimmed cream hat she'd worn for the journey, and sipped her wine before recounting all she had done, and the little Gorges had told her about the robbery itself. It was past two o'clock in the morning by the time she had finished. Shackleton, as she talked, constantly picked up various pieces of jewellery from the heap on the table and turned them under the light, marvelling at their sparkling changes of colour.

'Well, it seems everything has gone exactly to plan, if you ask me, Daisy. Once I get rid of the gems we're home and dry. But I'm forgetting, you must be tired out. Let me show you to your room.'

'I am a little fatigued, I must admit, Frank, but first some more wine.'

The couple drank another glass each before going to their separate beds. Daisy was too tired to want anything but sleep, and Shackleton was too excited about the deal he'd be doing with Rufus Levinson later that morning to think about taking advantage of his attractive guest. Unlike Gorges, he believed business and pleasure didn't mix. He placed the jewels in their bag and slept with it by his pillow.

After a light breakfast of boiled eggs and toast, Shackleton saw Daisy to a cab that would take her to Euston and the boat for Dublin. Over breakfast she had raised tentatively the question of her share of the money from the jewels.

'Don't worry, Daisy. You'll get it within a week in Dublin. By the way, you're not short of funds at the moment, are you?'

'No, I have a sufficiency, Frank.'

'Right then, Richard and I will contact you next week.'

Shackleton changed cabs three times on his way to No. 17c, Club Row. Thanks to Gorges's telegraph from Dublin, he had been able to give Levinson, the diamond merchant, more than twenty-four hours' notice to allow him to finalise his arrangements for disposing of the jewels. But the merchant was far from happy when Shackleton arrived at his little office.

'I needed more time,' complained Levinson. 'At least another day.'

'You don't want to take the jewels then?' asked Shackleton.

'Well, Mr Newman,' replied Levinson, using his visitor's previous pseudonym, 'I have been lucky, I admit. I've found a colleague who's going to Paris on the night train tonight but, at such short notice, it's costing a lot of money. It'll have to come out of your price.'

'How much?'

'Five hundred pounds!'

'Nonsense, Mr Levinson,' said Shackleton, firmly. 'Two hundred at the most.'

'All right – but I'm losing money,' said the diamond merchant in a grudging tone. In fact, he was happy at the figure agreed, since he intended to take the jewels to Paris himself and spend a fortnight's holiday there. The extra £200 would more than cover that at the very best hotel, he thought. Paris, he was sure, was the place to be while the initial hunt was on.

'So have you got the merchandise?'

'Certainly,' said Shackleton, placing his brown leather holdall on Levinson's grime-stained table. 'Have you got the money?' 'With some difficulty at such short notice – yes.' Levinson pulled a battered suitcase from under the table and placed it alongside Shackleton's holdall.

Shackleton took out the bag containing the jewels, weighing it in his hand, as Levinson snapped open the suitcase. Inside were neat piles of white £100 notes, held together with elastic bands.

Levinson produced a green baize square from the drawer of the table, and motioned Shackleton to empty the jewels onto it. He untied the leather knot and spilled them gently over the baize, spreading them apart with his left hand. There was a sharp intake of breath from the jeweller as he saw the haul of gems for the first time. He reached inside his waistcoat pocket, took out a jeweller's eye glass, screwed it into his right eye, and began examining the pieces of jewellery one by one, starting with the Star and the Badge.

'Superb,' he muttered. 'Absolutely superb. The craftsmanship is magnificent. You don't find pieces like these nowadays, Mr Newman.'

He removed his eye glass. 'I'm more than happy with these, Mr Newman. I am just sorry they have to be broken up – but then, that is business, is it not?'

Pushing the suitcase towards Shackleton, he continued, 'Here, count your money. It's in bundles of £1,000 each. All used notes, I might add.'

Shackleton picked out the bundles, counting each one, before placing them in his bag. He'd reached the fifteenth and last bundle when Levinson stopped him.

'Remember the £200 for my courier, Mr Newman.'

Shackleton smiled wryly and tore off two of the large white notes, tossing them on the table.

'I suspect it won't cost nearly that amount, Mr Levinson, but, unfortunately, I'm in your hands.'

'Correct. Oh, very correct, Mr Newman.'

The jeweller picked up the four corners of the green baize and tied them round the jewels. This bundle he pushed into the chamois bag and placed it in a drawer in the table, which he locked.

'These will be in Paris tomorrow and anywhere in Europe within a week. They'll be untraceable.'

'I thought', broke in Shackleton, 'experts could always identify a particular stone.'

'Not when they've been recut, my dear sir. And, luckily, there will not have to be much recutting to be done with all the Brazilian diamonds in the two ceremonial pieces.'

'I don't understand.'

'An ordinary diamond, say a South African white, is cut to have 58 facets, and a very definite character. The Brazilian stones aren't cut in the same way; they're not cut with the same disciplines, so they'll have fewer facets. When they've been prised from their setting they'll be completely unidentifiable. And that, be assured, will be done as soon as they reach Paris.'

'Now,' the jeweller continued, holding out his hand, 'I think our business is concluded. Good day, Mr Newman.'

'Thank you, Mr Levinson. I doubt if we shall meet again. I trust not anyway.'

Frank Shackleton hurried through the crowded streets around Levinson's office until he found a cab rank. On the way back to Park Lane he held his bag on his knees, wondering how to dispose of his share of the money. He was holding £14,500. Daisy Newman was owed £2,200, and that left £6,150 each for Gorges and himself. He was tempted to place the whole of his share directly into his account at Cox's Bank to support his overdraft, but such a large amount paid in at one time in cash would inevitably invite questions. It was a problem that would take some time to sort out, and until then the money would have to remain in the wall safe at his rooms. Not an ideal hiding place, thought Shackleton, with so many thieves around. He smiled to himself at the irony of the situation.

After putting the money in the safe, Shackleton changed quickly and went to Lady Ormonde's house in Upper Brook Street for a luncheon party. He was seated next to her daughter, Lady Constance Butler, and when the guests had finished a delicious main course of 'lamb medaillons de foie gras', their conversation turned to the next week's Royal Visit to Ireland.

'It should be a memorable occasion,' said Shackleton. 'The plans are very advanced.' The butler refilled his glass with claret. Shackleton was feeling a trifle light-headed after the first-class lunch, and that morning's successful transaction.

'Yes, we shall be travelling over for the visit, of course,' interrupted Lady Ormonde. 'I do hope Sir Arthur Vicars has arranged everything properly.'

'He always does, Mama,' said Lady Constance. 'He's so fussy. Anyone would think he was the Viceroy and not simply Ulster King of Arms.'

'Oh, come now, dear. You mustn't be unfair. He is fussy, I grant you, but he does have a post of great responsibility,' said Lady Ormonde. 'Isn't that so, Mr Shackleton?'

'It is indeed, Lady Ormonde. Great responsibility!'

'There, you see, Constance. Mr Shackleton agrees with me and he does work with Sir Arthur.'

Lady Ormonde continued, 'I mean, it's not only his own work, but also his responsibility for the Crown Jewels, you know.'

'Yes,' said Shackleton. 'He has a great deal of responsibility and he's very proud of his office.'

'You're so right, Mr Shackleton. He must be so proud looking after those magnificent jewels. They have to be guarded so carefully. . . .'

'They do indeed,' interrupted Shackleton, careless in wine. 'But I don't know . . . I shouldn't be surprised to hear they were stolen some day.'

Lady Ormonde and her guests laughed at such an outrageous suggestion. Shackleton joined in, realising at once how stupid and potentially damaging his remark had been.

'Stolen some day,' chuckled Lady Ormonde. 'Oh, Mr Shackleton, you can't mean that. Sir Arthur is much too fussy to allow that to happen.'

By late afternoon on Thursday 4 July, Captain Richard Gorges was becoming a very worried man. For some strange reason he could find no mention of the robbery in the Dublin evening newspapers. Surely, he thought, a full search of the Bedford Tower would have been made after the front door had been found unlocked the previous morning. He had been on duty in the rifle butts at the Curragh during the day, and had expected to return to his quarters and hear about the robbery from his fellow officers. Such news would have been the main topic of conversation in the mess, but no mention was made of it. It was imperative that the robbery should be discovered before Shackleton returned to Ireland so, the next day, Gorges hurried to Dublin to try to discover what had gone wrong. He went directly to the Castle, arriving just before the lunch hour and, to his surprise, met the debonair Peirce Gun Mahony just as he was passing under the archway.

'Peirce, my dear chap, how are you? I thought you were still convalescing in England.'

'No, Richard, I returned on Wednesday and came back to work here yesterday.'

'How are you now? I heard you caught a nasty bug.'

'Quite fine, thanks. Completely recovered. And you?'

'Mustn't grumble, old boy. Usual round of chores and all that. Trying to teach Irish farm boys to shoot straight isn't the most rewarding of tasks, after all.'

'I'll wager on that. How's Frank?'

'Shackleton? Oh, he's very well. Been away in London for the last couple of weeks. Due back for the Monarch's visit, I'm told.'

'I hope so. We've got enough work on to need him back.'

'Why? Are you folks in Bedford Tower in trouble or something?'

'Oh, not particularly, Richard. It's just that H.M. has changed his plans and is staying aboard the Royal Yacht rather than in Dublin.'

'Is that all?' asked Gorges sharply.

'Yes . . . why? Should there be anything else?'

'Not that I know of, old boy. Just inquiring.'

'Why not come and have lunch with me at the club, Richard? You're not doing anything special, are you?'

'Well, I was going to have a bite in the mess but since you've invited me . . . why not?'

The two men took a cab outside the Castle and ten minutes later were having a drink in the plush comfort of Mahony's club in Kildare Street. During lunch Gorges brought his companion up to date with all the gossip in Dublin, and also told him about the previous Sunday's party for Peter McEnnery.

'I'm afraid, Peirce, your uncle got a bit under the weather again.'

'As usual,' laughed Mahony.

'Yes . . . as usual.'

By the time they parted, Gorges was convinced from Mahony's attitude that the robbery had not been discovered yet. There was only one solution. He would have to break into the Bedford Tower again. This time, Gorges thought as he strolled along the banks of the Liffey, he wouldn't enter until eight o'clock or later, when he could be certain Detective Kerr had completed his check of the building. Gorges didn't want a repeat of the episode in the store cupboard full of rifles.

He sent a cabbie to Daisy Newman at Ballsbridge with a message that he would be calling later that night, and then dined early in the officers' mess at the Castle, afterwards taking coffee and brandy with two acquaintances in the mess lounge. Shortly before nine o'clock he excused himself and, in the gathering dusk, walked up to the Upper Castle Yard.

It was even more deserted, if that was possible, than on the night, three days previously, when he had committed the robbery. As before, he acknowledged the salutes of the sentries outside the Tower and walked casually round to the side leading to the basement store. No one was in sight so he went immediately down the steps, unlocked the door, and entered the basement. He listened for a few minutes at the door leading to the hallway but heard nothing. With less caution than before, he unlocked the door and went straight through the hallway and into the library. Gorges had been racking his brains over what to do next. He looked at the safe and wondered whether he should simply pull its door and swing it wide open. But that idea he quickly rejected. One of the sentries could look through the windows, see the open safe, and raise the alarm before Gorges could leave the Castle. Not likely, he thought, but possible, and he could leave nothing to chance.

'*My God . . . the jewels are gone!*'

Gorges moved out of the shadow of the library door and, crouched, made his way to the open office he knew was used by the messenger. Here, he was safe from the gaze of any peeking sentry. He looked at the strongroom with its inner grille guarding the Irish Sword of State, some valuable books, and miscellaneous regalia of the Order of St Patrick. He wondered if he had the key for the strongroom. Gorges took from his pocket all the keys that had been copied from Sir Arthur Vicars's key ring, and tried them in the lock of the strongroom door. The third one fitted and the door swung open. Was that enough to do? Gorges decided not. He reasoned that if an open front door could be ignored, then it might happen with a strongroom door. He tried his duplicate keys on the inner grille but none of them fitted.

He went back to the messenger's cubby hole of an office, and searched the drawers in his table. In the second drawer, pushed to the back and covered with papers, he found a key with another key attached to it with string. He tried these on the lock of the inner grille and the first one slipped in easily. He turned it and the lock clicked back. Gorges entered the strongroom and had a look at the magnificent Sword of State and the other contents of the glass case with its locks on each corner. There was little point in stealing them he decided, since it would be too risky without any plan for disposing of them. He left the strongroom, shutting the inner grille but leaving the key in the lock with the other key hanging from it. He decided to leave the strongroom door wide open. That must be enough, he reckoned to cause an alarm when it was discovered the next morning.

Gorges surveyed his handiwork for the last time, moved quickly to the library door, and ran on his toes into the hallway. It was nearly dark now inside the building, and he had to fumble for a moment to get the right key into the lock to open the way into the basement. He felt his way down the stairs, arms outstretched to touch both walls, taking one step carefully at a time, before he reached the basement, filled with shelves of military equipment. Here, the light wasn't that much better and Gorges cannoned off two shelves as he made his way to the outer door. Each time he had to grab the equipment on the shelf to stop it falling. Once it was a pile of metal canteen tins and Gorges breathed a thankful sigh of relief as he caught them in time and stacked them back into their places. He opened the basement door at his first attempt and locked it behind him. Outside, it was so dark that Gorges could hardly see the two sentries in the shadow of the pillars in front of the Bedford Tower as he walked round the building. But they saw him and saluted as he passed. In the darkness they wouldn't have seen his features clearly, thought Gorges, but they would have recognised him as an officer from the silhouette of his uniform cap. He walked calmly down to the archway, returning salutes, and out of the Castle.

This time the break-in had not been such a wearing ordeal, so he decided to take a cab to the Gresham Hotel for a drink before continuing to Daisy Newman's. He drank two brandies in the high-ceilinged lounge of the hotel while he smoked a cheroot, and then took a cab from outside to Ballsbridge, arriving there shortly after eleven o'clock.

As before, Daisy had waited up for him and opened the door almost immediately after his knock. They went into her drawing room off the hall.

'What's the matter?' she said in a worried tone as soon as the door was shut behind them. 'Your message that you were coming put me in a bit of a state. Has anything gone wrong?'

Gorges, his weariness making his shoulders slump a little, poured himself a drink before replying.

'What's gone wrong, Daisy, is that no one has discovered the robbery yet. I've had to break into the Tower again tonight to make sure that they do.'

'Oh, dear God. You must be exhausted.'

Gorges sank back into a corner of the sofa. 'To tell the truth, Daisy, I am a little tired. I never thought I'd have to go through the same thing twice though, I must admit, it wasn't so hazardous this time.'

Daisy was wearing her silk dressing gown and Gorges glimpsed a frilled, pink nightgown under it as she sat on the sofa next to him.

'No entertainments tonight, Daisy?'

'No. I wasn't sure when I'd return from London, so Millicent and John cancelled everything and went down to

Bray for the rest of the week. I'm on my own here. Perhaps that's why your message alarmed me so much.'

'Well, I don't think there's too much to worry about now, m'dear. They're bound to discover the robbery tomorrow, and Frank's alibi will be fine. By the way, I'm presuming everything went off well in London.'

'Oh, I delivered the jewels with no trouble at all. I left Frank before he passed them on – or at least I'm assuming that's what you intend to do.'

'Quite right, Daisy. They should be on the Continent by now. All we have to worry about is Frank's alibi. If he's in the clear then we're all safe. If he becomes suspected then they'll connect me with him for certain.'

'And me?' asked Daisy worriedly.

'You'll be safe whatever happens, Daisy. No one will be able to connect you with the robbery. We've been too careful for that.'

'Well, that's a relief,' said Daisy, rising from the sofa and picking up the decanter of brandy and another glass from the sideboard. 'Let's drink to that,' she added, refilling Gorges's glass and pouring a drink for herself. 'I suppose you intend to stay here for the night?'

'Is that a statement or an invitation, m'dear?'

'Seeing it's three days since we've been together, you can call it an invitation, dear Captain,' smiled Daisy.

'Then I shall accept with pleasure. Much pleasure.' Gorges, anticipation overcoming tiredness, leant over and kissed her.

'Not here again. Not on the carpet,' insisted Daisy. 'Come to bed properly if you must. . . .'

As Gorges began to waken the next morning, his arm draped across the smooth and warm nakedness of Daisy Newman, another day of routine began for the staff at the Office of Arms in the Bedford Tower. Normally they would work only until early afternoon on a Saturday but, with the imminent Royal Visit, they had a full day's work ahead on this day, 6 July 1907.

The first to arrive at the Tower was the cleaning woman, Mrs Mary Farrell, a fine-looking mother of three strapping sons, who believed that hard work was the cure for all ills and that, to be sure, cleanliness was next to godliness. Shortly before eight o'clock, she opened the front door of the office with her own latch key and, as usual, went directly to William Stivey's little office to see if the messenger had left any orders for her for special cleaning jobs. There were none this morning but, as soon as she entered the office, Mrs Farrell was shocked to see the door to the strongroom open and the key in the inner grille with another key hanging from it. What should she do? It was altogether too much for her limited intelligence. Only the previous Wednesday she'd found the front door unlocked and had told Mr Stivey. Nothing seemed to have been done about that, she recalled. Perhaps they hadn't believed her. Mrs Farrell decided to leave everything as it was while she pondered the problem during her cleaning chores.

But, eventually, her sense of rectitude overcame her fears of being thought foolish for a second time. When she had finished her cleaning and tidying she returned to the messenger's office and removed the keys from the lock of the inner grille, made sure it was locked, and then slammed shut the outer door of the strongroom. Mrs Farrell put the keys on the messenger's desk and, with a stub of pencil she always carried with her, wrote a message on his blotting pad. Tip of tongue clenched between her teeth, spelling each word to herself, she slowly wrote, 'Mr Stivey, I found the strongroom door open this morning. I have closed it and I closed the gate and leave the keys on your table.' She stood back to admire her work, the words a little uneven but still very legible for a woman of little formal education. She waited nearly half an hour for the messenger to arrive, but then had to leave to do her weekend shopping.

When Stivey arrived, just after ten o'clock, he read Mrs Farrell's message and checked immediately that all was well in the strongroom. Then he sat at his desk, stroking his waxed moustache, and thought about what he should do. His strict training in Her Majesty's Imperial Navy had taught him that the word of the commanding officer was law, and last Wednesday his superior, Sir Arthur Vicars, had been rather heavy-tongued and sarcastic when he'd reported the news about the front door. Perhaps, since nothing was missing, he should keep quiet on this occasion. He thought on his duty for quite a time and decided, somewhat half-heartedly, that he'd have to inform Ulster King of Arms. He marched, shoulders back, up the spiral staircase, and knocked on Sir Arthur's door.

'Yes? Come in.'

Stivey entered to find Sir Arthur deep in conference with Peirce Gun Mahony, Charles Horlock, his personal secretary, and Miss Gibbon, the typist.

'What is it, Stivey?' asked Sir Arthur sharply. 'Come on, man, can't you see we're busy?'

The messenger's resolution shrank in face of the crowded office.

'I'll tell you later, sir, when you're alone. I'm sorry to have interrupted you.' He left the room thankful for receiving only a baleful gaze from Sir Arthur and not another dose of sarcasm, especially in front of the others.

But an hour later, around one o'clock, Sir Arthur himself scurried down to the library to find a volume that might settle a complicated point of genealogical precedence. Stivey rose from behind his desk and approached him.

'Excuse me, sir. May I have a word?'

'Oh yes, Stivey,' said Sir Arthur, his mind on other things. 'You said you wanted to see me alone.'

'Yes, sir. It's Mrs Farrell again.'

'What do you mean, Mrs Farrell again?'

'Sir, this morning she found the door to the strongroom open and the key to the inner grille in the lock.'

'Is that so?' replied Sir Arthur brusquely.

'Nothing missing, sir, but you'll remember on Wednesday she found the front door unlocked.'

'Yes, Stivey, I do. Well?'

The messenger could see that his superior paid little attention to the news – or gave it any importance at all – and decided not to press the point and risk more sarcasm.

'Oh, nothing, sir.'

Sir Arthur turned and hurried upstairs again with his precious volume. He laid it on his desk and began turning its pages, seeking the passage that would settle his obscure problem. He pushed to one side the wooden case delivered that morning by a messenger from West's the jewellers. This contained the gold collar of the Order of St Patrick that had belonged to Lord de Ros, who had died recently. It had been sent to the jewellers to have his name engraved on the back of one of the links of the chain, and had now been returned to be used at the investiture into the Order of Lord Castletown. This ceremony was planned by Sir Arthur to be one of the most glittering to take place during the Royal Visit.

Just before two o'clock there was a knock on his door. It was Stivey again.

'Yes, Stivey,' said Sir Arthur, interrupting a discussion with his nephew, Peirce. 'What is it now?'

'Sir, it's nearly two o'clock and the Tower is closed to visitors. Can I go home?'

'Oh, very well, Stivey.' Sir Arthur looked at his over-crowded desk. 'But before you go put this in the safe, will you?' He handed Stivey the wooden case containing the gold collar. 'We're getting overcrowded here.'

Sir Arthur stood up, took out his keys, and handed them to Stivey, holding up the one that would open the safe.

'Certainly, sir,' said Stivey, rather surprised at Sir Arthur's order. He'd never been allowed to open the safe before but he thought he knew how to do so from watching Sir Arthur many times.

The messenger, still perplexed at his new responsibility, went down the staircase holding the wooden case tightly, and crossed the hall into the library. He put the case on a table near the safe and bent down to open it. He put the key first in the lower keyhole and tried to turn it to the left to unlock it, but it wouldn't move. Then he slipped the key into the upper lock and here the key would only turn to the right. He grasped the central lever, turned it and pulled, but the safe remained obstinately shut. Stivey was thoroughly bothered by now, but the thought crossed his mind that by turning the key in the upper lock he had just secured the safe rather than unlocking it. He picked up the case and went back towards the stairs. It was obvious to him that he needed help. The same thought had struck Sir Arthur in his office, and he was coming down the stairs to see how Stivey was coping. The two men met near the bottom step.

'Sir Arthur,' said a very worried Stivey, 'the last time you were at the safe you couldn't have locked the door.'

'Oh, I must have done,' replied Sir Arthur, becoming a little weary at what he thought was the messenger's obtuseness.

Stivey persisted, 'Well, Sir Arthur, I've found the safe door unlocked.'

'What do you mean?' said Ulster King of Arms, alarmed now by the obvious sincerity of the messenger. He hurried to the safe and turned the key in both locks. He pulled the central lever and the door swung open.

'I wonder if they're all right,' he muttered to himself as he saw the red morocco case, and the wooden cases piled neatly on the shelf. He opened the red case.

'My God, they're gone,' he cried. 'The jewels are gone!'

He frantically opened one of the wooden cases. 'Lord Cork's collar gone,' he exclaimed in anguish. 'Anything else?' As he opened each case he saw they were empty, save for the neatly wrapped tissue paper. 'This gone!' he half-sobbed, as he clicked open another case. 'This gone!' he repeated as another case was opened.

Sir Arthur, white-faced and shocked, turned to Stivey. 'Get the police and the detectives quickly.'

The messenger ran off as best he could as Sir Arthur went to the foot of the staircase.

'Peirce,' he shouted up the stairs. 'Peirce, come down here!'

As Peirce Gun Mahony, Cork Herald, entered the library he saw his uncle standing by the open safe, holding the empty red morocco case open in his hand. Sir Arthur swayed slightly with the shock and uttered one word in a strangled voice.

'Gone!'

7

King Edward fumes: 'They must be found.'

The choruses of Welsh hymns, played by a Royal Marines band, filled the *Victoria and Albert* as the Royal Yacht lay at anchor off the Welsh coast on the morning of Sunday 7 July 1907. King Edward VII, dressed in a navy blue barathea reefer jacket, light grey flannel trousers, white tan shoes, and wearing a peaked yachting cap with the badge of the Royal Yacht Squadron, strolled along the port deck to his private sitting room for breakfast just before ten o'clock. So far his tour of Wales had gone well, with enthusiastic receptions and fulsome civic addresses at every town and city he'd visited. The next day the Royal Yacht would steam majestically further up the coast to Caernarvon Bay, to allow King Edward a brief tour of north Wales, and then across the Irish Sea to Kingstown and Ireland.

It had been four years since the King had visited Ireland, and he was looking forward to his coming tour. He'd always had a soft spot for Ireland and its people ever since he'd been sent to the Curragh for military training forty-six years before. Military training, thought His Majesty with a wry smile, was the last thing he'd needed after his strict and lonely teenage years. And, he recalled, military training was the last thing he got. He delved into his memories – a habit to which he was becoming more attached as he approached his 66th birthday – pausing to look out to sea and lean on the varnished teak rail of the great yacht. What was her name, that actress procured by his fellow officers so long ago? Ah, yes – Nellie Clarke. A man, particularly a man who headed the greatest Empire the world had ever seen, should always remember the first woman he'd bedded. How silly Mama had been to blame his father's death on that scandal. As if, thought the King, a sweet few hours with a buxom actress could cause typhoid fever. Ah well, he sighed to himself, all that was past and gone. At his age, and after his kind of life, he looked more for companionship in a woman than anything else.

He resumed his portly way along the deck and into his sitting room, wondering what his chef, Monsieur Ménager, had prepared for breakfast. He'd ordered a light meal to please his doctors, who were becoming more and more concerned about his weight and his growing breathlessness. A footman in scarlet livery sprang to attention as King Edward entered the mahogany panelled room and made for the small dining table. The footman pulled back the King's chair as he sank into it, and then placed before him the morning's menu – fruit juices, kippers or steamed haddock, boiled eggs, toast, and tea. The King took little time to decide. 'The kippers are Manx, we presume? We'll have four of them and then two boiled eggs,' he ordered in his deep, slightly guttural voice. He adored the small, sweetly-cured fish from the Isle of Man, and M. Ménager always ensured a fresh supply was on hand. The King looked up as the door opened and his secretary, Sir Francis Knollys, entered the room.

'Good morning, sir. I trust you slept well.'

'Like a top, Francis. You know the sea air always does well for me. Have you breakfasted?'

'Thank you, sir. I took it in my cabin but perhaps some tea . . .?'

'Of course, Francis. Sit down.'

Sir Francis took the seat on the King's right, where cutlery had already been laid. A worried frown was set on his pleasant, though hawk-like, features. This was noticed quickly by King Edward, who knew intimately the range of expressions on his secretary's face.

'What's the trouble, Francis? From your look we know you've got something on your mind.'

'Sir, it's some rather upsetting news from Ireland.'

'Oh, good God, don't tell me Aberdeen wants to change the arrangements again.'

'No, sir, though the telegraph is from Lord Aberdeen.'

Sir Francis took a telegraph form from the folder he'd placed on the table.

'I'll read it, sir. It says: "Please inform His Majesty with regret that the Irish Crown Jewels have been found to be missing from Dublin Castle this afternoon. All steps are being taken for their recovery." The telegraph has yesterday's date and is signed by Lord Aberdeen.'

King Edward's large fist thumped the table with annoyance, making the silver cutlery jump and jingle. His small grey beard quivered with anger.

'What? What?' he exclaimed, his voice thickening in its rage. 'The fools in Dublin have lost the Crown Jewels? Well, that's damned fine news on the eve of our visit, eh, Francis?'

'Sir,' said his secretary soothingly, 'the telegraph does say all steps are being taken for their recovery.'

'All steps!' snorted the King. 'All steps . . . from our knowledge the police in Dublin have difficulty finding their own bootlaces to tie. Telegraph Aberdeen of our displeasure and make certain that Scotland Yard is called in at once. Those are some of our most beautiful jewels. They must be found.'

In fact, despite His Majesty's pessimism, the Dublin Police had done all that could be reasonably expected of them once the robbery had been reported. The first detective on the scene that Saturday afternoon had been Superintendent John Lowe, one of the 'G-men' to Fenian terrorists and ordinary criminals, because the detectives based at the Castle were officially in 'G' Division of the Dublin Metropolitan Police. William Stivey showed the burly detective into the library, where Sir Arthur Vicars and his staff were grouped disconsolately around the open and empty safe.

'A burglary has been committed here,' said Sir Arthur as soon as the detective entered. 'A burglary right under our noses.'

'What's happened, Sir Arthur?'

'The jewels have been stolen from the safe,' replied Ulster King of Arms, now very near the edge of hysteria. 'In fact, a clean sweep has been made of the safe.'

He showed Supt. Lowe the empty jewel cases and explained what they should have contained. The detective was struck immediately by the piece of blue ribbon that had been attached to the stolen Badge of the Order of St Patrick, but now lay in the forlorn emptiness of its red morocco case.

'How long would it take to remove the ribbon from the Badge, Sir Arthur?' he asked.

'About ten minutes, Superintendent, and whoever it was would have to know what he was doing. The screws are very fine and delicate.'

'Why should anyone remove that piece of ribbon?'

'I have no idea.'

'Well, I must tell you straight away, Sir Arthur, this has all the appearances of an "inside job". One of the staff working here must be involved in some way in the robbery.'

'That's impossible, Superintendent. I don't believe any of my staff is capable of theft.'

The detective looked at the anxious and strained faces of the staff of the Office of Arms who were in the library – Mahony, Burtchaell, Horlock, and Sir Arthur himself. He was positive the robbery must be an 'inside job'. No other explanation made sense. Just as he resumed his questioning, his superior officer arrived. The Assistant Commissioner, Mr William Harrel, strode into the room. Sir Arthur turned to him plaintively 'The Crown Jewels are gone,' he cried.

Once again Sir Arthur recounted how the robbery had been discovered, but now he was also beginning to try to apportion blame. 'This is the fault of the Board of Works. I asked them for a safe in the strongroom and they didn't give it.'

'When were the jewels last seen in the safe, Sir Arthur?' asked Mr Harrel bluntly.

'That's a problem. I can't remember when I showed them to my friend, Mr Hodgson, the librarian to the Duke of Northumberland.'

'Can't you send him a telegraph?'

'But that will make the matter public. . . .'

'Sir Arthur, this matter can hardly remain private. It's essential for us to know when the jewels were last seen here.'

'Oh, I don't know. . . .'

'Sir Arthur. It's essential.'

'But . . .?'

The two policemen could see that Ulster King of Arms was incapable of rational thought. They sat him, politely but firmly, at the table near the safe while the Assistant Commissioner dictated the telegraph to be sent to Mr Hodgson at Alnwick Castle.

'Am anxious to know latest date on which safe with jewels was opened. Do you recollect whether I showed them to you when here on 10th(27th) June. Wire reply. Letter follows. Vicars, Castle.'

The reply, when it came, surprised even the cynical and hardened detectives. It had been 11 June when Mr Hodgson had seen the jewels. That meant, on Sir Arthur's own account, that no one had checked the safe and its contents for 25 days.

Ulster King of Arms, now casting wildly about him for an explanation, found a new one for Detective Owen Kerr when he arrived in the library, two hours after the discovery of the robbery.

As he entered the handsome room, Sir Arthur hurried to his side. 'Kerr, the jewels are all gone. Some of the smart boys that have been over here for the King's visit have made a clean sweep of them.'

Detective Kerr was singularly unimpressed with this piece of fantasy.

'How was it discovered, Sir Arthur?' he asked.

'I sent Stivey with a collar and he came and found it open.'

'Though I've been here a little over six years,' the messenger interrupted, 'I never had the key in my hand before.'

'Yes, that's so,' agreed Sir Arthur. 'I was thronged owing to pressure of business, and I sent Stivey, but I was coming immediately after him. That key was always in my possession and I never let it out of it before.'

'What about the strongroom?' broke in Supt. Lowe. 'Were there any marks on the doors or anything missing from it?'

'No. It's a Milner strongroom,' replied Sir Arthur. 'It's quite secure. Milner or Chubb locks are burglar-proof.'

He failed to mention – and so did Stivey the messenger – that the strongroom door had been found unlocked and open that very morning. All he repeated was: 'It's burglar-proof and couldn't be opened, only by its own key.'

Late in the afternoon, the Chief Commissioner of the Dublin Metropolitan Police, Sir John Ross of Bladensburg, arrived at Bedford Tower. He thought the blue ribbon left in the jewel case, and the neatly folded pieces of tissue paper, were very significant clues.

'It's very different from the work of an ordinary burglar,' observed Sir John. 'They're usually in such a hurry that they never tidy up.'

The senior policemen questioned Sir Arthur into the early evening and then allowed him to return to his own office. Here, Ulster King of Arms scribbled a note to his friend, Mr Hodgson, explaining the reason for the urgent telegraph that had been sent earlier.

'It's awful for me,' he wrote, 'but what more can a mortal do when a safe is picked as appears to be the case, for no sign of tampering with safe or lock is visible. The police are hard at it and the hue and cry will be raised all over Europe, but for the present, please, keep this to yourself.'

Hardly had he put down his pen when there was a knock on his door and Assistant Commissioner Harrel, over 6ft 2ins tall and running slightly to fat, entered the office. He was far from satisfied with the security arrangements for the keys to the office in general, and the safe in particular.

'Can you tell me, Sir Arthur, about the key you carry to the safe?'

'Is it really necessary, Harrel? I've got so much work to do.'

'It is necessary, sir. Very necessary.'

'Well, the one I use is on my key ring and never leaves my possession. Indeed, at night, I sleep with it under my pillow.'

Mr Harrel persisted. 'Now is that really the case? It's not a thing many people could say.'

Sir Arthur was adamant. 'They have never left my possession. I have always been most careful.'

The questioning continued – Harrel firm and unyielding, Sir Arthur equally firm but wearying – for another half an hour until the Assistant Commissioner realised he was achieving little.

Ulster King of Arms left his office and returned to No. 7, St James's Terrace. There, he wrote again to Mr Hodgson at Alnwick Castle, and sent telegraphs to Frank Shackleton and

Frank Bennett-Goldney, as Dublin Herald and Athlone Pursuivant respectively, asking them to come to Ireland as quickly as possible. Shackleton was ordered to go to Scotland Yard with a full description of the jewels as contained in the printed Statutes of the Order of St Patrick. Then Sir Arthur dined alone and retired to bed early.

At Dublin Castle the gas lamps burned all night in the police offices as detectives pursued the few leads they had managed to discover. Already they were in contact with their informants in the underworld asking about the jewels. They had compiled a list of locksmiths, and were checking them systematically to see if anyone had been asked to copy a safe key in the recent past. The details of the theft, and an outline description of the missing jewels, had been telegraphed to Scotland Yard, and Sir John Ross had officially requested the help of the Metropolitan Police in London.

The robbery was a personal affront to Detective Owen Kerr, a stolid, reliable detective, whose grey hairs, coupled with his rank, showed him to be a man of little imagination or original intelligence, but rather one of dogged persistence. From the very beginning of his inquiries he believed the robbery to be an 'inside job'. He concentrated on interviewing members of the staff of the Office of Arms, but it wasn't until the middle of Sunday afternoon that he had time to interview Mrs Farrell, the cleaning woman.

'To be certain, Mr Kerr,' she told him, in the small drawing room of her neat, terraced house, 'I've been worried about the jewels all last week. Didn't I find the front door unlatched on Wednesday? And then, only yesterday, wasn't the strongroom door open when I arrived for work?'

The news came as a complete shock to the detective, and he returned hurriedly to Dublin Castle to tell his superiors.

These latest revelations passed from Supt. Lowe to Mr Harrel to Sir John Ross in quick succession, and the Chief Commissioner decided it was time for a conference. The three officers reviewed all the information that had been gathered, sitting in Sir John's comfortably furnished office in the Castle.

'To be frank, gentlemen,' said Sir John, 'I've very little optimism about this case. The robbery could have occurred at any time between yesterday and 11 June, though Mrs Farrell's evidence does suggest it happened in the last week. But why did the thief leave the front door open on one night and then return to open the strongroom on another? It had to be the thief, you know, if we accept Kerr's assurances that everything was in proper order after his visits to the Tower.'

'I agree, sir,' interrupted Supt. Lowe. 'The robbery must have been in the last week. But where did the keys come from to enter the building and open those locks? That seems the main point to me.'

'Well, let's not mince words,' Sir John resumed, leaning his tall, spare figure over his desk. 'The keys could only have come from someone who works in the Office of Arms. And as to the safe – presuming it was opened with a key – the key is held only by Ulster King of Arms.'

Mr Harrel broke in, 'He says, of course, that he never let the keys out of his possession.'

'Just so,' said Sir John, putting his hands together and raising them to his lips as if in prayer. 'Just so. But I'm willing to wager my pension that Ulster had nothing to do with this. At least, not knowingly, that is.'

The three men agreed on this, although they also agreed that Sir Arthur Vicars had an awful lot of questions to answer still.

The Dublin detectives would have been able to think up even more questions for Sir Arthur if they'd been acquainted with the file lying on the desk of Chief Inspector John Kane in his tiny, third-floor office at Scotland Yard in London. The Irish-born detective had been called from his Sunday at home in Lambeth, just south of the River Thames, to take charge of the Yard inquiries. First, he read the full telegraph from the Dublin police, setting out the details of the robbery. Then he drafted a first description of the jewels, to be circulated immediately to his police colleagues in every European capital. After that he leaned back in his swivel chair, lit his pipe, and thought. The name that kept recurring in the telegraph from Dublin was Sir Arthur Vicars, a name known to the chief inspector through another inquiry he'd been helping on. He sent his sergeant, Alec Sanders, to get the file on that inquiry from the Records Office.

Across the front of this buff-coloured file were the words 'Most Confidential' in large red lettering. It contained the names of men prominent in public life whom Scotland Yard believed to be practising homosexuals. These men had been followed, and the file listed addresses where they met for their discreet parties. Four of the men had visited Dublin that year, the chief inspector noted, and had spent most of their nights at No. 7, St James's Terrace, Clonskeagh, the home of Sir Arthur Vicars. All this and the Crown Jewels too, he thought, puffing at his briar pipe.

After an early breakfast on Monday 8 July 1907, Frank Shackleton boarded a train for London at Battle, deep in rural Sussex. He had every reason that morning for feeling on top of the world. His fellow guest for the weekend, and now his travelling companion on the train, was the Duke of Argyll, brother-in-law of King Edward VII. They had spent the last two days at Hammerfield, the beautiful country residence of Lord Ronald Gower, an eccentric and bohemian member of the aristocracy, youngest son of the second Duke of Sutherland, art lover, and, at 62 years of age, the devoted friend of Frank Hird, one-time Rome correspondent of the London *Morning Post*. So devoted, in fact, was Lord Ronald to his friend that he had adopted him as his legal son, a move that had caused more than a few raised eyebrows just before the turn of the century.

The weekend at Hammerfield had gone well for Shackleton. He had been introduced into the set by Lady Ormonde, Lord Ronald's neice, and intended to make full use of his good fortune. During his stay he had managed to interest his host and his companion in his romantic and lucrative dream of taming the Mexican forest, and Lord Ronald had virtually assured him of his financial support. With this – and the money hidden in the safe at his rooms – Shackleton believed he was nearly at the point of total success for his grandiose scheme. And, from the point of his social standing, Shackleton believed he'd never been nearer the top of the ladder.

Lord Ronald's carriage pulled right up to the station entrance at Battle, and the station master, wearing his official bowler hat, opened its door and ushered the royal personage of the Duke of Argyll into his reserved first-class compartment, along with his younger and taller travelling companion. The Duke settled back into the upholstered and tasselled comfort of the train compartment, and unfolded the copy of *The Times* he'd been handed by the station master.

'First-class weekend, eh, Shackleton?' said the Duke, as the train puffed out of the station.

'First-class, sir.'

'Funny old stick, my uncle Ronald, you know. Always been the one to shake up the family, but I must say he's been very decent to me always.'

'He's a very widely travelled man, sir. I find his company absolutely stimulating,' said Shackleton, trying to please his companion sitting opposite him.

'You're right, Shackleton. Stimulating is the very word for him.'

The Duke opened his newspaper, its front page filled with advertisements, and began perusing the news columns.

'Good lord, Shackleton. Listen to this – Sensation in Dublin – Crown Jewels found stolen. I say, that's going it a bit, what?'

'The Crown Jewels in Dublin stolen? My God!' exclaimed Shackleton, his reaction of total surprise and shock not all play acting. He'd never expected to hear the news officially from the brother-in-law of the owner of the jewels.

The Duke continued reading the column of type aloud to Shackleton, who had now recovered his composure and was making carefully studied responses of unbelieving horror, appropriate to someone whose job involved responsibility for guarding the Crown Jewels.

When he had finished reading the column, the Duke threw down the newspaper on the seat beside him.

'Well, Shackleton, that's going to put the cat amongst the pigeons and no mistake with His Majesty due in Dublin at any time. Knowing him, he's going to be furious about this. Absolutely furious. One of his main passions is medals, jewels, pageantry . . . all that sort of thing. Why I remember when he even told off the Duke of Devonshire for wearing some decoration or other upside down. He's going to be livid.'

'It's such a shock. Terrible news,' said Shackleton, playing his role to the hilt. 'I suppose it'll mean I'll have to return to Dublin immediately. Poor old Sir Arthur. . . .'

'Yes, I wouldn't be in Vicars's shoes for anything. Tell me, were the jewels properly guarded?'

Shackleton explained the security arrangements and concluded: 'With all those soldiers and police around you would have thought they'd been safe. But obviously not, sir.'

'Obviously.'

The remainder of the journey passed quickly as the two men discussed the robbery. They parted on cordial terms when the train reached London, and Shackleton took a cab immediately to the Junior Army and Navy Club in St James's Street, expecting to find a telegraph from Richard Gorges. Instead the message from Sir Arthur Vicars was awaiting him at the porter's desk. Shackleton smiled to himself as he read it. Now it was just a matter of brazening it through, he reckoned. The robbery had been discovered in time, he knew, for his alibi to be watertight.

He took a cab to his rooms in Park Lane, and went directly to his small wall safe and opened it. Inside were the bundles of white bank notes, share certificates, and, at the back, a copy of the Statutes of the Order of St Patrick. He took this, slipped it into the inside pocket of his frock coat, and left quickly, to hail another cab and head for Scotland Yard. The cab jingled and swayed its way past Buckingham Palace, and Shackleton noted that the Royal Standard was not flying on the Palace flagstaff, denoting the fact that the Sovereign was not in residence. Then, on through Admiralty Arch into Trafalgar Square, with Lord Nelson high on his column, and down Whitehall to the headquarters of the Metropolitan Police.

Shackleton announced himself to the sergeant behind the desk in the dark and gloomy entrance hall, told him his business, and, after waiting a few minutes, was escorted upstairs by a young constable. Their steps echoed on the stone floor as they passed down corridors, painted white and brown. Small offices opened off the corridors, and through half-opened doors Shackleton saw the detectives at work, some writing reports, some interviewing people. After what seemed a long climb and walk, the constable stopped at a door with the number 312 on it. He knocked, turned the door handle, and indicated to Shackleton that he should enter. A man of medium height, balding and slim, wearing a dark suit shiny with use, rose from behind his desk in the small room.

'Mr Shackleton, the Dublin Herald. Very nice of you to come. I'm Chief Inspector Kane. John Kane.'

'How do you do, Chief Inspector,' said Shackleton, shaking his hand. 'I've come here on the instructions of Sir Arthur Vicars, the Ulster King of Arms, to give you a full description of the missing jewellery.'

'Well, well,' smiled Kane amiably, his Irish accent noticeable despite his years in London. 'That's very thoughtful of Sir Arthur.'

Shackleton handed him a copy of the Statute. 'You'll find everything you need in there, Chief Inspector.'

'Perhaps, Mr Shackleton, perhaps, and then again, perhaps not. Have you time for a chat? A cup of tea, maybe?'

'That's kind of you. I can spare a little time, and then I must start on my way to Dublin.'

'Good. I'll arrange some tea and then we'll talk.'

The detective left the room for a minute and returned to find Shackleton sitting in the chair by his desk.

'So, Mr Shackleton, you've come all this way to bring me a description of the jewels.'

'From Dublin? Oh no, Mr Kane. I've been in London for the last fortnight. I've just returned from the country, and found the instructions from Sir Arthur to come here waiting at my club'.

'I see. By the way, you don't mind if I take a few notes as we talk? I've got a poor memory for things, you know,' said Kane confidingly.

'Of course not. Anything to help. . . .'

'Yes, of course. As a matter of routine, you understand, can I inquire where you were in the country?'

'Down in Sussex at Penhurst. The Duke of Argyll and I were the guests of Lord Ronald Gower at his home.'

'I see.' The detective scribbled on a pad of notepaper, trying to appear calm and nonchalant. But, in fact, this early mention of the King's brother-in-law had set alarm bells ringing in his brain.

'Where do you stay in London?'

Shackleton gave him the address in Park Lane, and told him the names of his clubs. 'Actually, I've been over here', he lied, 'to see if there was anything I could do to help my brother with his expedition to the Antarctic.'

'You're Ernest Shackleton's brother?'

'Yes. His younger one. But I don't have any aspirations about larking around in the snow and ice, I'm glad to say.'

Chief Inspector Kane smiled thinly. Mr Frank Shackleton, he thought to himself, you're an extremely smooth gentleman who's not afraid to throw in his high cards of social connection early on in the game.

'And in Dublin, Mr Shackleton, where do you stay?'

'No. 7, St James's Terrace, Clonskeagh.'

'But . . . but . . . isn't that the home of Sir Arthur Vicars?'

'Yes, we share the house.'

The detective looked up sharply. 'Share?'

'Yes. I find it much more convenient than staying in hotels over there.'

This latest information set even more alarm bells ringing for the Chief Inspector. He was tempted to mention the names in the buff-coloured file to Shackleton, and see what reaction he got, but the temptation faded with a knock on the door and Sgt Sanders arriving with a tray holding two cups of tea, a bowl of sugar, and a plate of plain tea biscuits.

While they drank their tea, the detective and Shackleton discussed the security arrangements at the Bedford Tower, and the staff employed in the Office of Arms. They talked for nearly an hour and Chief Inspector Kane was impressed by Shackleton's apparent frankness and willingness to help. But after he had left the detective sat back in his chair and wondered. He'd have to know a lot more about Frank Shackleton, he decided. Even from his sketchy knowledge of the robbery, it appeared clear to him that someone close to Sir Arthur Vicars must be involved in some way. Perhaps even the Dublin Herald, he thought. He would ask the department that specialised in City and business affairs if they could discover anything about Shackleton. It had been a useful meeting for the man from the Yard.

The stone corridors and lobbies of the House of Commons at Westminster were buzzing with the news of the robbery by the afternoon of Monday 8 July. The Irish Nationalist Members of Parliament could scarcely conceal their glee over this obvious embarrassment to the British Government.

Just before four o'clock, during question time, Patrick O'Brien, a leading Nationalist, rose to his feet and, with a disarming smile, caught the Speaker's eye. Sitting opposite him on the Government front benches was Augustine Birrell, the Irish Secretary of State. O'Brien pointed at him as he asked in a loud Irish brogue:

'How many people were guarding the Crown Jewels when they were stolen from Dublin Castle?'

The Irish Secretary began to rise from his padded bench, and then sat down again amidst growing laughter from the Opposition Members, and even from his own supporters seated at his back. Mr Birrell had no reply to either the question or the laughter.

As Augustine Birrell suffered his discomfiture in embarrassed silence, Rufus Levinson sat in the warm sunshine at a table under the pavement canopy of the Café des Voyageurs in the Boulevard St Germain, in Paris. He sipped a cognac and watched the Parisians stroll by. In his pocket was a small bag of uncut South African diamonds, valued by himself at a little under £20,000 when they had been cut and polished. His contact in Paris, François Jourdain, had been delighted with the merchandise Levinson had shown him, in the back room of his jeweller's shop just off the Boulevard St Michel. There had been little haggling over the price, and already M. Jourdain's trusted workforce had reduced the Crown Jewels into a mere pile of glittering diamonds, emeralds, and rubies. The enamel settings had been cut up and melted down. The same fate had awaited the 120 gold ornaments in the five collars of the Order of St Patrick, and the diamonds and pearls of the Mahony family jewels. The gold remained in Paris, the white and rose diamonds were on their way to Amsterdam, and M. Jourdain was making arrangements to send the pearls, emeralds and rubies, when they had been re-threaded or re-cut, to New York.

A very satisfactory transaction, thought Rufus Levinson, as he pondered what to do with the rest of his holiday. He'd already tasted the delights of a young seamstress, who was supplementing her family's income on the streets in the Montmartre district, and that evening he was planning to visit a house off the Rue du Faubourg St Honoré, where the entertainments were highly recommended by M. Jourdain, himself a regular patron.

All the business done, reflected Levinson, and well before news of the robbery reached Paris. Just as that Mr Newman – or whatever his name was – had said it would be. He drained his glass and beckoned to a white-aproned waiter.

Frank Shackleton, later that day, stood in the swaying corridor of the boat train to Dublin as it clattered its way towards Holyhead, on the Isle of Anglesey in north Wales, and the steamer that would cross the Irish Sea. In his hands were two brown holdall bags. One contained his night clothes, the other £14,500 in bank notes. He had reserved a sleeping compartment on the train, and was now looking at a list of his fellow travellers in similar accommodation. He was delighted to see the names of Lady Ormonde and her daughter, Lady Constance Butler, on the list. The next morning he searched them out on the boat and approached them as they sat in the lounge taking tea. To be useful, he believed, social connections had to be constantly renewed.

'Good morning, my dear Lady Ormonde,' said Shackleton as he reached the two women. 'And you, Lady Constance. I trust you've both journeyed well.'

'Oh, Mr Shackleton,' exclaimed Lady Ormonde, motioning him to sit beside her. 'How extraordinary meeting you like this! Poor Sir Arthur . . . I feel so sorry for him! Constance and I were just talking about the robbery and saying how odd it was that remark of yours at lunch the other day.'

'Remark, my lady?' replied Shackleton, deliberately obtuse.

'You remember, surely? You said you wouldn't be surprised if the jewels were stolen some day.'

Shackleton smiled weakly. 'Yes I do recall some jest like that. Probably due to your excellent hospitality, Lady Ormonde.'

He tried to turn the conversation quickly away from his indiscretion. 'How right you are to say "poor Sir Arthur". He must be in a frightful state. I'm returning to Dublin to see if I can help in any way.'

'Yes, of course,' said Lady Ormonde, sympathetically. 'He'll need all the help and support of his colleagues. By the way, Mr Shackleton, did my cousin enjoy his weekend?'

'Yes, indeed. His Grace, in fact, travelled with me to London yesterday and broke the news about the robbery while he was reading his newspaper.'

'Quite a shock, I would surmise,' interrupted Lady Constance.

'It was. Indeed it was,' said Shackleton.

After the train had pulled into Dublin, Shackleton went directly to No. 7, St James's Terrace, where he found Ulster King of Arms still in bed, and in a mood of total despair. The previous day both he and William Stivey had been questioned at length about their omitting to tell the police immediately about the unlocked front door and the open strongroom door. Sir Arthur had explained to Detective Kerr, 'I was so thronged owing to preparing the King's visit.' Stivey had been fairly blunt about the matter. He told the detective that he didn't think it was his duty to tell them at the time the robbery was discovered. He had told his superior and, as far as he was concerned, Ulster King of Arms should have informed the police.

The Dublin detectives were, in fact, very puzzled over Sir Arthur's attitude. It was bad enough not being informed about the previous week's two incidents at the time they'd happened, but not to mention them when the robbery was discovered seemed totally out of character with the usually fussy, and seemingly conscientious head of the Office of Arms. Their puzzlement had deepened as well after two experts had examined the safe in the library of the Bedford Tower. Both Cornelius Gallagher of the Ratner Safe Company and Frank O'Hare from Messrs Milner had taken the lock apart and examined the levers inside. They used magnifying glasses to look for any scratches on the highly polished surfaces of the levers, and found none. Therefore, they told the police, the lock hadn't been picked or forced.

'Could a key made from a wax impression have opened the lock?' asked Supt. Lowe.

'No, sir,' the experts chorussed. 'Such a key would be bound to leave scratches on the levers,' explained Mr Gallagher. 'The only key that opened this safe was either its proper key or one that was a perfect duplicate. And that duplicate couldn't have been made from a wax impression.' The police failed to ask – and the experts to volunteer – how a perfect duplicate could be made.

The conference of senior detectives that took place, while Frank Shackleton was still heading for Dublin, was forced to admit that it was baffled on a number of points. Why hadn't they been told about the front door and the strongroom? Why hadn't the jewels been checked for 25 days? Why had the piece of blue ribbon been removed and left behind? And, most important of all, how was the key obtained to open the safe?

These questions were put bluntly to Ulster King of Arms by Sir John Ross immediately after the police conference, and Sir Arthur couldn't answer one of them to the satisfaction of the Chief Commissioner.

Sir Arthur left the interview in a depressed and bewildered state of mind. So many questions, he thought, and so few answers. The only explanation he could provide for Lord Aberdeen later that day was that it was all another jape.

'That's the only thing that makes sense, my lord,' he told the Viceroy, as he stood before his desk in the Viceregal Lodge in Phoenix Park. He'd expected a stern reprimand from Lord Aberdeen, but the Viceroy, a naïve and kindly man, had noticed his obvious distress and decided that sympathy was more in order than a tongue-lashing.

'It could be you're right, Ulster,' he agreed. 'We've had one before. It could be a jape in, I must say, remarkably bad taste.'

Ulster King of Arms grasped at the straw. 'Yes, my lord,' he said, his countenance brightening visibly. 'I wouldn't be a bit surprised if they arrived at my house by parcel post in the morning.'

His mood of total despair, when Shackleton arrived at their villa at Clonskeagh, was caused by the apparent failure of his optimistic forecast. The jewels did not arrive in the parcel post for Sir Arthur that Tuesday, and Shackleton, while outwardly sympathetic, wondered to himself how someone like Ulster King of Arms could be so naïve to believe that they ever would.

King Edward fumes: 'They must be found'

Not long after dawn on Wednesday 10 July 1907, the Royal Yacht slid serenely past the breakwater at Kingstown and dropped anchor in the harbour. The twin-funnelled escort ship, HMS *Melampus*, took up station astern of the *Victoria and Albert*. By six o'clock crowds were already gathering on the promenade at Kingstown, and jostling for the best positions on the three terraces of the Pavilion on the sea front. Just before eight o'clock a 21-gun royal salute boomed out over the water, fired by a battery from the Royal Artillery. The salute awakened King Edward as he slept alone in his own cabin, adjoining that of Queen Alexandra. He breakfasted with his wife and his daughter, Princess Victoria, checked the day's itinerary with Sir Francis Knollys, and then retired to dress. He put on grey striped trousers, a white shirt, a black waistcoat, a black silk stock – fixed in position with an ostentatiously large pearl pin – and then a frock coat, with a large white carnation in its lapel. His valet handed him his black silk top hat with its brim curled at the sides and his dark gloves with ornamental stitching as he left his dressing cabin and made his way on deck a few minutes before mid-day.

King Edward sat on the sun deck with his family – Queen Alexandra wearing a black and white striped long silk dress with Irish lace at the bodice – and awaited the arrival of the pinnace he could see approaching the Royal Yacht. Lord Aberdeen was piped aboard the *Victoria and Albert*, and escorted into the King's presence.

The Viceroy doffed his plumed cockade uniform hat as he bowed and took the outstreched hand of his King.

'Hello, Aberdeen. We trust you are well.'

'Yes, Your Majesty. Thank you.'

Lord Aberdeen straightened up and noticed the King staring hard at the three decorations pinned on the right breast of his full dress uniform. One of them was his personal Badge of the Order of St Patrick, a silver replica of the missing Crown Jewels. The King looked intently at it, bending slightly as he did so.

'Is it not right, sir?' asked Lord Aberdeen, slightly alarmed, knowing the King's Hanoverian fetish about dress and medals.

'Oh, yes, it's quite right,' replied King Edward, unsmiling. 'But we were just thinking of our jewels.'

The King said no more to indicate that the royal cup of displeasure was about to overflow, subsequently to drown careers, reputations, and even lives.

8

Fingers of suspicion

As the first day of the Royal Visit to Ireland drew to a close on 10 July 1907, thousands of holidaymakers and sightseers still crammed the seafront and promenade at Kingstown. The more fortunate and taller had already caught a glimpse of the royal party as it left its convoy of motor cars and embarked in a pinnace to return to the *Victoria and Albert* lying sleekly at anchor in the calm waters of the harbour. Shortly after half past eight the gathering dusk of the fine summer evening was illuminated by hundreds of tiny lanterns being lit in the Royal Yacht and her escort, outlining their graceful lines. Then, with a whoosh and a crack like thunder, the fireworks display began. Rockets trailed their orange wake into the night sky, bursting to send hundreds of green, red and yellow balls of smoking fire dropping gently back into the sea. Vast catherine wheels whirled on the superstructure of HMS *Melampus*. Huge roman candles cascaded their showers of burning light against a backcloth of a clear night sky pinpricked with stars. At times, to the watchers on shore, the rockets seem to meet directly above the Royal Yacht pulling a fiery and sparkling canopy over her. Those spectators near the Victoria Wharf kept one eye on the fireworks and the other on the comings and goings of the pinnace from the Royal Yacht as it scurried back and forth across the harbour, like a smoking water beetle, picking up the guests for a private dinner party King Edward VII was giving aboard *Victoria and Albert* that night.

King Edward, sipping a glass of hock and soda water, sat with his family under a canopy on the foredeck, watching the fireworks display and reviewing the day's events in his mind.

The visit to the Irish International Exhibition at Ballsbridge had gone well enough, although the luncheon in the Grand Palace Restaurant at the Exhibition had been somewhat stodgy, both in company and fare. More to the King's liking had been the garden party held in the magnificent grounds of the Vice-Regal Lodge in Phoenix Park. His good humour at meeting so many old acquaintances had not been marred even by Lady Aberdeen insisting on trailing around with a pack of her snappy little terrier dogs. The King had refrained from making any comment about them, since he knew Queen Alexandra had been looking forward to seeing this new breed of small dog. Labradors who could pick up pheasants during a day's shoot were more to his liking. The King thought he'd behaved with commendable restraint throughout the day, not once mentioning the missing Crown Jewels in the presence of the Viceroy's party, though he did make the time to have a sharp word on the subject with Augustine Birrell, the Irish Secretary, who by now wished fervently that William the Fourth had kept his spare jewellery to himself. They had met before lunch in a restaurant anteroom where the King sipped a sweet sherry while his wife and daughter and their ladies in waiting did what all women do before sitting down to luncheon. Sir Francis Knollys had sought out Mr Birrell at the King's insistence and escorted the politician into the royal presence.

'Now, look here, Birrell,' said the King, pulling himself out of a deep armchair with no little difficulty. 'We're very concerned about these jewels. We want to know what's going on. Dammit, you're the man who really runs this country, not Aberdeen. You sit in Cabinet so you take the decisions. We all know that. But now it means it's up to you to recover our jewels, discover who's responsible for the outrage, and see that they're punished.'

The Irish Secretary whitened at the King's obvious anger.

'Sir, everything that can be done is being done,' he replied stiffly, his hands clutching and unclutching nervously behind his back. 'Posters offering a reward of £1,000 in return for information have been placed throughout Ireland. Scotland Yard are sending one of their best detectives over here and the Dublin police have interviewed everyone in the Office of

Arms who could possibly have been involved. Your Majesty, what more can be done?'

King Edward snorted derisively, 'It's been four days since the robbery was discovered – and the police have no idea who might have done it. Are we not right, Birrell?'

'You are, sir, but the police do tend to discount the Fenians or organisations like that. That's a start, surely? According to Sir John Ross when I spoke to him this morning, the Dublin Metropolitan Police believe the robbery was what they call an "inside job".'

'A what?'

'An "inside job", sir. A robbery perpetrated by someone working within the building.'

'They're certain of this, Birrell?'

'Well, sir, they can see no other explanation.'

'And what do Scotland Yard believe?'

'I have no idea, sir.'

The King turned away to pick up his half-filled glass and grunted disparagingly, 'We think you'd better find out, Birrell, and let Sir Francis here know as quickly as possible. We shall want to see copies of the reports concerning the robbery. All of them, Birrell.'

'Of course, Your Majesty.'

The King's attitude softened. At heart, he was a fair and kindly man whose rages died as quickly as they flared. 'For goodness sake, Birrell, get a drink and relax. You look like the condemned man.' He laughed throatily, 'Of course, if the police don't solve this, then you might be. . . .'

He slapped the Irish Secretary on the shoulder and Sir Francis joined in his laughter. Mr Augustine Birrell merely smiled.

Yes, thought King Edward as he sat on the Royal Yacht that evening, no one can accuse us of making a meal of this robbery, although we've every right to be angry. He resolved to put the jewels from his mind during dinner but, unhappily, this was to prove impossible.

Lady Ormonde, one of the sixteen guests, raised the matter first as the company finished their main course of beef marinaded in a Madeira wine sauce and then encased in a light shortcrust pastry. As befitting her family's connection with

King Edward, she was seated two places from His Majesty next to Major Guillamore O'Grady, one of the liveliest and richest men in Dublin's social set.

'I wonder if Your Majesty believes in second sight,' she said during a lull in the conversation, a smile playing around her mouth. She'd been saving her tasty piece of gossip throughout the evening.

'What, Elizabeth? Second sight?'

'Yes, sir – you know, the power to foretell events before they happen.'

'Sounds a load of Irish baloney to me,' laughed the King, in good humour at the excellence of M. Ménager's cooking and the liveliness of the company. 'But, pray, do go on and convince us, dear Elizabeth.'

'Well, sir, I gave lunch last week to Frank Shackleton who's Dublin Herald at the Office of Arms.'

'Go on,' said King Edward, leaning forward, his interest quickening.

'Well, he said he wouldn't be surprised if the Crown Jewels were stolen one day and, lo and behold, two days later they are found to be stolen.'

The King looked quizzically down the table, across gleaming silverware and shiny, stiff linen, catching the eye of Sir Francis Knollys, then turned sharply back to Lady Ormonde. 'He said that, did he?'

'Yes. All my guests laughed at him but it seems to me he did have second sight on this occasion.'

'Most interesting,' said the King. 'This Shackleton . . . he's the brother of the explorer, isn't he?'

'That's right. He's also a friend of John Argyll, as well. Funnily enough, they've just spent a weekend in the country together and my cousin John broke the news of the robbery to him as they were returning to London.'

'How very interesting, Elizabeth,' the King said quietly. The table was silent waiting for his next question. 'And where did John and this fellow stay for the weekend?'

'They were down at Ronnie Gower's in Sussex.'

'Gower, eh,' said the King, half to himself. 'Ronnie Gower. . . .' King Edward had been an old shooting companion of Lord Ronald Gower before the latter's increasingly eccentric behaviour and unusual sexual habits had meant his virtual banishment from Court circles.

A frown grew on the King's face. 'It seems this Shackleton fellow moves in some very unusual company for a Dublin Herald, Elizabeth. What say you, Francis?'

Sir Francis Knollys put down his glass of claret. 'He seems to be a most remarkable chap to have this second sight, sir,' he said, ever the diplomat.

'Yes, Francis, most remarkable.' The King turned to Lady Ormonde. 'And you, my dear Elizabeth, are one of the most remarkable women we know. You discover some of the most interesting people at your luncheons. We shall have to learn more about Mr Shackleton and his second sight. A most remarkable gift.'

The conversation turned away from the Jewels and Shackleton to the forthcoming Leopardstown Races where King Edward had two of his horses running, but the information he had received stayed firmly in the King's mind.

When the last of his guests had left, well after midnight, he suggested that Sir Francis should join him in his sitting room for a last brandy.

'A good evening, Francis, and most interesting, don't you think?'

'Sir?'

'Elizabeth Ormonde's story about this Dublin Herald chap.'

'That . . . oh, most interesting, sir.'

'We want you to get on to Birrell as soon as possible and tell him to find out all he can about this man. His means, his friends, that sort of thing. Something worries me about Elizabeth's gossip. We don't mind brother-in-law John visiting his uncle Ronald but how would Shackleton get to know the old goat? Remember Birrell saying this morning – or rather yesterday morning – that the police thought the robbery was perpetrated by someone inside Dublin Castle. We've a very uneasy feeling about this. Very uneasy.'

'I'll contact Birrell as soon as his office opens.'

'Good man, Francis. Now what about a last one before we retire . . .?'

As King Edward sipped his night-cap, the object of his curiosity, Frank Shackleton, wasn't so many miles away, enjoying the skilled ministrations of Daisy Newman. He lay on his back in her spacious bed as Daisy nipped and caressed his excited body with her lips and mouth. His hands were closed tightly in her auburn hair, occasionally guiding her, but more often just holding her as he felt her tremble in rhythm with Richard Gorges as he thrust into her from behind. Through eyes half-glazed with pleasure, he could see her brother, John, leaning on one elbow over him, helping the excitement to its inevitable climax with caresses and kisses. Suddenly, he felt himself dissolve into Daisy's mouth as she moaned deeply feeling Gorges's shuddering inside her. The four fell apart and lay panting on the bed for a few minutes. Then the door of the bedroom opened and Millicent, who'd started the evening of celebration by staging an entertainment with her brother, walked, naked, up to the bed with a freshly chilled bottle of champagne. Like a group on a picnic, they sat or knelt on the bed sipping their refreshing glasses.

'Marvellous, as always,' beamed Gorges, wiping champagne mingled with sweat from his moustache. He raised his glass, 'Here's to the incredible family Newman. Everything a man could possibly want.'

'To the Newmans,' echoed Shackleton, lifting his glass as he propped himself against the headboard of the bed. The thought struck him, looking at the naked men and women around him, that the human body, male or female, was always pendulous when satiated.

'Thank you, kind sirs,' replied Daisy, getting off the bed and slipping into her dressing gown. She executed a mock curtsey, one finger under her chin.

'You two, Millicent and John, off to bed now,' she ordered. 'And you two, off and get bathed. We have something to discuss, I believe, and that would be better done in the drawing room.'

Gorges groaned, 'You and your business and pleasure, Daisy. You'll ruin a man, I swear.'

Daisy smiled, 'Dear Captain . . . off to your bath. I insist.'

Twenty minutes later, Shackleton and Gorges sat, fully dressed, in the drawing room, their hair slicked down from their own sweat and the steam of their baths. Daisy, dressed in her favourite green silk evening dress, poured each of them a glass of brandy and then sat opposite them in an armchair.

'It's getting late, gentlemen, and I must confess your exertions, pleasurable as they were, have tired me somewhat. I think you have something for me.'

'That's right, m'dear,' murmured Shackleton, rising from the sofa and going out into the hallway. He returned carrying his brown holdall which he clicked open and upended over the carpet in front of Daisy Newman. The bundles of large bank notes fell with a succession of light thuds.

'There it is, Daisy. The money.'

'It's not so pretty as jewellery,' said Daisy, slipping onto her knees from the armchair. 'But it's much, much more useful.' She picked up one of the bundles of £100 notes and riffled through it. 'A thousand pounds a bundle, if I'm not mistaken.'

'Correct, as always, Daisy,' said Shackleton, leaning over and picking up three bundles of notes. Gorges was silent, his eyes wide at the sight of the money. 'This is yours,' Shackleton continued, handing Daisy two bundles and pulling two notes from the third. '£2,200 is the amount, I believe. That's thirty years of honest toil for the ordinary chap, Daisy. Look after it.'

'Oh, I will. I certainly will.'

'And now, Richard, our share out,' said Shackleton, brushing a lock of hair from his forehead. 'With perhaps a slight problem.'

'What's that, old boy?' queried Gorges, waking from his reverie.

'The problem of what to do with all this cash.'

'How much is left?' asked Daisy.

'Over £12,000, m'dear.'

'I can't see the problem,' said Gorges. 'It'll spend like any other money.'

'I should have thought you'd have seen the problem, Richard. We'll soon be the objects of police attention if we waltz round Dublin or London changing £100 notes.' He paused and then went on, 'And, quite frankly, as I told you earlier, I've had quite enough police attention with one session at Scotland Yard and another with the Dublin detectives when I arrived back here.'

'Why not put it straight in the bank?' asked Gorges, rather annoyed at Shackleton for making, what seemed to him, a mountain out of a molehill.

'Dear Richard,' said Shackleton sarcastically, 'that's almost as bad as spending the money in wads of £100 notes. If I arrived at my bank with more than £6,000 in notes the bank manager would be bound to want to know where I had obtained so much ready cash.'

'Well, I don't see. . . .', began Gorges.

'My bank manager wouldn't,' interrupted Daisy Newman.

Gorges started again. 'Frank, I don't think that. . . .' Again he was interrupted by Daisy. Shackleton held up one hand. 'Now hang on you two. One at a time. Daisy, you were saying. . . .'

'I was just about to say', replied Daisy quietly, 'that my bank manager wouldn't ask questions if I wanted to deposit so much money in notes into my account.'

Gorges and Shackleton looked intently at her as she went on, 'You see, apart from being a customer at his bank, I entertain the manager here as one of my customers. Like my locksmith, he'll do 'most anything I want. He wouldn't betray me, just as my locksmith has kept our secret under questioning by the police.'

Shackleton clapped his hands, 'Again Daisy has the answer.'

'Yes, I might have for a consideration,' said Daisy, poking her shoe into the pile of notes on the floor. 'A consideration, say, of two more of those lovely white notes.'

'£200,' muttered Gorges.

'It would be worth it, dear Captain. It would solve your problem. Give me the money and in return I'll give you a banker's draft or, even better perhaps, I'll give you a banker's draft each. You, Frank, could say it came from a business deal, and you, captain, could say it was a gift from a distant aunt or whatever.'

The two men hesitated. 'I can see you want to talk about it, gentlemen,' said Daisy. 'I'll go down to the cellar and get another bottle while you have your discussion.' She swept out of the room, back straight, head in the air.

'Now look what you've done, Frank,' Gorges exclaimed. 'You've got Daisy thinking we don't trust her.'

'Well, do we?'

'We have done so far with no reason to regret it.'

'Yes, Richard, but this time we're trusting her with money. A huge amount of money.'

'Perhaps, old boy.' Gorges thought for a moment. 'But what if we escort her to the bank with the money and then insist she gives us the banker's drafts as soon as she comes out? That would be safe, surely?'

'She might refuse once the money was safe in her account. She might tell us to go and walk round the Ring of Kerry. And then what would we do? Go and tell the police that she's swindled us out of the proceeds of our stealing the Crown Jewels? Oh, no, Richard, it's not safe.'

'What's the answer then, old boy?'

'She'll have to give us the banker's drafts before she puts the money in the bank.'

'But, if your theory is correct and we can't trust her, she could cancel the drafts before they reach our banks and still keep the money.'

'Not if we insist that the drafts are certified by her bank. If they're certified she can't cancel them nor can her bank.'

'Well, that's the answer then, Frank. We'll ask her to do that. But I do think you're being a little hard on Daisy. . . .'

He stopped in mid-sentence as the door swung open and Daisy entered carrying an ice bucket with the neck of a champagne bottle peeping out.

'You're taking my name in vain again, dear Captain,' she smiled, her annoyance of a few minutes before apparently gone.

She put the ice bucket on the sideboard. 'Let's leave it for a little to allow it to become really chilled and you can tell me what you've decided.'

Shackleton looked at Gorges, who nodded. 'Right, Daisy. We'll accept your idea gratefully but with one condition.'

'Condition, Frank?'

'Yes. Before we give you the money you give us two certified banker's drafts for £6,050 each.'

'An odd amount,' wondered Daisy.

'That's the money split in two after we've paid you an extra £200.

1 The collar and insignia of the Order of St Patrick: the Irish Crown Jewels

2a Bedford Tower, Dublin Castle. The library occupies the right-hand side of the building. The sentries stood by the front columns

2b Captain Richard Howard Gorges, as an officer of Thorneycroft's Mounted Regiment before Spion Kop

3a Sir Arthur Vicars, Ulster King of Arms — '. . . and gazes into the distance with little confidence' (Chapter 14)
(From a portrait by an unknown artist in Dublin Castle)

3b Frank Shackleton (right, in cloth cap) arriving in Liverpool, January 1913, with Det. Insp. Albert Cooper (in bowler hat)— . . . a gaunt scarecrow of a man' (Chapter 11)
(Picture: Radio Times Hulton Picture Library)

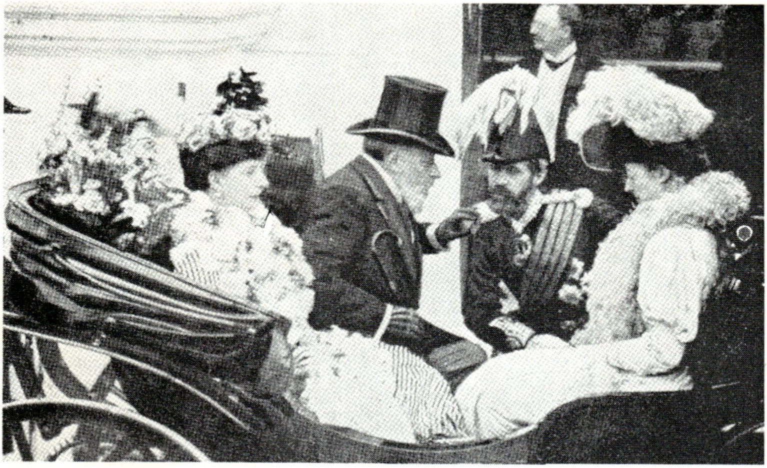

4a The Viceroy, Lord Aberdeen, bids farewell to the Royal Party at the end of their visit to the Irish International Exhibition — '. . . somewhat stodgy, said the King' (Chapter 8)

4b Kilmorna House, near Listowel. The last home of Sir Arthur Vicars — and the scene of his violent death. The house was destroyed by the IRA, 14 April 1921

Daisy shrugged her bare shoulders. 'That's perfectly acceptable to me. It'll take a couple of days your way, but if you're in no hurry. . . .'

'We're not, m'dear,' murmured Gorges. 'We've waited a long time already. A couple of days makes little difference.'

'Good,' said Daisy, beginning to uncork the champagne bottle. 'That just leaves the problem of sleeping accommodation for tonight – or rather what's left of it.'

'That's no problem,' laughed Gorges. 'No problem at all.'

Daisy looked at both men in turn and then joined in their laughter. 'I don't know, to be sure. I really don't. You two. . . .'

Still laughing, she poured out three glasses of champagne. Richard Gorges began loosening his collar.

Detective Chief Inspector John Kane, with Sergeant Sanders and four other Scotland Yard detectives, stepped off the mail boat at Kingstown on Friday 12 July 1907, and hurried for the Dublin train. The chief inspector had delayed his arrival in Ireland deliberately until the main part of the Royal Visit had ended. He'd surmised that no one at Dublin Castle would be in any mood to see him while His Majesty was in the Irish capital. Once in Dublin, the men from the Yard went directly to the Castle and introduced themselves to Superintendent Lowe. He showed them to a small office that had been set aside for them and then suggested that Kane should meet Sir John Ross immediately.

The man from London sensed a wariness in the Chief Commissioner as soon as they shook hands. 'It's very good of you to come over, Mr Kane,' said Sir John. 'I only hope it's going to be worthwhile.'

Assistant Commissioner Harrel and Supt. Lowe stood at one side of his large desk as he continued, 'First of all, I presume you'll want to know how we're getting on.'

'It would be a help, sir,' replied Kane. 'I wouldn't want to duplicate your efforts. I'm sure you'll have covered all the ground.' Kane believed that flattery got you almost anywhere, particularly with Chief Commissioners who quite obviously thought that all men from Scotland Yard were glory-seeking smart alecks.

'Well, I think it's fair to say we've left no stone unturned,' said Sir John expansively. 'We've interviewed every locksmith in Dublin, Belfast, Londonderry and Cork. Not one of them says he has been asked to copy anything remotely resembling the key to the safe. We've seen all the men known to us as handlers of stolen goods and they swear they haven't even been offered the Crown Jewels, let alone buying them. We're inclined to accept this, Mr Kane, as we virtually offered them an amnesty and the £1,000 reward if they could help us. We've talked to every member of the staff of the Office of Arms and none of them can shed any light on the affair.'

'Sir Arthur Vicars?' interrupted Kane, sharply.

'I'm afraid he's running around in ever-decreasing circles,' smiled Sir John. 'We've little doubt he's been somewhat negligent in looking after the Crown Jewels but we've no evidence at all – nor any belief – that he was involved in the robbery.'

Kane wondered to himself how the police and the military garrison at Dublin Castle apportioned blame amongst themselves for their own negligence in caring for the Crown Jewels, but aloud his tone was still warm and a little obsequious.

'You seem to have covered pretty well every angle, sir,' he said. 'What are you planning to do now?'

'The only thing we can do – and that's to spread our inquiries wider than the Office of Arms.'

'Is that wise, sir?' queried Kane. 'I share your original conviction that this was a robbery planned – if not executed – by someone within Dublin Castle. I think the piece of blue ribbon that was left behind is conclusive proof of this.'

'Yes. That ribbon did puzzle us,' Assistant Commissioner Harrel broke in. 'Our concern was why anyone should leave such an obvious clue. The ribbon points clearly to an "inside job".'

'Precisely, gentlemen,' said Kane, trying consciously to avoid a patronising tone. 'But I think our thief or thieves are extremely clever. He or they are trying to confuse us with too many clues. They are trying to lead us away from the basic situation of this robbery. That is, it must have involved someone with an intimate knowledge of the security arrangements at the Bedford Tower and with a close enough acquaintanceship with Sir Arthur Vicars to obtain either the original or a first-class duplicate of the safe key. All the clues – the ribbon, the unlatched front door, the open strongroom door – have been placed to lead us away from those two basic facts.'

Kane paused and opened a file lying on his crossed knees. 'To refresh our memories – the jewels were not seen for 25 days before the robbery was discovered. But in the week before the robbery was discovered we have these two strange incidents of the doors left open for all the world to see. What was the thief or thieves trying to do? There can be only one explanation, surely. He or they wanted the robbery to be discovered.'

'Why?' asked Supt. Lowe in a puzzled voice.

'Because it was important that it should be. And the only reason for that must surely be that. . . .'

'An alibi,' interrupted Assistant Commissioner Harrel, the light dawning. 'Someone involved had an alibi that wouldn't hold water unless the robbery was discovered when it was.'

'Exactly my deduction, Mr Harrel.'

'So we can eliminate all those who didn't have alibis, if your theory is correct,' exclaimed Sir John.

'Again correct, sir. And if my information is correct that leaves just two people with whom we should be concerned.'

'Athlone Pursuivant and Dublin Herald. Bennett-Goldney and Shackleton,' said Supt. Lowe.

'Precisely, gentlemen,' agreed Kane in a quiet, level voice. 'Francis Bennett-Goldney, the Mayor of Canterbury and wealthy in his own right, and Francis Shackleton, highly connected in society and would-be millionaire. A happy choice, I think you'll say!'

The Chief Inspector shut the file in his hands and addressed himself directly to Sir John Ross. 'I think at this point, sir, I should talk to you privately. I'm sure you'll agree with me when you hear what I have to say.'

The Chief Commissioner looked at his subordinates, shrugged, and nodded to them. The two senior detectives left the office.

'Now, Mr Kane, what have you to tell me that shouldn't be heard by my senior colleagues?' asked Sir John, his voice icy with disapproval.

Kane took out his pipe. 'Do you mind . . .?'

'No. Carry on.'

The Chief Inspector tamped some Navy Cut tobacco into his briar pipe and lit it. 'Well, sir, I'm sure you'll agree this is a most delicate case. . . .'

'Of course,' interrupted Sir John, impatiently.

'. . . with His Majesty very interested at the outcome.'

'They're his jewels.'

'Quite, Sir John. So you'll agree that we have to be very circumspect in our investigations.'

'Yes. Go on, Mr Kane,' said Sir John, becoming more and more impatient with what he thought were the meanderings of a detective who was trying to impress with his own importance.

'Well, sir, to be blunt, I have to inform you that our investigations have uncovered quite a nest of vipers in Dublin Castle.'

An alarmed expression flitted across Sir John's face. 'Vipers? A nest of vipers, Mr Kane?'

'We have evidence that Sir Arthur Vicars has entertained men known to us as practising homosexuals at his home at Clonskeagh, and that at these parties abominable acts took place between various guests including Mr Shackleton, who shares the house with Sir Arthur, as you'll know, the Cork Herald, Mr Peirce Mahony, a captain in the Army called Richard Gorges, and a gentleman called Peter McEnnery.'

'Good God!' cried Sir John. 'Are you sure?'

'We have reports of observations at the house and a statement I took this week from a gentleman in London who participated in these abominable and unnatural acts. We are certain of our evidence.'

The Chief Commissioner clasped both hands to his forehead and pulled them back through his grey hair. 'This is terrible news, Mr Kane,' he said quietly. He was silent for more than a minute, looking down at his blotter, the enormity of the situation permeating slowly into his mind. 'This is terrible,' he repeated.

'Yes, sir, particularly since one part of the alibi of Mr Shackleton concerning the robbery is that he was spending the weekend in the company of His Majesty's brother-in-law.'

Sir John was unable to grasp fully the awful implications of what Kane had told him. Instead his shocked mind took refuge in a petty point of police procedure.

After his silence, he raised his head slowly and looked directly into Kane's face. 'You said, Mr Kane, you have reports of observations on Sir Arthur Vicars's house. Who made these observations?'

'Officers from Scotland Yard.'

'On whose orders?' demanded Sir John, his voice rising. 'On whose orders, Chief Inspector, since their presence was not known to me?'

'On the orders of the Commissioner of the Metropolitan Police, sir,' said Kane, aware of the anger that was about to break over him. He had anticipated this situation.

'He had no right, Chief Inspector, to send men to Dublin without my permission or knowledge.'

'Sir.'

'That's not good enough, Chief Inspector. Not good enough at all. Did your Commissioner just take it into his head to send men here in secret?'

'I believe not, sir,' said Kane, straightening up in his chair and slipping his pipe into his coat pocket.

'Stop prevaricating, man,' exclaimed Sir John, rising from his chair and stalking round his desk to loom over Kane. His face was white with strain and anger. 'Just tell me all you know, Chief Inspector.'

'It's not really my place to do so, sir. I merely carry out my orders.'

'Chief Inspector, unless you tell me all you know I shall order your men and yourself from Dublin at this instant.'

'Sir, from my knowledge the Commissioner was acting under direct orders from the Home Office and the Home Secretary. This was felt to be an investigation that should be handled in the most confidential manner.'

Sir John Ross stared down at Kane for a moment, turned away abruptly and walked back to his desk. He sat down and pulled his writing pad towards him.

'I am communicating immediately with Mr Gladstone, the Home Secretary, to protest at this secretive inquiry by Scotland Yard. I shall also mention that, in my opinion, you are being less than frank with me even now.' Kane began to protest but the Chief Commissioner continued, 'I shall demand that this inquiry be left entirely to this police force and the Royal Irish

Constabulary as far as investigations in Ireland are concerned. Is that clear, Chief Inspector?'

'Sir.'

'You may leave.'

'Sir, before I do, may I say how much I regret the stance you have chosen to adopt. I believe with full co-operation between us we can clear up this robbery within a very few days.'

'You may do as you wish, Chief Inspector. My officers will continue their investigation under my orders and at my direction. Clear?'

'Sir,' replied Kane flatly. He began moving towards the door.

'And, Chief Inspector,' Sir John called just as Kane was opening the door, 'I wouldn't plan on your stay in Dublin being any longer than it takes for the Home Secretary to reply to my letter.'

Kane turned back towards the desk, thought better of it, and merely replied again, 'Sir.' When he returned to his temporary office, down the gloomy stone corridors of Dublin Castle, his detectives could see that something had gone seriously wrong. Normally, Kane was a most affable and friendly man to work for. Now, he was tense and brusque to the point of rudeness. Sgt Sanders noticed his hands trembled as he lit his pipe

'Everything all right, sir?' he asked tentatively.

'No, it's not, Sanders. You might as well all know. The Dublin police have taken objection to our presence here. I shall say no more except to say we have a great deal of work to do in a short time. I estimate we shall be leaving by Wednesday at the latest and by then I want to be in a position to make an interim report.'

His men looked at him expectantly, one of them taking his notebook from his jacket pocket.

'First, let me have the statement we took on Wednesday from Sir Reginald Fitzhunter and the memorandum from our City Department concerning Francis Shackleton.'

Sanders, who had already organised a rudimentary filing system for the papers the Yard men had brought with them, handed the documents to Kane.

'Ah, yes,' he said, his good humour beginning to return. 'Sir Reginald Fitzhunter. Poor man. His sins certainly caught up with him.' Forty-eight hours previously Sir Reginald had called at Scotland Yard at Kane's request. The detective had been uncharacteristically blunt with him, reading out dates, addresses and details from the buff-coloured file, all clearly proving Sir Reginald was a practising homosexual. At first he'd tried to bluff it out, Kane recalled, but that had soon stopped when he'd said the only way to check Sir Reginald's veracity was to question his wife and his colleagues on the Stock Exchange. Sir Reginald had broken down and threatened suicide. But Kane, with the prior approval of the Commissioner, had promised him he wouldn't be exposed if he co-operated with the detectives. Of course, Kane had explained, he would be expected to leave public life and resign from his clubs, but otherwise nothing would happen to him if he told all he knew about the parties at No. 7, St James's Terrace, Clonskeagh, Dublin. Sir Reginald, far from an Adonis-like figure, portly and below average height, had agreed readily and given Kane the names of Shackleton, Gorges, McEnnery and Mahony.

'Who invited you to Dublin, Sir Reginald?' Kane had asked.

'Frank Shackleton.'

'What about Sir Arthur Vicars?'

'He wasn't there on one occasion, and on the other he went to bed before . . . before . . . well, before anything happened.'

'Who's Richard Gorges?'

'As far as I know he's just a captain in the Army. From what I gathered he's a special friend of Shackleton's.'

A perfect combination for the robbery, thought Kane as he perused Sir Reginald's statement again. A man with insider's knowledge and a man of action.

Kane turned to the memorandum about Shackleton from the Yard's City Department. It listed his directorships in the Celtic Investment Trust and the North Mexico Land and Timber Company but also included mention of a rumour in the City that Shackleton was having difficulty in raising funds. It was thought, said the memorandum, that he'd had to resort to a moneylender.

All the information fitted into the theory in Kane's mind that was swiftly becoming a firm conviction. Now he needed evidence. He ordered Sgt Sanders to make discreet inquiries about Gorges around Dublin Castle and even down at Army Headquarters at the Curragh. The other detectives were to question all the sentries who had been on duty at the gates of Dublin Castle and outside the Bedford Tower during the fortnight before the robbery had been discovered. Kane himself wanted to concentrate on Sir Arthur Vicars. He strolled along the corridor and knocked on the door of Supt. Lowe's office.

'Hello, Kane, come in. Sit down.'

'Thank you, Superintendent.'

'What on earth have you done to Sir John? He's just read the riot act about you to Mr Harrel and myself. Do you think you'll actually be recalled?'

'I wouldn't be in the least surprised,' said Kane with a smile. 'We knew we were going to tread on some corns during this inquiry.'

'Tell me, what was all that private stuff about?'

'That, Superintendent, will have to come from your man. Not that I wouldn't like to tell you, you understand, but I've upset enough people for one day.'

Supt. Lowe laughed. 'You men from the Yard always were close chaps. Anyway, I'm told to offer you only minimum co-operation.'

'Well now, Superintendent, would that minimum co-operation extend to letting me buy you a drink at Jury's? It's a long time since I've been in Dublin. . . .'

'Why not? Now?'

'Why not? We'd better not be seen leaving together. I'll meet you there.'

Kane returned to his office to collect his homburg hat and discovered a message on his desk from the Irish Secretary's office saying he was expected at Mr Birrell's lodge in Phoenix Park at noon the next day. The envelope containing the note was marked 'Private' so Kane presumed that the fact of the meeting was to be kept confidential.

By late afternoon, after several pints of Guinness, Kane and Lowe were firm friends. Kane had given the Superintendent a general outline of how his mind was working and had hinted quite broadly at the sexual scandal that might lie behind it. Supt. Lowe had agreed to examine the notebooks of the constables who regularly patrolled St James's Terrace to see if anything untoward had been noticed, but he'd flatly refused to allow Kane permission to interview Sir Arthur Vicars.

'The Chief Commissioner would put me back in uniform patrolling the North Wall if I allowed you to do that, John.' The men had slipped easily into Christian-name terms amidst the mirrored and mahogany conviviality of the bar.

'Is there nothing you can do, John? Anything at all. . . .'

'Well, I must admit we haven't yet taken a formal signed statement from Sir Arthur. I could arrange to do that tomorrow and I suppose you could sit in, as it were.'

'That would be fine, John. Just fine.'

'I'll get my sergeant, Sheehan, to arrange that for, say, the middle afternoon then.'

That evening, as Kane and his team worked late before retiring to a small commercial hotel off St Stephen's Green, Shackleton and Gorges celebrated at the Spa Hotel. They had met Daisy Newman that afternoon, as if by chance, outside the Abbey Theatre. She had handed them two envelopes and Shackleton had given her his brown holdall containing the money.

'There are your certified banker's drafts, gentlemen. Shall I expect you this evening?'

'No, I don't think so, Daisy,' said Shackleton. 'I'm told at the Castle that detectives from Scotland Yard have arrived in Dublin so I think it better if we don't meet while they're around.'

'So be it,' said Daisy, slightly disappointed. 'But don't leave it too long, as I'm making arrangements to sell up in Ballsbridge and move to London.'

'We won't,' promised Gorges, as he saluted and Shackleton raised his top hat. To anyone watching it would have seemed a casual meeting between acquaintances, a few polite words exchanged, and nothing more. In fact, Shackleton had reluctantly decided that it was to be the last meeting with Daisy, at least in Dublin.

'Why, old boy?' protested Gorges as he heard his friend's decision over dinner in the hotel restaurant. 'We've never had a finer time since we were in Cape Town.'

'I agree, Richard, but now Scotland Yard are here we've got to be very careful. I'm bound to be under scrutiny because I live with Sir Arthur and work in the Office of Arms. The clues you deliberately left have confused the Dublin police long enough for all the business transactions to have been completed but I can't think they'll fool this Chief Inspector Kane for very long. I even think that after tonight we'd better not be seen together until Scotland Yard has finished its inquiries here.'

'Is that really necessary, Frank?'

'I believe it's absolutely vital. But still . . . drink up. We've got the rest of the evening. Let's have another bottle.'

'Why don't we have it sent up to my room . . . if we're not going to be able to be together for some time?'

'Why not indeed, dear Richard.'

The next morning, Saturday 13 July 1907, Kane presented himself at Augustine Birrell's official residence in Phoenix Park and was shown by a footman into the study. Mr Birrell was sitting behind his desk as Kane entered.

'Mr Kane. How good of you to come,' said the Irish Secretary, advancing across the room to shake his hand. 'Please seat yourself. A glass of sherry, perhaps?'

'Thank you, sir. Most kind.'

Mr Birrell turned away to pour two sherries from a decanter on a silver tray on his desk. 'I trust you realise this is a strictly informal meeting, Mr Kane,' he said over his shoulder.

'I assumed that, sir, from the manner of the invitation. Only my sergeant knows I am here.'

'Good man,' said Mr Birrell, handing him his glass of sherry.

'Your health, sir,' toasted Kane.

'And yours, Chief Inspector. Though I hear Sir John Ross would have it otherwise.'

'You have good information, sir.'

'Not much happens in that gossip factory called Dublin Castle that doesn't reach my ears.' He laughed conspiratorially. 'I heard the Chief Commissioner wants you out of Ireland.'

Kane smiled. 'Between you and I, sir, I expect him to succeed, knowing how anxious the people at the Home Office are to avoid trouble.'

'Will it affect your investigation?'

'Not too much, I think. It'll just mean we'll have to work a little quicker and a little longer.'

'Good man. That's the spirit.' The politician sat down in the armchair opposite Kane.

'Now you realise, Mr Kane, that I have little, if any, official standing in this matter. You have your own clearly defined chain of command – and rightly so. But I have been asked – or should I say commanded? – by an interested party in this affair to find out what lines you're working on.'

Mr Birrell didn't have to elaborate about whose orders he was working under. Kane realised at once that all he said in the study would be reported back to King Edward VII, from the politician's deliberate use of the word 'commanded'.

'I am hoping to draw up an interim report within a few days that will give a clear idea of the lines along which our investigation is proceeding. I daresay a copy could be sent here.'

'First class, my dear chap. We understand each other. Now, tell me of your suspicions.' Mr Birrell was anxious to make an interim report himself for Sir Francis Knollys after feeling the lash of His Majesty's displeasure about the robbery.

'Since this meeting is not officially taking place, sir, I think I can tell you my early thoughts.'

'Good. Pray continue.'

Kane told the Irish Secretary of his suspicions concerning Shackleton and Gorges and of the parties at No. 7, St James's Terrace. Mr Birrell's mouth opened in shocked amazement at Kane's recital.

'This could cause an awful scandal, Chief Inspector,' he said as Kane finished.

'Indeed, sir. If it ever comes out. Unhappily, as yet, I have little evidence to back up my suspicions. And our inquiries so far have proved fruitless. None of the sentries at Dublin Castle recall seeing Captain Gorges during the period when the robbery could have been perpetrated. I fear he was too familiar a figure at the Castle for anyone to notice him particularly. It's a not uncommon occurrence I've come across in my career before – the invisibility of the commonplace. And as for Mr Shackleton . . . I fear his alibi is watertight for the period of the robbery, and it would be embarrassing to test it with His Majesty's brother-in-law included in it.'

'Have you heard about the remarks Shackleton made to Lady Ormonde?'

'No, sir.'

'Apparently he was lunching with her during the week before the robbery was discovered when he said he wouldn't be surprised if the jewels were stolen some day.'

'Very cheeky, sir, if my suspicions are correct.'

'Chief Inspector, can't you face them with your suspicions?'

'An unwise move at present, sir. We could fairly accuse them of being perverts but that won't help us to discover what happened to the Crown Jewels. I fear they would brazen it out. This is going to be a most difficult investigation, sir.'

'Quite obviously, Mr Kane,' said the Irish Secretary, rising from his armchair. 'Please don't let me detain you any longer. You've spared me more than enough of your valuable time.'

That afternoon, Mr Birrell drafted a report of the conversation for Sir Francis Knollys, hoping it would reach him before the royal household left for Sussex and the Royal Goodwood race meeting, and Kane met Sir Arthur Vicars for the first time.

Sergeant Sheehan went to Ulster King of Arms's office to obtain the signed statement and showed Kane the safe in the library, now securely locked with nothing in it except a few documents. Sheehan introduced Kane to Sir Arthur.

'To save time, sir, the Chief Inspector would like to be present while I take your statement,' he explained.

'Perfectly all right with me, Sheehan,' said Sir Arthur. He turned to Kane, 'I hope you'll be able to get to the bottom of this mystery, Chief Inspector. We expect a lot from Scotland Yard, you know.'

'We'll do our best, sir.'

'Well, come along, Sheehan. Let's get started.'

It took more than an hour for the detailed statement to be laboriously written out by Sgt Sheehan. In it, Sir Arthur detailed the contents of the safe, the security arrangements for the keys, and his version of how the robbery had been discovered. He repeated his theory that the safe had been opened with a key made from a wax impression of the original held by himself.

During the hour or more, Kane had ample opportunity to study Ulster King of Arms and rather liked what he saw. Sir Arthur was obviously a fussy man; a man who cared for the small detail rather than the broad plan; a man, Kane recognised, of total integrity, devoid of cunning, but also a man of great naïveté.

When Sir Arthur had signed his statement, Kane asked if it would be in order to put a few questions of his own.

'Of course, my dear chap,' said Sir Arthur, relieved that he'd completed his statement. 'Anything you want to know, you just inquire.'

'Can I ask you, sir, if you know Sir Reginald Fitzhunter?'

'What a strange question, Chief Inspector. Yes, I do know him. He's a friend of Frank Shackleton. On the Stock Exchange, I remember. Shackleton brought him to dinner once.' Sir Arthur, Kane noted, answered without a flicker of hesitation or embarrassment.

'Peter McEnnery, sir?'

'Of course. Peter's a good friend. Gave him dinner on his birthday only a fortnight or so ago. His father's a very big landowner.' Again, Kane noted, no trace of embarrassment in the answer.

'And Captain Richard Gorges?'

A frown flitted across Sir Arthur's face. 'I know Gorges. He's a friend of Shackleton from the South African War. To be frank, Chief Inspector, he's not one of my favourite acquaintances. I've had occasion to warn Shackleton about him.'

'Why, sir?'

'Oh, nothing in particular,' said Sir Arthur hurriedly. 'I just don't think he's a very good influence. Bit of a wild man, don't you know.'

'Thank you, sir,' said Kane, well satisfied with the answers.

'Is that all?' asked Sir Arthur in amazement.

'For the moment, sir. Thank you.'

When Kane returned to his office, almost next door to the Bedford Tower, he found Sgt Sanders waiting for him.

'Well, Sanders, seen enough of the Army or do you want to join up?'

'Not particularly, sir, though the officers do seem to have a fairly pleasant time over here.'

'That's peacetime soldiering for you. Anyway, what have you discovered about friend Gorges?'

'Frankly, not too much, sir.' Sanders flicked open his notebook and looked at the few lines he'd scribbled.

'He's unmarried, popular with his fellow officers, seems to live within his means, frequently visits Dublin like the rest of them, drinks quite heavily – though I think most of the officers do, sir – and is generally regarded as a sound man in his job as a musketry instructor. Apparently he was a bit of a hero in the Boer War. He was at Spion Kop with a unit called Thorneycroft's Mounted Horse.'

Sgt Sanders looked at his notebook again and ended lamely, 'I think that's about all, sir.'

'Not a lot, is it, sergeant?'

'Not a lot,' admitted Sanders, feeling a little crestfallen.

'But then', said Kane brightly, 'if Gorges is as clever as I think he might be then I wouldn't expect a lot. Well done, Sergeant, that's a start at least. When we get back to London check his record in South Africa. That's apparently where he met Shackleton.'

After attending Mass, Kane devoted the next day to writing his interim report. He listed the circumstances of the robbery and the inquiries that had been made in London and Dublin, then he noted the lack of information coming from underworld sources about the Crown Jewels, and, finally, expounded the theory that, since the robbery bore all the hallmarks of an 'inside job', the weight of future investigations should be directed to the activities of Francis Shackleton, Dublin Herald, and the group of perverts around him, with particular emphasis on Captain Richard Gorges of the Royal Irish Regiment.

He made four copies. One for the Commissioner of the Metropolitan Police, one for Sir John Ross, one for the Irish Secretary, and the last for his own files.

The next morning, Monday 15 July 1907, he arrived early at Dublin Castle and went directly to the office of Sir John Ross. He handed the inspector who ran Sir John's administrative office a copy of the report in an envelope marked 'Highly Confidential'.

'Inspector, can you tell Sir John that I'm returning with my detectives to London today. Please pass on to him my thanks for his co-operation,' said Kane, a broad smile on his face. He'd decided overnight that it would be better to avoid any further scenes with the Chief Commissioner by leaving Dublin of his own volition.

He returned to his temporary office to see how Sgt Sanders was progressing with clearing up the files.

'Have you seen this?' said Sanders, as he entered the office. The sergeant held out a copy of the *Daily Express*.

'What is it, sergeant?' he said taking the proffered newspaper.

'Seems that Sir Arthur Vicars has been talking to the reporters, sir. Reckons we should call in Sherlock Holmes.'

'What?'

'It's all there, sir.'

Kane read the news column and a direct quote attributed to Sir Arthur: 'Curiously enough I have received a communication from Sir Arthur Conan Doyle, who is a distant relative of mine, asking if he could give any advice . . . my own opinion is that whoever has got the Crown Jewels will find he has got a white elephant, for I have sufficient faith in the rarity and beauty of the stones to feel that they cannot change hands without detection. Whoever has got them, the best thing they can do is to return them by parcel post and get the reward.'

Kane threw the newspaper on the table. A bewildered expression crossed his face. He rubbed his hand across his bald pate and burst into laughter.

'Just imagine, Sanders, what Sir John Ross would ruddy well say if Sherlock Holmes turned up in his office.'

Sgt Sanders began laughing as well. The swear word sounded so strange coming from Kane.

'That's all we ruddy well need . . . Sherlock Holmes,' gasped Kane, still laughing. 'I wonder what he'd make of this mess?'

9

Hot breath of scandal

The story in the *Daily Express* about Sir Arthur Vicars wishing to call in Sir Arthur Conan Doyle, creator of the immortal detective Sherlock Holmes, to help solve the robbery of the Crown Jewels, produced cynical laughter amongst the civil servants and the police at Dublin Castle. But it also brought Sir Arthur's plight to the attention of ordinary people, and, in response, a shoal of letters, some sympathetic, others abusive, flooded into the Office of Arms.

Miss Gibbon, the office typist, was given the task of sorting the mail and she, wisely, only gave the letters to Sir Arthur that offered him condolences and sympathy. The others, pithy to the point of obscenity, mostly came from Irishmen who welcomed any embarrassment to the British Establishment in their country. They were put discreetly in the wastepaper basket. On Wednesday 17 July 1907 Miss Gibbon was sorting through yet another batch of letters when she opened an ill-addressed envelope to Sir Arthur. With difficulty, she read through the letter and decided, immediately, that it contained something that should be brought directly to the attention of the hard-pressed Ulster King of Arms.

'What is it, Miss Gibbon?' asked Sir Arthur, as the typist hurried into his office that morning with the letter.

'Read it, sir. It's from someone who says she can help find the Crown Jewels.'

'Good Lord. Hand it here.'

Sir Arthur pored over the letter, trying to understand the ill-written English. After some minutes he had absorbed the basic message.

'Amazing, Miss Gibbon,' he said to his typist, hovering expectantly by his desk. 'This woman says her daughter has had a vision about the jewels. She wants to talk to me.'

He paused and rubbed his chin reflectively. 'Do you believe in all this spiritualism and visions, Miss Gibbon?'

The typist, like many a maiden lady who saw little prospect of being otherwise, did so, fervently. She nodded excitedly. 'My Aunt Agnes once got in touch with her dear Uncle Frank on the other side.'

'The other side?' queried a perplexed Sir Arthur. 'The other side of what, Miss Gibbon?'

'You know, sir, after Uncle Frank had passed over.'

'Passed over?' Sir Arthur looked puzzled.

'After he'd died, sir.'

'Oh, I see, Miss Gibbon. Most interesting. After he'd passed over . . . well, I never. But tell me, do you believe in visions?'

'Of course, Sir Arthur. Very definitely.'

'Well then, I suppose we'd better see this girl with her vision. What's her name?' He picked up the letter again and peered at it. 'Ah, yes. Lucia Pentozzi. She works on the Italian section of the International Exhibition.'

'Are you going down to Ballsbridge then, Sir Arthur? Shall I order your carriage?'

'Wait a minute, Miss Gibbon. I'm not sure if it's appropriate for me to see her first. The police might not understand if it transpires that this girl really has had a vision. We must be circumspect.'

'Of course, Sir Arthur.'

'I wonder if Dublin Herald is in his office.'

'I'll see, sir. I'll tell him you want to see him.'

Frank Shackleton was shown the letter and, scarcely concealing his amusement, agreed to take Sir Arthur's carriage to Ballsbridge and meet the girl with the vision.

He found Lucia Pentozzi and her mother working as waitresses in the small restaurant attached to the ornate, rococo, Italian part of the exhibition. Both were dressed in stiff, black taffeta dresses, with little white aprons pinned to the front and tiny squares of white lace set in their shiny black hair. Mother and daughter were of the same height, but child-bearing had taken its toll of Signora Pentozzi's figure, and sweat glistened on the perceptible black moustache on her upper lip.

'You come to see my daughter, sir?' the mother asked in reasonable English, spoken with a heavy Italian accent spiced with Cockney undertones.

'Yes, signora. It's about your letter to Sir Arthur Vicars.'

'Her vision about Crown Jewels, yes?'

'Yes.'

'My Lucia always have visions, sir. She see things others not see.'

'Of course, signora,' said Shackleton, turning to the girl in her mid-teens standing demurely by her mother. He was struck by her petite beauty and smooth olive complexion.

'Now, Lucia, tell me about this vision.'

'Sir?'

'Your vision, Lucia. Tell me about it. You saw the jewels. . . .'

'Oh yes, sir. I saw jewels. They sparkle in grass.'

'What?'

Her mother interrupted, 'She say she saw jewels in grass, sir.'

'Where?'

'In grass, sir.'

'No, I mean – where was the grass?'

'In country, sir,' said Lucia quietly, looking up at the tall man.

'Which country, m'dear?'

'Just country, sir.'

'Oh, I see. How obtuse of me.'

Lucia's mother sensed the story was making little impact. 'Lucia have vision again if you help.'

'How's that, signora?'

'You get other people with visions help her. Have a seeince.'

'Seeince? Oh, you mean a seance.'

'Yes, sir. A seeince.'

'Yes, well, signora. We'll see. I'll tell Sir Arthur Vicars and let him decide. When could you have your seance?'

'Only Sunday, sir. We work rest of time.'

'Well, Lucia, Signora Pentozzi, thank you for seeing me. I'll be in touch.'

'Sir?'

'I said I'll come down here again.'

'Oh, thank you, sir.'

Shackleton travelled back to Dublin Castle in a high state of merriment, chuckling to himself for most of the journey. Phillips, the coachman, wondered more than once if his passenger had had too much to drink. At the Office of Arms, Shackleton found Sir Arthur in an excited state. Ulster King of Arms had been hearing more success stories about spiritualists and visionaries from the enthusiastic Miss Gibbon.

'What do you think, Frank? Has she seen the jewels?'

'She says she has, Sir Arthur.'

'Where?'

'Well, the girl – pretty little thing she is – says they were lying in the grass somewhere in the country.'

'Abandoned, eh,' said Sir Arthur, his mind racing ahead. 'I knew the thief would realise he'd stolen something too hot.'

Shackleton explained to Ulster King of Arms that he'd have to arrange a seance with other spiritualists if the girl was to conjure up her vision for a second time.

'Miss Gibbon will arrange it,' said Sir Arthur firmly. 'She's got relations who dabble in this sort of thing.'

So it was on Sunday 21 July 1907 that six middle-aged women – the best spiritualists in Dublin – were summoned to No. 7, St James's Terrace, Clonskeagh. They arrived in mid-afternoon to be greeted by Sir Arthur himself, who ushered them into the drawing room. The last guests to arrive were Lucia Pentozzi and her mother, driven by Phillips, in Sir Arthur's carriage, from their lodgings in Ballsbridge.

Miss Gibbon had instructed Sir Arthur in the niceties of a seance, so, after the introductions had been completed, he closed the heavy velvet curtains and invited the women to sit around the covered table. He withdrew to a corner of the room with Shackleton to watch the proceedings, lit now only by a few trickles of sunlight that squeezed into the room.

The women joined hands and closed their eyes. The Italian girl looked even more diminutive in the circle of older women, still wearing their flowery wide-brimmed hats. The air in the room was filled with their perfumes mingling with the heavy scent of a large bowl of violets standing on a single table by the curtains. Suddenly, Sir Arthur noticed Lucia begin to sway a little from side to side, her head thrown back showing her firm jaw line. He sensed a change of temperature in the room. It seemed colder. A strange keening sound came from the Italian girl's throat as she began to sway more violently, held from falling from the chair only by the support of the hands clasping hers. The noise from her throat rose in pitch and then stopped. Lucia's swaying ended, and she sat rigid in her chair, her back arched, her arms stretched straight out at the sides. Even Shackleton held his breath at the scene before him. And then a voice spoke to the room from, it appeared, a point in the curtains just above Lucia's head.

In perfect, unaccented English, the voice said clearly, 'Look for what you seek near Clonsilla. They sparkle in the old churchyard.'

'Good lord,' Sir Arthur whispered to Shackleton. 'Clonsilla!'

As soon as the unearthly voice had delivered its message, Lucia slumped in her chair. The other women obviously had been expecting this to happen, as they quickly unclasped their hands and gathered round the girl. Sir Arthur moved to open the curtains.

'Don't do that yet, sir,' said one of the women. 'Let the young girl recover first before she sees the bright light.'

In five minutes Lucia had opened her eyes and, though still a little dazed, was clearly recovered. Her mother approached Shackleton.

'I tell truth, sir?' she said. 'My Lucia see things.'

'Quite right, signora. Quite amazing. Quite.'

Sir Arthur was almost trembling with excitement as he showed the women out of the house with indecent haste. He pressed a gold sovereign into each of the spiritualists' palms, and gave Lucia and her mother a gold £2 coin each.

'Quick, Frank, get a map,' he ordered as the door closed behind the last of the women. The two men spread it out on the table.

'Now the voice, or whatever it was, said a churchyard near Clonsilla.'

'Here it is,' said Shackleton, pointing out the small dot on the map just outside Dublin.

'But look, Frank, there's Mulhuddart before you reach Clonsilla, and that's got a churchyard as well. That might be the one. We'll have to search both, that's what we'll do.'

'When, Sir Arthur?'

'Straight away when Phillips returns with the carriage.' Sir Arthur paused for a moment and looked at his fob watch. 'On second thoughts, Frank, better not. What if we find the jewels? Sir John Ross will never believe it was because of some disembodied voice. If we discover them on our own, Frank, he'll think we had something to do with their removal and now have got cold feet.'

'Yes. It would be better to take a detective with you.'

'I'll contact the police, and tell them a clairvoyant has given us this information and would they help us check it. We'll go tomorrow.'

Shackleton had been casting around in his mind for any excuse to get out of what he knew would be a ludicrous expedition into the Irish countryside.

'I won't be able to accompany you, Sir Arthur,' he said, trying to force regret into his voice. 'Remember I'm returning to London tomorrow. I've got a lot of clearing up to do.'

'Of course, Frank. I forgot. I'll ask Peirce to accompany me.'

The next morning, Monday 22 July 1907, Sir Arthur's carriage clattered off into the green Irish countryside, with the two men from the Office of Arms and Sergeant Patrick Murphy from 'G' Division of the Dublin Metropolitan Police. The day was sunny and warm and Mrs Darcy had prepared a picnic lunch for the searchers. Sir Arthur's excitement grew as the carriage moved through the hedged lanes, and passed neat villas that stretched away from Dublin, until he caught the first glimpse of the church steeple at Mulhuddart. The churchyard was disused, but the iron gates at the entrance were still slightly open.

Sgt Murphy, with some effort, pushed them open wide enough for the others to squeeze through and stand amongst the long grass, brambles, and wild rose bushes. Bees and insects buzzed through the lush vegetation as the sun beat down, its heat raising the smell of the fecund soil to the searchers' nostrils. They were joined by Phillips, the coachman, and began beating their way with sticks through the undergrowth. They looked under the ornate family headstones and the raised stones of the graves. Occasionally, a stick would chink against glass, and Sir Arthur's spirits would rise momentarily only to fall again when the searcher uncovered an empty bottle. For well over an hour, the four men, perspiring in their tweed suits, searched the churchyard, collecting an assortment of bottles and rusting pieces of metal. Slowly, a crowd of inquisitive village children gathered at the gates to watch the curious spectacle of the four men clambering over the graves, brambles tugging at their clothes, their tempers rapidly becoming shorter. Eventually, it was the detective who called a halt.

'I don't see we're going to find them here,' he called over to Ulster King of Arms.

Sir Arthur, stooping over a grave, straightened up and wiped his brow with a handkerchief. . . .

'I think you're right, Murphy. After all, the clairvoyant did say Clonsilla. We'll move on there and eat our lunch in the carriage.'

The performance was repeated at the overgrown churchyard in the next village, but by mid-afternoon, after another fruitless search under the eyes of curious and occasionally jeering children, Sir Arthur was forced to admit defeat. Lucia Pentozzi's voice might have seen the Crown Jewels sparkle, but not in an old churchyard near Clonsilla.

It was a silent party that travelled back to Dublin. Sir Arthur, hot, sticky and discouraged, didn't appreciate the tentative efforts of Sgt Murphy to raise his flagging spirits.

'Nothing gained, nothing lost, sir,' the detective kept saying. 'It was worth a try, indeed.' Murphy, in reality, had enjoyed his day out in the country. It was a change from searching the seamier bars of Dublin for underworld informants who might know about the Crown Jewels.

Sir Arthur reported the expedition's failure to Shackleton when his carriage returned to St James's Terrace. 'It's not your fault, Frank,' he said, taking Shackleton's evinced sympathy for genuine emotion. 'As Murphy would keep reminding me, it was worth a try.'

'What are you going to do now, Sir Arthur?' asked Shackleton.

'I don't know, Frank. I just don't know,' Sir Arthur replied wearily. 'The first thing I'm going to do is to get out of these sticky clothes and have a bath. It really was boiling in the country. You get off to London, my dear chap, and thanks for waiting for my return before leaving. Most appreciated.'

'Well, you know where to find me, Sir Arthur,' said Shackleton, handing his suitcases to Pitt to put in the carriage. 'I'm sorry I have to leave you at a time like this, but my business affairs are most pressing.'

'Quite understand, Frank. Don't worry about me. I'll be fine. We'll find the jewels yet.'

The letter from Augustine Birrell, detailing his weekend's conversation with Chief Inspector Kane, deeply shocked King Edward VII. He considered himself a broad-minded man – indeed, he had every reason to be so – but homosexuality to him was totally beyond the pale of civilised behaviour. The thought of grown men going to bed together made him, the great libertine of his time, squirm with disgust. He was worldly enough to realise that it went on, but to think it was prevalent amongst the highest in the land was abhorrent to him.

His Majesty had read Birrell's letter in grim silence and, after finishing it, had sat for minutes without speaking. Sir Francis Knollys, opposite him across the desk at Windsor Castle, knew better than to break such a silence. Finally, the King had pushed the letter away from him, an expression of distaste on his features.

'Destroy it, Francis,' he ordered quietly. 'At once.'

Sir Francis picked up the letter, and carried it over to the large fireplace in the vast room overlooking the southern slopes of the gardens at Windsor. He pulled aside the ornamental fire shield in front of the empty grate, placed the letter carefully on the grate, and set light to it with a match. King Edward stared dully at the flame as it curled, and then blackened the letter. Sir Francis took a poker by the fireplace and jabbed at the charred paper until it broke into hundreds of fragments.

'We don't suppose, Francis, there's any reason, the slightest reason to think that Birrell and the Chief Inspector are wrong?'

'I fear not, sir.'

'This is very serious. Very serious, you realise.'

'Of course, sir.'

'God, that we were King of England four hundred years ago!' exclaimed His Majesty, his voice rising for the first time.

'Sir?'

'Then, Francis, the solution would have been simple. In those so-called uncivilised times it would have been very simple. The rack and irons to get to the truth, and then the axe to settle all debts.'

Sir Francis didn't reply. 'Now,' the King went on, 'we're what's called a constitutional monarchy. Our hands are tied except for one thing, Francis. Our displeasure. And, make little mistake, our displeasure is now very great.'

'But, sir, may I counsel caution. It's the Duke of Argyll I'm thinking of. . . .'

'We're not a bloody imbecile yet, Francis,' said the King sharply. 'Of course, we're aware of the Duke's position.'

'I'm sure it's just a casual acquaintanceship, sir. Nothing more.'

'So are we. We trust John Argyll implicitly. But we have to protect him from the results of this misguided friendship. Dammit, Francis, we've got to protect ourselves from it.'

'Of course, sir.'

'Think of the scandal in Germany last winter. Prince von Eulenberg-Hertefeld and Willie's two aides de camp. We have little time for the Kaiser, as you well know, Francis, but we must admire his swift action when he discovered he was surrounded by these . . . these . . . these prancing perverts. He dismissed the lot of them. Got rid of them.' The King crashed his fist on the desk. 'Bang! Just like that. He squashed them.'

'But the Kaiser rules differently from you, sir.'

'We know, Francis. We know. Sometimes we wish we had his powers.' He pointed a finger across the desk at his private secretary. 'But make no mistake, Francis, we shall squash these perverts in Dublin just as Willie did in Berlin. It may take longer, but we shall do it.'

Sir Francis tried to turn the King's anger into more rational channels. 'What of the Duke, sir?'

'We shall want to see him as soon as possible. We believe he's in London presently. Ask him to come here and see us.'

'Immediately, sir. I'll send a messenger at once.'

'Yes. Better not trust it to the telephone.'

On Tuesday 23 July 1907 the Duke of Argyll, now in late middle age, sat with the King on the East Terrace of Windsor Castle as the morning sunshine warmed the huge building, with its turrets and battlements standing high on a hill overlooking the narrow streets of the town. Below them the gardeners worked on the flower beds in the East Terrace Gardens, and away from them, stretching into the distance, they saw the avenue of lime trees that went nearly to the banks of the River Thames.

The Duke joined the King in a glass of hock and soda water though, after hearing the reason for his summons, he wished he'd settled for a stiff Scotch and soda.

'You've flabbergasted me, Bertie. Frank Shackleton . . . good heavens.'

'Yes, John, and the rest of them. All under the roof of our Ulster King of Arms. He must be one of them, or else totally blind and naïve.'

'It's almost unbelievable.'

'We wish it was, John. Sadly, it's all too horribly true.'

'What about the Crown Jewels?'

'We've little hope of seeing them again, we fear. And, anyway, that's not now the main consideration.'

'Isn't it, Bertie?'

'No, it's blasted well not.' The King's anger flared and then died again. 'We're sorry, John, but can't you see you've been compromised?' he said gently.

'But I hardly know the fellow,' protested the Duke.

'Doesn't matter, John. If Shackleton's brought to book for the robbery on a load of mish-mash evidence, then he's bound to use you in his alibi. And that must be avoided at all costs, for the sake of the family.'

'I see that, Bertie. But how?'

'One thing we're determined upon is that no one will escape our displeasure, but we shall have to be very careful about the police inquiries. We're lucky to some extent that the Dublin Police and Scotland Yard have apparently already fallen out.

We're pretty sure they're not going to find sufficient evidence to tie friend Shackleton firmly enough into the robbery to put him in charge.'

'What if they do?'

'Then we'll just have to face what comes. But we've already seen the Home Secretary and let him know our feelings. Mr Herbert Gladstone is not a bad chap, and understood us perfectly. Scotland Yard will continue its inquiries, of course, but we're certain that, short of a confession, they'll not reach a successful conclusion.'

'But how will they be punished, these people in Dublin? And what of the robbers?'

'We are still considering that, John. Be sure we shall find a way,' said the King, a note of grim anticipation in his voice. He smiled at his brother-in-law. 'And now, John, you're staying for lunch, of course. Alix is always saying we never see enough of you.'

Peter McEnnery found it a difficult decision to make – to voice his suspicions publicly. With his close and intimate relationships with two of the staff in the Office of Arms, he had been particularly keen to read everything that was written in the newspapers about the theft of the Crown Jewels, putting down all the relevant dates and facts in a notebook, to study them more closely. He searched his mind, remembering half-forgotten incidents over the previous days, weeks and months. Slowly, the conviction grew in his mind that only one person could have planned the robbery – Frank Shackleton. He knew he'd been short of funds, because Shackleton had tried to borrow a substantial amount from him in 1906. He realised that it would take someone with a close knowledge of the Bedford Tower to plan the robbery and, during a chat with Peirce Mahony at the Gresham Hotel in Sackville Street, he learned how the safe was opened with the original, or a perfectly made duplicate key.

'That's the mystery, Peter,' Mahony had said. 'How did they get the key, or an impression of the key, when Sir Arthur always kept it near him? It had to be someone who's been a guest at St James's Terrace.'

McEnnery's mind went back to his birthday party on 30 June and, suddenly, he remembered the absence of Richard Gorges just after midnight. Gorges, he knew, was Shackleton's closest friend, and as he pondered the problem the solution became clear. But how to tell anyone without revealing himself as a homosexual? Whatever he might be, McEnnery thought, he was also a man who knew where his duty lay. On Thursday 25 July 1907 he steeled himself, and called on Sir Arthur Vicars at his office in Dublin Castle. Ulster King of Arms was delighted, as always, to see his young friend.

'I fear this is not a pleasant business I have to discuss with you, Sir Arthur,' said McEnnery, his face ruddier than usual.

'My dear boy, you're obviously flustered,' said Sir Arthur. 'What's troubling you? Can I help?'

'I think it's I who can help you, sir.'

'How, Peter?'

'Sir Arthur, you recall that dinner you kindly gave me on my birthday?'

'Of course, dear boy. Delightful evening.'

'Can I ask you if you invited Richard Gorges on your own account, or did someone else?'

'Peter, I wouldn't have invited Gorges if I'd had my way. You'll probably know I don't care for him particularly. It was Frank who suggested he came. He prevailed upon me by saying Gorges was a particular friend of yours.'

This was the final confirmation for McEnnery. 'Then I must tell you, Sir Arthur,' he blurted out, 'I think it was Shackleton and Gorges who stole the Crown Jewels. I don't know how but. . . .'

'Peter, do you realise what you're saying?' interrupted Ulster King of Arms, his face beginning to set into a shocked mask.

'Yes, sir, I do. I realise it's a most serious allegation.'

'Good Lord, Peter, why do you say it?'

McEnnery then told him about Gorges's absence from the company, after Sir Arthur had retired early to bed, and explained his theory about Shackleton and Gorges executing the robbery.

Sir Arthur slumped back in his chair, pressing his head into his hands. 'It makes sense, Peter,' he said, his voice muffled by his hands. 'All too clearly it makes sense.'

He raised his head, and McEnnery could see the anguish in his eyes. 'Will you tell the detectives this?'

'If I must.'

Sir Arthur picked up the telephone on his desk, and whirled the handle on its side to raise the main switchboard at the Castle. After a wait, he was connected with Superintendent Lowe at the 'G' Division offices. Sir Arthur told him, in brief, what McEnnery had said, and agreed to let the detective use his office to take a statement.

Peter McEnnery found he didn't have to mention his homosexual behaviour in his statement. The Superintendent was satisfied with his saying merely that the birthday party had continued after Sir Arthur had gone to bed, and that Gorges had absented himself from the celebrations at the house for nearly half an hour.

The young farmer and landowner from Dunboyne left Dublin Castle feeling rather proud that he'd done his duty, and more than somewhat relieved that he hadn't been pressed for more details about the birthday party. His reputation had remained intact.

Sir Arthur stayed in his office, nursing his new suspicions about Frank Shackleton. The fact that McEnnery had been prepared to make a statement to the police went a long way to convincing him that the allegations were correct. He wondered why no one had made them before. It seemed so obvious to him now.

Superintendent Lowe didn't tell him that McEnnery's statement came as little surprise to the police, and Sir Arthur didn't know that his nephew had reached the self-same conclusions about the identity of the thieves.

For Peirce Gun Mahony had decided, a week before, that they had to be Shackleton and Gorges. Following the same line of deduction as McEnnery, he'd weighed up his position as a member of the legal profession in Dublin, his outwardly happy family life, and his reputation, and decided they were more important than catching two thieves. His legal training told him that if he voiced his suspicions – or rather his certainty –

then he risked being exposed as a homosexual. That, for Peirce Mahony in 1907, was unthinkable. It outweighed everything, even his affection for his uncle.

Lord Aberdeen sat in his office in the Vice-Regal Lodge in Phoenix Park on Wednesday 28 August 1907, looking more than usually sad, with his solemn beard and spaniel-like eyes. Nearly eight weeks had passed since the theft of the jewels had been discovered, and the police were no nearer making any arrests. The Viceroy had talked at length with Sir John Ross, and was aware of all the suspicions and gossip, but so far neither the Dublin Police nor Scotland Yard had unearthed any hard evidence. And now, in front of him on his desk, was another letter from Sir Francis Knollys. The first, a fortnight earlier, had simply asked, on behalf of His Majesty, if there was any news of the jewels. Lord Aberdeen had sent a stalling reply that everything was being done that could be. Obviously, he thought, looking at the letter now in front of him, this had not fooled the King.

Sir Francis had written bluntly: 'His Majesty is not, I am afraid, satisfied with your explanation, and he desires me to let you know that there is a mystery and apparent lukewarmness about the enquiry, and in fact the whole of the proceedings, which he does not understand. He says that at the end of nearly two months, surely, if there is ever to be a clue, it must have been discovered by this time. His Majesty also says that somebody must have been careless in the custody of the Crown Jewels, and if so he would be glad to know who, and whether, whoever it may be, anything in the way of punishment or reprimand has been given to him.'

Undoubtedly, thought the Viceroy, King Edward was out for blood. The royal axe was being sharpened over the neck of poor old Vicars. He put down the letter from Sir Francis, and glumly began trying to draft a reply that might buy some more time. If the jewels were found the King's anger would subside, he reckoned. Half-way through his work, he was interrupted by his Assistant Under-Secretary, Sir James Dougherty, knocking and hurrying into the office.

'Yes, James?'

'Sir, it's a telegraph from England about the jewels.'

Lord Aberdeen almost snatched the form out of Sir James's hand. He noted quickly that it had been sent from Malvern in Worcestershire, and then his heart leapt as he read: 'Jewels are in box, 9, Hadley Street, Dublin.' The telegraph was unsigned.

'Get me Ross on the telephone, James,' he ordered. 'This may be what we've been waiting for.'

'Yes, sir.'

The information in the telegraph caused consternation in the Chief Commissioner's office in Dublin Castle. Quickly he called a conference with Assistant Commissioner Harrel and Superintendent Lowe.

'I want this house and the immediate streets surrounded,' said Sir John. 'If the jewels are there, then so may be the thieves.'

'See to the men, superintendent,' ordered Mr Harrel.

Supt. Lowe strode out of the office to collect every available constable in Dublin Castle, as Sir John walked over to the large map of Dublin pinned on one wall of his office.

'Now, Bill, let's have a look at the area. I think we should go down there ourselves and supervise the operation.'

'Of course, Sir John,' said the Assistant Commissioner, always glad to bask in any glory that was being reflected.

'Now where was this house?' Sir John looked down at the notepaper in his hand. 'Ah, No. 9, Hadley Street.'

'Is it near the North Wall, sir? I think I've heard of it there.'

The two men peered closely at the map. Neither of them could immediately see Hadley Street.

'Let me look at the index, sir.' said Mr Harrel. He flicked through the pages, and then went down the list of streets beginning with 'H'. A puzzled expression crossed his face and he checked again, running his finger down the list.

'There's no Hadley Street in the index, Sir John!'

'What?'

'It doesn't exist, sir.'

The door burst open and Supt. Lowe returned. 'I've got the men in the wagons, sir, but there's a problem. None of the drivers has ever heard of Hadley Street.'

'But there must be,' insisted the Chief Commissioner.

'There's not, sir,' chorussed the Assistant Commissioner and the Superintendent.

'Oh, my God!' exclaimed Sir John. 'Not another bloody hoax!'

When the three detectives had recovered from their disappointment they looked at the telegraph again.

'It's most odd, sir,' said Supt Lowe. 'Why should anyone send the Viceroy an anonymous telegraph about an address that doesn't exist.'

'I think we should arrange for the original to be sent to Mr Kane at Scotland Yard,' said Mr Harrel. 'Let him check it using all those detectives he keeps sending over here.'

The idea appealed to the Chief Commissioner. 'First class, Bill. Give the fellow something to do rather than getting in our hair.'

The General Post Office found the original telegraph quickly, and sent it on to Chief Inspector Kane. He studied it with interest in his tiny office. Somewhere, he thought, I've seen that handwriting before.

'Sanders,' he ordered, 'Get me the carbon copies of all the statements taken by the Dublin Police.'

Kane scrutinised the statements from Stivey, Mahony, McEnnery, Shackleton, and Sir Arthur Vicars, then he hurried out of Scotland Yard, hailed a cab, and went to Mayfair.

On Friday 30 August 1907, Frank Shackleton was preparing to leave his rooms at 44, Park Lane, to lunch in the City, but he agreed to accompany Kane back to his office. There Kane asked him to wait in the adjoining office for a minute, went to his desk, and folded the telegraph form so that only the word 'Dublin' was visible. Then he called Shackleton in.

'Do you know who wrote this?' he asked, showing Shackleton the one word.

Shackleton peered at the writing for a moment. 'It's mine, I think. It looks like my writing.'

Kane unfolded the whole telegraph form and handed it to Shackleton. 'Well?'

'Good Lord. It seems to be my writing but I've never seen this telegraph before.'

'Didn't you send it, Mr Shackleton?'

'No. I swear I didn't.'

'But you say it's your writing.'

'It looks like it, but it can't be. I've never seen this before.'

'Come, come, Mr Shackleton. If it's your writing you must have sent it. Why?'

'But, Chief Inspector, I didn't.' A small line of perspiration was forming under Shackleton's hair line.

'So it's your writing but then it's not. Very strange, don't you agree, Mr Shackleton?'

'It is, Mr Kane, but I swear. . . .'

'Mr Shackleton, I shall have to test this further. Can you return here at mid-day tomorrow?'

'If you insist, but I can't see. . . .'

'I insist, sir.'

Shackleton left Scotland Yard a very perplexed and worried man. Until now, everything had been going so well. The cheque for £6,050 had been cleared through his bank, and had served to thaw the ice that was beginning to form in his relationship with Mr Johnson, the manager of Cox's Bank. His return to London had been greeted with dozens of invitations to luncheon and dinner from his acquaintances in society, all eager to hear the latest news about the Crown Jewels. His account of the seance with Lucia Pentozzi, and the subsequent search, had been so finely-honed that it was almost a set conversation piece, guaranteed to enthral the most blasé of company. It was all going so well, he reflected, and now this stupid telegraph!

When Shackleton had left the Yard, Kane sent a telegraph to Supt. Lowe in Dublin, asking him to request Sir Arthur Vicars to travel immediately to London. Lowe's reply showed that Sir Arthur was already in England, staying on holiday with Francis Bennett-Goldney at his home, Abbots Barton, at Canterbury. So Kane sent another telegraph and, in response, Sir Arthur arrived at his office shortly after noon on Saturday 31 August 1907.

He was more than surprised to see Shackleton waiting in the detective's office. Sir Arthur was at a loss how to greet his former friend, whom he now regarded with grave suspicion, which had been fanned into an active dislike by weeks of brooding. In the end he merely nodded to Shackleton.

'Sir Arthur, good of you to come,' said Kane, noting the antipathy between his two visitors. 'It won't take a moment, sir. I just want you to have a look at this.'

He showed him the telegraph form, folded once again to display only the word 'Dublin'. 'Who wrote this, sir?'

Sir Arthur bent his head to look closely at the word. Then he turned to Shackleton. 'I suppose you did.'

Kane looked at the two men. Sir Arthur glared at Shackleton, who shrugged his shoulders helplessly.

'Thank you, Sir Arthur,' said Kane, a note of triumph in his voice. 'I won't detain you any longer. Sergeant Sanders will see you out.'

When Ulster King of Arms had left, without a backward glance at Shackleton, Kane said sharply: 'Again I ask, sir. Why did you write this?'

'Again, Chief Inspector, I can only say I didn't,' protested Shackleton, now thoroughly bewildered at the turn of events.

'It's your writing?'

'Well, it appears to be. . . .'

'And yet you didn't write it?'

'No.'

'Well, Mr Shackleton, I think you'd better sit down and we'll go through your statement again.'

Point by point, name by name, Kane led Shackleton through his previous statement about his movements before the robbery was discovered. Finally, Kane decided to play his ace.

'Do you know Sir Reginald Fitzhunter, Mr Shackleton?'

Shackleton started in his chair, alarm flooding his features. 'He's an acquaintance.'

'Yes. An acquaintance. Well, sir, he's an acquaintance of ours as well. In fact he's told us some very interesting facts about certain happenings at No. 7, St James's Terrace and elsewhere. Do you follow me?'

'I don't know what you're talking about,' Shackleton blustered. 'He's merely an acquaintance. I can't see what you're driving at.'

'Can't you, sir? Well, we'll leave it at that for the present, I have little doubt I shall be seeing you again shortly.'

Shackleton sat in the cab taking him to the Junior Army and Navy Club and realised for the first time that he was a firm suspect in the eyes of Scotland Yard, and that his friendship with Sir Arthur Vicars was at an end. And all because of some silly telegraph, he thought.

Scotland Yard redoubled its checks on Shackleton but, during the next few days, the detectives could only confirm every detail of his alibi. Kane himself called at Shackleton's bank and questioned the manager. It was a circuitous interview, because Kane couldn't insist on any answers about his suspect's financial affairs. But Mr Johnson did indicate to him that Shackleton was a valued customer, whose account fluctuated a great deal, with large sums being credited and debited at fairly frequent intervals. There was little joy for Chief Inspector Kane in the interview.

And then, on Wednesday 4 September 1907, the mystery of the telegraph was solved. On that day a second telegraph was received by Lord Aberdeen, bearing the identical message about Hadley Street, Dublin, but this time with the signature 'Bullock Webster' and the clear postmark 'Great Malvern'. Kane took a train immediately to Worcestershire and, with the help of the county police force, soon traced Mr Bullock Webster and his wife to one of the hotels at the fashionable spa town. The interview was brief and to the point.

'Did you send these two telegraphs, Mr Webster?'

'Of course, chief inspector.'

'Why, may I ask?'

'Well, my wife had a dream one night in which she saw the Crown Jewels in a box at that address I wrote down. She insisted I sent the first telegraph, but I wasn't sure so I didn't sign it. Then we didn't see anything in the newspapers about it, so I sent the second telegraph.'

'Your wife had a dream, Mr Webster. . . .'

'Yes, she often sees things in her sleep.'

Chief Inspector Kane scratched his bald head in amazement. A wife who saw things in her sleep, and a husband who wrote in the same hand as Frank Shackleton. For once, he was lost for words.

Richard Gorges rolled over disconsolately on the large bed and smiled apologetically at Daisy Newman. 'It's no good, dear Daisy. Can't seem to get interested.'

'What's the matter, dear Captain? Too much wine?' asked Daisy, leaning over to comfort him, her erect nipples brushing his chest.

'No. Not that, Daisy. It's never that.'

'But this is supposed to be a celebration, Captain. My last evening in Dublin before a new life in London.'

'I know only too well. Don't rub it in.'

'That's obviously what we'll have to do if this is going to be a proper celebration,' Daisy laughed. 'John, see what you can do,' she asked her brother, who lay the other side of Gorges.

'Didn't you like Millicent's entertainment?' she prattled on, bending to kiss Gorges's moustache. 'She's not used to that rubber thing yet, but other gentlemen have found it most interesting. One of them suggested I should call the entertainment "A Maiden Alone".'

'No, that was fine, Daisy,' said Gorges as he felt her young brother's hand encircle his flaccidity, and gently begin to move up and down, occasionally scratching with his short-cut nails. He turned his head to smile in gratitude at the teenager, as the boy moved his head on the pillow and kissed him on the lips.

'Well, what is it?'

'It's nothing really, Daisy, and yet it's something.'

'Tell me.'

'Well, you know a Scotland Yard detective has been to the Curragh asking questions about me?'

'You mentioned it. Surely he couldn't have discovered anything to your detriment?'

'No, of course not. But his visit has caused suspicions, as it was bound to do. Probably it was meant to. Now some of my fellow officers, if you can call the swine that, are spreading rumours about my personal life.'

'You mean, here?' said Daisy, becoming alarmed.

'No, Daisy. No one knows about you. Shackleton doesn't even know I'm still visiting here. It's all to do with something that's supposed to have happened years ago, in South Africa. Some swine in the Hussars started it, and now they're all at it.'

'What are they saying?'

'That I was involved in a scandal with a coloured boy, and got kicked out of my regiment.'

'Were you?'

'Would I tell you all this if I had been?' lied Gorges. 'It's all so unfair.'

'What are you going to do about it?'

'What can I do? I've even noticed the colonel giving me odd glances in the mess now. I'll either have to challenge them, and that would lead to a public scandal. . . .'

'You don't want that because. . . .' Daisy looked across at her brother. He was intent in his pleasure-giving, his eyes closed, the tip of his tongue flicking across his lips.

'Yes, I know because, Daisy. Because it would lead to other things coming out. That's what's so unfair. I can't challenge them in public.'

'So what can you do?'

'I don't know. Life is becoming so unbearable with all this gossip. I might have to resign my commission. I could afford to do that now, of course. I've got enough to keep me going for a few years anyway.'

'My poor Captain,' crooned Daisy sympathetically, leaning over again to kiss him. 'Put it all from your mind for tonight and enjoy yourself. John will help you, won't you?'

Gorges started as he felt the boy's warm, moist lips close voraciously on him. His worries began to recede as waves of pleasure spread over him. For a few precious moments, on the evening of Monday 9 September 1907, Richard Gorges was able to forget that his past was catching up on him.

A light Highland drizzle was falling as the carriage that had met him at the station took Lord Aberdeen up the long drive to Balmoral Castle, the royal residence in Scotland. The Viceroy was in a resigned mood on Tuesday 24 September 1907, as he approached what he knew would be a difficult audience with King Edward VII. In the inside pocket of his tail coat he carried the letter from Sir Francis Knollys that had summoned him this day. It had been blunt to the point of curtness. In His Majesty's view, the search for those responsible for the theft of the Crown Jewels was not being carried on with enough drive. The King wished Ulster King of Arms to be suspended from office, and commanded Lord Aberdeen to present himself at Balmoral to explain what he was doing about it. The sands were running out, the Viceroy realised, but he still would try to gain more time, hoping against hope that the jewels might be found.

Before he left Dublin, he had mentioned his dilemma to Sir Anthony McDonnell, the Under-Secretary of State, who was standing in for Augustine Birrell, the Irish Secretary, while the latter was on holiday. Sir Anthony, a large man with imposing eyebrows, had held high office in India and Burma, and was regarded by the Viceroy as just the man to help in a crisis.

'There's one way out of the difficulty,' Sir Anthony had advised him. 'That would be to dispense with Vicars on another pretext. If he's sacked for failing to safeguard the jewels, what then about the police and the military? Wouldn't we have to punish their commanders for lax security at the Castle?'

'I see the point, Anthony,' the Viceroy had replied.

'And if we do that, sir, there'll be heads rolling all over the place. A major scandal would brew up!'

'You're right, of course. I'll mention it to His Majesty. Perhaps we can buy time and get rid of Vicars quietly. Though, personally, I don't want to. He's first class at his job, a thorough gentleman, and, frankly, I don't really blame him for the loss of the jewels. The general security just wasn't good enough from a number of aspects, not least of all the police and military patrols.'

'I agree about Vicars, sir. But it does seem His Majesty is determined.'

'I'm afraid so. Anyway, Anthony, while I'm away in Scotland, see if you can find a solution, will you?'

'Naturally, sir.'

Lord Aberdeen pulled himself out of his thoughts, noticing the drizzle that ran down the windows of his carriage as it drew up in front of the steps at Balmoral. That won't help the King's humour, he thought. Not at all the weather for shooting grouse on the moors.

After waiting for a few minutes, he was ushered into King Edward's office, overlooking the main lawns. The dull light through the high windows made the stone walls of the room look greyer than usual. The King had done his best to brighten up Balmoral after his mother, Queen Victoria, had died, but it remained a gloomy building, full of foreboding, particularly on a dank Highland day.

King Edward rose from his desk to greet the Viceroy, and led him over to a chair by the roaring and spitting wood fire.

'Not very nice, John, is it? But this is the warmest room in the castle.' The King's demeanour was grave. There were few pleasantries, apart from the ritual inquiries about the well-being of wives and families.

'We're sorry to drag you all this way in such gloomy weather, John,' said the King, when the two men were settled in their chairs either side of the fireplace. He used the Viceroy's Christian name deliberately to soften the harshness of what he was about to say. 'It was necessary, though, because of our deep concern about the situation in Dublin.'

'I quite understand, sir.'

'We wonder if you do. You know about the group of perverts?'

'Yes, sir. I've been fully briefed on the Scotland Yard report by the Chief Commissioner of Police.'

'Good. You'll realise then why we want this stamped on quickly and decisively.'

'Of course, sir. But there are two problems here, surely? One is the recovery of the jewels: the other is apportioning the blame for their loss.'

'Precisely, John. And the third is the group of perverts. They've involved, however slightly, a member of the Royal Family. That, you might think, is the most important point.'

'As you say, sir.'

'We do say, John. Most vehemently, we do say.'

The King was silent for a moment, the flames of the fire flickering the shadows of the gloomy room across his face and beard. Then he continued quietly. 'Although our letters have expressed dissatisfaction at the apparent lack of success of the police inquiries, that is not our paramount concern. The Royal Family must not be dragged into this affair because of that debauched ruffian Shackleton's casual house-party friendship with the Duke of Argyll.'

'What do you suggest, sir?'

'We've already told the Home Secretary that we would consider any prosecution to be most unwise unless the evidence against the culprits – presuming they are Shackleton and his

Army paramour – is so cast-iron that it would be pointless for Shackleton to involve the Duke as a witness to his alibi.'

'That seems unlikely, sir. The evidence, I mean.'

'It does. Indeed it does. Thus we have to take action ourselves against the people responsible.'

'Sir?'

'We will brook no further delay, John. We command you to get rid of all this filth in Dublin Castle.' The King punched his right fist into his left palm to emphasise the point. 'No further delay, John. Get them out.'

'But is dismissing Shackleton enough, sir?'

'It's a beginning, John. We intend to take other action as well in the future, to show our displeasure.'

'And Sir Arthur Vicars? Do you intend to take further action against him?'

'No, we think not. We're of the view that he has been merely a tool for Shackleton. He's a naïve and blind fool. His removal from public life will be sufficient punishment. We command that he's dismissed along with his nephew Mahony, Shackleton, Bennett-Goldney, and that stupid messenger, whatever his name is.'

'You've left out the army officer, Gorges, sir.'

'He will be dealt with. No regiment on earth will have him when the proper people hear of his conduct.'

'Your commands will be carried out, sir . . .'

'Thank you, John.'

'. . . but can I ask for a fortnight's leeway?'

'Why?' the King asked sharply.

'I've asked Sir Anthony McDonnell to try to find a way of dispensing with Vicars on another pretext. It might save a hullaballoo, sir.'

'Good man, that McDonnell,' murmured the King. 'That's acceptable to us, John. As long as the end result is the same we don't mind how you get rid of Vicars. But we don't want this matter lingering on. You have our command.'

'Of course, Your Majesty.'

The Viceroy arrived back in Dublin still pleased with himself at having gained a little breathing space. If the jewels could be found then Sir Arthur Vicars might yet be saved, he thought, as he arrived at the Vice-Regal Lodge.

Directly he was seated in his office, Lord Aberdeen told the Under-Secretary of State of his guarded optimism.

'At least, I've got a little more time for him,' he told Sir Anthony McDonnell.

'Are you sure, sir?'

'What do you mean, Anthony?'

'While you've been away, rumours about Sir Arthur have spread throughout Dublin.'

'What rumours?'

Sir Anthony handed a file to the Viceroy. 'I've written a report for you listing the more mentionable rumours. Some of the others are quite vile.'

Lord Aberdeen read the report with growing horror. It made clear that everyone who was anyone in Dublin had heard that Scotland Yard believed there was a link between Sir Arthur Vicars and a circle of homosexuals. The report also mentioned another rumour that homosexual parties had been held in the Office of Arms after working hours.

'This is dreadful, Anthony. These stories are everywhere?'

'Everywhere, sir.'

'Then I'm afraid there's nothing to be done. Even if the jewels are found, Sir Arthur is finished.'

'Quite.'

The satisfied tone of Sir Anthony's voice made Lord Aberdeen look at him quizzically. 'Anthony, can I ask where these rumours started?'

'I've no idea. A casual word here or there, I suppose. Anyway, sir, it does give you a pretext for getting rid of him.'

The Viceroy swallowed. 'Of course, Anthony. Thank you.' He realised then that it was McDonnell himself who'd started the rumours. Anyway, he thought wearily, it would probably have ended like this whatever he'd done.

Lord Aberdeen waited a fortnight until a further letter arrived from Sir Francis Knollys, indicating that the King's command could wait no longer.

William Stivey, the messenger, was the first to be dismissed, and then, on Wednesday 23 October 1907, Sir James Dougherty, the Assistant Under-Secretary, dictated brief letters to Sir Arthur Vicars, Frank Shackleton, Peirce Gun Mahony and Francis Bennett-Goldney.

All the letters ended with the identical and crushing words: 'His Majesty has come to the conclusion that he will reconstitute your office. I beg to inform you that your services are no longer in regard.'

The juggernaut of royal displeasure had begun to destroy its victims.

10

Enter O'Mahony, fighter of causes

The idea that Sir Arthur Vicars would fight the King's displeasure never crossed the mind of anyone amongst the bureaucracy of Dublin Castle. As far as Lord Aberdeen and his staff were concerned, Sir Arthur had been dismissed and that was that. An unpleasant episode in the unpleasant history of the Castle was closed. But Sir Arthur, fussy and naïve that he was, had a stubborn streak in him. Immediately he received his letter of dismissal, he replied demanding a full public inquiry into all the facts surrounding the robbery of the Crown Jewels. Then he wrote directly to King Edward VII and, somewhat naïvely, asked the man whose command had meant his downfall to inquire into the matter personally.

On Friday 25 October 1907, the letter sent by Sir James Dougherty, the Assistant Under-Secretary, to Sir Arthur would have ended the fight of most men. It said curtly, 'His Excellency is advised that your office has been legally and properly terminated and I am, therefore, to inform you that your request for an inquiry cannot be complied with.'

Sir Arthur, alone in his agony at St James's Terrace, was dismayed but unbowed. Five days after he had been sacked he requested, and received, an audience with the Viceroy. Augustine Birrell, the Irish Secretary, now returned from holiday, had insisted on the audience being granted, his sense of fair play outraged by the rumour-spreading tactics of his deputy, Sir Anthony McDonnell. But it was not to be the happiest of meetings between three men who once held honest regard for each other.

'There's nothing that can be done, Vicars,' Lord Aberdeen explained, trying to be firm and unrelenting in an effort to cover his embarrassment at meeting a man he had just helped to ruin.

Sir Arthur stood stiffly in front of the Viceroy's desk. 'I am aware, my lord, that rumours, scurrilous, awful rumours, have been spread about me throughout Dublin. I shall not demean myself by denying them. They are beneath contempt. I am here to discover why I've been dismissed.'

The Viceroy coughed into his handkerchief, his soulful eyes pleading for help from Augustine Birrell who stood by his desk.

'Sir Arthur,' the Irish Secretary said gently, 'your dismissal is because of your negligence in safeguarding the Crown Jewels. That is all. We have little regard for the rumours, unpleasant though they are.'

'What negligence?' demanded Sir Arthur, beginning to sense that there wasn't total accord between the two men in front of him. 'How could I be negligent when the jewels were obviously stolen out of working hours? Surely the police and the Army were negligent?'

Mr Birrell picked up a typewritten document lying on the side of the Viceroy's desk and began reading it aloud. He detailed how Sir Arthur had failed to make regular and frequent inspections of the Crown Jewels in their safe and how he had not taken immediate action when the front door and the strongroom door in the Bedford Tower had been discovered open during the first week of July.

'Is that all?' asked Sir Arthur contemptuously when the Irish Secretary had finished reading the document.

'That's enough, Sir Arthur, to justify a charge of negligence, surely?' replied Mr Birrell, his tone still gentle.

'And you dismiss me after nearly fifteen years' unblemished service for this?'

'Yes,' said Lord Aberdeen. 'We do.'

'Then I demand a public inquiry. That is my right.'

'It is your right, Vicars,' said the Viceroy huffily, attempting to bring the audience to an end. 'But it is also my right to refuse you.'

'Then I shall fight you, sir,' replied Sir Arthur pompously.

'That too is your right, Sir Arthur,' said Mr Birrell, 'but I fear you won't win.'

The audience ended in an atmosphere of polite animosity. Sir Arthur returned sadly to Clonskeagh, only to discover an unexpected ally had returned from the Balkans and was waiting for him in the drawing room, his stepbrother, Peirce O'Mahony, father of Cork Herald, Peirce Gun Mahony.

Mr O'Mahony, later to become The O'Mahony of Kerry, was a formidable man in his late fifties who had held office in Ireland as an Assistant Land Commissioner and then as Member of Parliament for North Meath. In the opening years of the twentieth century he had gone to Russia to claim a fortune in gold, silver and property amassed by a forebear called Peirce Lacey. He had fought as a general in the army of Catherine the Great after the failure of the Jacobite revolt. The inheritance was valued at more than £300,000 in 1905, a huge fortune by any standards. O'Mahony soon spent a deal of it in the newly-discovered cause of helping Bulgaria achieve her independence from the Turkish Empire. His fighting spirit made him one of the last of the great Wild Geese, the Irishmen who had travelled the world fighting for other people's causes. Now O'Mahony, through his brother, George, had discovered a cause to fight on his own doorstep.

The stepbrothers greeted each other coolly at first, because there had been bad blood between them ever since Peirce Mahony had defied his father's wishes and joined Sir Arthur in the Office of Arms. But then, as Sir Arthur realised that his brother passionately wanted to help him, the icy atmosphere melted and then warmed.

'Arthur,' declared Peirce O'Mahony, 'We're going to fight this together. It's outrageous that you've been treated in this way.'

'My dear Peirce, it's so good for me to hear you say that. At times in the last few days I've felt so alone and helpless. I've been betrayed by my friends and, it seems, by my King.'

'Now, don't you worry any more, Arthur,' said O'Mahony. 'Together we'll make the people in Dublin Castle tremble.' His craggy features split into a broad grin. 'My God, Arthur, we'll even make the King think twice about this. But first you'd better tell me everything that's gone on.'

Sir Arthur sipped a sherry and O'Mahony a large Irish whisky as they discussed the robbery of the Crown Jewels and its aftermath.

Eventually O'Mahony had all the facts and rumours. 'It's one cooking pot of a mess, isn't it, Arthur? Your so-called friend Shackleton has really pushed you into the dung heap up to your neck and no mistake. What a swine!'

'I'm afraid so, Peirce. It's so bad that I can't see what we can do.'

'Do, Arthur? Do?' laughed O'Mahony. 'We're going to shake the walls of the Castle, that's what we're going to do. Then we'll see who falls off its walls.'

Peirce O'Mahony, bristling with action, first approached John Redmond, the leader of the Irish Party at the House of Commons. But after two meetings it became clear that Redmond had been fully briefed by the Viceroy's staff. With the shadow of a homosexual scandal hanging over the affair, he refused the help of the MPs under his sway.

Next, O'Mahony, becoming angrier by the day, sought an interview with Augustine Birrell. The Irish Secretary was in the unenviable position of justifying a situation not of his own making and which he personally deplored. The meeting took place on Saturday 2 November 1907, at Dublin Castle.

'Mr Redmond tells me there are other charges against my brother apart from that of negligence,' said O'Mahony, glaring at the hapless politician. 'What are they, sir?'

'Mr O'Mahony, this is terribly difficult, you know.'

'I'm a grown man, Mr Birrell. Don't spare your words.'

'Well, the serious charge is that Sir Arthur has associated with a man of undesirable character.'

'You mean Shackleton,' said O'Mahony as a statement of fact.

'A man of undesirable character,' repeated Mr Birrell, refusing to be drawn into naming names.

'Good Lord, man,' boomed O'Mahony. 'You know my brother thought this man to be of good character. I also presume this man's other friends, like Lord Ronald Gower and the Duke of Argyll, thought he was of good character, too.'

The Irish Secretary winced at the use of the two names. 'That is neither here nor there, Mr O'Mahony. All I can say is that the charge of associating with a man of undesirable character was laid before His Majesty as well as the accusation of being negligent in safeguarding the Crown Jewels.'

'Mr Birrell, in all justice, you must have a public inquiry into this whole farrago of rumours and lies. You must seek out the truth. You're a man of understanding, sir. Can't you see the injustice of condemning a man like Sir Arthur on charges to which he has never had the opportunity to reply?'

Augustine Birrell flushed and began to reply angrily, 'Mr O'Mahony, for my part. . . .' He stopped and leaned back wearily in his chair. 'Mr O'Mahony, there's nothing more I can say. The Viceroy has taken the decision, on advice, that there'll be no inquiry.'

A week later, under continuous pressure for a public inquiry from Peirce O'Mahony, Lord Aberdeen offered a deal to Sir Arthur Vicars. If he would go quietly then his pension would still be paid.

'It's very tempting, Peirce,' Sir Arthur mused. 'I've little money left and little prospect of ever earning money again because of this scandal. I've spent most of what I had on buying books for the Office of Arms and, of course, my antiques.'

'It's Judas money, Arthur. Don't betray yourself for it,' urged his brother. 'I'll give you the money equivalent to your pension. Don't worry about the money. I've got more than enough for all of us. Let's just concentrate on fighting to clear your name.'

'But what of the names of the others, Bennett-Goldney and your son? Isn't there a risk that a public inquiry will blacken them?'

'There's a risk, of course, Arthur, but I doubt very much whether there'll be any mention of a homosexual scandal at any inquiry. It would be the last thing the King would allow.'

'Are you sure? I mean . . . your son, my nephew?'

'Peirce is a grown man. He is responsible for his own behaviour. If the rumours are true and he has got involved then I am sorry for him and I shall endeavour to help him if he is exposed,' said O'Mahony gravely. 'But I repeat, Arthur, I don't think the inquiry dare touch on these rumours.'

And so the battle continued into December 1907, with Lord Aberdeen becoming more and more alarmed at the persistence of the two stepbrothers. The straw that broke his back came on Monday 2 December. In a fiery letter, O'Mahony wrote, 'I personally am determined to leave no stone unturned to bring the true state of affairs under the notice of His Majesty, and I now definitely ask Your Excellency to convey to His Majesty my humble request for an audience at which I may be allowed to state my brother's side of the case.'

The Viceroy realised that nothing he could offer, except an inquiry, would satisfy O'Mahony. He wrote immediately to King Edward VII asking him if he would authorise a Court of Inquiry.

'This is a total disgrace,' stormed the King after he had read the Viceroy's letter in his light and airy office at Buckingham Palace. 'Aberdeen, Birrell, McDonnell – the whole pack of them – have mishandled the whole blasted affair.'

Sir Francis Knollys tried to calm his anger. 'There was little they could do, sir, surely? I mean, if Vicars and Mahony want an inquiry so badly then Dublin Castle can hardly refuse them.'

'You think not, Francis. We think otherwise. We think if they'd been strong enough and firm enough this Vicars would have been sent packing by now.'

The King handed Lord Aberdeen's letter back to his private secretary. 'Anyway, Francis, this affair has dragged on for too long. At this rate it'll still be around our necks in five years' time. We wash our hands of it. Tell Aberdeen that. We wash our hands of it. He can have his inquiry with all the scandal it'll lead to.'

'I'll write to him directly, sir. But there is one other course of action we could adopt that might help.'

'Nothing will help, Francis. It's a complete mess,' said the King disconsolately.

'Sir, what if the inquiry is held in private and is given simply the brief to look at whether Vicars was negligent and whether the building was secure enough? That will save the whole unsavoury story becoming public.'

'You're right, of course, Francis.' His Majesty brightened visibly. 'You're so right. We'll give them an inquiry but strictly on our terms.' He ran his hand over his beard, 'Yes Francis, that's the answer. But make sure at the same time that

Aberdeen understands our feelings about it all. We're very dissatisfied.'

'Be sure I shall, sir.'

The tone of the letter from Sir Francis Knollys sank Lord Aberdeen into an even deeper depression. He determined to make one last effort to persuade Sir Arthur Vicars to end his campaign. On Saturday 7 December 1907, he wrote to Peirce O'Mahony telling him that unless his stepbrother resigned within 48 hours then his office would be declared vacant in the *Dublin Gazette*. The Viceroy hoped this threat of public humiliation would bring Sir Arthur to heel, but O'Mahony countered with his master-stroke. It was a petition signed by sixteen of the twenty-one Knights of the Order of St Patrick.

To the King's Most Excellent Majesty
The Humble Petition of
The Knights of the Most Illustrious Order of St Patrick
Sheweth

That it has been brought to the notice of the Companions of Your Majesty's Most Illustrious Order that His Excellency the Grand Master has received Your Majesty's approval of the reconstitution of the Office of Arms, Dublin Castle, which will involve Ulster King of Arms being relieved of the office which he now holds.

That having regard to the fact that Ulster King of Arms, as Executive Officer of the Order, in addition to his other heraldic duties, has invariably discharged his functions for the last fifteen years in a manner which has called forth the special approbation of the various Grand Masters under whom he served, and has received the signal commendation of Their Royal Highnesses The Prince of Wales, K.P., and the Duke of Connaught, K.P.

That Your Petitioners feel that an inquiry into all the circumstances connected with the recent disappearance of the Insignia of the Order, at which Ulster may be given an opportunity of being heard before any steps be taken to relieve him from his office, would only be fair and just.

> Your Petitioners therefore humbly pray that Your Majesty may be graciously pleased to direct such an inquiry to be held.

Those who signed the petition were the Earls of Bandon, Carysfort, Dunraven, Enniskillen, Erne, Gosford, Listowel, Longford, Lucan, Mayo, Meath and Rosse; the Marquesses of Ormonde and Waterford, Lord Monteagle of Brandon, and Field-Marshal Earl Roberts.

The petition threw Dublin Castle into a complete tizzy when it arrived from O'Mahony with a letter requesting that it be forwarded to King Edward. Lord Aberdeen had virtually conceded that an inquiry should be set up and, to him, the petition was merely furthering his embarrassment. He refused to send it to His Majesty, although King Edward had already heard of it through Sir Francis Knollys's excellent intelligence service.

But O'Mahony was not to be thwarted, immediately sending the petition to the Home Secretary, Mr Herbert Gladstone, with a long statement making all the points in Sir Arthur's defence: 'That it was no part of Ulster's original duty to have the custody of the Crown Jewels; that under the new Statutes of the Order of St Patrick in 1905 the jewels were consigned to the care of Ulster, who never received any pay for this onerous duty, and therefore ought to be regarded as a voluntary trustee; that a trustee is never by law required to take better care of his trust property than an ordinary man takes of his own property; and that if the authorities required Ulster to take expert care of the jewels, such as is required from a bank manager, they should have laid down regulations to that effect.'

The powerful statement ended with a plea for Sir Arthur: 'By the nature of his work, he is now unfitted to seek other employment and, if deprived of his position of Ulster, he will be driven out penniless and broken.'

O'Mahony regarded the statement with satisfaction. 'That should give those mandarins in Whitehall something to think about,' he told Sir Arthur just before he posted it on Sunday 19 December 1907.

'The Viceroy won't be at all pleased about us going over his head, Peirce.'

'Well, that's his damned fault, Arthur. He's had every opportunity to do the proper thing. I think he's so scared of the King and any possible scandal that he's frozen into total paralysis. We'll soon jerk him out of that. The Home Secretary is bound to take notice.'

Indeed Mr Gladstone did take notice, raising the question of the petition at the next Cabinet meeting at No. 10, Downing Street on Thursday 2 January 1908. He criticised Lord Aberdeen for refusing to forward the petition and told the meeting that only a full public inquiry could save a row in Parliament, a possible vote of censure, and a split in the Cabinet. O'Mahony and his bullying tactics had won the day. On Monday 6 January a proclamation was issued from Dublin Castle setting up an official inquiry.

Frank Shackleton was sitting on the terrace overlooking the beautiful grounds of the Villa Bianca in the hills above San Remo in Italy when the summons reached him to attend the Official inquiry into the loss of the Crown Jewels. The winter sun of the Italian Riviera warmed him as he read the long, officially-worded document. A worried frown crossed the even features of his face as he studied the terms of reference for the commissioners of the inquiry: 'To inquire whether Sir Arthur Vicars exercised due vigilance and proper care; to examine witnesses, call for and examine all such books and documents as you shall judge likely to afford you the fullest information. . . .'

'What's the matter, Frank?' asked Lord Ronald Gower, noticing his guest's frown.

'He looks like he's lost a sovereign and found a penny,' smiled Frank Hird, as he removed his panama hat and wiped his brow.

'No – it's nothing much,' Shackleton reassured them. 'They've set up an inquiry into the loss of the Crown Jewels. I've been summoned to attend.'

'So dear old Bertie had to give way in the end, did he?' said Lord Ronald. 'Well, well, that's a bit tricky, Frank.'

'It could be, Ronnie.'

'Particularly if they inquire into your sleeping habits, Frank,' laughed Lord Ronald's 'son'.

'It won't come to that, I'm sure, Frank. I don't think they'll want to drag out all those vicious rumours again.'

'I damned well hope not,' growled Lord Ronald. 'I had my share of being the object of public gossip when Frank and I got together.' He leaned over the table where they were sitting and squeezed Hird's hand. 'Don't worry. I'm sure nothing will hurt us now.'

He turned to Shackleton, releasing his companion's hand. 'I can't see why you should be too concerned. You were with us and John Argyll when the robbery was discovered. They can't possibly say you had anything to do with it.'

'I don't see why I've ever been suspected at all, as you know, Ronnie. Why should I want to steal the Crown Jewels even if I could have done?' lied Shackleton. 'I've got my Mexican venture and now you've guaranteed the overdraft at Cox's, that's plain sailing.'

'The reason you were suspected, Frank, is quite simple. You don't fit into the great moral code of our time,' said Lord Ronald. 'You're not a blasted hypocrite, parading your loving family in public and then dashing off to some little harlot or painted boy in a grubby cottage in St John's Wood. Frank and I are the same, virtual outcasts because we happen to love each other.'

Lord Ronald picked up his glass of white chianti and took a sip before continuing. 'One day, mark my words, people like Havelock Ellis and Edward Carpenter will be recognised as great men. Ellis is pilloried at present because his books dare to say that homosexuality is as congenital as colour blindness, and Carpenter, well . . . when he writes that we're publicly useful because we're free from family ties and only a source of social evil because we're suppressed, then he's guaranteed not to get a Royal Warrant, isn't he?'

'Your sister, Elizabeth, told me a good story the other day, Ronnie,' interrupted Frank Hird. 'It illustrates the whole code of this great and so-called free era. Apparently some girl tells another that she's totally confused because her boy-friend says that love is the only thing that matters and her parents tell her that's all poppycock. According to them, behaviour is the only thing that matters.'

The three men laughed at the anecdote. 'That's quite true,

of course,' said Shackleton. 'It's not what you do nowadays that counts. It's what you're seen to do.'

He threw the summons on to the table, 'But all that doesn't solve my immediate problem. What am I going to do about that?'

'You'll have to go, of course, Frank,' said Lord Ronald. 'If you stay away it'll just fan the rumours. Take my advice – it'll be straightforward enough. They daren't ask you questions that are too personal. Old Bertie would have them in the Tower of London if they did.'

'I suppose you're right,' said Shackleton. 'Of course, you're right. I'd better start getting packed.'

'You don't have to go immediately, do you, Frank? Tomorrow will do, surely?' asked Hird, a sly smile on his face.

'Oh, I forgot . . . tonight.'

'Yes. Tonight, Frank,' laughed Lord Ronald and his companion. 'You forgot you invited that beautiful young sculptor to dinner, didn't you?'

Shackleton joined in the laughter. 'I must confess I did forget for a moment. I can always go tomorrow, can't I?'

'That's if you're strong enough after tonight,' grinned Frank Hird.

Chief Inspector John Kane felt his ill humour of the past week beginning to lift as he read the latest edition of the *Pall Mall Gazette* in his office at Scotland Yard. The leading article about the Crown Jewels robbery, written by the publication's famous editor, W. T. Stead, was exactly to his liking.

> Ireland is poor and its criminals clumsy. Thus it rarely comes about that the Dublin Police are called upon to investigate cases of such extreme complexity. It was therefore a great pity that Scotland Yard were not put in sole charge of the case. . . .

That's the understatement of the year so far, thought Kane, as he read on:

> Curiously enough it is not even acting now. Scotland Yard has been 'invited to confer' and advise only when

> asked by the Irish Police. No one has denied that the thief had an accurate knowledge of the department and had the opportunity of obtaining duplicate keys. This led not only to the careful examination of every person connected with the College of Arms but to searching inquiries into the antecedents of every officer and servant of the Office. For all this the Government are now forced to admit they have no evidence to secure the conviction of anyone, so they have now settled down to their secondary duty, the fixing of responsibility for a loss so amazingly brought about.

Kane put the paper aside with a smile on his face. His lunch with Mr Stead the previous week had not been wasted. The fact was that the Chief Inspector's investigation had ground to a halt. He'd done all he could, he reckoned. He'd even had examined all the telegraphs sent from the Post Offices at St James's and at South Audley Street in London during the period from 6 July to 29 October 1907, trying to find any sent by Frank Shackleton. After a huge job of sifting through the telegraphs, his detectives had found twelve sent by the suspect. None of them could have been construed as having anything remotely to do with the Crown Jewels. And now he was under instructions from the Home Office about his evidence before the Court of Inquiry. Kane had been told that, naturally, he should answer fully any questions asked of him but that he should not go out of his way to volunteer any information about the homosexual group surrounding Sir Arthur Vicars. Mr Arthur Banks, the Under-Secretary who had briefed him, had been firm on this point.

'The Home Secretary, Chief Inspector, doesn't think it's relevant to the terms of reference of the inquiry,' he explained.

'But what if I'm asked about the perverts, sir? Surely I'll have to answer?'

'We doubt here if you will be asked,' said Banks, handing the Scotland Yard man a glass of sherry. 'We think the Commissioners at the inquiry will stick very closely to their terms of reference.'

'And Shackleton, Mr Banks . . . what if I'm asked about these continual accusations made against him by Sir Arthur Vicars?'

'Then you state the truth, don't you, Mr Kane?'

'The truth?'

'Yes. That Sir Arthur has produced no evidence against him.'

'Well, that's true enough, sir. But what of my own suspicions?'

'We agree here with your suspicions. The Home Secretary has every reason to believe that they're true. He thinks you've done a first-class job in the circumstances. But, Mr Kane, they are only suspicions, after all. You couldn't bring a charge against him.'

'No – and that's the unhappy truth,' replied Kane.

'Then we don't think it would be correct to mention these suspicions.'

'Of course, sir.'

'By the way, Chief Inspector, I believe I have reason to congratulate you.'

'Congratulate, sir?'

'Yes. Haven't you been told yet?'

'Oh, you mean my transfer?'

'Yes. To head of detectives at 'F' Division, I believe.'

'That's correct, sir. I take over my new command as soon as I return from Dublin.'

'I expect it'll be a welcome change from this inquiry,' said the civil servant.

'Believe me, sir, it will be.'

Chief Inspector Kane packed his files into his briefcase before catching the boat train to Dublin on Thursday 9 January 1908, knowing only too well that the inquiry was to be the final act in the Crown Jewels investigation. He was professional enough, and well versed enough in the internal politics of Scotland Yard and the Home Office, to realise that his coming transfer to the quieter pastures of 'F' Division in West London meant that the Scotland Yard investigation was at an end.

The library in the Bedford Tower at Dublin Castle buzzed with conversation on the morning of Friday 10 January 1908. Barristers, in grey wigs and black gowns, chatted together in small groups, their files tied with ribbon under their arms.

Sir Arthur Vicars sat on the front row of the chairs laid out in the library talking quietly with Peirce O'Mahony. At the table just in front of him his counsel, Mr James Campbell KC, MP, a handsome, saturnine man, conferred with Mr Timothy Healy, another King's Counsel and Member of Parliament, who had agreed to represent Sir Arthur at the Court of Inquiry. At another table a few yards away the Solicitor-General for Ireland, Mr Redmond Barry KC, MP, laughed suddenly at a sally from the Chief Crown Solicitor, Mr Malachi Kelly. There was the relaxed yet expectant atmosphere of a great legal occasion, everyone trying to appear nonchalant and friendly, smiling sympathetically at Sir Arthur whenever they caught his eye. The men of the law knew full well that he was the sacrificial lamb to be slaughtered but it was important to them that he should know they didn't bear any personal malice. That was the tradition of British Justice, impartial, detached, yet deadly. Sir Arthur's eyes kept flicking around his beloved library, noting his prized volumes behind the glass of the book shelves, but always returning to dwell on the safe that stood a few feet from him, the empty and useless safe.

'Be upstanding for His Majesty's Commissioners,' roared a police sergeant standing by the door of the library, and everyone rose to their feet. The Commissioners entered, led by His Honour Judge James Shaw, the county court judge for Co. Kerry, dressed in his red and black robes, and followed by his two fellow Commissioners, Mr Robert Starkie and Mr Chester Jones. They took their places at a long table piled high with documents, set under the library windows looking on to the front entrance of the Bedford Tower, and stood as the Royal Warrant setting out the inquiry's terms of reference was read out by an usher. Then the Commissioners sat down and with a scraping of chairs, a low murmur of conversation, and a rustling of papers, the inquiry began its hearing.

Sir Arthur's leading counsel, Mr Campbell, jumped to his feet immediately.

'Yes, Mr Campbell?' asked Judge Shaw, looking over his half-moon glasses, a small figure in his voluminous robes.

'M'lud,' said Campbell, pausing to gaze round the people in the library, 'I can see no members of the public or the press here. Is this inquiry to be heard in private?'

'It is, Mr Campbell,' replied the judge. 'Although we are perfectly prepared to consider any application you may care to make on the matter.'

'Thank you, m'lud. I then make formal application that this inquiry be held in public. In making this application may I further say that I find the wording of the warrant instituting this inquiry to be somewhat unsatisfactory. It neither gives you the power, m'lud, to compel the attendance of witnesses nor the power to examine them under oath.'

'Isn't that a matter for us, Mr Campbell?'

'As m'lud pleases, but I speak generally of the terms of reference of the inquiry. It would be an intolerable act of injustice to have an inquiry which would appear to exclude consideration of the very terrible suggestions and insinuations affecting the moral character of Sir Arthur, though it is notorious that they were part and parcel of the information upon which action was taken in the month of October last.'

The barrister paused and hitched his robe round his shoulders. 'Indeed, m'lud, one of the charges against my client, a charge not formulated but insinuated against him, is an allegation that he introduced an undesirable person into the privacy of his office. That is a fact, m'lud, you may care to consider while remembering that the actual theft of the Crown Jewels is a crime which is alleged to have baffled the police from the date of its commission up to the present.'

'We are not here to find out who the thief was,' interrupted Mr Chester Jones. 'That's a job for the police.'

Judge Shaw added quickly, 'Mr Campbell, we are not investigating the crime. I do not think the terms of reference give us any such power whatsoever.'

'Then, m'lud,' exclaimed Campbell, 'What is the object of this inquiry? It is clear that Sir Arthur is not to be allowed the opportunity to vindicate his character or to answer the unformulated allegations which, I submit, were the real cause of his dismissal. If that is the case, neither Sir Arthur, my learned friend Mr Healy, or myself, can see any usefulness in this inquiry.'

Campbell looked down at his papers, shuffled them together, and addressed the room in ringing tones, turning slightly away from the Commissioners. 'I can see no purpose nor usefulness in my client taking any further part in the proceedings.'

The Solicitor General, Redmond Barry, leapt to his feet. 'Surely, m'lud, Mr Campbell knows that a public judicial inquiry such as he wants can only be instituted with the sanction of Parliament.'

'Then why not ask Parliament for it? We will support you,' interrupted Campbell, as a murmur of speculation grew in the background.

'M'lud,' Barry almost shouted, 'Sir Arthur Vicars will be failing in his duty if he follows the course suggested by my learned friend and withdraws from this inquiry.'

Judge Shaw banged his gavel as the level of noise rose around the library. Campbell turned to Sir Arthur and Peirce O'Mahony and nodded. The two counsel gathered their papers and legal books, bowed to the Commissioners, and walked out of the library followed by the two stepbrothers. The room was stunned into silence by the gesture and then, after a moment, pandemonium broke loose. The Commissioners began talking excitedly together, Redmond Barry threw down his brief on his desk with a loud thud, looking helplessly at the Chief Crown Solicitor beside him, and the other lawyers and police officers in the library chattered loudly about Sir Arthur's dramatic exit.

After nearly five minutes, Judge Shaw restored order by banging his gavel repeatedly. Redmond Barry rose to ask the Commissioners to hear all the evidence he had to present and pointed out that, at least, they would be able to consider the statements made by Sir Arthur to the police. Reluctantly, Judge Shaw decided the inquiry should continue without the presence of its likely scapegoat.

Outside the Bedford Tower, Sir Arthur and his party were besieged by reporters from the Dublin and London press. He answered their excited questions about his walk-out and handed them written statements explaining his objection to the private inquiry. The next day's newspapers were of one accord in attacking the Government for holding the inquiry in such secrecy. The *Daily Graphic* said it could only be because the thief's identity was already known to the Government who didn't intend to make it public.

Meanwhile the inquiry continued to hear evidence from Sir George Holmes of the Board of Works about why the safe was not placed in the strongroom; from Detective Owen Kerr, who got so confused he invented a fifth key to the strongroom; from the messenger, William Stivey, now ensconced in an old soldiers' home in Co. Kildare; from Mrs Mary Farrell who explained how she had found the doors open; from Sir John Ross and his senior detectives who introduced all the statements taken from the staff of the Office of Arms; from Frank Bennett-Goldney who gave his evidence anxious, as a prospective Member of Parliament, to make sure no blame attached to himself; and from Chief Inspector Kane.

He was questioned about the piece of blue ribbon left behind in the red morocco case that had once contained the jewels.

'It confirmed my belief', the Chief Inspector told Redmond Barry, 'that the thief must either be a member of the staff or someone introduced by one of them. I told Sir Arthur this but he said he had implicit confidence in every member of his staff.'

'Did Sir Arthur remain in this belief?'

'No, sir. Later he made continual visits to me at Scotland Yard accusing Francis Richard Shackleton of responsibility for the theft.'

'Could he justify them, Chief Inspector?'

'I've repeated to Sir Arthur Vicars and his friends, over and over again, when they pestered me with not only suggestions but direct accusations of Mr Shackleton, that they might as well accuse me, so far as the evidence they produced went to justify them.'

Kane left the witness box feeling less than proud with himself. But he'd done what he'd been instructed to do. His job in 'F' Division beckoned. And anyway, he thought, the Commissioners had quite enough leads to question Shackleton themselves if they wanted to.

On Tuesday 14 January 1908, the fourth day of the inquiry, Shackleton waited in the circular hallway outside the library, nervous beneath his calm exterior. When the usher called his name he strode into the inquiry, a handsome figure in an immaculate charcoal-grey suit from Huntsman's the tailors, a red carnation in his button hole. His striking appearance brought a buzz of anticipation amongst the audience of lawyers and policemen at the inquiry. Chief Inspector Kane, sitting at the back of the room, smiled cynically to himself and nudged Superintendent Lowe beside him.

'Here comes Flash Harry, John,' he whispered. 'To look at him you would think butter wouldn't melt in his mouth.'

Shackleton bowed solemnly to the Commissioners and began giving his evidence. He detailed meticulously the housekeeping arrangements between Sir Arthur Vicars and himself at St James's Terrace and how they shared exactly half the costs. It was the evidence of a man who apparently watched his expenditure very carefully.

'May I ask you, Mr Shackleton, are you well off?' said Judge Shaw, slightly bemused at the evidence so far. It was at complete variance with Frank Bennett-Goldney's story that Sir Arthur virtually supported Shackleton.

'Well, it depends on what you call well off,' Shackleton answered with a disarming smile. 'I have enough to live on.'

'Were you in monetary difficulties in 1907?' persisted the Judge.

'Yes,' Shackleton answered immediately. 'I had been for two years, I may say, in difficulties. I borrowed money, not from my banker, but from a moneylender. The sums were . . . one was £650. . . .'

He stopped, noticing a shorthand writer taking down his evidence. 'None of this will appear in the press, m'lud?'

'This will be taken down.'

'But I don't mind a bit so long as it doesn't appear in the press. It could be very unpleasant for me if these things came out.'

'Then I must warn you before you go any further,' said Judge Shaw. 'It will be printed and it may be published.'

'I was given to understand that the investigation was private.'

'It is private in the sense that the public aren't present here. But the evidence is being taken down and will be printed.'

'Then I think that that statement should have been given to me before. My reason is this, that it would be very injurious to me in business were it known that, at a period when I was engaged in a rather large business transaction, I was in difficulties.'

Judge Shaw shrugged his shoulders, 'You are aware of the position now, Mr Shackleton.'

The questioning continued, with Shackleton exhibiting an air of hurt, though total, frankness. He was asked about his remarks at Lady Ormonde's luncheon party before the robbery was discovered.

'You obviously thought the jewels were unsafe,' said Redmond Barry. 'Why?'

'Well, for many reasons. I considered there were too many keys of the outer door.'

'Could you have taken an impression of Sir Arthur's keys?'

'I could have done so, but I didn't, sir.'

The barristers and Commissioners questioned him at length about his movements to and from Dublin during the period before and after the robbery was discovered. Shackleton answered them all with easy charm. He gave a graphic account of Lucia Pentozzi's seance and recounted the confusion over the telegraphs from Mr Bullock Webster about his wife's dream.

After more than three hours, his evidence was ended. On the surface, thought Kane, a very searching examination. And he had to concede that Shackleton had given a good impression of a totally open demeanour. But, as the Home Office had forecast – or arranged, he thought cynically but accurately – no questions nor even any suggestion about the relationships Shackleton had had in Dublin. No mention of Richard Gorges, Lord Ronald Gower, the Duke of Argyll, or the vile parties in the sedate southern suburb of Clonskeagh.

Kane smiled at John Lowe. 'Well, that's your man away scot-free,' he murmured as Shackleton walked from the library.

'I think not, John,' replied Lowe, a mysterious smile on his face.

'What do you mean?'

'I'll tell you later. Let's just say there are plans for Flash Harry.'

Kane looked quizzically at Lowe, who smiled and shook his head. 'Later, John, later.'

Shackleton thought he had every reason to feel pleased with himself as the doors of the library closed behind him and he stepped into the hallway of the Bedford Tower. He regretted his frankness about his financial difficulties because he anticipated it wouldn't please his bank manager. But otherwise, he thought, everything had gone just as Ronnie Gower had predicted. What he needed was a stiff drink, he reckoned, and then he'd try to contact Richard Gorges. Now his evidence was over, he looked forward to a night at the Spa Hotel with his friend.

He stepped confidently out of the Bedford Tower to be met by Detective Owen Kerr.

'Hello, Kerr. How are you?'

'Well, sir, very well. Can you spare a few minutes?'

'Of course. What can I do for you?'

'Perhaps you'd come with me, sir. The Assistant Commissioner would like a word if you don't mind.'

'Lead on, Kerr,' said Shackleton, walking with the detective the fifty yards to the police headquarters in Upper Castle Yard of Dublin Castle.

'Mr Shackleton, please sit down,' said Assistant Commissioner Harrel. 'You've finished your evidence?'

'Yes. I told the Commissioners all I could. They seemed satisfied.'

'Naturally they would, Mr Shackleton,' said Mr Harrel, gesturing to Kerr to stand by the door of his office. 'But then they don't know the whole story, do they?'

Shackleton began to grow alarmed. 'What's that meant to mean, Mr Harrel?' he asked sharply.

The Assistant Commissioner opened a file on his desk. 'It means precisely what I said. They don't know the whole story.'

'I don't see . . .,' Shackleton began to protest.

'Will you be quiet, sir. Your charm and fine manners may have hoodwinked the inquiry but they won't wash in this office.' Mr Harrel's face was hard and menacing.

'You can't say that. You don't have. . . .'

'Will you be quiet. We have everything, Shackleton,' said the Assistant Commissioner, dropping all pretence of politeness. 'We have everything about your abominable behaviour in Dublin. We know about the parties at Clonskeagh. We know about your assignations with Captain Gorges at the Spa Hotel.

We know about your friend Daisy Newman and her family at Ballsbridge.'

He picked up the file in front of him and let it drop on the desk. It was the result of extensive checking by the Dublin detectives of every hotel in the Dublin area until the descriptions of Shackleton and Gorges were recognised, and of a four-month surveillance, twenty-four hours a day, of Gorges's movements.

'This is monstrous,' spluttered Shackleton. 'I won't stay and be. . . .'

'Sit down, Shackleton,' Detective Kerr moved behind his chair and placed a restraining hand on his shoulder, pushing him back into the seat.

'Fortunately for you,' said Mr Harrel grimly, 'the Newman entourage left Dublin shortly before I was able to call on them, but my subsequent inquiries have given me an idea of the perverted activities that took place there. Anyway, I have enough evidence already to charge you with the grossest of indecent behaviour.'

Shackleton was silent, his face reddening.

'You, Shackleton, for all your high and mighty airs, are a filthy pervert. Nothing more, nothing less. Heaven knows how many times you've committed the abominable crime of sodomy but I have firm evidence of at least two occasions.'

The Assistant Commissioner picked from the file the statement of Sir Reginald Fitzhunter and waved it at Shackleton. 'Here is the testimony of one of your friends from London whom you invited to Dublin for your unspeakable orgies. It's all here in black and white.'

He put the statement back in the file and looked contemptuously at Shackleton. 'You are an abominable creature, Shackleton, and we want no more of you. We cannot prove you connived at the robbery of the Crown Jewels but we know you did. You are not going to laugh up your sleeve at us, though. I'm instructing you to leave Ireland and never to return. If you do, you will be immediately arrested and charged with sodomy.'

Shackleton, white with shock, buried his face in his hands.

'Yes, Shackleton,' said Mr Harrel. 'You are not going to strut round Dublin with your airs and graces any more. And, for your information, neither will your friend and likely partner in robbery, Captain Gorges. When I've finished with you I shall be visiting his commanding officer and acquainting him with the contents of this file. I fancy your Captain will be dismissed forthwith from his regiment.'

'But who . . .?' Shackleton muttered, beginning to rally under the onslaught.

'Who instructed me, I presume you mean.'

'Yes,' said Shackleton, his voice husky with shock.

'That's none of your concern, you degenerate pervert. But I shall tell you none the less. My instructions come directly from the highest in the land.'

'Oh, my God,' exclaimed Shackleton.

'Yes, Shackleton. You are finished here and probably elsewhere. Now get out of my sight before I arrange for you to get the beating you deserve.'

Francis Richard Shackleton half stumbled down the stairs leading back to the courtyard. He drew inquisitive glances as he walked stiffly out of Dublin Castle, silent tears running down his face and dropping on to his suit jacket. As he walked towards the cab rank, he wrenched the red carnation from his buttonhole, crunched it in his hand, and threw it in the mud of the gutter.

On Tuesday 14 January 1908 Frank Shackleton stepped on to the boat at Kingstown to start his journey away from his native Ireland for ever and towards ultimate ruin and disgrace at the King's displeasure.

Strangely, on that very day, his brother Ernest was taking some of his first steps on the snow and ice of Cape Royds in the Ross Sea in Antarctica that would lead him to fame, riches and the honour of a knighthood from the same King.

11

The King plots a downfall

King Edward VII puffed on his first cigar of the day at noon on Monday 27 January 1908, in the ornate splendour of the saloon at Sandringham House, his favourite royal residence set amidst a vast estate in north-west Norfolk. He reclined on a red and white striped sofa by the wood fire blazing in the grate of the marble fireplace. Above the mantelpiece was a large portrait of himself and Queen Alexandra with two of their sons dressed in kilts, and above that, to remind him still further of Scotland, were three mounted stags' heads, their antlers jutting out from the wall, their glass eyes gazing balefully over the fine room cluttered with furniture. The King studied his advance copy of the Commission of Inquiry into the loss of the Crown Jewels and found it good reading, particularly the main conclusion which he'd turned to first.

'We feel bound to report to Your Excellency that, in our opinion, Sir Arthur Vicars did not exercise due vigilance or proper care as the custodian of the Regalia.'

That puts paid to Vicars, His Majesty thought, tapping the ash of his cigar into a speckled onyx ash tray. He turned the pages, scanning the report from back to front, and smiled as he came to the section dealing with Shackleton's evidence.

'We think it only due to that gentleman to say that there was no evidence before us which could support the suggestion that he was the person who stole the jewels.'

Well, the King reflected, that ends any chance of a court case involving brother-in-law John. It'll also give Shackleton enough spare rope to hang himself.

The King had already seen the confidential letter from Mr Augustine Birrell, the Irish Secretary, telling him that Shackleton had been interviewed after giving his evidence and virtually exiled from Ireland, and that, two days later, Captain Richard Gorges had been dismissed from his regiment.

Yes, King Edward thought, this was the time to set some more wheels in motion. He rang the little silver bell on the table beside him and asked the footman in his scarlet uniform to summon Sir Francis Knollys.

'This report makes excellent reading,' His Majesty told his private secretary when he'd entered the saloon. 'That idea of yours about the inquiry, Francis, has worked perfectly. Well done, dear friend.'

'Thank you, sir.'

'Now, Francis. . . .' Suddenly the King began to cough and splutter. 'These blasted cigars . . . sometimes we think we'll follow our physician's advice and cut them out altogether . . . now, Francis, we must move on in the matter of our Crown Jewels. This report makes it quite clear that Shackleton has little money of his own. Been to the moneylenders and all that. It wouldn't take much of a push at the right moment to finally settle his boat. Would you tell the footman to ask Sir Ernest to join us, if he's still in the house.'

'I believe he's on the terrace, sir.'

'He must be mad sitting in the sea air with his chest. We love this house as you know, Francis, but give us the Villa Eugenie at Biarritz for climate any time.'

'Only a couple more months, sir. . . .'

'Yes, indeed, Francis. We wish you'd join us out there at least once.'

'My place is in England, sir, watching your affairs.'

'As you always say, Francis, as you always say.'

A portly figure appeared at the door of the saloon – Sir Ernest Cassel, dressed in a thick tweed suit and carrying a thick cane.

'Come in, Ernest, my dear chap,' said the King. 'Sit yourself down and have a warm. What have you been doing out on the garden terrace on a freezing day like today?'

'Just taking the air, sir, and reading *The Times*,' said the great financier. 'Not much of interest in the rag. I see, though, the Kaiser's been making one of his speeches again.'

'Yes. We read it, Ernest. Young Willie's going to talk Europe into a war if he's not careful. He's a strange chap. When he was staying at Windsor before Christmas he was all sweetness and bonhomie. And then he gets back amongst his damned Prussian generals and starts acting the military man again. We're only glad Mama's not alive to see it, that's all.'

Sir Ernest noticed the King holding the bulky report of the inquiry. 'Francis got you doing more work, sir? You really should take a firm line with him.' Sir Ernest smiled at Knollys. 'His Majesty is supposed to be having a rest, you know, Francis.'

'We know, Ernest,' said the King. 'It's not Francis's fault. These papers just follow us around. We shouldn't really complain though. We were denied them long enough when we were Prince of Wales.'

'Anyway,' His Majesty continued, 'This is the report into the robbery of our Irish Crown Jewels. Very interesting reading. Puts the blame in all the right places and still stays very discreet. First-class piece of work. We'll want you to read it later.'

'I'd be most interested, sir.'

'Yes, well, we want you to be more than interested, Ernest. You've helped us out of many financial scrapes. . . .'

'My duty, sir,' Sir Ernest interrupted.

'Your friendship, you mean, Ernest. You know we're eternally grateful to you. Now we've got another little assignment for you.'

'Anything, sir.'

'Well, when you do read the report, pay particular attention to the evidence of one Francis Shackleton.'

'Sir . . .?'

'We want your help in bringing him down. He's an unmitigated swine whom, as you well know, almost compromised our family through his unspeakable habits. He has no place in our society.'

'How can I help?' asked Sir Ernest, not at all surprised at the King's request. He'd carried out many delicate assignments for this man whom he loved and admired.

'You'll see he's a man of straw from his evidence in the report. We want you to pull the rug from under his feet when you judge it'll cause the most serious effect. We know well how you operate. A word here, a nod there, and a man's a millionaire or in the hands of the bankruptcy court. We want you to take your time. You judge the moment. It can be this year, next year, whenever you think fit. But we want Shackleton brought to his knees.'

'I'll do as you request, sir.'

'Ernest, our gratitude and friendship is yours. We shall dismiss Shackleton from our mind knowing we can trust in your support. Now, since it's too cold to take a turn around the garden, let's have a game of skittles in the bowling alley before lunch.'

The morning's letters lay on a silver tray in the hallway of No. 7, St James's Terrace, Clonskeagh, as Sir Arthur Vicars came down the stairs on Friday 31 January 1908. He picked them up as he passed into the dining room to take breakfast with his stepbrother, Peirce O'Mahony. Mrs Darcy had prepared kedgeree, knowing this mixture of rice and flaked haddock fish was one of Sir Arthur's favourites and hoping to tempt his appetite as he recovered from a bout of bronchitis. Sir Arthur helped himself from the hotplate and sat down to eat and open his mail at the same time. He sorted through the letters and immediately noticed the large envelope bearing the seal of the Viceroy's office. As yet, Sir Arthur hadn't been informed of the findings of the Commission of Inquiry so he pushed his plate aside and quickly slit open the letter with his fish knife thinking it must contain those findings.

Peirce O'Mahony watched him from the other end of the dining table as he read the letter. Suddenly, he slumped in his chair, the letter dropping from his fingers into the plate of kedgeree.

'Good heavens, Arthur, what is it?' asked O'Mahony, alarmed at the grey colour flooding into his stepbrother's face. He pushed back his chair and hurried to him.

'What is it, Arthur?'

'God . . . why? . . . why, God?' mumbled Sir Arthur, beginning to cough violently.

O'Mahony picked up the letter, wiped some grains of rice from it, and read,

> I am directed by the Lord Justices to state that Letters Patent have this day passed the Great Seal of Ireland revoking the Letters Patent constituting you Ulster King of Arms, and appointing a successor to you in that office. I am to inform you that, by direction of Their Excellencies, the Office of Arms will be closed tomorrow (Friday), and I am to request you to arrange, either by attendance at the Office, or otherwise, as may be most convenient to you, to hand over to your successor the keys belonging to the office and the Crown Property in your custody, at 12 o'clock on Saturday next, 1 February.

The letter was signed by Sir James Dougherty.

Even O'Mahony, fighter of causes that he was, realised that the letter was brutally final. The irrevocable decision had been taken. Sir Arthur Vicars had been sacrificed for all the world to see. O'Mahony rang the bell for the footman and told Pitt to bring a glass of brandy immediately. Sir Arthur's teeth were chattering with shock and half the brandy O'Mahony tried to pour into his mouth spilled on to the napkin tucked into his collar. With Pitt supporting one side and O'Mahony the other, Sir Arthur was helped into the drawing room and settled on the sofa. Mrs Darcy, hearing the commotion, came to the door and looked anxiously at her master.

'It's some bad news,' explained O'Mahony. 'Very bad news. Make some strong, sweet tea, Mrs Darcy, will you? That'll help.'

After half an hour a semblance of normal colour had returned to Sir Arthur's cheeks.

'Shall I run for the doctor?' inquired Pitt.

'No. I don't think he'll be needed now,' replied O'Mahony. 'Are you feeling better, Arthur?'

'Thank you, Peirce,' said Sir Arthur weakly. 'I'm so sorry. Very foolish of me. Must have been the shock of that letter from Dougherty.'

'He could have phrased it less brutally, Arthur.'

'No, don't blame him. He's only carrying out his orders. It means the end, you realise. The end of everything.'

'It's not good,' O'Mahony conceded. 'But we can still fight on.'

'What's the point, Peirce? They've appointed my successor. That could only happen in Privy Council and that means the King has approved it. Obviously the inquiry went against me.'

'Don't give up. We can still hurt them.'

Sir Arthur shook his head wearily, his dishevelled hair falling over his high forehead. 'I don't know, Peirce. What can we do now?'

'We can show the world how shabbily you've been treated. At the very least, that's what we can do. You'll see. Have some breakfast now and we'll talk later.'

To Mrs Darcy's dismay, Sir Arthur only picked at the kedgeree. The shock of the letter and the after-effects of bronchitis made him feel less than hungry, but later in the morning, under his stepbrother's jollying influence and another large brandy, he began to revive.

'What we'll do, Arthur, is send this damnable letter to the press with a statement from you appealing for help. That should arouse some sympathy, don't you think?' asked O'Mahony.

The next morning, Saturday 1 February 1908, the Dublin press gave prominent display to the letter from Sir James Dougherty and Sir Arthur's statement.

> As an Irishman by family and birth I appeal to my fellow countrymen to demand for me the right to be judged in public by an impartial tribunal, a right which those now responsible for the government of this country have hitherto denied me.

His appeal drew much sympathy but its effect was muted by the newspapers printing very fully in the same editions the report of the Commission of Inquiry.

That Saturday, the new Ulster King of Arms, Captain Neville Rodwell Wilkinson, late of the Coldstream Guards, son-in-law of the Earl of Pembroke, the largest landlord in Dublin, sat in his office at the Bedford Tower, waiting for Sir Arthur to call on him and hand over the keys to the office. Captain Wilkinson, who knew little of heraldry or genealogy, waited in vain. Sir Arthur Vicars never passed through the gates of Dublin Castle again for the remainder of his life.

The publication of the Commissioners' report brought condemnation from all sections of the press, who saw through its patently obvious conclusions. The press questioned why the report blamed only Sir Arthur and not the police or the military guarding the Bedford Tower and it railed at the Commissioners for not giving any indication who the thief or thieves were.

O'Mahony's final shot in his campaign to embarrass the Government came in a lengthy and outspoken statement which the newspapers printed with barely restrained glee.

> I state deliberately that the Government do not wish to find the thief, because one suspected man and one of his associates, also suspected, are known to the police as men of unclean lives, and have threatened to involve Society in an unsavoury scandal.
>
> And so, in the twentieth century, under the enlightened rule of the most constitutional monarch in Europe, an official of hitherto unblemished character is to be dismissed and ruined and denied an opportunity of meeting his accusers in the open – a right accorded to the meanest criminal – because a few titled members of what are called so falsely the 'Upper Ten' and who circle round the throne, possess characters so absolutely rotten and degraded that they fear to face the threats of two men whom the Rt Hon. A. Birrell has described as 'abandoned ruffians'. My brother's honour is of no account to them – titled corruption must be shielded from the public gaze. Not thus, however, can they stem the fetid tide.

With that last devastating attack, Peirce O'Mahony retired from the immediate fray, leaving the Government to stonewall an avalanche of pointed questions in the House of Commons.

Sir Arthur Vicars sold his beloved books and book-plates at Sotheby's auction rooms, raising less than £800, and in May 1908 retired, a broken man, to live on O'Mahony's charity at the family home, Grange Con, in Co. Wicklow.

'Do you think we're safe now, Frank?' asked Richard Gorges,

trailing a finger down his friend's neck as they lay in bed together.

'I should think so. There hasn't been a question in Parliament for months now. I think it's all dead and forgotten,' replied Shackleton, smiling up at Gorges.

'At one time, I must confess, I thought we were really in for it, you know,' said Gorges.

'Yes. It wasn't very pleasant, was it? Both of us kicked out of Ireland. . . .'

'Actually, Frank, my commanding officer wasn't too bad about it. No damned histrionics anyway. Very correct and polite. Mind you, I'd half expected it for some time.'

'Well, I didn't. It was the shock of that swine Harrel that really unnerved me. I can tell you I almost cried like a baby. And when he mentioned Daisy Newman. . . .'

'Yes. I'm sorry about that. If I'd stayed away from her as you said they would never have traced her. I'm glad she got away in time.'

'It was pretty traumatic at the time.'

'Now, now, dear Frank,' murmured Gorges, bending over to kiss his cheek. 'It's all over and done with. Don't think about it.'

'It's hard to forget, but at least the inquiry cleared me. That's the main thing as far as my family is concerned. As far as they know I'm innocent and that's that.'

'All the rumours have stopped?'

'Well, I don't seem to be welcome at Elizabeth Ormonde's any more but Ronnie Gower's been a real brick about it.'

Shackleton leaned over the side of the bed to reach the bottle of wine on the bedside table. Gorges looked down at his smooth back and the twin globes of his firm buttocks half-covered by the silk sheet. He felt a stirring of excitement. Their love-making, after so many years together, still held its moments of abandoned, threshing passion. Shackleton turned round, holding the bottle, and smiled affectionately as he saw Gorges's jutting manhood. He leaned over and kissed it.

'You really are amazing, Richard. Do you think you'll ever lose the urge?'

'Not with you,' said Gorges, his hand pushing the smooth sheet from Shackleton's body. He bent and kissed his firm belly.

'Have a glass first,' Shackleton whispered, holding back his excitement with great difficulty. 'It prolongs it so deliciously.'

Gorges laughed, grasping his friend gently, 'You don't need to prolong that, do you, Frank?'

The two men sipped their champagne, Gorges kneeling up on the bed.

'Isn't it marvellous, Frank, to be financially independent? My investments are bringing me £700 a year and I've hardly touched the capital. If this is public disgrace, give me more of it.'

'Well, it hasn't harmed me either,' said Shackleton. 'At least I've got the new automobile and the new address.'

'Yes. Park Lane was hard to beat but you've managed it with Palace Court. Great style and you've furnished it beautifully.'

'Surprising how much credit you can get as the brother of Shackleton of the Antarctic.'

'You're not going in over your head?' asked Gorges anxiously. 'Remember you got out of Ireland just in front of the writs.'

Shackleton laughed. 'Yes. Harrel did me a favour on that score. No, don't worry. I'm well fixed. Soon the Mexican deal will come to fruition and the last of my worries will be gone.'

'Let's drink to that!'

'I thought we were drinking to something else,' smiled Shackleton, turning to put his glass on the bedside table.

'That too,' said Gorges, his hands beginning to move over his friend's body.

Through 1908 and 1909 life was good for Frank Shackleton and Richard Gorges. Shackleton lived comfortably at 29, Palace Court, London, W., and Gorges, when he wasn't staying with his friend, maintained a set of rooms in Knightsbridge, a convenient base for entertaining young, impressionable guardsmen. Together they visited, at least once a month, Daisy Newman's new establishment, flourishing in a large house just off The Mount in Ealing in West London, and generally behaved as reasonably well-off men about town.

Shackleton's finances remained balanced on a knife-edge with his overdraft at Cox's Bank now standing at £40,000 but secured with the unimpeachable personal guarantee of Lord Ronald Gower. Shackleton paid for the expedition to go to Mexico to inspect the forest lands on which he held an option and, as he'd predicted, the survey report had been first-class. Mr Frank Alden's stockbroking firm in Throgmorton Street renewed, without hesitation, their agreement to underwrite the shares of the company when they were offered to the public. Shackleton estimated he would need to raise £1,000,000 to fully exploit the vast timber concessions.

Gradually, any doubts entertained about him by his former friends in London society began to fade. They vanished finally when Ernest Shackleton's expedition ship *Nimrod* returned to England in the autumn of 1909. Frank Shackleton was on the crowded platform of Charing Cross Station to greet his brother when he returned to London, the new hero of the British Empire. The Shackleton expedition had reached the magnetic South Pole for the first time but Ernest, with two companions, had failed by only a few miles to reach the true geographic Pole. However, their trek of 117 days across the Antarctic, pulling their own sledges with rations for only 99 days, rightly captured the imagination of the whole world.

A fortnight after his return Ernest Shackleton was knighted by King Edward VII in the great ballroom of Buckingham Palace. Frank Shackleton tactfully declined his brother's invitation to accompany him to the Palace, reckoning discretion was the better part of valour. He had every reason to believe that the King's wrath had subsided during the two years but thought it wiser not to remind the Royal Household of his continuing presence in society.

As 1909 drew to a close Shackleton was invited to spend Christmas and New Year at Hammerfield, in Sussex, with Lord Ronald Gower and Frank Hird. The other guest was Miss Mary Josephine Browne, a wealthy lady in her sixties, an old friend of Hird's family. Shackleton had been often in the past to her home – Osborne Villa in Tavistock, Devonshire – when he'd visited his brother while he was fitting out his Antarctic expedition in the West Country. It was a happy Christmas amongst friends for Shackleton with, as always, a little business to spice the proceedings.

One evening, as the four friends sat by the roaring fire in the main drawing room of the splendid country house, Miss Browne raised the subject of money.

'I hear you're so clever about finance, Frank, that I wonder if I can ask your advice?'

'Of course, Mary.'

'I don't think he'll be interested in any small amount,' interrupted Frank Hird. 'Our Frank is after bigger game in Mexico, aren't you, Shackleton?'

'Anything I can do to help, Mary, I shall,' said Shackleton, ignoring the interruption.

'You see, I lent an old friend of mine, Charlie Drewitt, some money – £1,000 to be precise – to help him start a farm in Canada. Now he's died – God rest his soul – and his executors are repaying the loan from his insurance policies. I really don't know what to do with it.'

'Whenever you get it,' said Shackleton with a confident smile, 'let me have it. I'll invest it for you in something that'll give you a good return. Don't, on any account, go lending it out again.'

Two months later, Miss Browne sent a cheque for £1,000 to Shackleton and later he told her he'd invested it in the Celtic Investment Trust which was financing the Mexican venture.

'If you've got any more spare cash, Mary, I'd advise you to put it into this undertaking,' he told her on 24 April 1910, when he visited her in Tavistock. 'It can't lose, believe me.'

Miss Browne, trusting her close friend, sold shares worth more than £11,000 and passed the money over to Shackleton. All that remained of her modest fortune was a little capital and 100 shares in the Tavistock Conservative Club.

The money came in the nick of time for Shackleton. Although he had told Miss Browne he'd invested the money in the Celtic Trust he, in fact, put it straight into his own bank account. His guaranteed overdraft of £40,000 was drawn to the limit and his further overspending had been secured with another 60,000 shares in the Montevideo Public Works Corporation, a stock whose value had decreased over the years. Miss Browne's £12,000 reduced his overdraft and to help it even further he sold 5,000 of the virtually worthless Montevideo shares to Lord Ronald Gower for more than £5,000. Frank Hird worried about this transaction when he heard of it.

'Are you sure this Montevideo thing is safe, Frank?' he asked.

'Safe as houses, my dear friend,' replied Shackleton airily. 'Booming continent, South America. You just wait and see the returns. Anyway you don't think I'd put Ronnie into something shaky, do you?'

'Of course not,' said Hird soothingly. 'But remember you've got power of attorney now over all his finances. You've got to be careful.'

'I know. Frankly I wish I wasn't saddled with the responsibility. If Ronnie's financial man, Culverwell, hadn't died so inopportunely I wouldn't have got involved. But someone's got to help Ronnie. You know well enough, he's got no head for business.'

'That's true, Frank,' said Hird. 'But I just wonder if you've got too much to worry about, what with all your own enterprises.'

'We'll cope. Don't be alarmed.'

'Of course. Please don't think I was carping at you.' said Hird apologetically. 'I'm sure you'll do your best.'

Shackleton, indeed, was doing his very best to juggle the monies at his disposal, out of one account and into another, trying to keep all his financial balls in the air at the same time.

To those in the City, who took a keen interest in such affairs, Shackleton's plight was becoming well known. Until his Mexican deal was finalised and he could raise public capital, they knew he was walking a financial tightrope.

Sir Ernest Cassel, with his tentacles spread throughout the financial world, was acquainted intimately with Shackleton's problems. Long ago he had assigned a man to watch him, remembering his pledge to King Edward two years before. The King had never mentioned Shackleton to Sir Ernest since that conversation at Sandringham House, trusting his friend implicitly to carry out his wishes.

In fact, His Majesty was never to witness the final results of his royal displeasure. On 6 May 1910 he died at Buckingham Palace, four days after catching bronchitis at his beloved home in Norfolk. Fittingly, for a man who so loved the good life, the last words he heard brought him the news that his horse, Witch of Air, had won at the Kempton Park races.

His death sent shock waves through the capitals of the world. 'Teddy the Peacemaker' was dead. Would anything be the same again? Could his son, George, exert the same influence over the fractious monarchs of Europe, binding them together in an uneasy peace? These were the questions asked in the immediate mourning of his death. Financial men became jittery and began selling shares and buying gold against any eventuality. Shaky companies, like the Montevideo Public Works Corporation, were bound to suffer. Two days after King Edward's death a nervous creditor won judgment against that company for £5,000. For two months the directors of the company strove to raise the money to satisfy the demands of an ever-increasing list of creditors, all panicking together, but on 6 July 1910 they had to admit defeat. The company went into liquidation with debts totalling more than £940,000. All Shackleton's shares pledged to Cox's Bank and sold to Lord Ronald Gower were worth only the paper they were printed on.

It was now Sir Ernest Cassel made his move with a telephone call to the stockbroker Frank Alden.

'Sir Ernest,' said Alden, overwhelmed with a personal call from the great financier. 'What can I do for you?'

'How is business, Mr Alden?'

'Troublesome, Sir Ernest. The confidence has vanished from the country. Everyone wants to sell, not buy.'

'A temporary phase, Mr Alden. A natural reaction to the passing of a great king.'

'I agree, Sir Ernest. How can I help you?'

'I've been watching your firm for some time, Mr Alden, and I like the way you do business.'

'Thank you for saying so, Sir Ernest. We aim to serve.'

'I'm thinking of putting some of my business your way, if you think you can handle it.'

'Sir Ernest, of course.' Frank Alden was overjoyed. To handle part of the Cassel account would make him the envy of every stockbroker in the world.

'There's just one thing. I hear you're thinking of handling the public float of a company called North Mexico Land and Timber.'

'That's correct. Your information is impeccable, as always, Sir Ernest.'

'Well, my opinion is that it's a very speculative enterprise. I wouldn't want my stockbroker lending his name to it.'

Frank Alden was nonplussed as to why Sir Ernest Cassel should single out Shackleton's promising company for his disfavour. But, businessman that he was, he took the point directly.

'Nothing's been finalised yet, sir. I can always pull out and let them find another underwriter.'

'Good man. And now about those investments. Perhaps we could have luncheon next week and discuss the matter.'

'Of course, Sir Ernest. I look forward to being of service.'

Sir Ernest Cassel replaced his telephone with a grim smile. He'd fulfilled his last duty to his dead sovereign.

Alden wrote immediately to Shackleton: 'Owing to a variety of circumstances, of which the death of our beloved King Edward is by no means the least, I regret to inform you that this firm no longer feels able to underwrite the public flotation of North Mexico Land and Timber Company.'

The letter dealt a mortal blow to Shackleton's business enterprises. Cox's Bank was pressing for its money, and now part of its overdraft security had collapsed; Lord Ronald Gower was anxiously trying to contact him about his own and Miss Browne's investments; and finally Alden had deserted him.

Shackleton sat in the palatial comfort of 29, Palace Court, biting his knuckles, not knowing which way to turn. In fact, there was no way out.

On 6 August 1910 Shackleton was called to a meeting of creditors in an office at the Bankruptcy Court. His debts amounted to £84,442. He was finished and he knew it. But he asked for, and received, a postponement of his public examination of bankruptcy until 4 May 1911, because he said he was to enter hospital for an operation.

'Is that true?' asked Gorges the next evening, as they sat together in the drawing room of Daisy Newman's establishment.

'No, of course not, Richard,' said Shackleton impatiently, the strain of the past months beginning to show. 'I had to have some excuse to play for time.'

'What are you going to do now, then, Frank?' asked Daisy Newman.

'There's only one thing I can do. Run for it.'

'But all your money is tied up, surely?' said Gorges. 'It's all frozen in the bank, isn't it? You won't get far in this country.'

'Of course I haven't got any money to draw on. It'll have to be abroad and it'll have to be with your help, my friends,' said Shackleton firmly.

'I don't want to get involved again, Frank,' said Daisy, getting out of her chair and walking to a trolley carrying bottles of drink. 'I've changed since I came to London three years ago. I'm not a Dublin slut any more. I've got a good business.' She paused. 'And besides there's another reason I'll tell you about later.'

Shackleton looked at her as she poured out two brandies and some wine for herself. You certainly have changed, he thought. Daisy's auburn hair was now coiffeured in the latest style, no longer hanging loose, and her pink French chiffon gown with puffed sleeves and roses at the bodice was almost demure.

'I'm getting too old for this kind of life,' she continued. 'I'm going to hand over to Millicent and John if they want it.'

'You're not too old, Daisy,' protested Gorges. 'Bloom of youth and all that.'

She smiled at him. 'Thank you, dear Captain, if I can still call you that, but a mirror is a better judge of that rather than an out-and-out lecher like you.'

'So what are you going to do, Daisy?' asked Shackleton.

She sipped her glass of hock reflectively for a moment. 'I wasn't going to tell you until the evening was over . . . tonight is my last entertainment. I've decided to get married.'

'What?' chorussed the two men.

'Don't look so surprised,' pouted Daisy. 'I'm going to marry someone who's been after me for a long time.'

'And pray, who is this noble fellow?' inquired Gorges sarcastically.

'A locksmith from Dublin called Frank Robinson.'

'Not the locksmith? Our locksmith?'

'Yes. Your locksmith. With the money I've got he's going to open an ironmonger's shop in Ealing. We're going to be respectable tradespeople.'

Shackleton gulped his brandy and held out his glass for another. 'You flabbergast me, Daisy. You really do.'

'My mind's made up, Frank. I've seen what can happen leading your sort of life. You've got the bailiffs in and probably worse, the dear Captain's without a regiment, and I just escaped from Dublin one step in front of the constables. I want to settle down.'

'So you won't help me, Daisy?' said Shackleton, looking downcast.

'I didn't say that. I said I didn't want to get involved. If you simply want some money, you can have it. Would £500 be a help?'

'It would indeed.' Shackleton brightened as he turned to Gorges. 'And you, Richard?'

'Oh, well, put me down for £500 as well,' he said reluctantly. 'I can't afford much more anyway. My investments have looked pretty sad since the old King died. I've had to eat into my capital.'

'Well, £1,000 should get you away, Frank,' exclaimed Daisy. 'Where will you go?'

'Africa, I guess.'

'Not South Africa, old boy?'

'No, of course not. I'd be picked up pretty quickly there. Thought of trying my luck further up the continent. Somewhere like Portuguese West Africa, perhaps. Pretty civilised lot, the Portuguese. Oldest allies and all that. . . .'

'Not bad, Frank. But why go at all? Face it out. I know you're busted but. . . .'

'I fear when the accountants get to my books,' interrupted Shackleton, 'they'll find one or two little irregularities.'

'Oh, like that?'

'Yes. Like that. It had to be in the last year to keep the ship afloat. It still would be if Frank Alden hadn't pulled out at the last moment. Still can't understand it. He's never been able to give me a proper reason.'

'Well,' said Gorges, rubbing his hands together, 'tonight looks like the farewell performance, what? Our Daisy going into honourable retirement and Frank off to pastures new.'

'Some wine to celebrate, you mean, dear Captain?'

'Exactly, Daisy. And then the entertainment. What have you in mind, if you don't mind me asking. Something new?'

'I call it "A Woman's Revenge". John complains sometimes because Millicent gets carried away and whips him too hard, but I think you'll find it stimulating. Particularly when Millicent forgives him. Do you know, that's one thing I've learned about gentlemen in London. They do like their little bit of flagellation.'

'Probably their public school upbringing,' said Gorges with a quiet, expectant smile.

In November 1910 Shackleton bade farewell to his father, Dr Henry Shackleton, telling him he was going to holiday for the winter with friends on the Continent, and took the train to Paris. There, he caught another train across Europe to Lisbon. He spent a last few days of luxury in the Grand Hotel at Estoril before sailing from the River Tagus in the SS *Vespucci* bound for Benguela in Portuguese West Africa. During the fortnight's voyage he studied Portuguese from a book and took lessons from a friendly steward. By the time he arrived in Benguela, just before Christmas, he had enough command of the language to find his way round the thriving, though still primitive, seaport.

Shackleton's arrival amongst the white community aroused considerable attention, his fine London-tailored clothes and easy manners setting him apart from the rougher colonists who were trying to hack their fortunes from the incredibly rich and fertile country. The life in Benguela was pleasant and relaxed for Shackleton, his limited funds still adequate enough to allow him to join the established settlers in their pursuits of drinking, card-playing, and chasing the more attractive native women, or in Shackleton's case, men. The climate was temperate with the breezes off the Atlantic keeping the stifling tropical heat of the jungle at bay. But by March 1911 Shackleton realised he would have to find work, and one of his new-found friends offered him the job of assistant manager at a banana plantation up country near Hanha. In accepting the offer gratefully, Shackleton saw two advantages; first, the money, and second, the opportunity to move from Benguela where too many people were arriving fresh from Europe. He reasoned that one day someone might come who might know something of his past life.

At first, he found life on the banana plantation hard but interesting as he learned his duties. His drive and obvious intelligence were rewarded within three months by promotion to plantation manager. But gradually the unremitting heat and humidity began to take its toll. Shackleton found little companionship in his new assistant Manuel Garcia and his wife, a stolid unimaginative couple, and the native labourers were unlike the cosmopolitan, easy-going Africans he'd come to know and like at Benguela. He took more and more to the native liquor, fermented from bananas into a gin-like drink, and passed his days in a haze of alcohol and sweating, cloying heat. He stopped shaving every day, didn't bother to change his clothes, and quickly became a gaunt scarecrow of a man suffering successive attacks of fever.

The plantation became a living hell for Shackleton, but where was his escape? He wrote to his father begging for help but, when no reply arrived, assumed that door too was closed to him. In his moments of lucidity, Shackleton traced his downfall and began to nurse a bitterness towards his brother, Ernest. If he hadn't tried to emulate him, he reasoned, he wouldn't have been tempted into his grandiose dream of fortune in Mexico, and if he hadn't pursued that dream then he wouldn't have fallen in with Richard Gorges's plan to steal the Crown Jewels. It was all very clear to a mind twisted with alcohol and sickness. Soon it was set in his self-pitying brain that if it hadn't been for Ernest he could still have been leading the pleasant and rewarding life of Dublin Herald, dabbling in genealogy and enjoying the social whirl amongst Ireland's aristocracy.

But reality was catching up with him. On 21 September 1912 a warrant was issued for his arrest in London on a charge of having fraudulently converted to his own use a cheque to the value of £1,000, the property of Miss Mary Josephine Browne of Osborne Villa, Tavistock.

Detective Inspector Albert Cooper of Scotland Yard was given the task of bringing him to justice and soon learned of his whereabouts from Dr Henry Shackleton. The doctor had decided that the best way to help his errant son was to hand him over to the police so that he could pay whatever penalty was imposed on him and then start a new life.

On 31 October, under the long-standing extradition treaty between Britain and Portugal, Shackleton was arrested at the banana plantation and held in the jail at Hanha. Later he was moved to Benguela to await the arrival of the man from Scotland Yard. On 9 December 1912 Detective Inspector Cooper, his heavy moustache wilting in the heat and his bowler hat sticking to his sweaty forehead, arrived at Benguela prison to claim his man.

'Thank God, you've come,' exclaimed Shackleton, falling on him like a long-lost friend. 'I'll do anything to get out of this place. If I stay here much longer I'll die.'

Shackleton waived all his legal rights to an extradition hearing in Benguela and sailed for Liverpool a fortnight later in the SS *Grandtully*.

In England Shackleton's spirits quickly revived and he pleaded not guilty at the Inner London Sessions on 21 January 1913 to three charges of defrauding Miss Browne of £1,000, and of conspiring to defraud Lord Ronald Gower of £50,000 and Frank Hird of £6,000. The weight of evidence was overwhelming and the verdict of guilty inevitable.

Francis Richard Shackleton, lately Dublin Herald, brother of a hero of the British Empire, pervert and thief, was sent to prison for fifteen months.

As he was taken from the dock to the cells below, he glanced up at the public gallery and saw Richard Gorges. A brief, tight smile passed between them.

12

Gorges: twin deaths – and degradation

Richard Gorges strode down Scrubs Lane in the Hammersmith district of West London on Tuesday 26 August 1913, approaching the forbidding grey bulk of Wormwood Scrubs Prison. From a distance, he could see the narrow, barred windows above the walls, high up in the cell blocks with their dark grey slate roofs. Occasionally he saw a white face pressed against a window as a prisoner looked out on the world denied to him outside the big prison. Gorges, his cuffs a little frayed, his trousers and jacket elbows a little shiny, still presented a tall, immaculate figure compared with the majority of the people waiting outside the prison that fine afternoon. A bell rang inside the prison at two o'clock and an arched side gate in the large doors of the prison opened. The queue of people, most of them women in tattered dresses with small, dirty-faced children in their arms, pressed forward towards a prison warder in his blue uniform as he stepped through the gate.

'Now get back into line,' shouted the warder, pushing the women back as if they were cattle. 'No shoving. If you've got your passes you'll all be allowed in.'

When Gorges's turn came he presented the warder with a small slip of paper, bearing the stamp of the Home Office and the indecipherable scrawl of a civil servant's signature. The warder looked up at him sharply.

'Right, sir. Captain Gorges to see prisoner 100277 Shackleton, eh? Just follow the others to the visiting room, sir. You'll be allowed ten minutes with him.'

The warder smiled ingratiatingly, 'I'm sorry you've had to

wait outside with the rabble, sir. If you come again, Captain, we'll get you through first.'

'Thank you,' said Gorges coldly. He wasn't relishing what lay before him.

'Just ask for Warder Todd, sir. That's me. I'm usually on duty at visiting times. Can't have gentlemen like you mixing with these poor wretches.'

'Thank you again, Todd.'

'Pleasure to be of service, Captain,' said the warder, who'd fancied being a soldier if only he hadn't had flat feet. He snapped his version of a military salute at Gorges as he ducked his head and passed through the small gateway into the prison courtyard.

The visiting room was a babble of noise. In the middle of the room was a wooden and narrow-meshed wire partition stretching from floor to ceiling. The few chairs on the visitors' side were already taken by women. Their children, some sucking their thumbs, looked curiously at the prisoners standing in their faded grey uniforms on the other side of the partition. The mesh was so small that they were able only to crook their little fingers through the wire to touch the hands of their loved ones. Gorges gave his slip of paper to a bored-looking warder who shouted immediately above the hubbub, '100277 Shackleton'.

A door on the prisoner's side of the partition opened and Gorges recognised Frank Shackleton at once as he stepped through it.

'Just ten minutes, sir,' said the warder beside him. 'And don't try to pass anything to the prisoner. Not that you would, of course. As routine, all prisoners are stripped and searched after having visitors.'

Shackleton was pushed into a corner of the partition where it met the brown-painted stone wall.

'Hello, Frank,' said Gorges, thoroughly ill at ease in what he thought were loathsome conditions.

'Richard, how good of you to come.'

Shackleton looked thin, his cheekbones prominent under his white prison pallor. He ran his hand – Gorges noticed it was calloused with dirty, broken nails – through his close-cropped hair.

'Afraid I don't present the best of appearances, do I, Richard?' he said in a quiet voice that hardly carried over the noise of the room.

'You look fine, Frank. Just fine,' said Gorges, pressing close to the partition.

'Thanks for lying, old friend, but I know I look a frightful mess.'

Gorges, in truth, was shocked at his friend's appearance. Prison life had aged him considerably and he now had a slight stoop. But his fine, blue eyes were still the same, gazing through the wire with pleasure at seeing his visitor.

'How are they treating you?'

'I believe the expression is as well as can be expected. I sew mail bags for twelve hours a day but I'm hopeful I might soon get work in the kitchens, such as they are.'

'Anyway, not long now, Frank.'

'Another year, nearly. I'm counting the days. But let's not talk about me. I'll survive. What's happening on the great outside?'

'Well, as you can see, Frank, I'm not in the best of conditions, either.' Gorges held up his frayed cuffs to illustrate his point. 'Most of the money's gone. Blasted investments went totally wrong. I've had to loot the family a bit to keep going.'

'Things will change, Richard.'

'Damn well hope so. While you were gallivanting around Africa I almost ended up in here. Couldn't pay an hotel bill and did a flit, as it were. Bit embarrassing in court when they brought out the service record and all that. Gallant soldier rubbish, you know. Anyway, it got me a conditional discharge.'

'Yes, my father told me he'd read you were in a little trouble.'

'Family still visiting, then?'

'Actually, they've been very good. Ernest, or should I call him Sir Ernest, is raising funds for another trip to the Antarctic. No, they've been pretty decent. Sticking by me when I come out, they say.'

'Got any plans?'

'Well, obviously I'm finished in the City and all that. Father says he knows an accountant in Tunbridge Wells who might take me on as a clerk. Wants me to change my name, though, to save Ernest embarrassment.'

'Will you?'

'Suppose I'll have to . . . anyway, that's enough about me. What are you going to do?'

'Reckon it's time for pastures old but new, Frank. I'm thinking of returning to Ireland. After all, I wasn't barred from the place like you. Trouble brewing up there, the newspapers say. Might find something worthwhile.'

'Trouble brewing up everywhere, father tells me.'

'Yes. It looks like the Kaiser's up to something. No one to hold him in check with King Teddy gone.'

'You could enlist again if there's war.'

'I doubt it. Name's pretty well known now, I fear.'

Shackleton leant against the wire, looking intently at Gorges.

'Do you regret it, Richard? Our friendship and all that? The affair in Dublin?'

'Not at all, old boy. Fun while it lasted, that's how I see it.'

'So do I, funnily enough. Remember those times with Daisy?'

'Do I just, old boy. Do I just.'

'Have you seen her?'

'Thought about it, of course. Even went to Ealing a year or two back. The shop seemed to be doing well. On reflection, I thought it best not to go in. Dragging up the past, what.'

'You were probably right. By the way, father tells me that old Sir Arthur's been in the newspapers again.'

'Yes. Quite a rumpus. Lucky, he was too. Winning a libel action like that. Wish I'd got the money.'

Gorges smiled and continued, 'Trouble would be, Frank, if anyone libelled me they'd be telling the truth, what?'

Shackleton laughed. 'And me, too.'

'A fine pair.'

'I fear so, Richard.'

'Still we had some good times.'

'Yes. We did at that.'

A hand tapped Gorges on the shoulder. It was the bored-looking warder.

'Time's up, Captain.'

'Already?'

'Only ten minutes.'

'Right,' said Gorges turning back to Shackleton. 'Well, I have to be off now, Frank. It's been good seeing you.'

'And you, Richard. Come again.'

'Try to. Dashed hard getting permission though.'

'I know. One visit a month isn't a lot.'

'That's enough, Shackleton,' snapped the warder, standing by Gorges.

'Yes, sir,' said Shackleton, stiffening to attention, fear flicking over his face.

'Keep smiling, old boy,' said Gorges, quietly, as he watched Shackleton turn sharply on his heel and walk stiffly to the door on his side of the partition. It opened and he went through without a backward glance.

'Come along now, sir,' said the warder firmly.

'Right-ho,' said Gorges. 'Glad to leave this depressing place.'

'Most of them are, sir. Doesn't do to spend too long in here. Not a place for a gentleman.'

'He's a gentleman,' replied Gorges, gesturing at the door which had just closed behind Shackleton.

'Not any more, sir. He's a convict now. Just a convict like the rest of them.'

Gorges was glad to breathe fresh air again, ridding his nostrils of the musty, disinfected smell of the prison. He walked away from Wormwood Scrubs feeling very depressed. The sight of his old friend had hurt him deeply. It hadn't been worth it after all, he thought, if you ended up like that. He stepped out along Wood Lane, past the small terraced villas, and headed for the nearest public house. What he needed now were two or three stiff whiskies, he decided. And, he remembered, he'd better buy another bottle before he returned to his meagre lodgings in Notting Hill Gate. He had high hopes of an entertaining evening with that slim young man from the grocery shop who'd promised to call.

Gorges began to whistle to himself as he mingled with the crowds around Hammersmith Broadway. Things could be worse, he decided. At least he wasn't cooped up like poor old Shackleton.

Sir Arthur Vicars hadn't enjoyed the libel action one little bit, although the £5,000 damages he'd been awarded against the *London Mail* had gone some way to ease his embarrassment at the article that gossip sheet had published in its issue of Monday 11 November 1912.

He had hardly settled into his life as the Master of Kilmorna House in Co. Kerry in the west of Ireland, given to him for life by his sister, Mrs Edith de Janase, on the death of George Mahony, when the article had been published asking a series of, to him, highly offensive questions:

> What happened in Dublin Castle the night before the Crown Jewels were stolen? And why was the lady who carried out such an elaborate scheme of revenge against Sir Arthur Vicars allowed to go unpunished?
>
> Further, what led Sir Arthur Vicars to shield this lady, and that at the cost of his post and his honour, and what return did the lady make him for this sacrifice?
>
> And why did those officials, all enjoying the highest posts in the Irish Administration, remain mute through the whole affair, allowing the word 'robbery' to be bruited about and yet all the time knowing that the jewels were never off the Castle premises?
>
> And, as a last query, that wants a great deal of explaining: Why did Lord and Lady Aberdeen display such extraordinary and inhuman vindictiveness against Sir Arthur Vicars when their son, Lord Haddo, did all he could to vindicate the accused man?
>
> Will anyone have the courage to tell the whole truth about this wretched business, revolving as it has round love, jealousy, and a culminating tragedy of fiendish revenge?

The article completely flummoxed Sir Arthur. He could think of nothing that had happened remotely resembling the insinuations that he'd shielded a lady during the period before or after the robbery. On the advice of his stepbrother, Peirce O'Mahony, he issued an immediate writ against the *London Mail* claiming damages for libel, and demanded that the gossip sheet's editor, an egregious journalist called A. Moreton Mandeville, should produce Particulars of Justification setting out his proposed defence against Sir Arthur's claim.

This document, sent on Monday 31 March 1913, was even more bewildering to Sir Arthur than the original article. Mr Mandeville maintained that a woman known as Molly Maloney had been Sir Arthur's mistress and had slept with him at Dublin Castle, obtaining the key to the safe the night before the robbery was discovered.

'It's quite monstrous, Peirce,' exclaimed Sir Arthur when he showed the legal document to his stepbrother. 'This editor fellow even says I spent the night with this woman after playing cards with Shackleton and Lord Ronald Gower. It really is quite fantastic.'

'All the better for you, Arthur. You'll be able to crush them with damages.'

'But what if they bring trumped-up evidence? Since there's no truth in the story, how can I deny it effectively?'

'Don't worry. Engage James Campbell as your counsel and he'll sort it out.'

'Oh, I don't know. It's all so painful. I don't know if I can face a court,' said Sir Arthur gloomily. 'The news of Shackleton's sentence has quite put me against it. He was a rotten swine to me but he was influenced by others. I just can't imagine him in prison.'

'Forget Shackleton. Everything that's happened to him, he brought on his own head. You have to proceed,' urged O'Mahony. 'For your own honour, first of all, and then think of what will happen when you win. You'll get favourable publicity, a jury will have decided in your favour and it'll give us another opportunity to petition for your re-instatement.'

Sir Arthur brightened. 'You're right, Peirce. I hadn't thought of it in those terms. It might just open up the whole affair again.'

But, unhappily for Sir Arthur, it didn't quite happen like that. Although Mr Moreton Mandeville gave every appearance of fighting his claim, he caved in directly the case began to be heard before Mr Justice Darling in the King's Bench Division of the High Court. The newspaper's barrister, Mr Montague Shearman, announced that no attempt would be made to justify any part of the offending article.

Mr James Campbell KC, MP pointed out the fact that the *London Mail* claimed a huge circulation amongst the society that was its prey for gossip. Then he called Sir Arthur, and Lord and Lady Haddo, to give brief evidence that there was not a word of truth in the allegations. It took the jury under ten minutes to decide to award Sir Arthur substantial damages.

Peirce O'Mahony gave a celebration dinner at the Ritz Hotel that evening to cheer his stepbrother out of his despondency over what he regarded as a thoroughly sordid affair.

'Now we can start badgering the Government again,' smiled O'Mahony, raising his glass of champagne. 'Let's have a toast to your vindication and success.'

After a plain though excellent dinner, the two men sat by the water fountain in the hotel's ornate lounge discussing their next moves.

Ten days after the favourable settlement of the libel case Peirce O'Mahony petitioned his old antagonist, the Irish Secretary, Mr Augustine Birrell: 'The verdict of a British jury in favour of my brother, Sir Arthur Vicars, seems to me to present a favourable opportunity of once more appealing to you to reconsider the harsh and unfair treatment meted out to him by the Irish Government. I appeal to you now, even at the eleventh hour, to do some small modicum of justice to my brother, and at least to secure for him that pension which you were willing to give him in 1907.'

This was followed, a fortnight later, by a petition from Sir Arthur to Lord Aberdeen asking him to request King George V to set up a new Commission of Inquiry. This time his petition was forwarded speedily to His Majesty, who was on a shooting and stalking holiday at Balmoral. But, accompanying the petition, was a note pointing out that Mr Birrell opposed a new inquiry.

'Those Irish Crown Jewels again, eh, Arthur?' the King remarked to his private secretary, Lord Stamfordham. 'We remember they gave Papa enough worry during his life. On one occasion he almost bit the carpet with rage over the handling of the damned affair.'

The King, brown-haired, neatly bearded and moustached in a naval style, read the petition and the relevant papers with it on Friday 22 August 1913.

'You know, Arthur,' he said, looking up from his desk, 'we can't help thinking this Vicars chap has had a bit of a raw deal.

He seems to have carried the blame for everything. No blame on the police or anybody else.'

'I think, sir,' replied Lord Stamfordham, 'it was partly his own fault. Remember he refused to appear before the inquiry in 1908.'

'Don't blame the damned fellow,' said the King gruffly. 'Seem to recall that Papa rigged the terms of reference so he didn't have much of a chance anyway.'

'There were other considerations, sir,' said his secretary in an arch tone, disapproving of His Majesty's occasionally down-to-earth manner acquired from his service in the Imperial Navy.

'Yes, we remember, Arthur. From your hoity-toity manner,' the King smiled thinly, 'you obviously think it was right to sacrifice Vicars to save a scandal in the family.'

'His late Majesty acted under the best advice available.'

'The best interests of the family, you mean.'

'Sir.'

'Anyway, Arthur, we've decided we're prepared to give Vicars a chance. It's all so long ago that nobody will bother about any juicy gossip that might arise from the evidence. We think there should be another Commission of Inquiry and this time let's have the witnesses examined under oath.'

'As you command, sir.'

'Yes, let it be. Though we doubt if our wishes will prevail,' the King continued pessimistically. 'The civil servants won't like it a bit.'

King George V knew his Civil Service well. The Home Secretary, Mr Reginald McKenna, after consulting his advisers, replied by pointing out all the details of the intricate legislation needed to set up a new inquiry. He added that this would all take up valuable parliamentary time. Without actually saying so, he made it perfectly plain that Whitehall was opposed to the King's idea. And so it was dropped.

Sir Arthur accepted the verdict with weary resignation.

'I told you so, Peirce,' he said when he received the letter at the end of September 1913, informing him that his petition was disallowed. 'There's no way past those scoundrels at Dublin Castle. They're too afraid of admitting they made a mistake.'

'It was worth a try,' replied O'Mahony. 'Don't give up hope.'

'Hope?' snorted Sir Arthur. 'There's no hope at all. You can't fight a King, even a dead one, along with his civil servants, and win.'

'There'll be other opportunities,' said O'Mahony soothingly, trying to raise his stepbrother's spirits. 'You'll find some way of showing your loyalty, mark my words. They'll realise your worth in the end.'

'Perhaps so, Peirce. Perhaps so,' said Sir Arthur in a disbelieving voice. 'Anyway I shall return to my exile at Kilmorna and get on with my work there. There's plenty to do.'

His old friends were surprised, and not a little dismayed, when Richard Gorges returned to Ireland in January 1914. Peter McEnnery, Derrick Moore, Patrick Walker, all now married with children, were more than a little embarrassed when he called on them at their homes in Dublin. Peirce Mahony was another who believed his youthful debauchery and part in the homosexual orgies at No. 7, St James's Terrace, Clonskeagh, was dead and forgotten. Not that Gorges was tactless enough to refer to the events of the past years in any explicit way. He surveyed their comfortable homes and high positions in Dublin society and compared them with his own highly vulnerable financial situation.

'Bit down on my luck at the moment,' he told Mahony when they met at the Gresham Hotel in Sackville Street. 'All my investments went to pot after King Teddy died. Lost a lot of money too, when poor Frank Shackleton crashed,' he lied with conviction.

'Sorry to hear that, Richard,' said Mahony warily.

'Yes. And that's why I decided to return to Dublin. Thought I'd gather material for some newspaper articles about the circumstances surrounding the theft of the Crown Jewels. Some friends in Fleet Street seem very interested in printing them.'

In fact, Gorges had already tried the newspaper industry, hawking his story up and down Fleet Street, with little success. After the *London Mail* libel action he found all the magazines and newspapers decidedly lukewarm towards printing anything at all about the more scandalous events in 1907. Gorges had told the various journalists he'd met about how the theft arose from a homosexual group, carefully omitting his leading part in it, but had found no response whatsoever. However, this was, naturally, not known to his former friends in Dublin.

The idea of his writing anything caused Mahony great alarm, just as Gorges calculated it would.

'Do you think it's a very good idea, Richard?' gulped Mahony when he heard the proposal. 'I mean to say that's all over and done with.'

'Oh, don't worry, Peirce. No intention of mentioning your name. You've been too good a friend,' said Gorges lightly. 'But a fellow's got to earn a crust, what!'

'You really are on your beam ends?' asked Mahony suspiciously.

'Down to my last tenner, old boy. But don't worry about it. I mean . . . well, it's none of your concern.'

Mahony felt tempted to ask him what he'd done with the proceeds from the robbery, the years that had passed making him even more convinced that Shackleton and Gorges had been the thieves. But he thought that would enrage Gorges, just when he wanted to stay on friendly terms.

'Can I help you in any way?' he said reluctantly, knowing full well he was trapped by his past.

'Well, that's awfully good of you, Peirce. Anything you can do to tide me over would be welcome.'

'How about £200?'

'Oh, my dear chap, that's too generous,' said Gorges, pretending surprise at what he knew would be an inevitable offer. 'That really would help out.'

'You'd still go ahead with your articles?'

'No need to, old boy, with your help. I'm sure some of our other friends might want to help out as well. Frankly,' he said in a confiding manner, nudging Mahony with his elbow, 'never fancied myself as a journalist chappie at all. Not quite the thing, is it?'

Mahony contacted McEnnery, Moore and Walker, who had all attended the parties in Clonskeagh, and soon Richard Gorges had £800 on deposit at the Royal Bank of Ireland in St Stephen's Green. He took rooms in Ballsbridge, only six roads away from Daisy Newman's old residence, and proceeded to live more in the style to which he was accustomed. It wasn't a fortune but it was enough to sustain him for a year or so with his increasingly heavy drinking habits. He amused himself for a while by dabbling in the darkening waters of Irish Nationalism, even suggesting a plan of how the Nationalists could take over Dublin Castle to begin their revolt against the British. Gorges's idea was as bold and sly as his whole raffish approach to life. He thought the Irish should strike on a Bank Holiday when the garrison would be under-manned, with most of the Army officers and senior Government officials away enjoying themselves. But, in 1914, his idea was received with little enthusiasm. The leading Nationalists had heard from Peirce O'Mahony of Gorges's unsavoury background. Two years later Gorges was to permit himself a rare smile when he heard that the eventual Irish revolt began on the Monday of Easter Bank Holiday, just as he'd suggested.

Gorges occasionally met old friends who would entertain him but he studiously avoided moving in any circles that might mean his bumping into any former Army colleagues. Gradually his drinking began to take its toll, his behaviour at dinner parties becoming more and more outrageous as his hosts watched him slur and slurp his way through the evening. Invitations became fewer and fewer and Gorges felt increasingly isolated. His bitterness deepened. His waning sexual needs were now satisfied with casual pick-ups in the sailors' bars along the North Wall in Dublin and with impotent fumblings in dingy hotels. Once, he woke to find his wallet stolen by his long-vanished bed companion.

It was not long before he was noticed by the police, and Assistant Commissioner William Harrel was notified of his presence in Dublin. But Mr Harrel, learning how far down the social ladder Gorges had slipped, decided to leave him in peace. He had bigger fish to catch at this time. As the Unionists in Ulster, under Sir Edward Carson, began arming themselves, so there were increasing rumours of guns being smuggled into the small ports around the southern coast of Ireland. Mr Harrel and his detectives were kept fully occupied trying to snuff out the fuse burning its way to the powder keg that was Ireland in 1914.

Gorges saw Peirce Mahony rarely, usually meeting him by chance in Dublin's shopping centre, but on Thursday 10 July 1914 he telephoned him asking for a meeting that evening at Buswell's Hotel. Mahony agreed reluctantly, fearing the occasion would cost him yet more money. But weightier problems were on Gorges's whisky-sodden brain.

'Who's this fellow lawyer of yours, Peirce, this John Wallace?' asked Gorges, who'd been drinking for most of the day.

'Oh, Wallace. He's a bit of an eccentric.'

'Well, I read in *The Times* that he's trying to take out a warrant for the arrest of the Viceroy and Sir John Ross for conspiring to steal the Crown Jewels.'

'That's right. He was on that particular hobby horse while you were away in England, Richard,' said Mahony, relieved that Gorges didn't seem to want to touch him for more money.

'What's his game, then?' Gorges slurred.

'He's pretty harmless. I say, Richard, you've had a bit much, haven't you . . .?'

'None of your damned business. Tell me about Wallace.'

'Don't you remember he tried to take out a writ before charging me with the theft? It never reached court.'

'What would happen if it did, old boy?' demanded Gorges, his blood-shot eyes peering at his square-faced, firm-jawed companion.

'Then I'd imagine there'd be a fair amount of mud-slinging. Wallace is a jaunty little fellow, quite nice, but he's under the impression that it's his life's work to champion the cause of poor old Sir Arthur. He reckons he can open up the affair again if he can get it into court.'

The news worried Gorges. He ordered another large Jameson whisky and took a mouthful. He sat silently for a moment, feeling the alcohol burn its way down his throat and into his empty stomach. Mahony looked at him sadly, remembering the Gorges of seven and eight years before, thinking against his will of the sight and feel then of his slim and hard naked body.

'I wouldn't worry about it, Richard,' he said soothingly, realising how agitated Gorges was. 'It'll never come to anything.'

'That's not the point, Peirce,' said his companion truculently. 'The point is what would happen if this mad lawyer does succeed in getting it to court. For instance, would you give evidence?'

'Suppose I'd have to.'

'And what would you say?' Gorges demanded aggressively, stabbing his finger at Mahony.

'Depends on what I was asked.'

'You're evading the issue. Would you drag Shackleton and me into it?'

'Why should I?'

'No reason, but would you?'

'Well, if I was asked I suppose I'd have to say you were around at the time.'

'Nothing more?' asked Gorges suspiciously.

'Really, Richard, you're becoming a bit of a bore over this. Why should I say anything more?'

'Just wanted to know. I've seen what happened to dear old Shackleton. He thought he had friends as well and then they turned against him.'

'Frank cheated in business,' said Mahony flatly.

'They all do. They all do. Why pick on poor old Frank? I reckon someone's got it in for Frank and me. . . .'

'You can't be serious?'

'I bloody well am serious.' Gorges voice rose with excitement and drink. Other people in the hotel's lounge began taking notice.

'Hush, Richard. Keep it down,' urged Mahony, colouring with embarrassment.

'Keep it down? That's just what I intend to do. I'll not let this Wallace fellow drag it all up again. Suffered enough already – and that's the bloody truth.'

A tail-coated waiter hovered by Mahony's chair and coughed discreetly.

'Excuse me, sir. I wonder if your friend would mind moderating his language. One or two guests are. . . .'

'Of course. He's a little excited, that's all.'

'Thank you, sir. Sorry to intrude.'

The waiter left and Mahony turned to Gorges. 'I think we'd better go, Richard. There's nothing more to discuss.'

'But I want another drink. . . .'

'I think you've had enough. Anyway, I'm leaving. I promised my wife I'd be in for dinner.'

'Wife, eh?' Gorges laughed thickly, cynically, fumbling in his jacket for a cheroot. 'Remember the times when the last thing you wanted was. . . .'

'Richard! That's enough,' Mahony interrupted sharply.

Gorges stared wildly round the lounge and realised everyone was looking at him. He pulled himself out of his chair with some difficulty and stood swaying for a moment. He peered with half-glazed eyes down at Mahony sitting elegantly with one leg crossed over the other.

'Yes, that's enough, Peirce, as you say. As you say,' he repeated, 'but if I thought you'd help this Wallace fellow. . . .'

He left the sentence unfinished but the ugly expression on his face left Mahony with little doubt about the threat behind his words.

'Don't be so silly, Richard.' He rose from his chair, leaving his half-filled glass on the table, put his hand under Gorges's elbow and guided the taller, heavier man from the lounge.

Outside on the pavement, Gorges muttered again, 'If I thought for one moment, Peirce. . . .'

'Don't think, Richard. Just go home and sleep it off,' said Mahony coldly, determined this was to be his last meeting with the addled, debauched figure from his past.

'Just you remember, Peirce,' Gorges called over his shoulder as he swayed towards a waiting cab. 'Just remember, I'm not bluffing.'

The next morning Gorges awoke with a monstrous hangover but still with the belief in his fuddled mind that the action by John Wallace was a danger to him, as was any possible involvement in the case by Peirce Mahony. The conviction increased over the next fortnight as Gorges tried to drown his unfounded fears in a series of fierce drinking bouts. By Friday 25 July 1914 he was certain he would have to take positive action to stamp out this threat of exposure. His plan was simple. He was going to inform Mahony that if he gave evidence in any case about the Jewels, then his wife would be acquainted with his homosexual habits. That, decided Gorges, was enough of a threat to shut Mahony's mouth.

On the afternoon of that Friday he telephoned Mahony's office in Dublin, only to be told by his legal clerk that Mahony had gone to his father's estate in Co. Wicklow for the weekend. Gorges thought on the matter, drinking almost a whole bottle of whisky in the process, and, with the impatience typical of the alcoholic, resolved to deliver his blackmailing threat as soon as possible. The next morning he boarded a train and headed south into the magnificent countryside beyond the Wicklow Mountains.

The reason for Peirce O'Mahony summoning his son to the family estate at Grange Con was not one of paternal love. There was a coolness between father and son still existing from the days when Peirce Gun Mahony had accepted the job of Cork Herald. But now The O'Mahony of Kerry was a worried man. During the weekend he planned to give his son the benefit of his shrewd far-sightedness by forecasting a European war in the near future, coupled with Civil War in Ireland. Peirce O'Mahony, as a respected Nationalist, knew of plans to land guns and ammunition at Howth, just north of Dublin, on the Sunday of that weekend, and he feared that, at any moment, the powder keg of political discontent would explode throughout Ireland. Such events as he foresaw would affect his family's fortune, so O'Mahony thought it only his duty to instruct his son and heir on the intricacies of the family's business affairs. He had already made as many provisions as he could to protect the fortune, but he knew himself to be in a vulnerable position as a well-known Nationalist. In the event of his death, the new O'Mahony of Kerry must be able to carry on. Through Friday night and Saturday morning he instructed his son what to do. Peirce Mahony thought his father was being alarmist and was glad of a chance to escape when some neighbours invited him to tea on the afternoon of Saturday 26 July 1914. He planned to row across his father's lake at Grange Con to the neighbouring estate, shooting a few wildfowl on the way.

Richard Gorges arrived at Grange Con, a weary, hot and drunken man. He'd been unable to find anyone to drive him from the station, and his temper had increased during the long, dusty walk, punctuated by frequent stops for refreshments from one of the two hip flasks he was carrying.

By chance, he was half-way up the drive of the estate, leading to the fine house with its wide terraces and ornamental gardens, when he saw Peirce Mahony walking across his path, a hundred yards away, carrying what appeared from that distance to be a shotgun. Gorges changed direction to follow him and caught up with him about twenty yards from the boathouse, sheltering under a weeping willow tree on the lakeside.

'Peirce,' he called as he approached, 'Peirce, wait a minute.'

Mahony turned and stared in amazement at the dishevelled figure of Gorges. Even from a distance, he could smell the whisky fumes.

'Good Lord, Richard, what on earth are you doing here?'

'Must talk to you,' said Gorges, approaching Mahony and gripping him just above the elbow of his left arm. The smell of stale whisky forced Mahony to turn his head away.

'Richard, you're absolutely soused.'

'Had one or two on the train, old boy. That's all.'

'More than one or two, I'd wager. Anyway, what do you mean by barging on to my father's estate like this?'

The two men had reached a low barbed wire fence surrounding the boat house. Just beyond the wire was the rowing boat which Mahony intended to use for his trip across the lake.

'Had to see you, Peirce, about this Wallace business. Been on my mind ever since we met.'

'Not that again, surely? You didn't come all the way down here just for that?' said Mahony, annoyed sarcasm in his voice.

'Don't take that attitude, old boy, or it could be the worse for you,' snapped Gorges.

'And what do you mean by that? More of your drunken threats. . . .'

'Drunken, maybe, if you're such a cad to say so.' Gorges swayed slightly as he reached inside his tweed jacket and pulled out a letter. 'But no threats this time, Peirce,' he sneered. 'Take a look at this letter.'

He waved the envelope in Mahony's face.

'Good God. It's addressed to my wife.'

'That's so right, my friend. And inside it is the pretty tale of Peirce Mahony – lawyer, respected citizen, fond father, and homosexual. It's all here. The truth about you, old boy. Pure and simple.'

Mahony tried to snatch the letter but Gorges pulled it out of reach.

'What do you mean to do with it, you swine?' shouted Mahony.

'Nothing, old boy, if you do what you're told. If you promise not to give evidence for this Wallace fellow.'

'That's blackmail, you drunken imbecile!'

'Call it what you like, old boy. Won't do you any good.'

'You unspeakable swine. Give it here,' cried Mahony, lunging at Gorges. The two men closed and struggled together. Then Gorges, the stronger even in drink, broke free and shoved Mahoney backwards. The younger man slipped on the damp grass by the lakeside, the back of his knees hit the barbed wire, and he began toppling backwards. As he fell, he grabbed wildly for any support. His right hand closed round the barrels of his shotgun, leaning against the fence, and he dragged it with him as he went backwards. Gorges saw what was happening, as if it was in slow motion, but he was powerless to prevent it. The shotgun, its twin barrels pointing directly at Mahony, dragged over the fence. A loose strand of wire caught in the triggers and the gun exploded. The two cartridges caught Mahony squarely in the chest, hurling him backwards, an expression of disbelief on his face, into the rowing boat. He seemed to crouch for a moment, clutching at his shattered chest, his expression changing to one of fierce agony as his eyes began to cloud over, and, with a low, gasping moan, he fell sideways out of the boat face downwards into the shallow water of the lake. His legs twitched and then he was still, his blood beginning to colour the muddy water around him.

Even in his befuddled, shocked state, Gorges knew from his experience that no one could possibly survive the impact of a twin charge of shot at such close range. He gazed quickly around to see if anyone had been alerted by the shots, stuffed the letter in his pocket, glanced for a last time at Peirce Mahony, a widening, reddening stain around him, and hurried off along the lakeside.

As he left Grange Con, he debated with himself for a moment whether he should get help for his former friend but quickly dismissed the thought from his mind. He knew there was nothing anyone could usefully do for Peirce Mahony except bury him. If he stayed, he knew there would be questions and suspicions that the accident had been more than simply that. An unfortunate, terrible accident. He felt sorry, in a maudlin way, for Mahony but he decided there was little point in sticking his own neck out. His slight twinges of conscience were eased by sips from his hip flasks as he tramped down the lanes towards the railway station and the train back to Dublin.

Peirce Mahony was not missed that afternoon or even that night. It was only when he failed to appear for breakfast by eleven o'clock on Sunday morning that a maid was sent to his room, only to discover his bed had not been slept on. A call to the neighbouring estate established he hadn't arrived for tea the day before and O'Mahony then ordered a search for his son. It was one of the Bulgarians living on the estate who found the body. The blood had been washed away by the ebb and flow of the lake and, at first, he thought that Mahony had drowned in some way. Only a closer examination found the gaping wounds in the dead man's chest.

The newspapers devoted few column inches to Peirce Mahony's death. On Monday 28 July 1914 they were filled with accounts of the successful gun-running operation at Howth and a later riot in Dublin in which three people were killed by Scottish troops. The newspapers were demanding a scapegoat and, as usual, one was served up to them. The choice fell on Assistant Commissioner William Harrel, who was dismissed from the Dublin Police for incompetent handling of the riot in Bachelor's Walk.

The inquest on Peirce Mahony decided his death was accidental, the jury presuming he'd got his shotgun tangled in the barbed wire as he stepped into the rowing boat. The fact was totally ignored that Mahony was an experienced hunter who would have had to break the habit of a lifetime ever to step over any fence with a shotgun pointing towards himself.

Richard Gorges read the inquest verdict in a Dublin evening newspaper and smiled wryly to himself. The jury, he knew, had found the right verdict but for the wrong reasons. He toyed with the idea of sending a wreath to Peirce Mahony's funeral but decided against it. It would be tempting the fates, he reckoned.

Five weeks later, England and Germany were at war, providing Gorges with just the escape route he needed. He travelled to London and, in the confusion of the urgent recruiting campaign that was in progress, was accepted without question. On Friday 5 September 1914 he was commissioned as a Captain in the London Rifle Regiment. He was back in uniform again. But by now this once hard-drinking professional soldier was a chronic alcoholic. At first, he succeeded in disguising his drinking habits by his vast military experience, but soon it became clear he was of little use to the Army. One night in the mess in January 1915 he fell into a drunken sleep before the Loyal Toast was proposed. After only four months, he was allowed to resign his commission by an understanding colonel. For the third time in his life, Richard Gorges had been rejected as unfit to serve his Sovereign.

He rented rooms in a house in Hampstead, telling his landlord that he'd been invalided out of the Army after being gassed in the trenches in Belgium. Inwardly, he was gnawed with bitterness and frustration as he read the war dispatches in the newspapers. Soldiering was his life and now he was denied a part in the biggest war so far in history. His drinking dulled the edges of his disappointment but it couldn't ease it altogether.

Gorges was a pitiable figure as he lived out his lie amidst the prevailing atmosphere of war-fever and overwhelming patriotism. In his drunken self-delusion, he took to secretly carrying a .32 revolver in his back pocket, the feel of it reminding him of his military past, his gallantry in the Boer War. The public houses of Hampstead came to know well his stories of past glories and most felt sorry for him, keeping his whisky glass well filled. His military bearing and bleary good looks still impressed young men of similar sexual tastes and many were happy to be seduced by him.

But, finally, it was the relics of his military life that were to be his undoing. One day in July 1915 his landlord discovered his service revolver and nearly 200 rounds of ammunition in his rooms and informed the police. On Wednesday 14 July 1915 two detectives from the local police station, armed with a warrant, entered his rooms while Gorges was out drinking.

They found the revolver and ammunition, which Gorges had purloined from one of his regiments and held without any proper firearms licence. The detectives left after an hour, telling the landlord they would return later.

Gorges returned home in the early evening after his drinking bout accompanied by a young acolyte who worked in a local menswear shop. Their hasty embraces led them into Gorges's bedroom and into bed where the elder man was well satisfied with the youngster's lithe, squirming body. When his friend left after two hours to return home to his parents, Gorges searched his rooms to find some whisky, only to discover his gun and ammunition were missing.

He rushed downstairs to confront his burly landlord, Charles Thorogood, a professional boxer.

'Have you been in my rooms, Thorogood, and removed some of my belongings?' he demanded angrily.

'Not me, Captain. It wasn't me,' insisted Thorogood. 'It must have been the police. They've been here with a warrant. They want to see you.'

Gorges face reddened with fury and alarm. What part of his life were the police investigating? His young men? His lies about his Army service? The Crown Jewels again?

'If any police lay hands on me,' he stormed at Thorogood, 'I'll shoot them dead.'

At a quarter to ten that evening, Detective Sergeant William Askew and Detective Constable Alfred Young returned to the lodgings. Gorges approached them as they entered the hallway, his hands behind his back, obviously concealing something.

'Stay at the door, Young,' ordered the sergeant. 'I'll take him.'

As the detective moved towards him, Gorges produced his .32 revolver from behind his back and aimed it at him. The detective rushed at him and grabbed Gorges's gun hand. The two men struggled, bouncing off the walls of the narrow hallway, the detective trying to wrest the gun from Gorges, banging his hand continually against the wall. Suddenly, the revolver went off, the noise of the shot reverberating around the hall. The shot brought Gorges to his senses and he stopped fighting. The sergeant was just about to speak to him when they both heard a low moan from the doorway. They turned and, to their horror, saw the young detective constable slumping slowly down the door, his hands at his chest covered with pulsing blood. The bullet from Gorges's revolver had hit a vital artery and Detective Constable Young bled to death in the hallway before a doctor could reach him.

Gorges was arrested and taken to Hampstead Police Station to be charged with manslaughter. When the station inspector read out the charge he used his military title.

'Don't call me captain,' cried Gorges, 'for the sake of the regiment.'

He explained to the grim-faced inspector, 'I had no more intention of shooting him than of shooting you. I was in liquor.'

The court proceedings reached an inevitable conclusion. Richard Gorges, sometime brave soldier and pervert, unshaven, hands shaking with alcoholic withdrawal, was found guilty of manslaughter and sentenced to twelve years' hard labour in prison. Gorges, later to serve his sentence on the rock piles of Dartmoor Prison, was sent first to Wormwood Scrubs.

There his belongings were taken from him. He was ordered to take a bath before being examined by the prison doctor and issued with his uniform. As he was drying himself with a small, rough towel, a prison warder strode into the open bath stall.

'Captain Gorges, isn't it?' he asked briskly.

'Yes,' Gorges replied, standing up straight, holding the towel over his genitals. He thought he'd seen the warder somewhere before.

The warder watched the dawning recognition in Gorges's eyes.

'That's correct. You do know me. The name's Warder Todd, remember? I always said ask for me the next time you came here.'

'That's right, Todd,' said Gorges sullenly.

'It's not Todd from now on. It's "sir", isn't it?'

'Yes, sir.'

'Good. And it's not Captain any more, is it? It's Convict Gorges.'

'Yes, sir.'

'That's fine. Just fine. We'll get along famously now,' said Todd, flashing his ingratiating smile again. 'Shot a policeman, didn't we?'

'Yes, sir.'

The smile remained on Todd's face.

'Bastard', he said, in a matter-of-fact voice, and kneed Gorges viciously in his unprotected groin.

13

The executioners

Sir Arthur Vicars loved Kilmorna House unashamedly. It was everything that could be wanted by a man who adored high station in society. Just to the east of Listowel, it stood in 600 acres of the beautiful, rolling countryside of Co. Kerry in the deep west of Ireland. Three lodge houses with pointed roofs stood by the slate- and stone-walled entrances on each side of gravel drives winding through rich, green farmland to three stone archways that led to the great house itself. Kilmorna was built of brick surfaced with smooth Kerry stones and through most of the year green ivy climbed high up its walls. Eight chimneys and a square tower, cut with mock battlements, pointed to a sky ever-changing with the weather scudding off the Atlantic fifteen miles away. On the west side of the house, a walk of lime trees paraded down to the banks of the River Feale, rich with salmon, bending and meandering through the estate. From the granite terraces of the house, the smooth lawns sloped gently down to the river, through shrubberies and flower beds and herbaceous borders, flanked by plantations of beech, oak and yew trees.

It was here in 1917 that Sir Arthur found some happiness after ten years in the wilderness of royal displeasure. He married, to the surprise of many, Miss Gertrude Wright of Kilmurry House, near Castleisland, Co. Kerry, the elder sister of Peirce Mahony's widow. At the age of 53 he found unselfish companionship for perhaps the first time in his adult life.

He knew little of the intricacies of running a great estate, but his manager and workers carried the burden for him, husbanding the rich land and its livestock with such devotion and skill that the estate made handsome profits, allowing Sir Arthur to play the country gentleman to the hilt. In return, he was a good and generous master, paying wages above the average for this backward area of Ireland, giving gifts of food and clothing to his workers at Christmas, organising a huge party for their children every St Stephen's Day, and even getting together a cricket team to play sides from the other great estates in Co. Kerry. The families who had worked for The O'Mahony of Kerry for generations were well satisfied with their new master.

In the community at large, as well, Sir Arthur took every opportunity to play a leading role. He liked to ride round neighbouring farms on his favourite bay horse, Gypsy, a dapper figure in hacking jacket and brown bowler hat, giving advice whether it was needed or not. Once or twice a week he would drive his spanking new automobile the four and a half miles into Listowel to do his personal shopping, invariably accompanied by four of his wife's tiny Yorkshire terriers, their top-knots tied with coloured ribbon. In the small, flat market town, with its mixture of very wide and very narrow streets, he became a leader of the Anglican community, presenting a brass lectern and decorated choir stalls to St John's Church in the middle of Market Square, which helped a little way to match the magnificence of the Roman Catholic Church of St Mary's, a bare thirty yards away in the same square. He became honorary secretary to the Boy Scout Association in Listowel, paying for uniforms and equipment for the poorer youngsters. In fact, Sir Arthur saw himself as Lord Bountiful to the community as a whole. He handed out the produce of Kilmorna's market garden and orchards to needy families, Protestant and Catholic alike. Large crates of fruit and vegetables were sent regularly to the police barracks in Tay Lane in Listowel and to the British troops garrisoned in the town. Sir Arthur always insisted that any meat and poultry sold to Browne's and Murphy's, the butchers, should reach the housewives at fair prices and if he heard of any really sad cases from Doctors Maguire and Dillon, the town's general medical practitioners, then he'd send those families cuts of meat with his compliments.

But there were sadder aspects to his life. The mean fates that befell Frank Shackleton, Richard Gorges, and his nephew Peirce Mahony faded from his consciousness as the years went by, but he remained filled with deep bitterness over what he regarded as the vicious injustice done to himself. He dreamed still of restoring himself in the eyes of Dublin Castle and his King. The bitterness became an obsession, manifesting itself in insomnia. Sir Arthur found he could sleep for only an hour at the most each night. He tried to find better sleep in different rooms at Kilmorna, his staff moving his favourite bedroom furniture from room to room at his whim. To occupy these sleepless night hours he began dabbling in spiritualism, even trying to summon the spirit of his dead nephew in the hope it might throw further light on the theft of the Crown Jewels.

'My dearest Arthur,' Lady Vicars remonstrated with him. 'Aren't you going too far? The servants are very religious, as you know, and they get very worried because they say you talk to the spirits all night.'

'Let them, m'dear,' replied Sir Arthur, hopping from one foot to the other in embarrassment. 'This is my house and I shall do as I wish in it.'

'But can't you forget the past? We have a good life here. Why spoil your health by harking back to the jewels? They're gone, dear, and nothing anyone can do can change that.'

'It's not the jewels,' said Sir Arthur, becoming agitated at what he regarded as his wife's obtuseness. 'A great injustice was done to me and I must find a way to erase it. One day, be sure, I shall be exonerated and regarded again as the loyal servant of His Majesty that I am.'

The stories of his unusual night-time pursuits became common knowledge throughout the area and the more ignorant talked of Sir Arthur trying to summon up 'the divil himself'. Others looked at Kilmorna with eyes more greedy than superstitious after they heard from estate workers that Sir Arthur had installed a strongroom of fire-brick and iron in the great house. In fact, Sir Arthur, with his bitter experience of the unreliability of safes, had built the strongroom to house his wife's jewels, Kilmorna's silver ornaments and valuable books, and some minor family paintings, when he was away from the house. It was natural, though, that wilder stories spread in the countryside amongst those who were, in essence, uneducated peasant farmers.

Could it be, some asked, that Sir Arthur really did steal the Crown Jewels and had now hidden them in Kilmorna's strongroom? Was this the real reason he was disgraced and dismissed by King Edward VII?

But the men who mattered in the west of Ireland at this time were more interested in whether Sir Arthur's strongroom contained guns that could be turned against the British. The spark of revolt ignited by the Easter Rising in Dublin in 1916 had now grown into the flame of open warfare, particularly in Co. Cork and Co. Kerry. Sir Arthur knew many of the local members of the Irish Republican Army, but believed he was above the savage war of ambush and counter-ambush, murder and retaliatory execution, that rended the country around Listowel. Hadn't he even sent a Christmas turkey to Paddy Landers, the genial blacksmith who commanded the IRA's local brigade? He even knew that some of his estate workers were Republican sympathisers if not actual Volunteers. But he still believed that the struggle was of little moment to the Master of Kilmorna. The great house was, after all, the property of the family of The O'Mahony of Kerry, a well-known and ardent Nationalist. And then, of course, Kilmorna provided employment and income, directly or indirectly, for hundreds of local people. It was an integral and important part of the area's economy. For these reasons Sir Arthur believed he was safe. Yet again, he had plunged his head so far into the sand that he failed to notice the shift in the prevailing wind.

On the evening of Friday 30 April 1920, twelve armed Volunteers of the Duagh Company of the IRA set off from their small village. They moved through a mile of sloping fields, splashed through the River Feale, crept through the shrubbery in front of the terrace at Kilmorna House, approaching the porchway made of coloured glass that led to the large, studded wooden front door of the house. They were commanded by Jimmy Costelloe, a thin, wiry man in his early thirties, sharp-featured with a mop of dark hair and a matching complexion.

With the butt of his .38 calibre revolver, he smashed a pane of green glass in the porchway, put his hand through and turned the brass key to open the outer door. The men filed into the porch and began banging on the front door with the butts of their revolvers, rifles and shotguns.

'Open this door,' shouted Costelloe. 'Open the door. This is the IRA.'

After a few minutes of thunderous banging, those still outside on the terrace saw a light go on in the hallway.

'Someone's coming,' they cried to Costelloe, and his men redoubled their hammering on the door.

'Who's there?' asked a muffled voice, querulous in tone, from inside the house. 'What do you want?'

'This is the Duagh Company of the Volunteers,' said Costelloe, calling through the keyhole. 'Open the door and no harm will come to anyone.'

'Who are you, and what do you want at this hour?' cried the voice again from the other side of the door.

One of the Volunteers, Jimmy McDonagh, recognised the voice. 'It's your man himself. Sir Arthur. It's Sir Arthur Vicars there,' he announced to his companions.

'Stop your banging, blast you,' said Costelloe angrily to the man beside him, Paddy MacMahon, who was almost splintering the butt of his shotgun as he hammered it against the metal studs. 'Let's have quiet here.'

When the hubbub in the porch had quietened, Costelloe spoke again: 'Sir Arthur, if that's you there, open the door. No harm will come to you. We just want to talk to you.'

'Who is this? What do you want here?' The question came again, muffled and still querulous, from behind the door.

'I represent the Volunteers, Sir Arthur,' called Costelloe. 'We must talk to you. If you won't let us in, I warn you we'll break the door down.'

For a moment there was silence from inside the house, and then the men in the porch heard the sound of metal bolts being drawn back. The key turned and the door swung open.

Sir Arthur moved back from the open door to the middle of the hallway. He stood there, white-faced but calm, a small figure with unkempt hair and ruffled moustache, wearing a quilted crimson dressing gown that hung below his knees.

The men in the porch fell silent as they saw the Master of Kilmorna before them, alone in the magnificence of the hall, suits of armour and oil paintings round the walls gleaming dully in the light from the gas lamp hanging from the ceiling. The courage vanished from the more timid-hearted as the enormity of what they were doing began to dawn on them. They pressed back into their companions trying to avoid Sir Arthur's eyes.

Sir Arthur broke the silence. 'Well then, what do you want?' he asked in a quiet, firm voice. He heard a rustling noise behind him, turned, and saw two of his manservants in their nightclothes peering nervously over the top of the banisters of the winding oak staircase. 'Go back to bed,' he ordered. 'You are not needed here.'

Jimmy Costelloe, sensing the failing courage of the men around him, stepped into the hall, on to a richly patterned rug covering most of the polished wooden floor.

'We have not come to harm you, sir,' he muttered, and then, realising he wasn't giving a resolute enough impression to his followers, he said more loudly, 'We want the keys to your strongroom.'

'You have the audacity to ask me that,' snapped Sir Arthur, anger replacing fear as he realised what a motley, ill-garbed group faced him. 'Well, I haven't got them with me, so you can go away again before I send for the authorities to deal with you. Get back to your homes.'

His defiant tone nonplussed the raiders. It was the last thing they expected. Some, still in the porchway, shifted nervously and looked over their shoulders, ready to leave.

Costelloe moved further into the hall and pointed his revolver at Sir Arthur's head. 'Do as I say or you're a dead man,' he shouted, furious at the small defiant man for weakening his authority.

'You're nothing but rebel scum,' shouted back Sir Arthur. 'I'll have you shot for this.'

It was an unfortunate remark, only serving to anger the men around Costelloe. 'Come on, boys. Don't let this old fool scare you,' he called to his company. The men pressed through the door to stand around him. They glowered sullenly at the Master of Kilmorna.

'Now, Sir high-and-mighty Vicars, give us the keys.'

'I haven't got them. They are not here.'

'Well, get them quickly if you want to stay alive.'

'I can't,' replied Sir Arthur, his voice faltering as he realised the mood of the Volunteers had become ugly and menacing. 'The keys are with Lady Vicars and she's away in Dublin.'

'You're lying,' said Costelloe. 'You're lying through your teeth. Come on, boys, we'll get the truth out of him.'

He turned to his men and motioned them forward, pushing them into line before Sir Arthur.

'This is your last chance. Unless you give us the keys, you will be shot.'

'I haven't got them I tell you.'

'Right, boys. We'll have a firing squad here. On my command, raise your weapons.'

'I tell you I haven't got the keys,' repeated Sir Arthur, his voice rising in alarm as he looked into the barrels of four revolvers, three rifles, and four shotguns. He saw the men's eyes squinting along the barrels from under the peaks of their cloth caps and realised that they weren't bluffing or play-acting.

'On the count of ten, boys,' said Costelloe, savouring the situation now he was in total command. He noticed Sir Arthur's hands begin to shake as they hung by his sides, the fingers twitching.

'One,' counted Costelloe. 'Two . . . three. . . .'

'I haven't got them. Don't you see that?' pleaded Sir Arthur.

'Four . . . five . . . six. . . .'

Paddy MacMahon lifted his head from the stock of his shotgun and looked quizzically at Costelloe. He'd come, like the others, for guns and loot, not a killing.

'Seven . . . eight. . . .'

'I'll take you to the strong room,' half-sobbed Sir Arthur. 'I'll take you there. Don't shoot.'

Two more men lifted their heads from their guns, their weapons wavering away from Sir Arthur. Bob Stack began lowering his revolver.

'Nine. . . .' And then Costelloe stopped counting. 'You'll take us there?'

'Yes. Yes. Don't shoot. I tell you I haven't got the keys.'

'Right, boys, relax,' ordered Costelloe. 'Maybe the old fool is telling the truth. He's not worth the killing.'

Sir Arthur stumbled back into the banisters of the staircase. His body had tensed rigid expecting the smashing blows of the bullets. Now it relaxed suddenly and, involuntarily, he broke wind.

The men, who, a moment ago, were to be his executioners, guffawed and laughed openly as they saw Sir Arthur's face turning scarlet with embarrassment.

'Jeeze,' roared Costelloe. 'The great squire almost shat himself.'

The hallway echoed with laughter as Costelloe went up to Sir Arthur and clapped him on the shoulder. 'Now don't you worry, Sir Arthur. We won't tell anyone.'

The laughter redoubled as Costelloe turned back to his men, pinching his nose with his thumb and forefinger. 'Don't come any closer boys. The squire here smells like a piggery.'

Tension vanished completely from the hallway. The Volunteers felt almost comradely towards the middle-aged man standing before them in his deep embarrassment. He was just a man after all, not the great master.

'Come on, then' said Costelloe, jabbing his revolver into Sir Arthur's slight pot belly. 'Let's be seeing this grand strongroom of yours.'

'Bring the hammers,' he called to the Sheehy brothers, John and Michael, at the back of the hall. They'd brought sledgehammers in anticipation of having to break down the door of Kilmorna House.

Sir Arthur led the raiders through the dining room and library at the front of the house. They clattered behind, rifle butts clanking on the carpets, until they reached the tower. There, facing them, was a wooden door.

'The strongroom is behind there,' said Sir Arthur pointing at the door.

'Right. Stand aside,' ordered Costelloe. 'We'll soon have that down and then we'll see what you've hidden away.'

'There's nothing much of value there,' replied Sir Arthur.

'Do you hear that, boys?' cried Costelloe. 'He says there's nothing much of value.' Some of the Volunteers laughed.

'What's of not much value to you, Sir Arthur, is priceless to these poor boys. Guns or jewels to buy guns, for instance. Your sort have bled us dry for long enough. You've grown pig rich on our broken backs and blistered hands. But with the help of guns our time is coming, you just see.'

The Sheehy brothers positioned themselves each side of the wooden door and swung their sledgehammers. The oak splintered and cracked under the blows and then the hammers struck metal with loud clangs that shot vibrations up the shafts.

'Jeeze,' shouted Michael Sheehy, dropping his hammer in pain as the vibrations jarred his shoulders.

'What's that metal?' demanded Costelloe.

'It's the real door to the strongroom,' explained Sir Arthur. 'The whole room is made of iron surrounded by brick.'

The Volunteers tore the splintered wood away from the shattered door with their bare hands and saw that he had spoken the truth. The rough cast-iron door with a large keyhole on its right-hand side shone darkly in the half-light of the gas lamp burning on the wall.

'Oh, Holy Mother of God,' exclaimed Costelloe.

'We'll never get through that without powder,' said Michael Sheehy, picking up his sledgehammer.

'Give that here,' exclaimed Costelloe, taking the hammer from him, reluctant to admit defeat and lose face.

He swung the hammer at the keyhole but it merely bounced off, not even denting the door or leaving a mark on it. With the other men, he took turns to batter at the strongroom door for over an hour.

Sir Arthur smiled to himself and then, quickly, set his features again, not wishing to enrage the men around him again.

'What are we going to do?' the Volunteers asked Costelloe.

'What do you fucking suggest?' their sweating leader replied exasperatedly. 'Blow the door open with the squire's farts?'

The men standing on the edge of the group around the strongroom saw the hopelessness of the situation. They turned and began shuffling away.

Costelloe peered at Sir Arthur in the dim light, anger contorting his features. 'You've beaten us this time, you bastard son of the divil.' He pointed his revolver at Sir Arthur's head and clicked back the hammer. 'I've got a mind to pay you out now.'

'No. Not now, Jimmy,' urged Paddy MacMahon. 'Let's leave here. It's been a wasted night's work. Your man's not worth a bullet.'

Costelloe realised his men had had enough. He uncocked his revolver and laughed. 'Well, at least we gave the squire here the fright of his life. Come on then, boys.'

The Volunteers straggled back through the house. Costelloe swung his revolver in frustration at a fine vase of Waterford glass standing on a table in the library, smashing it to the floor in glittering splinters.

Slowly the men wandered out through the porchway. Costelloe was the last to leave. He turned back to Sir Arthur, a forlorn figure standing alone in the hallway.

'We'll meet again,' he said threateningly. 'Yes, we'll certainly meet again, Sir Arthur bloody Vicars. That's if you don't take my warning and leave Ireland now. You know too much now. You've seen us all. Your time is coming unless you go.'

And then the Volunteers had gone into the night as suddenly as they had come. Kilmorna's servants emerged in ones and twos from their rooms about the house and began quietly clearing up the mess. Sir Arthur sat in a padded leather arm, chair in the library and drank a large brandy to restore his nerves.

Lord Askwith caught the eye of the Lord Chancellor sitting on the Woolsack in a packed House of Lords at Westminster on Thursday 6 May 1920, and rose to speak during a debate on the fast-deteriorating situation in Ireland. The assembled peers had heard already of the growing number of murders of members of the Royal Irish Constabulary throughout the country and of the increasing pressure on the garrisons of regular Army units and the irregular force, the Black and Tans, former British soldiers recruited specially to help the hard-pressed security forces.

Now they heard from Lord Askwith about the isolated positions of the great landlords on their estates. He told them that it was not surprising that many were now leaving Ireland, allowing their once flourishing estates to go to rack and ruin.

'But I have a shining example of courage that should encourage them all in their stand,' declaimed Lord Askwith, flourishing a letter above his head. 'This is a letter from Sir Arthur Vicars of Kilmorna House in Co. Kerry. Many of you will remember this noble gentleman as Ulster King of Arms before a terrible wrong was done to him in the affair of the Irish Crown Jewels.'

A murmur of assent ran through the chamber. Lord Askwith continued, 'This letter from Sir Arthur tells better than I could of the terrible lawlessness prevailing in Ireland at this very moment.'

He proceeded to read to the silent chamber Sir Arthur's graphic account of the night raid at Kilmorna.

Perhaps the shock of the occasion had added strength to Sir Arthur's pen because he wrote of how a mob of nearly one hundred, not merely twelve, had broken into the house.

'Shame,' muttered the Peers of the Realm. 'Shocking,' they cried, rustling their order papers. 'Law and order,' they exclaimed as Lord Askwith pressed on through Sir Arthur's letter.

As he finished reading, the House of Lords was in a ferment of outrage. Peer after peer rose to express their admiration for Sir Arthur and their heart-felt wishes for his continued safety.

The shock of the night raid had worsened Sir Arthur's insomnia. Now he was seen rarely about the estate until after two o'clock in the afternoon, having spent the preceding fourteen hours moving from room to room trying to find rest. But he continued to play his part in the community, often visiting Listowel, still a popinjay of a man, as the locals called him behind his back.

'Are you sure you're wise to stay here?' asked Listowel's Church of Ireland vicar, Canon Robert Adderley. 'There's a lot of talk in the town that you'd be better advised to leave and then return when the troubles are over.'

'Nonsense, my dear rector,' said Sir Arthur, as he sipped a glass of sherry with the Canon in the chintzy comfort of the rectory. 'With respect, of course,' he added hastily. 'The rebel curs don't frighten me. The soldiers, thanks to Captain Watson, are almost always on some part of my estate or another. We've also arranged a system of signalling from Kilmorna railway station to Listowel if the rebels have the temerity to call on me again.'

'But, Sir Arthur, that's precisely the point if you don't mind me saying so. Some of your friends here think you're giving the impression of being too close to the military garrison.'

'How can I be too close, as you call it, to the forces of His Majesty?' replied Sir Arthur coldly. 'It is everyone's duty to assist them to stamp out these rebels.'

'Do you not think it would be safer to leave that to the soldiers themselves?'

'I'm afraid you don't understand, rector. I believe it is my duty to help them and I shall continue to do so.'

'You're running a frightful risk, you know.'

Sir Arthur fumbled in his trouser pocket and pulled out a tiny religious statuette hanging from a chain.

'This statue of St Anthony will protect me. I always have it with me. No harm will come to me while I'm carrying it.'

He lowered his voice and spoke confidentially. 'That's what I've been told from the other side, rector. As long as I carry St Anthony I shall be safe.'

Canon Adderley, ever loath to dent any man's beliefs, particularly Sir Arthur's in the power of the Patron Saint of Finding Things, shifted uncomfortably in his chair and said nothing.

'And there's another consideration, rector,' Sir Arthur continued. 'It's in the best interests of the military to protect me.'

'What do you mean by that?'

'Oh, let's just say they appreciate my support,' replied Sir Arthur airily, fingering his moustache with a secretive smile.

Canon Adderley was not the only friend of Sir Arthur Vicars who tried to persuade him to leave Kilmorna. Many tradespeople, rebel sympathisers though they were, liked him despite his busy-body attitude and wanted no harm to come to him.

But, unknown to them all, Sir Arthur was working on a new scheme to win his way back into popularity and high esteem at Dublin Castle. He had explained it to his wife, shortly after the raid on Kilmorna.

'Now the rebels have had the gall to try to take action against me, I've decided to take positive action against them, m'dear,' he told her.

'Why not just forget them, darling?' said Lady Vicars. She simply wanted to care for her husband and her Yorkshire terriers. She'd even built a canine cemetery plot in Kilmorna's grounds where her dogs were buried with proper little headstones. 'The rebels won't interfere with you again if you leave them alone.'

'No. You're wrong, I'm afraid. This is my chance to show them in Dublin that they can't do without Sir Arthur Vicars.'

'Yes, darling,' murmured Lady Vicars, unsure of what her husband was trying to say.

'I've decided to send regular intelligence reports to Dublin Castle,' said Sir Arthur, unveiling his plan in a triumphant tone. 'That'll put me back in regard, you see.'

'Intelligence reports, dear?'

Sir Arthur loved his vague and gentle wife but wondered sometimes at her feminine obtuseness. Men could always grasp the point more quickly, he reckoned.

'You know, dear, intelligence reports . . . news about the activities of the rebels.'

'But how do you know what they're doing?'

'I don't,' said Sir Arthur, testily. 'However, on my travels around the countryside I'll soon find out which farmers are disloyal to the Crown. It'll be a great help to Dublin to know which people are rebel sympathisers, giving them food and shelter and even ammunition.'

'Are you sure it's wise, dear? The rebels won't be pleased if they find out.'

'How can they? Even they haven't access to the Royal Mail, blast them.'

'Now, dear. . . .'

'I'm sorry, m'dear. Upset and all that. But, darling, can't you see this is my great chance? It'll show Dublin my loyalty to His Majesty and when the rebels are beaten – as they surely will be – it'll give me some strong cards to play to get myself re-instated.'

Lady Vicars could see there was little point in arguing with her husband. She knew that whenever he got an idea fixed in his head nothing would shift it. 'If you think it's safe, dear. . . .'

'As safe as Kilmorna itself, m'dear. Don't you worry your pretty head about it. With my help we'll soon have these rebels out of Kerry.'

So, still dreaming of reversing his downfall over the theft of the Crown Jewels, Sir Arthur Vicars began writing to Dublin Castle giving news about rebel sympathisers in the villages surrounding Kilmorna House. And, as he'd anticipated, the intelligence officers at the Castle were grateful for his help.

If the truth be known, Dublin Castle was grateful for any help as the British forces faced an increasingly ugly situation. In the west of Ireland, particularly, there was now almost open warfare. In 1920 the third and sixth battalions of the Kerry Brigade of the IRA, the most active and ruthless units, banded together to form the North Kerry Flying Column. This was a force that lived on the countryside, at permanent war with the security forces, unlike the IRA Volunteers who went about their normal lives until called upon to carry out special assignments.

The Flying Column, numbering no more than thirty young men, set up ambushes for the British troops, took reprisals on the Black and Tans, whose indiscipline and drunken viciousness outraged even those uncommitted in the struggle going on around them, and attacked the police in their barracks. Soon the column became the main target for the security forces. But its members, who saw themselves as the front-line fighters in Ireland's battle for independence, evaded capture because of the support of the numerous close-knit farming communities in Co. Kerry on whom they depended for food, shelter and information.

Sir Arthur continued sending his reports to Dublin but, in the spring of 1921, his activities came under close scrutiny after a chambermaid at Kilmorna cleaned his study one day. In a wastepaper basket she found a torn-up letter bearing the crest of Dublin Castle. She took the pieces of paper to a friend, Tom Halpin, a Volunteer in the Duagh Company of the IRA. He pieced them together and discovered the letter was from

British Army headquarters thanking Sir Arthur for his most recent information about rebel activity around Kilmorna.

'How can we find out what he's telling them?' wondered the commander of the Duagh Company, Jimmy Costelloe, when he saw the letter.

'We could search the mail leaving Kilmorna,' suggested Halpin, a helpful, if not over-bright farm worker.

'And how do we do that, you idjit?' demanded Costelloe.

'Can't we ask May Aherne to open the sacks at Kilmorna railway station and take any letters addressed to Dublin Castle?' said Halpin with a rare flash of inspiration.

'You're right, Tom. That might work. I'll ask her to do it.'

Costelloe talked later that day to the young woman whose job it was to smuggle packets of ammunition, sent to the Volunteers from Dublin, past the Black and Tans guarding the station. She agreed to search the mail and four days later, on 5 April 1921, found a letter from Sir Arthur to Dublin Castle. It confirmed the IRA's suspicions, containing a list of farm buildings in the area that Sir Arthur rightly suspected of being used as overnight stops by the North Kerry Flying Column.

'I'll tell the boys in the column this,' said Costelloe with a grin of self-satisfaction, remembering his own abortive raid on Kilmorna. 'Jeeze, I don't think the boys will be at all pleased with your man. Not at all pleased.'

In fact, Costelloe didn't have the opportunity of passing his information to the Flying Column before it went into action near Kilmorna two days later. On Thursday 7 April 1921 the column received news from Timmie Carroll, the Captain of the Knockamure Company of Volunteers, that ten soldiers had been seen cycling to Kilmorna House that morning, led by Captain J. Biddewell Watson, the commander of the British garrison at Listowel. The soldiers planned to spend a relaxing day with Sir Arthur at Kilmorna House. The column determined to ambush them when they returned to Listowel that evening.

As dusk approached, seven of the Flying Column, ammunition belts slung diagonally over their tattered jackets and waistcoats, hid behind high hedges between two bends on the leafy road between Kilmorna and Listowel. Mick Galvin and Timmie Egan, both in their early twenties, took up positions just past the crown of the first bend and the others – Con Brosnan, Jackie Carroll, Donalin O'Grady, Mick Purtill and Paddy Reidy – spread themselves further along the road towards the second bend.

The section of the Flying Column waited for a little more than thirty minutes before they heard the whirring of approaching cyclists and the laughing banter of the soldiers as they rode back from their pleasant day, eating their fill and flirting with the servant girls at Kilmorna House.

Two soldiers cycled thirty yards in front of the main party and, as they rounded the first bend, Galvin and Egan opened fire with their rifles. The two soldiers fell seriously wounded in the road, their bicycles clattering down on top of their torn bodies. Egan dashed into the road and grabbed one of their .303 Lee-Enfield rifles.

The main party of troops dismounted quickly and advanced round the bend, running and crouching along either side of the hedgerows, firing as they came. The bullets from the troops in their khaki uniforms raked the hedges, sending leaves and twigs flying into the air. The returning bullets from the Flying Column spurted off the road, whining and cracking, as they kicked up splinters of tarmac and gravel.

Mick Galvin, hidden behind a gate post, got a clear shot at Captain Watson as the officer ran across a gap in the hedge on the opposite side of the road. He saw blood spurt from the captain's forehead as he fell forward behind the hedge. Exultantly Galvin stepped from behind his cover, intending to cross the road, grab the captain's revolver, and make certain he was dead. It was a foolhardy move taken in the heat of the short skirmish. Captain Watson had been merely grazed by Galvin's bullet. As the young rebel began to cross the road, the captain took careful aim, resting his revolver on his forearm, and shot him through the heart. Galvin's arms flew up in the air, his cloth cap and his rifle spun away from him as his body half-turned under the impact of the fatal bullet and tumbled back into the hedgerow.

When they saw their comrade killed, the remainder of the column faded away across the fields. The soldiers didn't give chase, more concerned to tend their two seriously wounded comrades and congratulate Captain Watson on his shooting.

They gathered around the crumpled body of Galvin, wondering about his identity, until a rough search of his bloodied and dusty clothes found a letter that bore his name.

The body was taken to the public mortuary established in Listowel Workhouse. The Royal Irish Constabulary rounded up well-known rebel sympathisers and forced them to view the body, hoping its positive identification would lead to Galvin's companions in the flying column. But no one identified the rebel soldier, fearing reprisals against his family or friends, although all knew it was Mick Galvin. Finally Captain Watson realised he would have to give the distasteful order.

'Get Galvin's mother over from Dromberg. Don't tell her what it's for,' he instructed one of his officers. 'Her reaction will tell us whether or not it's this Galvin fellow.'

Mrs Galvin, bewildered by being dragged from her small cottage, thrust into a car by the soldiers, and then driven pell-mell the two miles to Listowel, sensed that it must have something to do with her son, but no one in the military vehicle would answer her anxious questions. She thought he'd been captured and was totally unprepared for the sight of her dead son, eyes staring open, mouth fixed in a grin of death, blood all over his chest.

'Is that Michael Galvin?' asked Captain Watson gently, hating what he was doing.

The tiny, round woman caught her breath, swaying against the thick-set Army captain. Tears began running down her face, streaking her ruddy cheeks.

'It is not,' she whispered. 'The poor, poor boy. It is not my son. Rest his soul.'

Despite further questioning, Mrs Galvin refused to admit that the body was that of her son. Her fear of reprisals against her other children overcame her anguish, her longing to throw herself across her dead son's body, her need to sob her grief away.

'Then he shall be buried in an unmarked grave,' said Captain Watson, disliking every moment of this most unnerving but, to him, necessary scene.

The news of the treatment of Mick Galvin's mother infuriated the men of the North Kerry Flying Column, already shocked by his death. Their fury increased when they heard from Jimmy Costelloe of Sir Arthur Vicars's spying activities. Hadn't Sir Arthur, they asked, entertained the soldiers just before they killed Galvin? There was no doubt left in their minds. Sir Arthur was no longer the harmless and slightly eccentric Master of Kilmorna. He was part and parcel of the British security forces. The Flying Column debated with the local IRA Volunteers what to do. To burn Kilmorna House and force Sir Arthur to leave Ireland? Or to go even further?

The Flying Column favoured a ruthless reprisal in revenge for their dead comrade and what they regarded as Sir Arthur's perfidy. These men could be seen simply as heartless killers who enjoyed their way of life. The truth was more complex. They were countrymen, used to the harshness of nature, hardened by the savagery of the events around them. They were not born killers, nor fanatics, rather idealists who had become used to killing through the circumstances of the time. To them, it was a natural extension of the law of the jungle, kill or be killed.

The local Volunteers were not so immured in the savagery of the Anglo-Irish war. Mostly farmers, they had a love-hate relationship with the Master of Kilmorna and the great house. It was the traditional relationship of serf to master found around any great estate in any country. They felt proud to be part of such a magnificent way of life, yet they hated the fact that they could never dream of indulging in that life-style themselves. They favoured less drastic action, though they, too, felt betrayed by Sir Arthur.

After three days of hard debate, a compromise was reached. Kilmorna House would be burned, but a final warning to leave the district would be given to Sir Arthur before the raid. If he heeded it, well and good. If he ignored it, then be it on his own head.

On Monday 11 April 1921 one of the estate workers at Kilmorna House, Mick Lane, was told to warn Sir Arthur that a raid was imminent and that he should make his getaway.

'What do you mean by this, Lane?' asked Sir Arthur angrily when the warning was passed on to him. 'Are you one of these rebel curs, as well?'

'No, sir,' replied Lane, twisting his cap nervously in his hands, as he stood before Sir Arthur in the Long Hall at

Kilmorna House. 'I've just heard this from the Volunteers. They are most anxious for you to heed the warning.'

'Poppycock, man. They're just trying to frighten me away.'

'If you don't mind me saying so, sir, I don't think they are. I don't think they're bluffing. They were most careful in their warning.'

'Who warned you, Lane? Tell me his name and I'll have him put in charge,' stormed Sir Arthur, beside himself with rage at what he saw as gross impudence.

'I don't know him, sir,' the estate worker replied, lying lamely.

'Then I don't wish to hear any more about this ridiculous warning. Mark my words, those rebel scum won't dare come here. The military are most concerned about protecting me. Now get back to your work, Lane, and no more of this nonsense.'

Mick Lane shrugged his broad shoulders and left the house. If your man won't take the warning, he thought to himself, then it's too bad for all of us.

Lady Vicars had overheard the last part of the conversation as she entered the room.

'Do you think you're being wise, dear?' she asked anxiously. 'We could always travel to England for a few weeks. There's no harm in that, surely?'

'And show the rebels I heed their words? Never, m'dear. Besides I've far too much important work to do here.'

'But the estate virtually runs itself, darling. . . .'

'No. Not the estate. I must keep sending the intelligence reports to Dublin. They're becoming very appreciative of them. I really do think I am in regard again. A few more months and I think I may draft another petition asking that I may be reinstated as Ulster King of Arms or, at the very least, requesting a public hearing. I'm confident any petition will be given favourable consideration this time because of my work in the last year.'

'If you think so, dear,' said Lady Vicars. 'But do consider that warning again.'

'For you, m'dear, of course. I'll think about it during the day,' replied Sir Arthur, wanting to assuage his wife's fears. 'I'll think about it.'

Sir Arthur, despite his air of unconcern, did worry about the warning, and during the next nights suffered worse than usual bouts of insomnia.

He was still in bed at ten o'clock on the morning of Thursday 14 April 1921, discussing the business of the estate with his manager, Michael Murphy, when Lady Vicars hurried into his room.

'Quick, my darling, there are men with pistols all around the house,' she cried excitedly.

Murphy rushed to the window and saw two armed men at the front of the house.

'Get dressed, Sir Arthur,' he called. 'I'll go down and secure the doors.'

The estate manager took the stairs from the third floor at a gallop, only to find two of the raiders were already inside the house.

Lar Broder, of the Knockamure Company of the Volunteers, strode up to Murphy, his revolver hanging by his side. He held out his hand.

'Don't worry. It's all right. We've only come to burn the house.'

'No one's going to be harmed?' asked Murphy.

'I can guarantee that,' said Broder shaking Murphy's hand. 'But you'd better hurry up. You've only got two minutes to get out.'

As far as Broder was concerned he was telling the truth. His eight companions from Knockamure – Jack Aherne, Jack Broder, Jack, Patrick and Timmie Carroll, Denis and Hugh Goulding and James Sheehan – were to set fire to Kilmorna House. The eight Volunteers from the Duagh Company – Paul Broder, Jimmy Costelloe, Matt Finucane, Tom Halpin, Jim Hickie, Davy Lanigan, Paddy McElligott and Michael Sheehy – were to guard the outside of the house.

Michael Murphy rushed up the stairs again, taking them two at a time, and burst into the bedroom again. Sir Arthur and Lady Vicars were by the window, looking out, their arms clasped protectively around each other.

'They've only come to burn the house,' he gasped breathlessly. 'They say no one will be harmed, Sir Arthur.'

'Right, Murphy. Get my silver and the books and take them outside.'

Murphy began gathering up the valuables. Sir Arthur turned to his wife who was crying silently. 'Don't worry, m'dear. No harm will come to us. They've promised that.'

The manager took the valuables downstairs and piled them outside the front door. He began dashing up the stairs again when he was stopped by Jackie Sheehan, one of the North Kerry Flying Column, a .38 revolver in his hand. Sheehan, stocky and brown-haired, wore a dirty bandage round his forehead, the result of a police bullet chipping a brick near his head during a raid on Ballylongford Barracks a week previously. He waved Murphy back down the stairs and on to the front terrace. There he stood guard over him.

Meanwhile, upstairs, Sir Arthur's valet, Edward Murphy, had smelt burning as the Volunteers set light to curtains and furniture they'd soaked with petrol. He ran to his master and told him to hurry up.

'Help me save the paintings,' ordered Sir Arthur, still in his long crimson dressing gown. They threw two paintings out of the third floor window into the shrubbery by the front terrace.

'Now go downstairs, Edward,' said Sir Arthur, surprisingly calm still. 'Get the paintings of The O'Mahony's and Lady Rossmore in the dining room and save them.'

'What about you, sir?'

'I'll be along in a minute.'

Sir Arthur comforted his wife. 'You go along down, dear. The house is burning. You go along.'

Lady Vicars clung to her husband, loath to leave him. 'Now go along, dear. Hurry up,' insisted Sir Arthur. 'I'll see you outside.'

When his wife had left the bedroom, Sir Arthur scooped up a few small silver ornaments from his dressing table and took a last look out of the window. He could see smoke billowing from the ground floor, flames beginning to dart out of the windows. On the lawn there was a small group of armed men. He heaved a sigh as he looked round his bedroom for the last time, then went downstairs. He left the house by the french windows which led on to the front terrace from the Long Hall. He could see his wife standing under a yew tree seventy-five yards away.

Jackie Sheehan saw him hurrying through the billowing smoke.

'Who's that in the dressing gown?' he asked Michael Murphy.

'That's Sir Arthur,' replied the estate manager.

'Right, boys. This way,' called Sheehan to two men standing twenty yards away, Jack Brehony and Paddy Deane, also members of the Flying Column. They ran down the terrace steps after Sir Arthur, catching up with him by the two brown beech trees planted in front of the terrace by the Irish Nationalist leader Charles Stewart Parnell forty years before.

'Sir Arthur Vicars?' shouted Sheehan pointing his revolver at the retreating figure. Sir Arthur stopped, turned, and nodded.

'All right, Paddy,' said Sheehan, and Deane went forward and snapped handcuffs on Sir Arthur's wrists, pinning his arms behind his back. Unknown to the IRA Volunteers from Duagh and Knockamure, the North Kerry Flying Column had decided unilaterally on more ruthless action than simply burning Kilmorna House.

By this time the Army was on its way from Listowel, alerted by a message sent from Kilmorna railway station, two hundred yards from the estate, by a worker who had seen the Volunteers arrive. The three Army trucks roared at top speed towards Kilmorna, under eight minutes' drive away. As they approached the crossroads at Shanacool, half a mile from the estate, they came under fire from Jimmy Barrett, an IRA Volunteer, posted there to delay the Army's progress. The soldiers jumped down from their armoured trucks, suspecting a full-scale ambush, fanned out across the fields, and then chased Barrett who deliberately ran in full view up a hill towards his father's house. The soldiers wasted precious minutes in a chase that was to prove fruitless.

In those minutes, Sir Arthur stood under the guns of the three men from the North Kerry Flying Column, his back pressed against a beech tree. To his right, about fifty yards away, he could see his wife being restrained from running over to him by his estate manager.

'Sir Arthur Vicars, you have been found guilty by the Kerry Brigade of the Irish Republican Army of the offence of spying for the British Army of Occupation,' said Sheehan evenly. 'The sentence passed on you, Sir Arthur, is that you should be executed by firing squad.'

Sir Arthur blanched, his knees almost giving way. Deane and Brehony, cloth caps slanted on their heads, raised their rifles.

'You have a minute to find peace with your Maker,' said Sheehan.

Sir Arthur stared wildly at the men six feet in front of him. They looked back at him impassively, almost curiously. He knew there was no escape this time.

He looked beyond them and saw flames and smoke crackling out of his beloved house. He turned his head to the left and saw his wife in the distance, still struggling to reach him. The sight was too painful for him and he twisted his head away to look over the lawns sweeping down to the river. The sun reflected and danced off its surface. He heard the raucous cawing of the rooks as they flapped around the tree tops, frightened by the smoke and the yelling confusion. And he wasn't afraid any more.

Sir Arthur faced the three men, feeling dreadfully alone, and yet not lonely. He twisted his handcuffed arms awkwardly and felt the comforting weight of the statuette of St Anthony in his pocket. He raised his head to the light blue spring sky and listened to the wind off the Atlantic rustling the leaves of the tree above him.

'Go on then,' he said quietly. He closed his eyes shut. Suddenly he felt two tremendous hammer blows in his chest, pushing him back with terrible, irresistible force into the trunk of the tree. And then nothing.

Deane and Brehony had fired their rifles at point-blank range into Sir Arthur's chest. Sheehan had fired his revolver, the bullet catching its victim in the right side of the neck, just under the jaw bone.

Sir Arthur Vicars, his life blood gouting from the neck wound, slumped slowly down the tree trunk. He sat for a moment at its base, as if asleep in its shade, and then rolled slowly on to his left side, gurgling noises coming from deep inside his torn chest.

Jackie Sheehan stepped forward and stood over Sir Arthur. 'God rest your soul,' he muttered. The he fired two bullets into the dying man's face, one into his right eye, the other into the centre of his forehead. Sir Arthur's head and rolling eyes distorted with the impact of the *coup de grâce*. And then he was silent and still.

Brehony knelt down and slipped an ill-written sign round Sir Arthur's neck. It read 'Spy. Informers beware. IRA never forgets.'

The three executioners looked without remorse at the body, small and bent at the foot of the tree, blood spreading in the grass around its head, then moved off to join the main section of the Volunteers who were leaving the estate, splashing across the River Feale and up the rising fields towards Duagh.

Lady Vicars had screamed when she heard the shots and saw her husband fall but Murphy had managed to restrain her and shield her from the sight of the final two shots. Now, she ran across the lawn towards the beech tree, tears streaming down her face, sobbing deeply. Murphy ran with her and tried to shield the awful sight of her husband from her when they reached the tree. But she pushed past him to kneel by the body. She lifted her husband's shattered head gently and rested it between her knees, oblivious to the blood seeping on to her long tweed skirt.

'My poor darling,' she murmured, her tears falling on to Sir Arthur's face, mingling with his blood. 'My poor, foolish darling.'

14

The Queen's brooch

And so by half past ten on the morning of Thursday 14 April 1921, it was over. The self-deluding naïveté of Sir Arthur Vicars had made the tragedy inevitable ever since he had misplaced his trust in the young and handsome Frank Shackleton sixteen years before. The last of the players in this twentieth-century Greek tragedy was carried off the stage on a wide plank held shoulder high by the estate workers of Kilmorna House. As the great house still burned, its walls crumbling and crashing in the intense heat, his pitiful remains were borne to a stable, safe from the fire. There they lay for two days, covered with a Union Jack provided by the soldiers who had arrived too late, watched over by the men of the estate who wondered through the long hours of their wake at what might have been if only their dead master had shown common sense for once in his life. They wondered also at what would be now. Without the protection and bounty of the great house, what would they do to support their families?

The Army wondered, too, at what might remain in the smoking ruins of Kilmorna, so they blew open the strongroom. A slim private wormed his way through the small hole the explosives made in the door, shone his torch around, and saw nothing. Nothing whatsoever. The strongroom had been empty all the time.

The Army's last duty was to provide a guard of honour for Sir Arthur as his remains were carried to Kilmorna railway station and then across the Irish Sea for burial in his family's grave at Leamington Spa in Warwickshire.

As the funeral took place, Mr Lloyd George rose in the House of Commons on Tuesday 19 April 1921 to quote, in ringing, chapel tones, a leader written in the *Manchester Guardian* newspaper.

'For a crowd of armed men to attack an unarmed man in a lonely house, take him out of bed and jointly murder him, they must have debauched their minds to an extent which makes them a curse to any cause they pretend to honour.'

A murmur of assent echoed round the chamber. More emotional members shouted 'Shocking' and 'Murderous Thugs'. The House then moved on to other business.

The O'Mahony of Kerry, Peirce O'Mahony, called in his lawyers to formulate a claim for compensation against the British Government, valuing Kilmorna House at around £15,000. He swore that no O'Mahony of Kerry would ever live again in that troubled county. Nor did they.

From Listowel, the people came to gaze at the great blackened ruin. Their children played with dismembered pieces of suits of armour they found lying on the terrace. Some wandered amongst the tiny headstones of Lady Vicars's canine cemetery but mostly they stood looking silently at the devastation before them. Then they returned to their market town to find four houses blazing fiercely in and near Church Street, a retaliatory gesture by the Black and Tans. Sir Arthur was dead, the mourning done, let the bloody war continue.

The IRA, caught off balance by the wave of sympathy for Sir Arthur, issued a statement from their headquarters denying responsibility. Their local brigade commander, Paddy Landers, upbraided his company captains at Duagh and Knockamure for going too far when he was released from prison a few months later.

There was no need for the IRA to punish Jackie Sheehan, Sir Arthur's chief executioner. On Thursday 26 May 1921 he was surprised by British troops while he was paying a brief visit to his family's poor farm at Coilbee, near Listowel. As he fled, Sheehan was killed by a single bullet fired by an Army marksman at a range of nearly 500 yards.

Sixteen days later the North Kerry Flying Column relieved their vengeful feelings by executing, as an informer, an elderly, retired sergeant of the Royal Irish Constabulary called James

Kane. By accident or design, the almost senile man shot to death on Shanacool Bridge, near Kilmorna, happened to be the brother of Chief Inspector John Kane, lately of Scotland Yard and the Crown Jewels investigation.

In a last letter to his family, dictated to one of his executioners, Donalin O'Grady, James Kane wrote, 'My dear children, I am condemned to die. I had the priest today, thank God. Don't go to much expense of a funeral, and have no drink or public wake. I am told my body will be got near my home. I got the greatest kindness from the men who were in charge of me. Good-bye now, and God bless you and God bless Ireland.'

Thus, few who came into close contact with Sir Arthur Vicars lived their lives without feeling the hand of tragedy.

Peirce O'Mahony lost his dilettante son and his family's great house; Chief Inspector John Kane suffered the brutality of his brother's death; Frank Shackleton, brilliant but weak, lost his name and liberty, leaving prison required to live under an assumed name if he was to receive a family pension for the remaining twenty years of his life; Richard Gorges, bold but debauched, suffered a similar fate, dying in anonymity in an old people's home in the 1950s; and Sir Arthur himself lost all, his public reputation, his peace of mind, and his life.

Sir Arthur's tragedy showed the foolishness of believing legends like that of the three wise monkeys. Through his 57 years, he saw no evil, heard no evil, spoke no evil, and yet he was far from wise.

Today, a visitor to Listowel or Kilmorna will find little trace of Sir Arthur or the great house. There is still the brass lectern he presented to St John's Church in Listowel but no other memorial to him in the area. Instead there is a roadside cross marking the death of his executioner, Jackie Sheehan. Of Kilmorna House, there is nothing but two broken archways and some scattered stones in a green pasture by the River Feale. A portrait of Sir Arthur still hangs, however, in Dublin Castle, the scene of his downfall. He wears his ceremonial uniform and gazes into the distance with little confidence.

And what of the Crown Jewels? They adorn the throats and bosoms of the women of the rich throughout the world. There is a tale, though, related in Amsterdam and London by some diamond merchants, who should know about these things, that some of the Irish Crown Jewels have unknowingly returned to the British Royal Family, three generations after they were stolen.

A magnificent brooch, said to contain at least a dozen white Brazilian diamonds from the jewels, is worn frequently in public by Her Majesty Queen Elizabeth II. But that, after all, may be simply a diamond merchants' tale.

Author's footnote

Late one night, at the height of the terrorist bombing campaign in London, I was sitting in the newsroom of BBC Television News, waiting to write any news flashes if a bomb should explode in the British capital. It was a time of waiting and I happened to pick up a paperback copy of *King Edward VII*, by Sir Philip Magnus, which was lying around the newsroom. I flicked through it, reading sections here and there, when my eye was caught by a paragraph telling how King Edward had visited Ireland in 1907, only to discover his Irish Crown Jewels had been stolen, never to be recovered. The bell that all journalists seem to have in their head began ringing. The Irish Crown Jewels Robbery? I'd never heard of it, nor had any of my older colleagues whom I asked. Thus started eighteen months' work.

During these months, the almost unbelievable story related in this book began to unfold. It is made even more incredible, I would suggest, by the fact that it is a story based in known fact to a large extent. All the main characters – Sir Arthur Vicars, Frank Shackleton, Richard Gorges, Peirce Mahony – existed in real life, acting as they are depicted in this book and meeting the sad fates that are described. The civil servants, the politicians, the policemen, the prostitutes, the IRA fighters, the royal courtiers, and other ancillary characters, existed in real life as well, playing their allotted parts in the tragic story that spans more than twenty years at the beginning of this century. The only important characters that are figments of my imagination are Frank Robinson, the Dublin locksmith, and Rufus Levinson, the London diamond merchant. I am certain, however, that these characters existed at the time under different names.

It is impossible to discover, at this range of time, the exact documentary proof of what happened before, during, and after the robbery. The friends of King Edward VII perpetrated a 'cover-up' that makes the Watergate Affair appear the work of backward children. For guidance, I assembled all the circumstantial evidence available from official and unofficial sources and showed it to some of my detective friends at Scotland Yard. These officers, sadly, must remain anonymous for obvious reasons. Between us, using the dictum of method, motive and opportunity, we arrived at the conclusions about the robbery contained in the book. Naturally, I have used my imagination in re-creating many of the private conversations of the time, although a deal of them are based on official diaries and police statements. The attitudes revealed in these conversations were undoubtedly the prevailing attitudes of the various people involved at the time.

I must thank my former journalistic colleague, Mr Norman Dickson, for his initial researches on my behalf, and all those who, since then, have given freely of their time and memories. I recall particularly Miss May Quillinan and Mr Bryan MacMahon of Listowel, Co. Kerry, and Mr Jackie Murphy of Kilmorna, Co. Kerry. My equal thanks must also go to those who gave me information but insisted on remaining anonymous.

I would like to thank also the staffs of the newspaper sections of the British Museum and the National Library of Ireland, and the staffs of Maidenhead Library in Berkshire, England, and of Kerry County Library in Tralee, Co. Kerry. Their patience and guidance were invaluable.

Many books have been read during the past eighteen months but the one always closest to hand has been *Vicious Circle* by Francis Bamford and Viola Bankes, which contains most of the unvarnished and conflicting evidence about the Irish Crown Jewels Robbery. The painstaking research work done by these authors certainly shortened and eased my task. I list below other books that have been of help:

Listowel and its Vicinity by J. Anthony Gaughan.
With the Flag to Pretoria by H. W. Wilson.

Author's footnote

Battles of the Boer War by W. Baring Pemberton.
King Edward VII: A Biography by Sir Sidney Lee.
King Edward VII by Sir Philip Magnus.
Endurance by Alfred Lansing.
Scenes of Edwardian Life by Sir Charles Petrie.
Edward VII and his Circle by Virginia Cowles.
Edwardians in Love by Anita Leslie.
The Gentry Bell, a play, by Bryan MacMahon.
The Phoenix Park Murders by Tom Corfe.
The Making of Ireland and its Undoing by Mrs Alice Stopford Green.
A Spy in the Castle by David Neligan.

Finally, I would like to thank Mr Alan Protheroe of BBC Television News, who thought it was a good idea.